Ripper

A Novel

Isabel Allende

Translated from the Spanish by Ollie Brock and Frank Wynne

FOURTH ESTATE • *London*

Fourth Estate
An imprint of HarperCollins*Publishers*
1 London Bridge Street
London SE1 9GF

2

This Fourth Estate paperback edition published 2015
First published in Great Britain by Fourth Estate in 2014

B-format ISBN 978-0-00-754895-8
A-format ISBN 978-0-00-757917-4

Printed and bound in Great Britain by
Clays Ltd, St Ives plc

MIX
Paper from
responsible sources
FSC™ C007454

FSC™ is a non-profit international organisation established to promote
the responsible management of the world's forests. Products carrying the
FSC label are independently certified to assure consumers that they come
from forests that are managed to meet the social, economic and
ecological needs of present and future generations,
and other controlled sources.

Find out more about HarperCollins and the environment at
www.harpercollins.co.uk/green

ISABEL AL   ks of
fiction, four memoirs, and three young-adult novels, which have been
translated into thirty-five languages, with over 60 million copies sold.
In 2004 she was inducted into the American Academy of Arts and
Letters. Born in Peru and raised in Chile, she lives in California.

From the reviews of *Ripper*:

'A literary banquet overflowing with morsels of Nancy Drew, mouth-
fuls of Agatha Christie, a sprinkle of Barbara Cartland and dashes of
James Patterson and Tom Clancy ... [The] combination of detective
story and romantic saga is likely to intrigue Allende fans ... What
lingers is Allende's generosity with fictional detail, her warmth and
humanity.'
Observer

'Idiosyncratic, unflinching, glaringly contemporary ... and obviously
much better written than it needs to be. Allende excels at exacting
portraiture and barbed asides ... *Ripper* is something of a *jeu d'esprit*.'
Guardian

'As it gathers pace, the tale becomes gripping and delivers a clever final
twist.'
Sunday Times

'[A] thoroughly charming book ... a lot of fun to read. Also, it features
a teenage sleuth ... who is pretty much irresistible ... Allende blithely
dispenses with the more restrictive genre conventions to get to the fun
parts ... A canvas so crowded with life that even death seems to melt
into the background.'
New York Times

'Although this is Allende's first work of crime fiction, it's a similarly compulsive page-turner.'   *Vogue*

'The writing is seductive and the observations are wide-ranging ... it's an excellent read.'   *Literary Review*

'The author handles a complicated plot and complex characters with great skill.'   *Country Life Magazine*

'Literary icon Isabel Allende mesmerizes with her first crime novel ... this race-against-the-clock thriller is pure magic.'   *People Magazine*

'It must have been surprising to discover that [Allende's] particular literary strengths – a talent for dramatization, a delight in world-building and a passion for investigating relationships between family members – lend themselves so well to a genre she's never bothered with before. I am hoping she'll continue her killings.'

San Francisco Chronicle

'Given Allende's skill in creating warm, believable characters and setting them in a beautifully observed modern-day America, it's much, much more than a simple whodunit. While the main storyline rips along at a pace, the back stories, supporting cast and cultural references add weight and conviction ... Illusion, reality and multiple identities all play their part in this gripping read.'   *New Internationalist*

'[A] rip-roaring, entertaining crime novel ... Allende remains a remarkable spinner of stories. Her prose is sparkling and graceful ... her ability to portray passion and action undimmed. *Ripper* grabs you, toys with you, amuses you.'   *Minneapolis Star Tribune*

'*Ripper* is full of wry humour. Brimming over with humanity, it is very far from being a straightforward thriller ... All Allende's habitual concerns are on display: the interplay of character, the importance of family and the conflicting pulls of religion, spiritualism and alternative remedies ... Allende manages to pull it off as a terrific storyteller. She holds the reader from start to finish and throws in a neat twist at the end.'
Daily Express

'There are deliciously creepy elements in *Ripper*, much like those in the dark Scandinavian crime novels one of its characters loves.'
Seattle Times

'Allende's tightly plotted tale of crimes obvious and masked is sharply perceptive, utterly charming, and intensely suspenseful.' *Booklist*

'[Allende's] facility with plotting and pacing will keep readers turning the pages.' *Publishers Weekly*

'Appealing characters, a fast-paced plot, and a successfully imagined killer add up to great entertainment.' *Library Journal*

'Allende doesn't miss a beat, smoothly exposing the underbelly of the city and the shenanigans of its wealthy elite. You might guess the identity of the killer before the last pages, but you won't care – the shocks and unexpected twists will keep you riveted until the end.'
More Magazine

To William C. Gordon, my partner in love and crime

Ripper

"*Mom is still alive, but* she's going to be murdered at midnight on Good Friday," Amanda Martín told the deputy chief, who didn't even think to question the girl; she'd already proved she knew more than he and all his colleagues in Homicide put together. The woman in question was being held at an unknown location somewhere in the seven thousand square miles of the San Francisco Bay Area; if they were to find her alive, they had only a few hours, and the deputy chief had no idea where or how to begin.

///////////////

They referred to the first murder as the Case of the Misplaced Baseball Bat, so as not to insult the victim by giving it a more explicit name. "They" were five teenagers and an elderly man who met up online for a role-playing game called Ripper.

On the morning of October 11, 2011, at 8:15 a.m., the fourth-grade students of Golden Hills Elementary School raced into the gym to whistle blasts from their coach in the doorway. The vast, modern, well-equipped gym—built using a generous donation from a former pupil who had made a fortune in the property market before the bubble burst—was also used for graduation ceremonies, school plays, and concerts. Normally the fourth-graders would run two laps around the basketball court to warm up, but this morning they came to a shuddering halt in the middle of the hall, shocked by the grisly sight of a man sprawled across a vaulting horse, his pants pooled around his ankles, his buttocks bared, and the handle of a baseball bat inserted into his rectum. The stunned children stood motionless around the corpse until one nine-year-old boy, more daring than his classmates, bent down, ran his finger through the dark stain on the floor, and realized that it was not chocolate but congealed blood; a second boy picked up a spent bullet cartridge and slipped it into his pocket, intending to swap it during recess for a porn magazine, while a girl filmed the scene on her cell phone. Just then the coach bounded over to the little group of students, whistle trilling with every breath, and, seeing this strange spectacle—which did not look like a prank—suffered a panic attack. The fourth-graders raised the alarm; other teachers quickly appeared and dragged the children kicking and screaming from the gym, followed reluctantly by the coach. The teachers removed the baseball bat, and as they laid the corpse out on the floor, they noticed a bullet hole in the center of the victim's forehead. They covered the body with a pair of sweatpants, closed the door, and waited for the police, who arrived precisely nineteen minutes later, by which time the crime scene had been so completely contaminated it was impossible to tell what the hell had happened.

A little later, during the first press conference, Bob Martín announced that the victim had been identified as one Ed Staton, forty-nine, a school security guard. "Tell us about the baseball bat!" a prurient tabloid journalist yelled. Furious to discover that information about the case had been leaked, which was not only humiliating to Ed Staton but possibly damaging to the reputation of the school, the deputy chief snapped that such details would be addressed during the autopsy.

"What about suspects?"

"This security guard, was he gay?"

Deputy Chief Martín ignored the barrage of questions and brought the press conference to a close, assuring those present that the Personal Crimes Division would keep the media informed of all pertinent facts in the investigation now under way—an investigation he would personally oversee.

A group of twelfth-graders from a nearby high school had been in the gym the night before, rehearsing a Halloween musical involving zombies and rock 'n' roll, but they did not find out what had happened until the following day. By midnight—some hours before the crime was committed, according to police—there was no one in the school building. Three teenagers in the parking lot, loading their instruments into a van, had been the last people to see Ed Staton alive. In their statements they said that the guard had waved to them before driving off in a small car at about twelve thirty. Although they were some way off, and there was no lighting in the parking lot, they had clearly recognized Staton's uniform in the moonlight, but could not agree on the color or make of the car he was driving or whether anyone had been in the vehicle with him. The police quickly worked out that it was not the victim's car, since Staton's silver-gray SUV was parked a few yards from the band's van. It was suggested that Staton had driven off with someone who was waiting for him, and who came back to the school later to pick up his car.

At a second press conference, the deputy chief of the Personal Crimes Division explained that the guard was not due to finish his shift until 6:00 a.m., and that they had no information about why he had left the school that night, returning later only to find death lying in wait. Martín's daughter Amanda, who was watching the press conference on TV, phoned her father to correct him: it was not death that had been lying in wait for Ed Staton, but a murderer.

////////////////////////

For the Ripper players, this first murder was the start of what would become a dangerous obsession. The questions they were faced with were those that also puzzled the police: Where did the guard go in the brief period between being seen by the band members and the estimated time of death? How did he get back to the school? Why had the guard not tried to defend himself before being shot through the head? What was the significance of a baseball bat being inserted into such an intimate orifice?

Perhaps Ed Staton had deserved his fate, but the kids who played Ripper were not interested in moral issues; they focused strictly on the facts. Up to this point the game had revolved around fictional nineteenth-century crimes in a fog-shrouded London where characters were faced with scoundrels armed with axes and icepicks, archetypal villains intent on disturbing the peace of the city. But when the players agreed to Amanda Martín's suggestion that they investigate murders in present-day San Francisco—a city no less shrouded in fog—the game took on a more realistic dimension. Celeste Roko, the famous astrologer, had predicted a bloodbath in the city, and Amanda decided to take this unique opportunity to put the art of divination to the test. To do so she enlisted the help of the other Ripper players and her best friend, Blake Jackson— her grandfather, coincidentally—little suspecting that the game would turn violent and that her mother, Indiana Jackson, would number among its victims.

The kids who played Ripper were a select group of freaks and geeks from around the world who had first met up online to hunt down and destroy the mysterious Jack the Ripper, tackling obstacles and enemies along the way. As games master, Amanda was responsible for plotting these adventures, carefully bearing in mind the strengths and weaknesses of the players' alter egos.

A boy in New Zealand who had been paralyzed by an accident and was confined to a wheelchair—but whose mind was still free to explore fantastical worlds, to live in the past or in the future— created the character of Esmeralda, a cunning and curious gypsy girl. A shy, lonely teenager who lived with his mother in New Jersey, and who for two years now had left his bedroom only to go to the bathroom, played Sir Edmond Paddington, a bigoted, cantankerous retired English colonel—an invaluable character, since he was an expert in weapons and military strategy. A nineteen-year-old girl in Montreal who had spent much of her short life in the hospital suffering from an eating disorder, had created Abatha, a psychic capable of reading minds, manipulating memories, and communicating with the dead. A thirteen-year-old African American orphan with an IQ of 156 and a scholarship to an academy in Reno for gifted children decided to be Sherlock Holmes, since logic and deductive reasoning came effortlessly to him.

In the beginning, Amanda did not have her own character. Her role was simply to oversee the game and make sure players respected the rules; but given the impending bloodbath, she allowed herself to bend those rules a little. She moved the action of the game from London, 1888, to San Francisco, 2011. Furthermore—now in direct breach of the rules—she created for herself a henchman named Kabel, a dim-witted but loyal and obedient hunchback she tasked with obeying her every whim, however ridiculous. It didn't escape her grandfather's notice that the henchman's name was an anagram of his own. At sixty-four, Blake Jackson was much too old for children's games, but he agreed to participate in Ripper so he and his granddaughter would have something more in common than horror movies, chess matches, and the brainteasers they set each other—puzzles and problems he sometimes managed to solve by consulting a couple of friends who were professors of philosophy and mathematics at Berkeley.

January

Monday, 2

Lying facedown on the massage table, Ryan Miller was dozing under the healing hands of Indiana Jackson, a first-degree Reiki practitioner, well versed in the techniques developed by the Japanese Buddhist Mikao Usui in 1922. Having read sixty-odd pages on the subject, Ryan knew that there was no scientific proof that Reiki was actually beneficial, but he figured it had to have some mysterious power, since it had been denounced by the US Conference of Catholic Bishops in 2009 as dangerous to Christian spiritual welfare.

Indiana worked in Treatment Room 8 on the second floor of North Beach's famous Holistic Clinic, in the heart of San Francisco's Little Italy. The door to the surgery was painted indigo— the color of spirituality—and the walls were pale green, the color of health. A sign in copperplate script read INDIANA, HEALER, and beneath it was a list of the therapies she offered: intuitive massage, Reiki, magnet therapy, crystal therapy, aromatherapy. One wall of the tiny waiting room was decorated with a garish tapestry, bought from an Asian store, of the Hindu goddess Shakti as a sensual young woman with long raven hair, dressed all in red and adorned with golden jewels. In one hand she held a sword, in another a flower. The goddess was depicted as having many arms, and each hand held one of the symbols of her power—which ranged from a musical instrument to something that looked like a cell phone. Indiana was such a devout disciple of Shakti that she had once considered taking her name until her father, Blake Jackson, managed to convince her that a Hindu goddess's name was not appropriate for a tall, voluptuous blond American with the looks of an inflatable doll.

Given the nature of his work and his background in the military, Ryan was a skeptic, yet he gratefully surrendered to Indiana's tender ministrations. He left each session feeling weightless and euphoric—something that could be explained either as a placebo effect combined with his puppyish infatuation with the healer, as his friend Pedro Alarcón suggested, or, as Indiana insisted, by the fact that his chakras were now correctly aligned. This peaceful hour was the most pleasurable in his solitary existence, and Ryan experienced more intimacy in his healing sessions with Indiana than he did in his strenuous sexual gymnastics with Jennifer Yang, the most regular of his lovers. He was a tall, heavyset man with the neck and shoulders of a wrestler, arms as thick and stout as tree trunks, and the delicate hands of a pastry chef. He had dark, close-cropped hair streaked with gray, teeth that seemed too white to be natural, pale gray eyes, a broken nose, and thirteen visible scars, including his stump. Indiana suspected he had other scars, but she hadn't seen him without his boxer shorts. Yet.

"How do you feel?" the healer asked.

"Great. I'm starving, though—that's probably because I smell like dessert."

"That's orange essential oil. If you're just going to make fun, I don't know why you bother coming."

"To see you, babe, why else?"

"In that case, my therapies aren't right for you," Indiana snapped.

"You know I'm just kidding, Indi."

"Orange oil is a youthful and happy essence—two qualities you seem to lack, Ryan. And I'll have you know that Reiki is so powerful that second-degree practitioners are capable of 'distance healing'; they can work without the patient even being present—though I'd probably need to spend twenty years studying in Japan to get to level two."

"Don't even think about distance healing. Without you here, this would be a lousy deal."

"Healing is not a deal!"

"Everyone's got to make a living. You charge less than your colleagues at the Holistic Clinic. Do you know how much Yumiko charges for a single acupuncture session?"

"I've no idea, and it's none of my business."

"Nearly twice as much as you," said Ryan. "Why don't you let me pay you more?"

"You're my friend. I'd rather you didn't pay at all, but if I didn't let you pay, you probably wouldn't come back. You won't allow yourself to be in anyone's debt. Pride is your great sin."

"Would you miss me?"

"No, because we'd still see each other as friends. But I bet you'd miss me. Come on, admit it, these sessions have really helped. Remember how much pain you were in when you first came? Next week, we'll do a session of magnet therapy."

"And a massage, please. You've got the hands of an angel."

"Okay, and a massage. Now get your clothes on, I've got another client waiting."

"Don't you find it weird that almost all your clients are men?"
asked Ryan, clambering down from the massage table.

"They're not all men—I treat women too, as well as a few children. And one arthritic poodle."

///////////////////////

Ryan was convinced that if Indiana's other male clients were anything like him, they paid simply to be near her, not because they
had any faith in her healing methods. This was what had first
brought him to Treatment Room 8, something he admitted to Indiana during their third session so there would be no misunderstandings, and also because his initial attraction had blossomed into
friendship. Indiana had burst out laughing—she was well used
to come-ons—and made a bet with him that after two or three
weeks, when he felt the results, he would change his mind. Ryan
accepted the bet, suggesting dinner at his favorite restaurant. "If
you can cure me, I'll pick up the tab, otherwise dinner is on you,"
he said, hoping to spend time with her somewhere more conducive
to conversation than these two cramped cubicles, watched over by
the omniscient Shakti.

Ryan and Indiana had met in 2009, on one of the trails that
wound through Samuel P. Taylor State Park among thousand-
year-old, three-hundred-foot-high trees. Indiana had taken her
bicycle on the ferry across San Francisco Bay, and once in Marin
County cycled the twenty or so miles to the park as part of her
training for a long bike ride to Los Angeles she planned to make a
few weeks later. As a rule, Indiana thought sports were pointless,
and she had no particular interest in keeping fit; but her daughter,
Amanda, was determined to take part in a charity bike ride for
AIDS, and Indiana was not about to let her go alone.

She had just stopped the bike to take a drink from her water
bottle, one foot on the ground, when Ryan raced past with Attila

on a leash. She didn't see the dog until it was practically on top of her; the shock sent her flying, and she ended up tangled in the bike frame. Ryan apologized, helped her to her feet, and tried to straighten the buckled wheel while Indiana dusted herself off. She was more concerned about Attila than with her own bumps and bruises. She'd never before seen such a disfigured animal: the dog had scars everywhere, bald patches on its belly, and two metallic fangs worthy of Dracula in an otherwise toothless maw; one of its ears was missing, as though hacked off with scissors. She stroked the animal's head gently and leaned down to kiss its snout, but Ryan quickly jerked her away.

"Don't get your face too close! Attila's a war dog."

"What breed is he?"

"Purebred Belgian Malinois. They're smarter and stronger than German shepherds, and they keep their backs straight, so they don't suffer from hip problems."

"What on earth happened to the poor thing?"

"He survived a land-mine explosion," Ryan said, dipping his handkerchief in the cold water of the river, where a week earlier he'd watched salmon leaping against the current in their arduous swim upstream to spawn. Miller handed Indiana the wet handkerchief to dab the grazes on her legs. He was wearing track pants, a sweatshirt, and something that looked like a bulletproof jacket—it weighed forty-five pounds, he explained, making it perfect for training because when he took it off to race, he felt like he was flying. They sat among the thick, tangled roots of a tree and talked, watched over by Attila, who studied Ryan's every move as though waiting for an order and from time to time nuzzled Indiana and discreetly sniffed her. The warm afternoon, heady with the scent of pine needles and dead leaves, was lit by shafts of sunlight that pierced the treetops like spears; the air quivered with birdsong, the hum of mosquitoes, the lapping of

the creek, and the wind in the leaves; it was the perfect setting for
a meeting in a romantic novel.

Ryan had been a Navy SEAL—a former member of SEAL
Team Six, the unit that in May 2011 launched the assault on
Osama bin Laden's compound in Pakistan. In fact, one of Ryan's
former teammates would be the one to kill the Al-Qaeda leader.
When he and Indiana met, however, Ryan could not have known
this would happen two years later; no one could, except perhaps
Celeste Roko, by studying the movement of the planets. Ryan
was granted an honorable discharge in 2007 after he lost a leg in
combat—an injury that didn't stop him continuing to compete as
a triathlete, as he told Indiana. Up to this point she had scarcely
looked at Ryan, focused as she was on the dog, but now she noticed that he wore only one shoe; his other leg ended in a curved
blade.

"It's called a Flex-Foot Cheetah—they model it on the way big
cats run in the wild," he explained, showing her the prosthesis.

"How does it fit?"

He hiked up the leg of his pants, and she studied the contraption
fastened to the stump.

"It's carbon fiber," Ryan explained. "It's so light and perfect
that officials tried to stop Oscar Pistorius, a South African double
amputee, from competing in the Olympics because they said his
prostheses gave him an unfair advantage over other runners. This
model is designed for running," he went on, explaining with a certain pride that this was cutting-edge technology. "I've got other
prosthetics for walking and cycling."

"Doesn't it hurt?"

"Sometimes. But there's other stuff that hurts more."

"Like what?"

"Things from my past. But that's enough about me—tell me
about you."

"Sorry, but I haven't got anything as interesting as a bionic leg," Indiana confessed, "and I've only got one scar, which I'm not going to show you. As a kid, I fell on my butt on some barbed wire."

Indiana and Ryan sat in the park, chatting about this and that under the watchful eye of Attila. She introduced herself—half joking, half serious—by telling him she was a Pisces, her ruling planet was Neptune, her lucky number 8, her element water, and her birthstones, silver-gray moonstone, which nurtures intuitive power, and aquamarine, which encourages visions, opens the mind, and promotes happiness. Indiana had no intention of seducing Ryan; for the past four years she had been in love with a man named Alan Keller and had chosen the path of fidelity. Had she wanted to seduce him, she would have talked about Shakti, goddess of beauty, sex, and fertility, since the mere mention of these attributes was enough to overcome the scruples of any man—Indiana was heterosexual—if her voluptuous body were not enough. Indiana never mentioned that Shakti was also the divine mother, the primordial life force, the sacred feminine—as these roles tended to put men off.

Usually Indiana didn't tell men that she was a healer by profession; she had met her fair share of cynics who listened to her talk about cosmic energy with a condescending smirk while they stared at her breasts. But somehow she sensed she could trust this Navy SEAL, so she gave him a brief account of her methods, though when put into words they sounded less than convincing even to her ears. To Ryan it sounded more like voodoo than medicine, but he pretended to be interested—the information gave him a perfect excuse to see her again. He told her about the cramps he suffered at night, the spasms that could sometimes bring him to a standstill in the middle of a race. Indiana prescribed a course of therapeutic massage and a diet of banana and kiwifruit smoothies.

They were so caught up in the moment that the sun had already begun to set when Indiana realized that she was going to miss the ferry back to San Francisco. She jumped to her feet and said good-bye, but Ryan, explaining that his van was just outside the park, offered to give her a ride—after all, they lived in the same city. The van had a souped-up engine, oversize wheels, a roof rack, a bicycle rack, and a tasseled pink velvet cushion for Attila that neither Ryan nor his dog had chosen—Ryan's girlfriend Jennifer Yang had given it to him in a fit of Chinese humor.

Three days later, unable to get Indiana out of his mind, Ryan turned up at the Holistic Clinic just to see the woman with the bicycle. She was the polar opposite of the usual subjects of his fantasies: he preferred slim Asian women like Jennifer Yang, who besides having perfect features—ivory skin, silken hair, and a bone structure to die for—was also a high-powered banker. Indiana, on the other hand, was a big-boned, curvaceous, good-hearted typical American girl of the type that usually bored him. Yet for some inexplicable reason he found her irresistible. "Creamy and delicious" was how he described her to Pedro Alarcón, adjectives more appropriate to high-cholesterol food, as his friend pointed out. Shortly after Ryan introduced them, Alarcón commented that Indiana, with her ample diva's bosom, her blond mane, her sinuous curves and long lashes, had the larger-than-life sexiness of a gangster's moll from a 1970s movie, but Ryan didn't know anything about the goddesses who'd graced the silver screen before he was born.

Ryan was somewhat surprised by the Holistic Clinic—having expected a sort of Buddhist temple, he found himself standing in front of a hideous three-story building the color of guacamole. He didn't know that it had been built in 1940 and for years attracted tourists who flocked to admire its art-deco style and its stained-glass windows, inspired by Gustav Klimt, but that in the earthquake of 1989 its magnificent facade had collapsed. Two of the windows had been smashed, and the remaining two had since been auctioned off, to be replaced with those tinted glass windows the color of chicken shit favored by button factories and military barracks. Meanwhile, during one of the building's many misguided renovations, the geometric black-and-white-tiled floor had been replaced with linoleum, since it was easier to clean. The decorative green granite pillars imported from India and the tall lacquered double doors had been sold to a Thai restaurant. All that remained of the clinic's former glory was the wrought-iron banister on the stairs and two period lamps that, if they had been genuine Lalique, would probably have suffered the same fate as the pillars and the doors. The doorman's lodge had been bricked up, and twenty feet lopped off the once bright, spacious lobby to build windowless, cavelike offices. But as Ryan arrived that morning, the sun shimmered on the yellow-gold windows, and for a magical half hour the space seemed suspended in amber, the walls dripping caramel and the lobby fleetingly recovering some of its former splendor.

Ryan went up to Treatment Room 8, prepared to agree to any therapy, however bizarre. He half expected to see Indiana decked out like a priestess; instead she greeted him wearing a white coat and a pair of white clogs, her hair pulled back into a ponytail and tied with a scrunchie. There was nothing of the sorceress about her. She got him to fill out a detailed form, then took him back out into the corridor and had him walk up and down to study his gait. Only then did she tell him to strip down to his boxer shorts and lie on the massage table. Having examined him, she discovered that one of his hips was slightly higher than the other, and his spine had a minor curvature—unsurprising in a man with only one leg. In addition she diagnosed an energy blockage in the sacral chakra, knotted shoulder muscles, tension and stiffness in the neck, and an exaggerated startle reflex. In a word, he was still a Navy SEAL.

Indiana assured him that some of her therapies would be helpful, but that if he wanted them to be successful, he had to learn to relax. She recommended acupuncture sessions with Yumiko Sato, two doors down, and without waiting for him to agree, picked up the phone and made an appointment for him with a Qigong master in Chinatown, five blocks from the Holistic Clinic. It was only to humor her that Ryan agreed to these therapies, but in both cases he was pleasantly surprised.

Yumiko Sato, a person of indeterminate age and gender who had close-cropped hair like his own, thick glasses, a dancer's delicate fingers, and a sepulchral serenity, took his pulse and arrived at the same diagnosis as Indiana. Ryan was advised that acupuncture could be used to treat his physical pain, but it would not heal the wounds in his mind. He flinched, thinking he had misheard. The phrase intrigued him, and some months later, after they had established a bond of trust, he asked Yumiko what she had meant. Yumiko Sato said simply that only fools have no mental wounds.

Ryan's Qigong lessons with Master Xai—who was originally from Laos and had a beatific face and the belly of a Laughing Buddha—were a revelation: the perfect combination of balance, breathing, movement, and meditation. It was the ideal exercise for body and mind, and Ryan quickly incorporated it into his daily routine.

/////////////////////

Indiana didn't manage to cure the spasms within three weeks as promised, but Ryan lied so he could take her out and pay for dinner, since by then he'd realized that financially she was bordering on poverty. The bustling yet intimate restaurant, the French-influenced Vietnamese food, and the bottle of Flowers pinot noir all played a part in cementing a friendship that in time Ryan would come to think of as his greatest treasure. He had lived his life among men. The fifteen Navy SEALs he'd trained with when he was twenty were his true family; like him they were inured to rigorous physical exertion, to the terror and exhilaration of war, to the tedium of hours spent idle. Some of his comrades, he had not seen in years, others he had seen only a few months earlier, but he kept in touch with them all; they would always be his brothers.

Before he lost his left leg, the navy vet's relationships with women had been uncomplicated: sexual, sporadic, and so brief that the features of these women blurred into a single face that looked not unlike Jennifer Yang's. They were usually just flings, and when from time to time he did fall for someone, the relationship never lasted. His life—constantly on the move, constantly fighting to the death—did not lend itself to emotional attachments, much less to marriage and children. He fought a constant war against his enemies, some real, others imaginary; this was how he had spent his youth.

In civilian life Ryan was awkward, a fish out of water. He found it difficult to make small talk, and his long silences sometimes seemed insulting to people who didn't know him well. The fact that San Francisco was the center of a thriving gay community meant it was teeming with beautiful, available, successful women very different from the girls Ryan was used to encountering in dive bars or hanging around the barracks. In the right light, Ryan could easily pass for handsome, and his disability—aside from giving him the martyred air of a man who has suffered for his country—offered a good excuse to strike up a conversation. He was never short of offers, but when he was with the sort of intelligent woman he found attractive, he worried so much about making a good impression that he ended up boring them. No California woman would rather spend the evening listening to war stories, however heroic, than go clubbing—no one, that is, except Jennifer Yang, who had inherited not only the infinite patience of her ancestors in the Celestial Empire but also the ability to pretend she was listening when actually she was thinking about something else. Yet from the very first time they met among the sequoias in Samuel P. Taylor State Park, Ryan had felt comfortable with Indiana Jackson. A few weeks later, at the Vietnamese restaurant, he realized he didn't need to rack his brains for things to talk about; half a glass of wine was all it took to loosen Indiana's tongue. The time flew by, and when he checked his watch, Ryan saw it was past midnight and the only other people in the restaurant were two Mexican waiters clearing tables with the disgruntled air of men who had finished their shift and were anxious to get home. It was on that night, three years ago, that Ryan and Indiana had become firm friends.

For all his initial skepticism, after three or four months the ex-soldier was forced to admit that Indiana was not just some crazy New Age hippie; she genuinely had the gift of healing. Her therapies relaxed him; he slept more soundly, and the cramps and spasms had all but disappeared. But the most wonderful thing about their sessions together was the peace they brought him: her hands radiated affection, and her sympathetic presence stilled the voices from his past.

As for Indiana, she came to rely on this strong, silent friend, who kept her fit by forcing her to jog the endless paths and forest trails in the San Francisco area, and bailed her out when she had financial problems and couldn't bring herself to approach her father. They got along well, and though the words were never spoken, she sensed that their friendship might have blossomed into a passionate affair if she wasn't still hung up on her elusive lover Alan, and Ryan wasn't so determined to push away love in atonement for his sins.

The summer her mother met Ryan Miller, Amanda Martín had been fourteen, though she could have passed for ten. She was a skinny, gawky girl with thick glasses and a retainer who hid from the unbearable noise and glare of the world behind her mop of hair or the hood of her sweatshirt; she looked so unlike her mother that people often asked if she was adopted. From the first, Ryan treated Amanda with the exaggerated courtesy of a Japanese gentleman. He made no effort to help her during their long bike ride to Los Angeles, although, being an experienced triathlete, he had helped her to train and prepare for the trip, something that won him the girl's trust.

One Friday morning at seven, all three of them—Indiana, Amanda, and Ryan—set off from San Francisco with two thousand other keen cyclists wearing red AIDS awareness ribbons, escorted by a procession of cars and trucks filled with volunteers transporting tents and provisions. They arrived in Los Angeles the following Friday, their butts red-raw, their legs stiff, and their minds as free of thoughts as newborn babes. For seven days they had pedaled up hills and along highways, through stretches of beautiful countryside and others of hellish traffic. To Ryan—for whom a daily fifteen-hour bike ride was a breeze—the ride was effortless, but to mother and daughter it felt like a century of agonizing effort, and they only got to the finish line because Ryan was there, goading them like a drill sergeant whenever they flagged and recharging their energy with electrolyte drinks and energy bars.

Every night, like an exhausted flock of migrating birds, the two thousand cyclists descended on the makeshift campsites erected by the volunteers along the route, wolfed down five thousand calories, checked their bicycles, showered in trailers, and rubbed their calves and thighs with soothing ointment. Before they went to sleep, Ryan applied hot compresses to Indiana and Amanda and gave them little pep talks about the benefits of exercise and fresh air.

"What has any of this got to do with AIDS?" asked Indiana on the third day, having cycled for ten hours, weeping from sheer exhaustion and for all the woes in her life. "What do I know?" was Ryan's honest answer. "Ask your daughter."

The ride may have made only a modest contribution to the fight against AIDS, but it cemented the budding friendship between Ryan and Indiana, while for Amanda it led to something impossible: a new friend. This girl, who looked set to become a hermit, had precisely three friends in the world: her grandfather, Blake Jackson; Bradley, her future boyfriend; and now Ryan Miller, the Navy SEAL. The kids she played Ripper with didn't fall into the same category; she only knew them within the context of the game, and their relationship was entirely centered around crime.

Tuesday, 3

*A*manda's godmother, *Celeste Roko, the* most famous astrologer in California, made her "bloodbath" prediction the last day of September 2011. Her daily show aired early, before the morning weather forecast, and repeated after the evening news. At fiftysomething, thanks to a little nip and tuck, Roko looked good for her age. Charming on screen and a dragon in person, she was considered beautiful and elegant by her many admirers. She looked like Eva Perón with a few extra pounds. The set for her TV show featured a blown-up photo of the Golden Gate Bridge behind a fake picture window and a huge model of the solar system, with planets that could light up and be moved by remote control.

Psychics, astrologers, and other practitioners of the mysterious arts tend to make their predictions on New Year's Eve, but Madame Roko could not bring herself to wait three months before warning the citizens of San Francisco of the horrors that lay in store for them. Her prophecy was of such magnitude that it captured the public imagination, went viral on the Internet. Her pronounce-

ment provoked scathing editorials in the local press and hysterical headlines in the tabloids, speculating about terrible atrocities at
San Quentin State Prison, gang warfare between blacks and Latinos, and an apocalyptic earthquake along the San Andreas Fault.
But Celeste Roko, who exuded an air of infallibility thanks to a
former career as a Jungian analyst and an impressive number of
accurate predictions, was adamant that her vision concerned murders. This provoked a collective sigh of relief among devotees of
astrology, since it was the least dreadful of the calamities they had
feared. In northern California, the chance of being murdered was
one in twenty thousand; it was, everyone believed, a crime that
happened to other people.

It was on the day of this prediction that Amanda and her grandfather finally decided to challenge the power of Celeste Roko. They
were sick and tired of the influence Amanda's godmother wielded
over the family by pretending that she could foretell the future.
Madame Roko was a temperamental woman with the unshakable
belief in herself common to those who receive direct messages from
the universe or from God. She never managed to sway Blake Jackson, who would have no truck with astrology, but Indiana always
consulted Celeste before making important decisions, allowing
her life to be guided by the dictates of her horoscope. All too often
Celeste Roko's astrological readings thwarted Amanda's best-laid
plans. When she was younger, for example, the planets had deemed
it an inauspicious moment to buy a skateboard but a propitious time
to take up ballet—which left Amanda in a pink tutu, sobbing with
humiliation.

When she turned thirteen, Amanda discovered that her godmother was not in fact infallible. The planets had apparently
decided that Amanda should go to a public high school, but Encarnación Martín, her formidable paternal grandmother, insisted she
attend a Catholic boarding school. For once Amanda sided with

Celeste, since a co-ed school seemed slightly less terrifying than being taught by nuns. But Doña Encarnación triumphed over Celeste Roko—by producing a check for the tuition fees. Little did she suspect that the nuns would turn out to be feminists in pants who challenged the pope, and used science class to demonstrate the correct use of a condom with the aid of a banana.

Encouraged by the skepticism of her grandfather, who rarely dared to directly challenge Celeste, Amanda questioned the relationship between the heavenly bodies and the fates of human beings; to her, astrology seemed as much mumbo-jumbo as her mother's white magic. Celeste's most recent prognostication offered grandfather and granddaughter a perfect opportunity to refute the predictive powers of the stars. It is one thing to announce that the coming week is a favorable one for letter-writing, quite another to predict a bloodbath in San Francisco. That's not something that happens every day.

When Amanda, her grandfather, and her online buddies transformed Ripper from a game into a criminal investigation, they could never have imagined what they were getting themselves into. Precisely eleven days after Celeste Roko's pronouncement, Ed Staton was murdered. This might have been considered a coincidence, but given the unusual nature of the crime—the baseball bat—Amanda began to put together a case file using information published in the papers, what little she managed to wheedle out of her father, who was conducting the investigation, and whatever her grandfather could dig up.

Blake Jackson was a pharmacist by profession, a book lover, and a frustrated writer until he finally took the opportunity to chronicle the tumultuous events predicted by Celeste Roko. In his novel, he described his granddaughter Amanda as "idiosyncratic of appearance, timorous of character, but magnificent of mind"—his baroque use of language distinguishing him from his peers. His account of these fateful events would end up being much longer than he expected, even though—excepting a few flashbacks—it spanned a period of only three months. The critics were vicious, dismissing his work as magical realism—a literary style deemed passé—but no one could prove he had distorted the events to make them seem supernatural, since the San Francisco Police Department and the daily newspapers documented them.

In January 2012, Amanda Martín was sixteen and a high school senior. As an only child, Amanda had been dreadfully spoiled, but her grandfather was convinced that when she graduated from high school and went out into the world that would sort itself out. She was vegetarian now only because she didn't have to cook for herself; when she was forced to do so, she would be less persnickety about her diet. From an early age Amanda had been a passionate reader, with all the dangers such a pastime entails. Although the San Francisco murders would have been committed in any case, Amanda would not have been involved if an obsession with Scandinavian crime novels had not developed into a morbid interest in evil in general and premeditated murder in particular. Though her grandfather was no advocate of censorship, it worried him that Amanda was reading books like this at fourteen. His granddaughter put him in his place by reminding him that he was reading them too, so all Blake Jackson could do was give her a stern warning about their content—which of course made her all the more curious. The fact that Amanda's father was deputy chief of the homicide detail in San Francisco's Personal Crimes Division fueled her obsession; through him she discovered how much evil there was in this idyllic city, which could seem immune to it. But if heinous crimes happened in enlightened countries like Sweden and Norway, there was no point in expecting things to be different in San Francisco—a city founded by rapacious prospectors, polygamous preachers, and women of easy virtue, all lured by the gold rush of the mid-nineteenth century.

Amanda went to an all-girls boarding school—one of a handful that still remained since America had opted for the muddle of mixed education—at which she had somehow survived for four years by managing to be invisible to her classmates, although not to the teachers and the few nuns who still worked there. She had an excellent grade-point average, although the sainted sisters never saw her open a textbook and knew she spent most nights staring at her computer, engrossed in mysterious games, or reading unsavory books. They never dared to ask what she was reading so avidly, suspecting that she read the very books they enjoyed in secret. Only the girl's questionable reading habits could explain her morbid fascination for guns, drugs, poison, autopsies, methods of torture, and means of disposing of dead bodies.

///////////////////

Amanda closed her eyes and took a deep breath of fresh winter-morning air. The smell of pine needles told her that they were driving through the park; the stench of dung, that they were passing the riding stables. Thus she could calculate that it was exactly 8:23 a.m. She had given up wearing a watch two years earlier so she could train herself to tell time instinctively, the same way she calculated temperature and distance; she'd also refined her sense of taste so that she could distinguish suspect ingredients in her food. She cataloged people by scent: her grandfather, Blake, smelled of gentleness—a mixture of wool sweaters and chamomile; Bob, her father, of strength—metal, tobacco, and aftershave; Bradley, her boyfriend, of sensuality, sweat and chlorine; and Ryan smelled of reliability and confidence, a doggy aroma that was the most wonderful fragrance in the world. As for her mother Indiana, steeped in the essential oils of her treatment room, she smelled of magic.

After her grandfather's spluttering '95 Ford passed the stables, Amanda mentally counted off three minutes and eighteen seconds, then opened her eyes and saw the school gates. "We're here," said Jackson, as though this fact might have escaped her notice. Her grandfather, who kept fit playing squash, took Amanda's heavy schoolbag and nimbly bounded up to the second floor while she trudged after him, violin in one hand, laptop in the other. The dorm room was deserted: since the new semester did not begin until tomorrow morning, the rest of the boarders would not be back from Christmas vacation until tonight. This was another of Amanda's manias: wherever she went, she had to be the first to arrive so she could reconnoiter the terrain before potential enemies showed up. Amanda found it irritating to have to share the dorm room with others—their clothes strewn across the floor, their constant racket; the smells of shampoo, nail polish, and stale candy; the girls' incessant chatter, their lives like some corny soap opera filled with jealousy, gossip, and betrayal from which she felt excluded.

"My dad thinks that Ed Staton's murder was some sort of gay revenge killing," Amanda told her grandfather before he left.

"What's he basing that theory on?"

"On the baseball bat shoved—you know where," Amanda said, blushing to her roots as she thought of the video she'd seen online.

"Let's not jump to conclusions, Amanda. There's still a lot we don't know."

"Exactly. Like, how did the killer get in?"

"Ed Staton was supposed to lock the doors and set the alarm when he started his shift," said Blake. "Since there was no sign of forced entry, we have to assume the killer hid in the school before Staton locked up."

"But if the murder really was premeditated, why didn't the guy kill Staton before he drove off? He couldn't have known Staton intended to come back."

"Maybe it wasn't premeditated. Maybe someone sneaked into the school intending to rob the place, and Staton caught him in the act."

"Dad says that in all the years he's worked in homicide, though he's seen murderers who panicked and lashed out violently, he's never come across a murderer who took the time to hang around and cruelly humiliate his victim."

"What other pearls of wisdom did Bob come up with?"

"You know what Dad's like—I have to surgically extract every scrap of information from him. He doesn't think it's an appropriate subject for a girl my age. Dad's a troglodyte."

"He's got a point, Amanda. This whole thing is a bit sordid."

"It's public domain, it was on TV, and if you think you can handle it, there's a video on the Internet some little girl shot on her cell phone."

"Jeez, that's cold-blooded. Kids these days are so used to violence that nothing scares them. Now, back in my day . . ." Jackson trailed off with a sigh.

"This is your day! It really bugs me when you talk like an old man. So, have you checked out the juvenile detention center, Kabel?"

"I've got work to do—I can't just leave the drugstore unattended. But I'll get to it as soon as I can."

"Well, hurry up, or I might just find myself a new henchman."

"You can try! I'd like to see anyone else who's prepared to put up with you."

"You love me, Gramps?"

"Nope."

"Me neither," Amanda said, and flung her arms around his neck.

///////////////

Blake Jackson buried his nose in his granddaughter's mane of frizzy hair, which smelled of salad—she washed it with vinegar—and thought about the fact that in a few months she would be off to college, and he would no longer be around to protect her. He missed her already, and she had not even left yet. He flicked through fleeting memories of her short life, back to an image of the sullen, skeptical little girl who would spend hours hiding in a makeshift tent of bedsheets where no one was admitted except Save-the-Tuna, the invisible friend who followed her around for years, her cat Gina, and sometimes Blake himself, when he was lucky enough to be invited to drink make-believe tea from tiny plastic cups.

Where on earth does she get it from? Blake Jackson had wondered when Amanda—aged six—first beat him at chess. It could hardly be from Indiana, who floated in the stratosphere preaching love and peace half a century after the hippies had died out, and it wasn't from Bob Martín, who had never finished a book in his life. "I wouldn't worry too much about it," said Celeste Roko, who had a habit of showing up unannounced, and who terrified Blake Jackson almost as much as the devil himself. "Lots of kids are precocious at that age, but it doesn't last. Just wait till her hormones kick in, and she'll nosedive to the usual level of teenage stupidity."

But in this case the psychic had been wrong: Amanda's intelligence had continued to develop throughout her teenage years, and the only impact her hormones had was on her appearance. At puberty she grew quickly, and at fifteen she got contact lenses to replace her glasses, had her retainer removed, learned to tame her shock of curly hair, and emerged as a slim young woman with delicate features, her father's dark hair, and her mother's pale skin, a young woman who had no idea how beautiful she was. At seventeen she still shambled along, still bit her nails, and still dressed in bizarre castoffs she bought in thrift stores and accessorized according to her mood.

When her grandfather left, Amanda felt, for a few hours at least, that she was master of her own space. Three months from now she'd graduate from high school—where she'd been happy, on the whole, despite the frustration of having to share a dorm room—and soon she'd be heading for Massachusetts, to MIT, where her virtual boyfriend, Bradley, was already enrolled. He'd told her all about the MIT Media Lab, a haven of imagination and creativity, everything she had ever dreamed of. Bradley was the perfect man: he was a bit of a geek, like her, had a quirky sense of humor and a great body. His broad shoulders and healthy tan, he owed to being on the swim team; his fluorescent yellow hair to the strange cocktail of chemicals in swimming pools. He could easily pass for Australian. Sometime in the distant future Amanda planned to marry Bradley, though she hadn't told him this yet. In the meantime, they hooked up online to play Go, talked about hermetic subjects and about books.

Bradley was a science-fiction fan—something Amanda found depressing; more often than not science fiction involved a universe where the earth had been reduced to rubble and machines controlled the population. She'd read a lot of science fiction between the ages of eight and eleven before moving on to fantasy—imaginary eras with little technology where the difference between heroes and villains was clear—a genre Bradley considered puerile and pernicious. He preferred bleak dystopias. Amanda didn't dare tell him that she'd read all four Twilight novels and the Millennium trilogy; Bradley had no time for vampires and psychopaths.

Their romantic e-mails full of virtual kisses were also heavily laced with irony so as not to seem soppy; certainly nothing explicit. The Reverend Mother had expelled a classmate of Amanda's the previous December for uploading a video of herself naked, spread-eagled, and masturbating. Bradley had not been particularly shocked by the story, since some of his buddies' girlfriends had made similar sex tapes. Amanda had been a little surprised to discover that her friend was completely shaven, and that she'd made no attempt to hide her face, but she was more shocked by the hysterical reaction of the nuns, who had the reputation of being tolerant.

While she messaged Bradley online, Amanda filed away the information her grandfather had managed to dig up on the Case of the Misplaced Baseball Bat, along with a number of grisly press cuttings she'd been collecting since her godmother first broadcast her grim prophecy. The kids who played Ripper were still trying to come up with answers to several questions about Ed Staton, but already Amanda was preparing a new dossier for their next case: the murders of Doris and Michael Constante.

///////////////

Matheus Pereira, a painter of Brazilian origin, was another of Indiana Jackson's admirers. But their love was strictly platonic, since Matheus devoted all his energies to his painting. Matheus believed that artistic creativity was fueled by sexual energy, and when forced to choose between painting and seducing Indiana—who didn't seem interested in an affair—he chose the former. In any case, marijuana kept him in a permanent state of zoned-out bliss that didn't lend itself to amorous schemes. Matheus and Indiana were close friends; they saw each other most days, and they looked out for each other. He was constantly harassed by the police, while she sometimes had problems with clients who got too fresh, and with Deputy Chief Martín, who felt he still had the right to interfere in his ex-wife's affairs.

"I'm worried about Amanda," Indiana said as she massaged Matheus with eucalyptus oil to relieve his sciatica. "Her new obsession is crime."

"So she's over the whole vampire thing?"

"That was last year. But this is more serious—she's fixated on real-life crimes."

"She's her father's daughter."

"I never know what she's up to. That's the problem with the Internet—some pervert could be grooming my daughter right now, and I'd be the last to know."

"It's not like that, Indi. They're just a bunch of kids playing games. By the way, I saw Amanda in Café Rossini last Saturday, having breakfast with your ex-husband. I swear that guy's got it in for me, Indi."

"No, he hasn't. Bob's pulled strings to keep you out of jail more than once."

"Only because you asked him. Anyway, like I was saying, Amanda and I chatted for a bit, and she told me about their role-playing game, Ripper. Did you know that in one of the murders, the killer shoved a bat—"

"Yes, Matheus, I do know," Indiana interrupted. "But that's just what I mean—do you really think it's healthy for Amanda to be obsessed with gruesome things like that? Most girls her age have crushes on movie stars."

Matheus Pereira lived in an unauthorized extension on the flat roof of the Holistic Clinic, and in practice he also acted as the building supervisor. This ramshackle shed that he called his studio got exceptionally good light for painting and for growing marijuana—which was purely for his personal use and that of his friends.

In the late 1990s, after passing through various hands, the building had been sold to a Chinese businessman with a good eye for an investment, who had the idea of turning it into one of the health and wellness centers flourishing all over California. He had the exterior painted and hung up a sign that read HOLISTIC CLINIC to distinguish it from the fishmongers in Chinatown. The people to whom he rented the units on the second and third floors, all practitioners of the healing arts and sciences, did the rest of the work. A yoga studio and an art gallery occupied the two ground-floor units. The former also offered popular tantric dance classes, while the latter—inexplicably called the Hairy Caterpillar—mounted exhibitions of work by local artists. On Friday and Saturday nights, musicians and arty types thronged the gallery, sipping complimentary acrid wine from paper cups. Anyone looking for illicit drugs could buy them at the Hairy Caterpillar at bargain prices right under the noses of the police, who tolerated low-level trafficking as long as it was done discreetly. The two top floors of the Holistic Clinic were subdivided into small consulting suites that comprised a waiting room barely big enough for a school desk and a couple of chairs, and a treatment room. Access to the treatment rooms was somewhat restricted by the fact there was no elevator in the building—a major drawback to some patients, but one that had the advantage of discouraging the seriously ill, who were unlikely to get much benefit from alternative medicine.

Matheus Pereira had lived in the building for thirty years, successfully resisting every attempt by the previous owners to evict him. The Chinese businessman didn't even try—it suited him to have someone in the building outside office hours, so he appointed Matheus building supervisor, giving him master keys to the units and paying him a notional salary to lock up at night, turn out the lights, and act as a contact for tenants in case of emergency or if any repairs were needed.

Matheus exhibited his paintings—inspired by German Expressionism—at the Hairy Caterpillar from time to time, though they never sold. A few of his canvases also hung in the lobby, and though the anguished, misshapen figures painted in thick angry brushstrokes clashed not only with the Holistic Clinic's last vestiges of art deco but with its new ethos of promoting physical and emotional well-being in its clients, no one dared suggest taking them down for fear of offending the artist.

"This is all down to your ex-husband, Indi," Matheus said as he was leaving. "Where else do you think Amanda gets her morbid fascination with crime?"

"Bob's as worried about Amanda's new obsession as I am."

"It could be worse, she could be taking drugs—"

"Look who's talking!" Indiana laughed.

"Exactly! I'm an expert."

"If you want, I can give you a ten-minute massage tomorrow between clients," Indiana offered.

"You've been giving me free massages for years now, so I've decided—I want you to have one of my canvases!"

"No, no, Matheus!" said Indiana, managing to disguise the rising panic in her voice. "I couldn't possibly accept. I'm sure one day your paintings will be very valuable."

Wednesday, 4

*A*t *10:00 p.m., Blake Jackson* finished the novel he'd been reading and went into the kitchen to fix himself some oatmeal porridge—something that brought back childhood memories and consoled him when he felt overwhelmed by the stupidity of the human race. Some novels left him feeling this way. Wednesday evenings were usually reserved for squash games, but his squash partner was on vacation this week. Blake sat down with his bowl of oatmeal, inhaling the delicate aroma of honey and cinnamon, and dialed Amanda's cell phone number. He wasn't worried about waking her, knowing that at this hour she would be reading. Since Indiana's bedroom was some distance from the kitchen, there was no chance that she would overhear, but still Blake Jackson found himself whispering. It was best his daughter didn't know what he and his granddaughter were up to.

"Amanda? It's Kabel."

"I recognized the voice. So, what's the story?"

"It's about Ed Staton. Making the most of the unseasonably

warm weather—it was seventy degrees today, it felt like summer—"

"Get to the point, Kabel, I don't have all night to chat about global warming."

" . . . I went for a beer with your dad and discovered a few things I thought might interest you."

"What things?"

"The juvenile detention center where Staton worked before he moved to San Francisco was a place called Boys' Camp, smack in the middle of the Arizona desert. He worked there for a couple years until he got canned in 2010 in a scandal involving the death of a fifteen-year-old kid. And it wasn't the first time, Amanda— three boys have died at the facility in the past eight years, but it's still open. Every time, the judge has simply suspended its license temporarily for the duration of the investigation."

"Cause of death?"

"A military-style regime enforced by people who were either stupid or sadistic. A catalog of neglect, abuse, and torture. These boys were beaten, forced to exercise until they passed out, deprived of food and sleep. The boy who died in 2010 had contracted pneumonia; he was running a temperature and had collapsed more than once, and still they forced him to go on a run with the other inmates in the blazing, sweltering Arizona heat. When he collapsed, they kicked him while he was on the ground. He spent two weeks in the hospital before he died. Afterward, they discovered he had a couple of quarts of pus in his lungs."

"And Ed Staton was one of these sadists," concluded Amanda.

"He had a long record at Boys' Camp. His name crops up in a number of complaints made against the facility, alleging abuse of inmates, but it wasn't until 2010 that they fired him. Seems nobody gave a damn what happened to those poor boys. It's like that Charles Dickens novel—"

"Oliver Twist. Come on, Kabel, cut to the chase."

"So, anyway, they tried to hush up Staton's dismissal, but they couldn't—the boy's death stirred up a hornet's nest. But even with his reputation, Staton still managed to get a job at Golden Hills Elementary School in San Francisco. Doesn't that seem weird to you? I mean, they must have been aware of his record."

"Maybe he had the right connections."

"No one took the trouble to look into his background. The principal at Golden Hills liked the guy because he knew how to enforce discipline, but a number of students and teachers I talked to said he was a bully, one of those candy-asses who grovel to their superiors and become viciously cruel the moment they get a little power. The world's full of guys like that, unfortunately. In the end, the principal put him on the night shift to avoid any trouble. Staton's shift ran from eight p.m. to six a.m."

"Maybe he was killed by someone he'd bullied at this Boys' Camp."

"Your dad's looking into the possibility, though he's still clinging to the theory that the murder is gay-related. Staton was into gay porn, and he used hustlers."

"What?"

"Hustlers—male prostitutes. Staton's regular partners were two young Puerto Rican guys—your dad questioned them, but they've got solid alibis. Oh, and about the alarm in the school, you can tell the Ripper kids Staton was supposed to set it every night, only on the night in question he didn't. Maybe he was in a hurry, maybe he planned to set it after he got back."

"I know you're still holding out on me," Amanda said.

"Me?"

"Come on, Kabel, spit it out."

"It's something pretty weird—even your dad's stumped by it," said Blake Jackson. "The school gym is full of equipment—

baseball bats, gloves, balls—but the bat used on Staton didn't come from the school."

"Don't tell me: the bat was from some team in Arizona!"

"Like the Arizona Devils? That would make the connection to Boys' Camp obvious, Amanda, but it didn't."

"So where did it come from?"

"Arkansas State University."

///////////////////////

According to Celeste Roko, who had studied the astrological charts of all of her friends and relatives, Indiana Jackson's personality corresponded to her star sign, Pisces. This, she felt, explained her interest in the esoteric and her irrepressible need to help out every unfortunate wretch she encountered—including those who neither wanted nor appreciated her help. This made Carol Underwater the perfect focus for Indiana's indiscriminate bursts of compassion.

The two women had met one morning in December 2011. Indiana was locking up her bike and, out of the corner of her eye, noticed a woman leaning against a nearby tree as though she was about to faint. Indiana rushed over, offered the woman a shoulder to lean on, led her to the Holistic Clinic, and helped her up the two flights of stairs to Treatment Room 8, where the stranger slumped, exhausted, into one of the rickety chairs in the waiting room. After she got her breath back, the woman introduced herself and explained that she was suffering from an aggressive form of cancer and that the chemotherapy was proving worse than the disease. Touched, Indiana offered to let the woman lie down on the massage table and rest for a while. In a tremulous voice, Carol Underwater said she was fine in the chair but that she would be grateful for a hot drink. Indiana left the woman and went down the street to buy a herbal tea, feeling bad that there wasn't a hot plate in the consulting room so she could boil water. When she got back, she found that the woman had recovered a little and even put on brick-red lipstick in a pathetic attempt to smarten herself up. Pale and ravaged by the cancer, Carol Underwater looked simply grotesque, her eyes standing out like glass buttons on a rag doll. She told Indiana she was thirty-six, but the wig and the deep furrows made her look ten years older.

So began a relationship based on Carol Underwater's misfortune and Indiana's need to play the Good Samaritan. Indiana often offered therapies to bolster Carol's immune system, but she always managed to find some excuse for postponing them. At first, suspecting the woman couldn't afford to pay, Indiana offered the treatments for free, as she often did with patients in straitened circumstances, but when Carol continued to find excuses, Indi did not insist; she knew better than anyone that many people still distrusted alternative medicine.

The women shared a taste for sushi, walks in the park, and romantic comedies, and were both concerned about animal welfare. Carol—like Amanda—was a vegetarian but made an exception with sushi, while Indiana was happy just to protest against the suffering endured by battery hens and laboratory rats and the fashion industry's use of fur. One of her favorite organizations was PETA, which a year earlier had petitioned the mayor of San Francisco to change the name of the Tenderloin district: it was inexcusable that a neighborhood should be named after a prime cut from some suffering animal; the area should be renamed after a vegetable. The mayor did not respond.

Despite the things they had in common, Indiana and Carol's relationship was somewhat strained, with Indiana feeling she had to keep a certain distance, lest Carol stick to her like dandruff. The woman felt helpless and forsaken; her life was a catalog of rejections and disappointments. Carol saw herself as boring, with no charm, no talent, and few social skills, and suspected that her husband had only married her to get a green card. Indiana gently advised that she needed to rewrite this script that cast her as the victim, since the first step toward healing was to rid oneself of negative energy and bitterness. Instead, Indiana suggested, Carol needed a positive script, one that connected her to the oneness of the universe and to the divine light, but still Carol clung to her misfortune. Indiana sometimes worried she might be sucked into the bottomless chasm of this woman's need: Carol phoned Indiana at all hours to whine, and waited outside her treatment room for hours to bring her expensive chocolates that clearly represented a sizable percentage of her social security check. Indiana would politely eat these, counting every calorie and with no real pleasure, since she preferred the dark chocolates flecked with chili that she shared with Alan.

Carol had no children and no family, but she did have a couple of friends Indiana never met who accompanied her to the chemotherapy sessions. Carol's only topics of conversation were her cancer and her husband, a Colombian deported for drug dealing whom she was trying to bring back to the States. The cancer itself caused her no pain, but the poison being dripped into her veins was killing her. Carol's skin was deathly pale, she had no energy, and her voice quavered, but Indiana nurtured the hope that she might recover—her scent was different from that of the other cancer patients Indi had treated. What's more, Indiana's customary ability to tune in to other people's illnesses didn't work with Carol, something she took as a positive sign.

One day, as they were discussing this at the Café Rossini, Carol talked about her fear of dying and her hopes that Indiana would help her—a burden Indiana felt unable to take on.

"You're a very spiritual person, Indi," Carol said.

Indiana laughed. "Don't call me that! The only people I know who claim to be spiritual are sanctimonious and steal books about the occult from bookstores."

"Do you believe in reincarnation?" Carol asked.

"I believe in the immortality of the soul."

"I've frittered away this life, so if reincarnation really does exist, I'll come back as a cockroach."

Indiana lent Carol some books she always kept at her bedside, an eclectic mixture of tomes about Sufism, Platonism, Buddhism, and contemporary psychology, though she didn't tell the woman that she herself had been studying for nine years and had only recently taken the first steps on the long path to enlightenment; for her to attain "plenitude of being," and rid her soul of conflict and suffering, would take eons. Indiana hoped that her instincts as a healer would not fail her; that Carol would survive her battle with cancer and have time enough in this world to achieve the enlightenment she sought.

On that Wednesday in January, one of Indiana's clients had canceled a Reiki and aromatherapy session, so she and Carol arranged to meet at the Café Rossini at five. It had been Carol who suggested the meeting, explaining on the phone that she'd just started radiotherapy, having had two weeks' respite after her last course of chemo. Carol arrived first, wearing one of the usual ethnic outfits that did little to hide her angular figure and terrible posture: a cotton shift and trousers in a vaguely Moroccan style, a pair of sneakers, and lots of African seed necklaces and bracelets. Danny D'Angelo, a waiter who had served Carol on several occasions, greeted her with an effusiveness many of his customers had come to fear. Danny boasted that he was friends with half the population of North Beach—especially the regulars at the Café Rossini, where he'd been a waiter for so long that no one could remember a time before he worked there.

"Hey, girl, I gotta say that turban you got on is a lot better than that fright wig you been wearing lately," were his first words to

Carol Underwater. "Last time you were here, I thought to myself, 'Danny, you gotta tell that girl to ditch the dead skunk,' but in the end, I didn't have the heart."

"I have cancer," said Carol, offended.

" 'Course you do, princess, even a blind man can see that. But you could totally rock the shaved-head look—lots of women do it these days. So what can I get you?"

"A chamomile tea and a biscotti, but I'll wait till Indiana gets here."

"Indi's like Mother fucking Teresa, don't you think? I tell you, I owe that woman my life," said Danny. He would happily have sat down and told Carol Underwater stories of his beloved Indiana Jackson, but the café was crowded and the owner was already signaling to him to hurry up and serve the other tables.

Through the window, Danny saw Indiana crossing Columbus Avenue, heading toward the café. He rushed to make a double cappuccino con panna, the way she liked it, so he could greet her at the door, cup in hand. "Salute your queen, plebs!" Danny announced in a loud voice, as he usually did, and the regulars—accustomed to this ritual—obeyed. Indiana planted a kiss on his cheek and took the cappuccino over to the table where Carol was sitting.

"I feel sick all the time, Indi, and I've hardly got the strength to do anything." Carol sighed. "I don't know what to do—all I want is to throw myself off a bridge."

"Any particular bridge?" asked Danny as he passed their table, carrying a tray.

"It's just a figure of speech, Danny," snapped Indiana.

"Just saying, hon, because if she's thinking of jumping off the Golden Gate, I wouldn't advise it. They've got railings up and CCTV cameras to discourage jumpers. You get bipolars and depressives come from all over the world to throw themselves off that freakin' bridge, it's like a tourist attraction. And they always jump in toward the bay—never out to sea, because they're scared of sharks."

"Danny!" Indiana yelped, passing Carol a paper napkin to blow her nose.

The waiter wandered off with his tray, but a couple of minutes later he was hovering again, listening to Indiana try to comfort her hapless friend. She gave Carol a ceramic locket to wear around her neck and three dark glass vials containing niaouli, lavender, and mint. She explained that, being natural remedies, essential oils are quickly absorbed through the skin, making them ideal for people who can't take oral medication. She told Carol to put two drops of niaouli into the locket every day to ward off the nausea, put a few drops of lavender on her pillow, and rub the peppermint oil into the soles of her feet to lift her spirits. Did she know that peppermint oil was rubbed into the testicles of elderly bulls in order to—

"Indi!" Carol interrupted her. "I don't even what to think about what that must be like! Those poor bulls!"

Just at that moment the great wooden door with its beveled glass panels swung open—it was as ancient and tattered as everything in the Café Rossini—and in stepped Lulu Gardner, making her daily rounds of the neighborhood. Everyone except Carol Underwater immediately recognized the tiny, toothless old woman. Lulu was as wrinkled as a shriveled apple; the tip of her nose almost touched her chin, and she wore a scarlet bonnet and cape like Little Red Riding Hood. She'd lived in North Beach since the long-forgotten era of the beatniks and was the self-professed official photographer of the area. The curious old crone claimed she had been photographing the people of North Beach since the early twentieth century when Italian immigrants flooded in after the 1906 earthquake, not to mention snapping pictures of every famous resident from Jack Kerouac (an able typist, according to Lulu), Allen Ginsberg, her favorite poet and activist, and Joe DiMaggio, who'd lived here in the 1950s with Marilyn Monroe, to the Condor Club Girls—the first strippers to unionize, in the 1970s. Lulu had photographed them all, the saints and the sinners, watched over by the patron saint of the city, Saint Francis of Assisi, from his shrine down on Vallejo Street. She wandered around with a walking stick almost as tall as she was, clutching the sort of Polaroid camera no one makes these days and a huge photo album tucked under one arm.

There were all sorts of rumors about Lulu, and she never took the trouble to deny them. People said that though she looked like a bag lady, she had millions salted away somewhere; that she was a survivor from a concentration camp; that she'd lost her husband at Pearl Harbor. All anyone knew for certain was that Lulu was Jewish—not that this stopped her celebrating Christmas. The previous year Lulu had mysteriously disappeared, and after three weeks the neighbors gave her up for dead and decided to hold a memorial service in her honor. They set up a large photo of Lulu in a prominent place in Washington Park where people came to lay flowers, stuffed toys, reproductions of her photos, meaningful poems, and messages. At dusk the following Sunday, when a dozen people with candles had gathered to pay a reverent last farewell, Lulu Gardner showed up in the park and promptly began to photograph the mourners and ask them who had died. Feeling that she had mocked them, many of the neighbors never forgave her for still being alive.

Now the photographer stepped into the Café Rossini, weaving between the tables like a dancer to the slow blues from the loud-speakers, singing softly and offering her services. She approached Indiana and Carol, gazing at them with her beady, rheumy eyes. Before anyone could stop him, Danny D'Angelo crouched between the women, hunkering down to their level, and Lulu Gardner clicked the shutter. Startled by the flash, Carol Underwater leaped to her feet so suddenly she knocked over her chair. "I don't want your fucking photos, you old witch!" she yelled, trying to snatch the camera from a terrified Lulu, who backed away as Danny D'Angelo intervened. Astonished by this overreaction, Indiana tried to calm her friend, while a murmur of disapproval rippled through the café's customers, including some who had been offended by Lulu's resurrection. Mortified, Carol slumped back into her chair and buried her face in her hands. "My nerves are shot to shit," she sobbed.

Thursday, 5

*A*manda waited for her roommates to grow tired of gossiping about Tom Cruise's impending divorce and go to sleep before calling her grandfather.

"It's two a.m., Amanda, you woke me up. Don't you ever sleep, girl?"

"Sure, in class. You got any news for me?"

"I went and talked with Henrietta Post." Her grandfather yawned.

"The neighbor who discovered the Constantes' bodies?"

"That's her."

"So why didn't you call?" his granddaughter chided him. "What were you waiting for?"

"I was waiting for sunup!"

"But it's been weeks since the murders. You know this all happened back in November, right?"

"Yeah, Amanda, but I couldn't make it out there any earlier. Don't worry, the woman remembers everything. Got a shock that scared her half to death, but every last detail of what she saw that day is burned into her brain—the most terrifying day of her life, she told me."

"So give me the lowdown, Kabel."

"I can't. It's late, and your mom will be home any minute."

"It's Thursday—Mom's with Keller."

"But she doesn't always spend the night with him. 'Sides, I need my sleep. I can send you the notes from my conversation with Henrietta Post and what I managed to wheedle out of your father."

"You wrote it all down?"

"One of these days, I'm going to write a novel," said her hench-man. "I jot down anything that interests me, never know what might be useful to me in the future."

"Write your memoirs," suggested his granddaughter. "That's what most old codgers do."

"Nah—it would bomb, nothing worth writing about has ever happened to me. I'm the most pitifully boring widower in the world."

"True. Anyway, send me those notes on the Constantes. G'night, Hench. You love me?"

"Nope."

"Me neither."

Minutes later, the details of Blake Jackson's interview with the key witness to the Constantes murder were in Amanda's in-box.

On the morning of November 11 at about ten fifteen, Henri-etta Post, who lived on the same street as the Constantes, was out walking her dog when she noticed that the door to their place was wide open—something unusual in that neighborhood, where they'd had trouble with gangbangers and drug dealers. Henrietta rang the doorbell, intending to warn the Constantes, whom she knew well, and when no one answered she stepped inside, call-ing to see if anyone was home. She wandered through the living room, where the TV was blaring, through the dining room and the kitchen, then climbed the stairs—with some difficulty, given that she's seventy-eight and suffers from palpitations. The resounding silence made her uneasy in a house usually so bustling with life; more than once she'd had to complain about the racket.

She found the children's bedrooms empty and shuffled down the short passageway to the master bedroom, calling out to the Constantes with what little breath she had left. She knocked three times before opening the door and poking her head in. She says the bedroom was in semi-darkness, with the shutters closed and the curtains drawn, and that it was cold and stuffy in there, as though it hadn't been aired in days. She took a couple steps into the room, her eyes adjusting to the darkness, then quickly retreated with a mumbled apology when she saw the outline of the couple lying in the bed.

She was about to creep out quietly, but instinct told her there was something strange about the stillness of the house, about the fact that the Constantes had not answered when she called and were sound asleep in the middle of a weekday morning. She crept back into the room, fumbling along the wall for the switch, and flicked on the light. Doris and Michael Constante were lying on their backs with the comforter pulled up to their necks, utterly rigid, their eyes wide open. Henrietta Post let out a strangled cry, felt a heavy jolt in her chest, and thought her heart was about to burst. She couldn't bring herself to move until she heard her dog barking—then she walked back along the corridor, stumbled down the stairs, and, grasping at the furniture for support, tottered as far as the phone in the kitchen.

She dialed 911 at precisely 10:29; her neighbors were dead, she said over and over, until finally the operator interrupted to ask two or three key questions and tell her to stay right where she was and not touch anything, that help was on its way. Six minutes later two patrol officers who happened to be in the neighborhood showed up, followed almost immediately by an ambulance and police backup. There was nothing the paramedics could do for the Constantes, but they rushed Henrietta Post to the emergency room with tachycardia and blood pressure that was going through the roof.

At about eleven, by which time the street had been taped off, Inspector Bob Martín arrived with Ingrid Dunn, the medical examiner, and a photographer from forensic services. Bob pulled on latex gloves and followed the medical examiner upstairs to the Constantes' bedroom. On seeing the couple lying in the bed, he initially assumed he was dealing with a double suicide, though he would have to wait for a verdict from Dunn, who was meticulously studying those parts of the bodies that were visible, careful not to move anything. Bob let the photographer get on with his job while the rest of the forensics team showed up; then the ME had the gurneys brought up, and the couple was taken to the morgue. The crime scene might belong to the San Francisco Police Department, but the bodies were hers.

The autopsy later revealed that Doris, forty-seven, and Michael, forty-eight, had both died of an overdose of heroin injected directly into the jugular vein, and that both had had their buttocks branded postmortem.

Ten minutes later the phone woke Blake Jackson again.

"Hey, Hench, I've got a question."

"Amanda, that's it—I've had enough!" roared her grandfather. "I resign as your henchman!"

His words were followed by a deathly silence.

"Amanda?" ventured her grandfather after a second or two.

"Yeah?" she said, her voice quavering.

"I'm just kidding. What did you want to ask?"

"Tell me about the burn marks on their butts."

"They were discovered at the morgue when the bodies were stripped," her grandfather said. "I forgot to mention in my notes that they found a couple of used syringes with traces of heroin on them in the bathroom, along with a butane blowtorch that was almost certainly used to make the burns. All of it wiped clean of prints."

"And you're saying this just slipped your mind?! That's vital evidence!"

"I meant to put it in, but I got sidetracked. I figure that stuff was left there on purpose, as a taunt—all neatly set out on a tray and covered with a white napkin."

"Thanks, Kabel."

" 'Night, boss."

" 'Night, Grandpa. I won't call again, promise. Sleep tight."

///////////////////////

It was one of those nights with Alan that Indiana looked forward to like a blushing bride, although they had long since established a routine in which there were few surprises, and the rhythms of their sex life were those of an old married couple. They had been together for four years: they *were* an old married couple. They knew each other intimately, loved each other in a leisurely fashion, and took the time to laugh, to eat, to talk. Alan would have said they made love sedately, like a couple of geriatrics; Indiana felt that for geriatrics they were pretty debauched. They were happy with the arrangement—early on they had tried out some porn-movie acrobatics that had left Indiana peeved and Alan half paralyzed; they had explored more or less everything a healthy imagination could dream up without involving third parties or animals, and had finally settled on a repertoire of four conventional positions with some variations, which they acted out at the Fairmont Hotel once or twice a week as their bodies demanded.

While they waited for the oysters and smoked salmon they had ordered from room service, Indiana recounted the tragic tale of Carol Underwater, and told Alan about Danny D'Angelo's tactless comments. Alan knew Danny, and not only because he often met Indiana at the Café Rossini. A year ago Danny had flamboyantly thrown up in Alan's new Lexus while Alan—at Indi's request— was driving him to the emergency room. He'd had to have the car washed several times to get rid of the stains and the stench.

It had happened that June, after the city's annual Gay Pride March, during which Danny had disappeared. He didn't come in to work the next day, and no one heard from him until six days later, when some guy with a Hispanic accent phoned to tell Indiana that her friend was in a bad way, ill and alone in his apartment, and to suggest she go round and look after him, or he could wind up dead. Danny lived in a crumbling building in the Tenderloin, where even the police were afraid to venture after dark, a neighborhood characterized by booze, drugs, brothels, and shady nightclubs that had always attracted drifters and delinquents. "The throbbing heart of Sin City," Danny called it with a certain pride, as though those living there deserved a medal for bravery. His apartment block had been built in the 1940s for sailors, but over time it had degenerated into a refuge for the destitute, the drugged-up, and the diseased. More than once Indiana had come by to bring food and medication to her friend, who often ended up a wreck after some sleazy binge.

When she got the anonymous call, Indiana once again rushed to Danny's side. She climbed the five flights of stairs scrawled with graffiti, four-letter words, and obscene drawings, past the seedy apartments of drunkards, doddering lunatics, and rent boys who turned tricks for drugs. Danny's room was dark and stank of vomit and patchouli oil. There was a bed in one corner, a closet, an ironing board, and a quaint little dressing table with a satin valance, a cracked mirror, and a vast collection of makeup jars. There were a dozen pairs of stilettos and two clothes racks from which the feathery sequined dresses Danny wore as a cabaret singer hung like ugly, lifeless birds. There was little natural light; the only window was caked with twenty years' worth of grime.

Indiana found Danny sprawled on the bed, filthy and still half dressed in the French maid's outfit he had worn to Gay Pride. He was burning up and severely dehydrated, a combination of pneumonia and the lethal cocktail of alcohol and drugs he had ingested. Each floor of the building had only one bathroom shared by twenty tenants, and Danny was too weak for Indiana to drag him there. He didn't respond when Indiana tried to get him to sit up, drink some water, and clean himself up. Realizing she could not deal with him on her own, she called Alan.

///////////////////////

Alan was bitterly disappointed to realize Indiana had called him only as a last resort. Her father's car was in the shop, probably, and that son of a bitch Ryan Miller was off traveling somewhere. The tacit agreement whereby their relationship was limited to a series of romantic encounters suited him, but it somehow offended him to realize that Indiana could happily exist without him. Indiana was constantly broke—a fact she never mentioned—but whenever he offered help, she dismissed the idea with a laugh. Instead she turned to her father for help, and—though he had no proof—Alan was convinced she was prepared to accept help from Miller. "I'm your lover, not some kept woman," Indiana would say whenever he offered to pay the rent on her consulting rooms or Amanda's dentist's bill. He'd wanted to buy her a Volkswagen Beetle for her birthday—a lemon-yellow one, or maybe that deep nail-polish red she loved—but Indiana dismissed the idea: public transport and her bicycle were more environmentally friendly. She refused to allow him to open a bank account in her name or give her a credit card, and she didn't like it when he gave her clothes, thinking—rightly—that he was trying to make her over. Indiana found the expensive silk and lace lingerie he bought for her faintly ridiculous, but to make him happy she wore it as part of their erotic games. Alan knew that the moment his back was turned, she would give it to Danny, who probably appreciated it more.

Although Alan admired Indiana's integrity, he was upset that she did not seem to need him. Being with this woman who was happier to give than to receive made him feel small, made him feel cheap. In all their years together, she had rarely asked for his help, so when she called from Danny's apartment, he rushed to her side.

//////////////////////

The Tenderloin district was notorious for Filipino, Chinese, and Vietnamese gangs, for robbery, assault, and murder; Alan had hardly ever set foot there, even though it was in the heart of San Francisco, only a few blocks from the banks, stores, and expensive restaurants he frequented. He still harbored a romantic, antiquated notion of the district: to him it was 1920 there, and the place was still full of gambling dens, speakeasies, boxing rings, brothels, and sundry other lowlife. He vaguely remembered that Dashiell Hammett had set one of his novels in the Tenderloin—maybe *The Maltese Falcon*. He did not realize that after the Vietnam War, the area had been flooded with Asian refugees drawn by cheap rents and the proximity to Chinatown; that nowadays up to ten people lived in the one-bedroom apartments. Seeing the hobos sprawled on the sidewalk with their sleeping bags and their overstuffed shopping carts, the shifty men hovering on street corners, and the toothless, disheveled women muttering to themselves, Alan realized it was probably best not to park on the street.

It took him a while to find a secure parking lot, and longer still to find Danny's building; the street numbers had been worn away by time and weather, and he could not bring himself to ask for directions. When he finally did stumble on the place, it was even seedier and more run-down than he had expected. Drunks, drifters, and shady-looking guys lurked in the doorways or shambled along the hallways, and he worried that some thug might jump him. He walked faster, careful to look no one in the eye, suppressing the urge to hold his nose, acutely aware of how ridiculous his Italian suede shoes and his Barbour jacket must look in a place like this. The five-floor climb up to Danny's room seemed fraught with danger, and when he finally got there, the reek of vomit stopped him in the doorway.

By the light of the bare bulb dangling from the ceiling he could see Indiana leaning over the bed, washing Danny's face with a damp cloth. "We have to get him to the hospital, Alan," she said quickly. "I need you to put a shirt and some pants on him." Alan felt his throat heave and had the urge to retch, but he could not be a coward and give up, not now. Careful not to get dirty, he helped Indiana to wash and dress the delirious man. Danny was skinny, but in his present state he seemed heavy as a horse. Between them they managed to get Danny on his feet and half carried, half dragged him along the hallway to the stairwell, then step by step down to the ground floor to sneering looks from the other tenants. Outside, they sat Danny down on the sidewalk between a couple of garbage cans, and Indiana stayed with him while Alan ran the few blocks to his car. It was while Danny was spraying the backseat of the gold Lexus with vomit that it occurred to Alan they could have called an ambulance. This thought had not even crossed Indiana's mind; calling an ambulance would cost a thousand dollars, and Danny had no medical insurance.

Danny D'Angelo spent a week in the hospital while doctors struggled to get his pneumonia, stomach infection, and blood pressure under control. Then he spent a second week staying with In-

diana's father, who reluctantly played nursemaid until Danny was
strong enough to manage on his own and go back to his rathole
and his job. Blake Jackson barely knew Danny D'Angelo at the
time, but he collected the man from the hospital because his daughter asked him to, and gave him a bed and took care of him for the
same reason.

Alan Keller had first been attracted by Indiana Jackson's looks: a
healthy, well-fed mermaid. Later he was captivated by her opti-
mistic personality; in fact, he liked her precisely because she was
the polar opposite of the skinny, neurotic women he usually dated.
He would never have admitted that he was "in love"——that would
be tasteless, he felt no need to put a name on what he felt. It was
enough that he enjoyed the carefully prearranged, slightly predict-
able times they spent together. During the weekly sessions with
his analyst, who, like most therapists in California, was a New
York Jew and a practicing Zen Buddhist, Alan had acknowledged
that he was "very fond" of Indiana, a euphemism that allowed him
to avoid using the word *passion*, something he appreciated only in
opera, where violent emotions shaped the destinies of tenor and so-
prano. Indiana's beauty inspired in him an aesthetic pleasure more
constant than sexual desire, her freshness moved him, and her admiration for him had become an addictive drug he would find difficult to give up. And yet he was constantly reminded of the gulf that
separated them. She was from a lower class. The curvaceous body
and shameless sensuality he so loved in private was embarrassing
when they were in public. Indiana ate with relish, sopped up sauce
with her bread, licked her fingers, and always ordered second help-
ings of dessert, to Alan's astonishment——he was used to the women
of his own class who thought anorexia was a virtue and death was
preferable to the terrible shame of a few extra pounds. You could
tell a woman was rich if you could see her bones. Though Indiana

was far from overweight, Alan knew his friends would not appreciate that unsettling beauty she had, like a Flemish milkmaid's, nor the bluntness that sometimes bordered on vulgarity, so he avoided taking her to places where they might run into anyone he knew. On those rare occasions when this was likely—at a concert or at the theater—he would buy her a suitable dress and ask her to pin her hair up. Indiana always acquiesced with the playfulness of a child dressing up, but over time these tasteful little black dresses began to constrict her body and sap her soul.

Alan's most thoughtful present had been the weekly flowers—an elegant ikebana arrangement from a florist in Japantown—delivered punctually to her treatment room at the Holistic Clinic every Monday by a young man with hayfever who wore gloves and a surgical mask. Another extraordinary gift had been a gold pendant—an apple encrusted with diamonds—to replace the studded collar she usually wore. Every Monday, Indiana waited impatiently for her ikebana; she loved the minimal arrangements—a gnarled twig, two leaves, a solitary flower. The diamond-encrusted apple, however, she had worn only once or twice to please Alan before storing it in the velvet case in her dressing-table drawer, since in the voluminous topography of her cleavage it looked like a stray insect. Besides, she had once seen a documentary about blood diamonds and the horrifying conditions in African mines. In the early days, Alan had tried to change her wardrobe, to teach her to be more respectable, instruct her in etiquette, but Indiana had obstinately refused. Given how much work it would take for her to become the woman he wanted, she argued, he would be better off looking for a woman more to his taste.

With his urbane sophistication and his aristocratic English looks, Alan was something of a catch. His female friends considered him the most eligible bachelor in San Francisco because, aside from his charm, he was rumored to be extremely wealthy. The precise extent of his fortune was a mystery, but he lived well, though not to excess: he rarely spent extravagantly and wore the same shabby suits year in, year out; not for him the quirks of fashion or the designer labels worn by the nouveau riche. Money bored him precisely because he had always had it. Thanks to his family name, maintaining his social standing required no effort on his part, and he had no need to worry about the future. Alan lacked the entre-preneurial acumen of his grandfather, who had made the family's fortune during Prohibition; the pliable morality of his father, who had added to it through shady dealings in Asia; and the visionary greed of his siblings, who maintained it by speculating on the stock market.

Here in his suite at the Fairmont, amid the honey-colored silk cur-tains, the antique, intricately carved furniture, the crystal lamp-shades, and the elegant French lithographs, Alan shuddered as he thought back to that unpleasant episode with Danny D'Angelo, which had further reinforced his belief that he and Indiana could never live together. He had no patience with promiscuous people like Danny, with ugliness and poverty, nor with Indiana's indis-criminate generosity, which at first had seemed like a virtue, but over time came to be an irritation. That night, as Indiana wal-lowed in the jacuzzi, Alan sat in an armchair, still dressed, holding a glass of chilled white wine—a sauvignon blanc produced in his own vineyard solely for his pleasure, and that of a few friends, and three exclusive San Francisco restaurants—while he waited for room service to arrive.

From where he sat, he could see Indiana's naked body in the wa-ter, her unruly shock of curly blond hair pinned on top of her head with a pencil, stray wisps framing her face. Her skin was flushed, her cheeks red, and her eyes sparkled with the pleasure of a little girl on a merry-go-round. Whenever they met at the hotel, the first thing she always did was turn on the hot tub, which seemed to her the height of decadence and luxury. Alan never joined her—the hot water would only raise his blood pressure, and his doctor had warned him to be careful—preferring to watch her from his armchair as she recounted some story involving Danny D'Angelo and some woman called Carol, a cancer victim who had joined the ranks of Indiana's weird friends. He could not really hear her over the swirling water. Not that he was particularly interested in the story; he simply wanted to gaze at her body reflected in the large beveled mirror behind the bathtub, waiting for the moment the oysters and smoked salmon would arrive, when he would uncork a second bottle of sauvignon and she would emerge from the water like Venus born out of the sea; then he would swathe her in a towel, wrap his arms around her, nuzzle her warm, wet, youthful skin. And so it would begin, the slow, familiar dance of foreplay. This was what he loved most in life: anticipated pleasure.

Saturday, 7

The Ripper players, including Kabel—a humble henchman with no role in the game beyond carrying out his mistress's orders—had agreed to meet up on Skype. At the appointed time, they were all sitting in front of their computers, with the games master holding the dice and the cards. For Amanda and Kabel in San Francisco, and for Sherlock Holmes in Reno, it was 8:00 p.m.; for Sir Edmond Paddington in New Jersey and Abatha in Montreal, it was 11:00 p.m.; and for Esmeralda, who lived in the future, in New Zealand, it was already 3:00 p.m. the next day. When the game first started, they had played in a private text-based chat room, but when—at Amanda's suggestion—they started to investigate real crimes, they decided to use video chat. They were so used to dealing with each other in character that every time they logged on there would be an astonished pause when they saw each other in person. It was difficult to see this boy confined to a wheelchair as the tempestuous gypsy Esmeralda, to imagine the black kid in the baseball cap as Conan Doyle's celebrated detective, or this scrawny, acne-ridden, agoraphobic teenager as a retired English colonel. Only the anorexic girl in Montreal looked a little like her character—Abatha, the psychic, a skeletal figure more spirit than substance. They said hello to the games master and aired their concern that they had made little progress in the Ed Staton case during the previous session.

"Let's discuss what's come up in the Case of the Misplaced Baseball Bat before moving on to the Constantes," suggested Amanda. "According to my dad, Ed Staton made no attempt to defend himself. There were no signs of a struggle, no bruises or contusions on the body."

"Which could mean he knew his killer," said Sherlock Holmes.

"But it doesn't explain why Staton was kneeling or sitting when he was shot in the head," said the games master.

"How do we know that he was?" asked Esmeralda.

"From the bullet's angle of entry. The shot was fired at close range—about fifteen inches—and the bullet lodged inside the skull; there was no exit wound. The weapon was a small semiautomatic pistol."

"That's a pretty common handgun," interrupted Colonel Paddington, "small, easy to conceal in a pocket or a handbag; it's not a serious weapon. A hardened criminal would use something more lethal than that."

"Maybe, but it was lethal enough to kill Staton. Afterward the murderer pitched him over the vaulting horse and . . . well, we all know what he did with the baseball bat. . . ."

"It can't have been easy to get his pants down and position him over the vaulting horse; Staton was tall, and he was heavy. Why do it?"

"A message," murmured Abatha. "A sign, a warning."

"Statistically, a baseball bat is often used in cases of domestic violence," said Colonel Paddington in his affected British accent.

"And why would the killer bring a bat rather than just using one he found at the school?"

"Maybe he didn't know there would be bats in the gym and brought one along," suggested Abatha.

"Which would indicate that the killer has some connection to Arkansas," said Sherlock. "Either that, or the bat has a particular significance."

"Permission to speak?" said Kabel.

"Go ahead."

"The weapon was an ordinary thirty-two-inch aluminum bat, the kind used by high school kids—light, powerful, durable."

"Hmm . . . the mystery of the baseball bat," mused Abatha. "I suspect the killer chose it for sentimental reasons."

"Ha! So you're saying our killer's a romantic?" mocked Sir Edmond Paddington.

"No one practices sodomy for sentimental reasons," said Sherlock, the only one who did not resort to euphemisms.

"How would you know?" asked Esmeralda.

"Surely it depends on the sentiment?" said Abatha.

They spent fifteen minutes debating the various possibilities until the games master, deciding they had spent long enough on Ed Staton, moved on to what they called the Case of Branding by Blowtorch, committed on November 10. Amanda asked her henchman to outline the facts. Kabel read from his notes, embellishing the tale with a few choice details like any aspiring writer would.

Starting from this scenario, they began to play. Ripper, the kids agreed, had evolved into something much more gripping than the original game, and the players no longer wanted to be limited by the dice and the cards that had previously dictated their moves. It was therefore decided that players could only use logic to solve cases, with the exception of Abatha, who was allowed to use her psychic powers. Three players were tasked with working up a detailed analysis of the murders; Abatha would appeal to the spirit world, and Kabel would continue his offline investigation, while Amanda would coordinate their efforts and plan a course of action.

///////////////////

Unlike his granddaughter, who had no time for the man, Blake Jackson liked Alan Keller and hoped that his affair with Indiana might end in marriage. His daughter needed some stability in her life, a levelheaded man to protect and care for her, he thought. She needed a second father, since he was not going to be around forever. Alan was only nine years younger than Blake, and he clearly had a number of irritating quirks that, as with anyone, would probably only get worse with age. But compared with the men in Indiana's past he was Prince Charming. He was the only one Blake could really talk to about books, or about culture in general. Indiana's previous boyfriends—beginning with Bob Martín—had all been jocks: strong as a bull and about as smart. His daughter did not usually appeal to intellectuals, so Alan's arrival had been a godsend.

As a little girl, Amanda had pestered Blake with questions about her parents; she was much too intelligent to believe the fairy-tale version told to her by her grandmother Encarnación. Amanda had been only three years old when Indiana and Bob split up, and could not remember a time when they had all lived under the same roof. In fact—despite Doña Encarnación's eloquence—Amanda found it difficult to imagine her parents together at all.

The fifteen years since her son's divorce had been agony for Encarnación, a devout Catholic who said the rosary every day and regularly prayed to Saint Jude—the patron saint of hopeless causes—lighting votive candles in the hope the couple would be reconciled.

Blake loved Bob Martín like the son he'd never had. He could not help himself: he found himself moved by his former son-in-law's spontaneous displays of affection, his utter devotion to Amanda, his loyal friendship for Indiana. But he did not want Saint Jude to miraculously bring them back together. The only thing they had in common was their daughter. Apart, they behaved like brother and sister; together, they would inevitably have come to blows.

They had met in high school when Indiana was fifteen, and Bob twenty. Officially, he should have already graduated, and any other school would have thrown him out when he turned eighteen, but Bob was the captain of the football team and the coach's blue-eyed boy; to the other teachers he was a nightmare they tolerated only because he was the finest athlete to play for the school since its founding in 1956. Good-looking and arrogant, Bob aroused violent passions in the girls, who plagued him with propositions and threats of suicide, while inspiring a mixture of fear and admiration in the boys, who bragged about his sporting prowess and his daring pranks but kept a wary distance, since, if his mood changed, Bob could knock them down with his little finger. Indiana, who had the face of an angel, the body of a grown woman, and a tendency to wear her heart on her sleeve, rivaled the football captain in popularity. She was a picture of innocence, while he had a reputation as the devil incarnate: no one was surprised when they fell in love, but anyone who hoped she would be a good influence on him was sorely disappointed. The opposite happened: Bob went right on being the bonehead he had always been, while Indiana plunged headfirst into love, alcohol, and pot.

Soon afterward, Blake noticed that his daughter's clothes suddenly seemed too tight, and she was often in tears. He questioned her relentlessly until finally she confessed that she hadn't had her period in three or four months, maybe five—she wasn't sure, since she'd always been irregular. Blake buried his face in his hands. His

only excuse for missing the obvious signs that Indiana was pregnant, just as he had turned a blind eye when she stumbled home
drunk or floating in a marijuana haze, was the fact that his wife,
Marianne, was seriously ill, and he spent all his time taking care
of her. He grabbed his daughter by the arm and took her first to a
gynecologist, who confirmed that the pregnancy was too far advanced to consider a termination; next, to the school principal; and
finally to confront the lothario responsible for her condition.

The Martín house in the Mission district came as a surprise to
Blake, who was expecting something more modest. Indiana had
told him only that Bob's mother had a business making tortillas,
so Blake had naturally expected to find an immigrant family in
straitened circumstances. When Bob heard that Indiana and her
father were coming to visit, he disappeared, leaving his mother
to defend him. Blake found himself face-to-face with a beautiful
middle-aged woman dressed all in black save for her fingernails
and her lips, which were painted flame red. She introduced herself
as Encarnación, widow of the late Señor Martín. The house was
warm and welcoming, with heavy furniture, threadbare carpets,
toys strewn over the floor, family photographs, a cabinet filled
with football trophies, and two plump cats lounging on the green
plush sofa. Enthroned on a high-backed chair with carved lion's-
paw feet, Bob's grandmother sat ramrod straight, dressed in black
like her daughter, her gray hair pulled back into a bun so tight
that from the front she looked almost bald. The old woman looked
Blake and Indiana up and down without a word.

"I am devastated by my son's actions, Señor Jackson," the
widow began. "I have failed as a mother, failed to instill in Bob
a sense of responsibility. What good are all these shiny trophies
if the boy has no sense of decency?" she wondered rhetorically,
gesturing to the cabinet.

Blake accepted the small cup of strong coffee brought by a maid from the kitchen and sat down on the sofa, which was covered in cat hair. Indiana remained standing, her cheeks flushed with embarrassment, her hands clasped over her blouse to hide her bump, while Doña Encarnación proceeded to give them a potted family history.

"My mother here—God preserve her—was a schoolteacher in Mexico, and my father—God forgive him—was a bandido who abandoned her just after they got married to seek his fortune here in America. At first she got one or two letters, but then months went by with no news. Meanwhile, I was born—Encarnación, at your service—and my mother sold what little she had and, with me in her arms, set off to find my father. She traveled all over California, and we stayed with Mexican families who took pity on us. Finally we arrived in San Francisco, and my mother found out that her husband was in jail for killing a man in a brawl. She visited him only once, told him to take care, then rolled up her sleeves and got to work. In America, she had no future as a schoolteacher, but she knew how to cook."

Since her daughter spoke of her as though she were dead, or a character in some myth, Blake took it for granted that the grandmother seated on her ceremonial throne spoke no English. Doña Encarnación went on to explain that she had grown up tied to her mother's apron strings and working from a very early age. Fifteen years later, when her father was released from prison, wizened, sickly, and covered in tattoos, he was duly deported. His wife did not go back with him to Mexico; by then her love for him had withered, and besides, she had a successful business selling tacos in the heart of the Mission district. Not long afterward, young Encarnación met José Manuel Martín, a second-generation Mexican who had a voice like a nightingale, a mariachi band, and American citizenship. They were married, and he joined his mother-in-law's thriving business. By the time of Señor Martín's untimely death, the Martíns had succeeded in amassing five children, three restaurants, and a tortilla factory.

"When it came, death found José Manuel—may God enfold him in his holy breast—singing *rancheras*," said the widow. Her two daughters, she added, now ran the Martín family business, while her two eldest sons had respectable jobs in their professions; all of them were devout Christians and devoted to their family. The only child who had ever caused her heartache was her youngest son, Bob, who had been only two years old when she was widowed and had therefore grown up without a father's firm hand.

"I'm sorry, Señora." Blake sighed. "To tell the truth, I'm not sure why we came. There is nothing anyone can do. My daughter's pregnancy is already too far advanced."

"What do you mean, nothing anyone can do, Señor Jackson? Bob must accept his responsibilities. In this family, a man does not go around fathering bastards. Pardon my language, but there is no other word, and I feel it best to be absolutely clear. Bob will have to marry the girl."

"Marry her?" Blake leaped to his feet. "But Indiana is barely fifteen!"

"I'll be sixteen in March," his daughter corrected him in a whisper.

"You shut your mouth!" roared her father, though he had never before raised his voice to her.

"My sainted mother has six great-grandchildren—my grandchildren," said the widow. "Together we have helped to raise them, just as we will help to raise this child when it comes along, by the grace of God."

In the silence that followed this pronouncement, the great-grandmother rose from her throne, walked over to Indiana, studied her coldly, and said in perfect English:

"What is your name, child?"

"Indi—Indiana Jackson."

"I don't much care for the name. Is there a Saint Indiana?"

"I'm not sure. My mom called me that because that's where she was born."

"Ah!" murmured the old lady, speechless. She stepped closer and stroked the girl's swollen belly. "The baby you are carrying is a girl. Make sure you give her a good Catholic name."

The following day, Bob Martín appeared at the Jackson house on Potrero Hill wearing a dark suit and a funereal tie, carrying a bunch of moribund flowers. He was flanked by his mother and by one of his brothers, who gripped the boy's arm like a prison warden. Indiana did not come downstairs—she had spent the whole night crying, and was in a terrible state. By now Blake was resigned to the idea of marriage, having failed to persuade his daughter that there were less permanent solutions. He had tried all the usual arguments, though he stopped short of threatening to have Bob charged with statutory rape. The couple was quietly married at City Hall, having promised Doña Encarnación that they would have a church wedding as soon as Indiana—who had been raised by agnostics—could be baptized.

Four months later, on May 30, 1994, Indiana gave birth to a little girl, just as Bob's grandmother had predicted. After hours of excruciating labor, the child emerged from her mother's belly and was dropped into the hands of Blake Jackson, who cut the umbilical cord using scissors given him by the duty doctor. Blake quickly took his granddaughter, swaddled in a pink blanket, a woolly cap pulled down over her eyebrows, to introduce her to the Martín family and to Indiana's school friends, who had flocked to the hospital, bringing balloons and cuddly toys. When she saw her only granddaughter, Doña Encarnación sobbed as though she were at a funeral—her other grandchildren counted for little, since all were boys. She had spent months preparing, had bought a traditional bassinet with a starched white canopy, two suitcases full of pretty dresses, and a pair of pearl earrings that she planned to put in the little girl's ears as soon as her mother's back was turned. Bob's brothers spent hours searching for him, trying to make sure he was present for the birth of his daughter, but it being Sunday, the new father was off celebrating another win with his football team and did not show up until the early hours.

As soon as Indiana could hobble out of the delivery room and sit in a wheelchair, her father took her and her newborn upstairs to the fourth floor, where Marianne, the child's other grandmother, lay dying.

"What are you going to call her?" asked Marianne, her voice scarcely audible.

"Amanda. It means bright, clever, deserving to be loved."

"That's pretty. In what language?"

"Sanskrit," explained her daughter, who had dreamed of India ever since she was a little girl, "or it could be Latin. But the Martíns think it's a Catholic name."

Marianne only just lived long enough to see her granddaughter. With her dying breath, she offered Indiana one last piece of advice. "You're going to need a lot of support to raise your daughter, Indi. You can rely on your papa and on the Martín family, but don't let Bob wash his hands of her. Amanda will need a father, and though he's a little immature, Bob is a good boy." She was right.

Sunday, 8

T hank God for the Internet, thought Amanda as she got ready, because if I'd had to ask the girls at school, I'd look like a complete idiot. Amanda had heard about raves, those secret hedonistic gatherings of teenagers, but could not picture what they were actually like until she looked up the term online and discovered everything she needed to know, including the appropriate dress code. She hunted down what she needed from her wardrobe, ripped the sleeves from an old T-shirt, shortened a skirt with irregular scissor slashes, and bought a tube of luminous paint. The idea of asking her father whether she could go to a rave was so absurd that it did not even occur to her. He would never have agreed; in fact, had he known, he would have shown up with a whole battalion of officers and ruined the party. She told him she didn't need a ride, that a friend would drop her back at school, and he didn't seem to notice that she looked more like she was heading to a carnival than back to boarding school—this was how his daughter usually dressed.

Amanda caught a cab that dropped her at Union Square at 6:00

p.m., prepared to wait for some time. By now she should already have been back at school, but she had taken the precaution of letting the teachers know she would not get back until Monday morning so no one would call her parents. She had left her violin in the dorm, but there was nothing she could do to get rid of her heavy backpack. She spent fifteen minutes watching the square's newest attraction: a young man smeared from head to foot in gold paint who stood frozen like a statue while tourists posed to have their picture taken. She strolled around Macy's and, in one of the restrooms, painted luminous stripes on her arms. Outside, it was dark now. To kill time, she went to a hole-in-the-wall that served Chinese food, and at nine arrived back at Union Square, by now empty but for a few dawdling tourists and the beggars who came from colder climates to winter in California, settling in their sleeping bags for the night.

She sat underneath a streetlamp, playing chess on her cell phone, wrapped in one of her grandfather's old cardigans, something that always soothed her. She checked the time every five minutes, anxiously wondering whether Cynthia and her friends would pick her up as promised. Cynthia was a girl from school who had bullied her for three years and then suddenly, without explanation, invited her to this rave, even offering her a ride to Tiburon, forty minutes' drive from San Francisco. Somewhat skeptical, since this was the first time they had included her, Amanda nevertheless immediately accepted.

If only Bradley, her childhood friend and future husband, were here, she would feel more confident. She had spoken to him a couple of times earlier in the day, though she said nothing about her plans for the evening, afraid that he might try to dissuade her from going. With Bradley, as with her father, it was best to recount the facts after the disaster had occurred. She missed the boy that Bradley had once been, someone warmer and funnier than the

straitlaced young man he had become almost as soon as he started
to shave. As children they had played at being married and found
other convoluted ways to satisfy their childish curiosity, but barely
had Bradley reached his teens—a couple of years before she did—
than their beautiful friendship began to flounder. In high school
Bradley was a high flyer: he was captain of the swim team, and
when he discovered he could attract girls whose anatomy was more
exciting, he began to treat Amanda like a little sister. But Amanda
had a good memory, and had not forgotten the secret games they
played at the bottom of the garden, something she planned to remind Bradley about when she went to MIT in September. In the
meantime, she did her best not to worry him with minor details
like this rave.

Her mom's fridge usually contained a few "magic brownies,"
gifts from Matheus Pereira, which Indiana would leave there for
months until they were covered with green mold and fit only for
the garbage. Amanda had tried them just to be in tune with the
rest of her generation, but she could not see what was so entertaining about wandering around out of her head. To her it was time
wasted that might be better spent playing Ripper. But that Sunday
evening, wrapped in her grandfather's threadbare cardigan, sitting
beneath the streetlamp on Union Square, she thought nostalgically
about Pereira's "space cakes"; they would have calmed her down.

By half past ten Amanda was on the point of crying, convinced
that Cynthia had made a fool of her out of sheer spite. When word
got around about her humiliation, she would be the laughingstock
of the school. I will not cry, I will not cry, she said to herself. Just
as she picked up her cell phone to call her grandfather and ask him
to come and get her, a van pulled up on the corner of Geary and
Powell and someone leaned halfway out the window, waving frantically to her.

Amanda rushed over, her heart pounding. Inside the van were

three boys wreathed in clouds of smoke, all high as kites, including the driver. One of them got out of the passenger seat and gestured for her to sit next to the driver, a young guy with black hair who was very handsome in a Goth sort of way. "Hey, I'm Clive, Cynthia's brother," he introduced himself, flooring the accelerator before Amanda even had time to close the door. Amanda recalled that Cynthia had introduced them at the school Christmas concert. Clive had shown up with his parents, wearing a blue suit, white shirt, and patent leather shoes, a very different look from this guy sitting next to her with his deathly pale complexion and bags under his eyes that looked like bruises. After the school concert Clive, with mocking, overstated formality, had congratulated her on her violin solo. "See you soon, I hope," he said, winking, as he left. Amanda was sure that she had misheard; as far as she was aware, until that moment no boy had ever looked at her twice. She decided that this must have something to do with Cynthia's unexpected invitation. This new, ghostly version of Clive, to say nothing of his erratic driving, worried her somewhat, but at least he was someone she knew, someone she could ask to drop her off tomorrow at school in time.

Clive drove on, letting out eerie howls and drinking from a hip flask the boys were passing around, but he managed to find the Golden Gate Bridge and get onto Route 101 without crashing the car or attracting the attention of the police. In Sausalito, Cynthia and another girl climbed into the van, settled into their seats, and immediately joined in the drinking without so much as glancing at Amanda or acknowledging her greeting. With a peremptory gesture, Clive passed the hip flask to Amanda, who didn't dare refuse. Hoping it might relax her a little, she took a sip that left her throat on fire and her eyes welling with tears; she felt foolish and out of place, as she often did when she was in a group. Worse still, she felt ridiculous, as neither of the girls had dressed up like she had. It was too late now to try and cover up her paint-streaked forearms, since she'd put her grandfather's cardigan into her backpack before getting into the van. She tried to ignore the sarcastic whispers from the backseat. Clive took the exit at Tiburon Boulevard and drove down the long road that hugged the shore of Richardson Bay, then turned up a hill and glanced around, trying to get his bearings. When they finally arrived at their destination, Amanda saw that it was a private residence shielded from the neighboring houses by a high, seemingly impenetrable wall. Dozens of cars and motorbikes were parked out on the street. She climbed out of the van, knees trembling, and followed Clive through a dark garden. At the foot of the steps leading up to the house, she hid her backpack under a bush, but she clung to her cell phone like a life raft.

Inside were throngs of teenagers, some dancing to the deafening thump of the music, others drinking, and a few sprawled on the stairs amid bottles and beer cans. There were no lasers, no psychedelic colors, just a deserted house stripped of furniture, with a few packing cases in the living room; the air was thick with smoke, and there was a rancid stench, a mixture of paint, dope, and garbage. Amanda froze, unable to move, but Clive hugged her to his body and began to twitch to the frenetic rhythm of the music, dragging her into the living room, where everyone was dancing alone, each lost in a private little world. Someone handed her a paper cup of rum and pineapple juice, and her mouth felt so dry she drained it in three gulps. She felt herself choke with fear and claustrophobia, something that used to happen to her when, as a little girl, she would hide in her makeshift tent to escape the terrible perils of the world, the crushing presence of human beings, their oppressive odors and booming voices.

Clive kissed her neck, searching for her lips, and she responded with a smack from her cell phone that almost broke his nose but did little to discourage him. Desperate, she extricated herself from the hands slipping into the neckline of her T-shirt and up her short skirt, trying to elbow her way out. Amanda tolerated physical contact only from her immediate family and some animals; finding herself being mauled, invaded, hemmed in by other bodies, she began to howl, but the blaring music drowned out her screams. She felt as though she were at the bottom of the sea, with no air, no voice, slowly drowning.

////////////////

Amanda, who usually prided herself on knowing the time without needing a watch, had no idea how long she'd spent in the house. She didn't know whether she'd seen Cynthia and Clive again that night, or how she had managed to force her way through the crowd to hide among the packing cases on which music equipment had been set up. For what seemed an eternity, she stayed huddled inside one of the crates, doubled up like an acrobat and trembling uncontrollably, her eyes tight shut, her hands clasped over her ears. It did not occur to her to run into the street, to call her grandfather or phone her parents.

At some point the police arrived in a deafening wail of sirens, surrounded the property, and burst in, but by then Amanda was in such a state that it was twenty minutes before she realized that the chatter of teenagers and the thump of music had been replaced by the sound of orders, by whistles and screams. She steeled herself, opening her eyes and peering between the planks of her hiding place to see flashlight beams and the legs of people being rounded up by uniformed officers. A few kids tried to make a run for it, but most meekly obeyed the order to go out and line up in the street, where they were frisked for weapons and drugs and questioned, those underage being separated from the rest. They all gave the same story—they had received an invitation from a friend by SMS or on Facebook, and did not know whose house it was, or that it

was unoccupied and currently up for sale, nor could they explain
how they had entered the premises.

Amanda remained deathly silent inside her shelter, and no one
thought to look among the crates, though two or three officers
searched the rest of the house from top to bottom, opening doors
and checking alcoves to make sure there were no stragglers. Grad-
ually the interior of the house became calm, the silence broken
only by the muffled sound of voices from the street, and Amanda
was able to think clearly. In the silence, without the menacing
presence of the partygoers, she felt the walls retreating, and she
could breathe again. She had decided to wait until everyone had
left before she emerged from her hiding place when suddenly she
heard an officer's commanding voice giving orders that the house
be locked and guarded until a technician could come to reset the
alarm system.

An hour and a half later, the police had arrested all the intoxicated kids, taken details of the others and let them go, and fer-
ried those who were underage down to the station to wait for their
parents. Someone from the security company bolted the windows
and doors and turned on the alarm and motion sensors. Locked
up in this dark abandoned mansion where the sickening stench of
the party still lingered, Amanda was unable to move or even open
a window without triggering the alarm. After the arrival of the
police, she'd felt that there was no way out; she could hardly ask
her mother, who did not have a car, to come pick her up; her father
would have been humiliated in front of his colleagues through his
daughter's stupidity; and she certainly could not call her grandfather, who would never forgive her for going to such a place without
telling him. She could think of only one person who would help
her without asking questions. She rang the number until her battery was dead, but every time she reached voice mail. *Come and
get me, come and get me*. Shivering with cold, she curled up in the

packing case once more and waited for dawn, praying that someone would come to let her out.

//////////////////////

Sometime between two and three in the morning, Ryan's cell phone
vibrated several times. It was far from his bed, plugged in to charge.
It was bitterly cold in the loft, a vast, sparsely furnished open-plan
apartment in a former printworks with exposed brick walls, cement floors, and a tangle of aluminum pipes running across the
ceiling, with no curtains, no carpets, and no heating. Ryan slept in
his boxer shorts, covered with an electric blanket, a pillow over his
head. At 5:00 a.m., Attila, who found the winter nights too long,
jumped up on the bed to let him know that it was time to begin his
morning rituals.

Ryan sat bolt upright, acting on military instinct, his head still
swimming with images from a disturbing dream. In the darkness,
he groped on the floor for his prosthetic leg and strapped it on. Attila was nudging him with his snout, and Ryan responded to this
greeting by patting the dog's back once or twice; then he flicked on
the light, pulled on sweatpants and thick socks, and padded to the
bathroom. Emerging again, he found Attila waiting with feigned
indifference, betrayed by his irrepressibly wagging tail. The routine was the same every morning. "I'm coming, fella," said Ryan,
drying his face with a towel. "Just hold on a second." He began
measuring out food into the dog's bowl, at which point Attila,
abandoning all pretense, began the complicated little dance with
which he always greeted breakfast, though he did not approach the
bowl until Ryan gave him the signal.

Before beginning the slow Qigong exercises, his daily half hour
of meditation in movement, Ryan glanced at his cell, at which point
he noticed that he had a long list of missed calls from Amanda.
Please come get me, I'm hiding, don't say anything to Mom,

please come get me.... He dialed and dialed her number, and when he could not get through, he felt his heart lurch in his chest before his habitual calm kicked in again, the calmness learned as part of the toughest military training anywhere in the world. Indiana's daughter was in trouble, he realized, but it was not serious: she had not been kidnapped, nor did she seem to be in any real danger, though she had to be very scared, given that she seemed unable to explain what was happening or where exactly she was.

He dressed in a matter of seconds and sat down in front of his computers. He had systems and software as sophisticated as any used by the Pentagon, making it possible for him to work remotely. Triangulating the location of a cell phone that had rung him eighteen times was easy. He called the station house in Tiburon, rattled off his CIA badge number, requested he be put through to the chief, and asked whether there had been any callouts during the night. The officer, assuming Ryan was concerned about one of the teenagers who had been arrested, told him about the rave, mentioning the address but downplaying the incident—this was not the first time something like this had happened, and there had been no vandalism. Everything was fine now, he said; the alarm had been switched on, and they had been in touch with the real estate agents selling the property so they could send round a cleaning crew. In all probability, charges would not be brought against the kids, but that decision was not a police matter. Ryan thanked him, and a moment later he had an aerial view of the property on his computer screen and a map of how to get there. "C'mon, Attila!" he called, and though the dog could not hear, he knew from Ryan's manner that they weren't going for a walk around the block: this was a call to action.

As he raced down to his truck, Ryan phoned Pedro Alarcón, who at this hour was probably preparing for class and sipping maté. His friend still clung to old habits from his native Uruguay, such as drinking this bitter greenish concoction, which Ryan personally thought tasted foul. He was punctilious about the ritual: he would only use the maté gourd and the silver straw he had inherited from his parents, yerba imported directly from Montevideo, and filtered water heated to a precise temperature.

"Get some clothes on—I'll be there to pick you up in eleven minutes," Ryan said by way of greeting, "and bring whatever you need to disable an alarm."

"It's early, man. . . . What's the deal?"

"Unlawful entry."

"What kind of an alarm system?"

"It's a private house, shouldn't be too complicated."

Pedro sighed. "At least we're not robbing a bank."

It was still dark, and Monday-morning rush hour had not yet started when Ryan, Pedro, and Attila crossed the Golden Gate Bridge. Yellowish floodlights lit the red steel structure, which looked as though it were suspended in midair, and from the distance came the wail of the lighthouse siren that guided vessels safely through the dense fog. By the time they reached the house in Tiburon, the sky was beginning to pale, a few stray cars were circulating, and the early-morning joggers were just setting out.

Assuming that the residents of such an elegant neighborhood would be suspicious of strangers, the Navy SEAL parked his truck a block from the house and pretended to be walking his dog while he reconnoitered the terrain.

Pedro Alarcón walked briskly toward the house as though he had been sent by the owner, slipped a picklock into the padlock securing the gate—child's play to this Houdini who could crack a safe with his eyes closed—and in less than a minute had it open. Security was Ryan's area of expertise; he worked with military and governmental agencies who hired him to protect their information.

His job was to get inside the head of the person who might want to steal such data—think like the enemy, imagine all the possible ways of gaining access—and then design a system to prevent it from happening. Watching Alarcón at work with his picklock, it occurred to Ryan that one man, with the necessary skills and determination, could break even the most sophisticated security codes. This was the danger of terrorism: it pitted the cunning of a single individual hiding in a crowd against the colossal might of the most powerful nations on earth.

Now fifty-nine, Pedro Alarcón had been forced to leave Uruguay during the bloody dictatorship in 1976. At eighteen he had joined the *tupamaros*, an urban Communist guerrilla organization waging an armed struggle against the government, convinced that only by violence could they change Uruguay's prevailing regime of abuse, corruption, and injustice. The *tupamaros* planted bombs, robbed banks, and kidnapped people before being crushed by the army: some had died fighting, some were executed, others captured and tortured, the rest forced into exile. Alarcón, who had begun his adult life assembling homemade bombs and forcing locks, still had a framed poster from the 1970s, now yellowed with age, showing him with three of his *tupamaro* comrades and offering a reward from the military for their capture. The pallid boy in the photo, with his long, shaggy hair, his beard, and his astonished expression, was very different from the man Ryan knew, a short, wiry gray-haired man, all bones and sinew, intelligent and imperturbable, with the manual dexterity of an illusionist.

These days Alarcón was professor of artificial intelligence at Stanford University and competed as a triathlete with Ryan, who was twenty years his junior. Aside from their shared passion for technology and sport, both were men of few words, which was why they got along so well. They both lived frugal lives and were bachelors; if anyone asked, they'd claim they'd seen too much of life to believe in schmaltzy love stories or to be tied down to one woman when there were so many willing beauties in the world, but deep down they suspected that they had ended up alone out of sheer bad luck. According to Indiana Jackson, growing old alone meant dying of heartache, and though they would never have admitted it, secretly they agreed.

Within minutes Pedro Alarcón had picked the lock on the main door and managed to disable the alarm, and both men stepped into the house. Ryan used his cell phone as a flashlight, keeping a tight grip on Attila, who was ready to do battle—straining at the leash, panting, teeth bared, a low growl coming from deep in his throat.

In a sudden flash, as had so often happened at the most inopportune moments, Ryan found himself back in Afghanistan. Part of his brain could process what was happening: post-traumatic stress disorder, the symptoms of which were flashbacks, night terrors, depression, and fits of crying or rage. Ryan had struggled to overcome the temptation to commit suicide, recovered from the addictions to alcohol and drugs that a few years earlier had all but killed him, but he knew they could come back at any time. He could never let his guard down; these symptoms were his enemy now.

He could hear his father's voice: no man fit to wear the uniform would bitch about having carried out orders or blame the navy for his nightmares, war is for the brave and the strong, if you're scared of blood, get a different job. Another part of his brain reeled off the statistics he knew by heart: 2.3 million American combatants in Iraq and Afghanistan over the past decade, 6,179 dead, 47,000 wounded, most with devastating injuries, 210,000 war vets being treated for the same syndrome he suffered from, to say nothing of the epidemic that had devastated the armed forces: an estimated 700,000 soldiers suffering psychological problems or with brain damage.

And still there was a small, dark corner of Ryan's mind—a part he could not control—that was trapped in the past, in that night in Afghanistan.

A group of Navy SEALs advances through the desert terrain, heading for a village in the foothills of the mountains. Their orders are to conduct a house-to-house search, dismantle the terrorist cell apparently operating in the region, and bring prisoners back for interrogation. Their ultimate objective is the elusive phantom of Osama bin Laden himself. It is a nocturnal mission, aiming to surprise the enemy and minimize collateral damage: at night there will be no women in the market, no children playing in the dust. This is a secret mission requiring speed and discretion, a specialty of SEAL Team Six, trained to operate in desert heat, in arctic cold, to deal with underwater currents, soaring peaks, the pestilential miasma of the jungle. The night is cloudless, moonlit; Ryan can make out the village silhouetted in the distance and, as they move closer, a dozen or so mud huts, a well, and some livestock pens. The bleating of a goat breaks the spectral silence of the night, making him start. He feels a tingling in his hands, in the back of his neck; he feels adrenaline course through his veins, his every muscle tense; he can sense the men advancing through the shadows with him, who are a part of him: sixteen brothers but a single beating heart. This was what the instructor had hammered home during BUD/S training, the infamous Hell Week during which they were pushed beyond the limits of human endurance, an ordeal that only 15 percent of men come through; they are the invincibles.

"Hey, Ryan, what's up, buddy?"

The voice came from far away, and had called his name twice before he managed to come back from the remote village in Afghanistan to the deserted mansion in Tiburon, California. Pedro Alarcón was shaking his shoulder. Ryan snapped out of his trance and sucked in a lungful of air, trying to dispel the memories and focus on the present. He heard Pedro calling to Amanda a couple of times, careful to keep his voice low so as not to scare her, and then he realized he had let Attila off the leash. He searched for him in the beam from his cell phone and saw the dog dashing around, nose pressed to the floor, bewildered by the combination of smells. Attila was trained to sniff out explosives or bodies, whether alive or dead. With two taps on his collar, Ryan let the dog know they were looking for a person. He had no need to use words; he simply picked up the leash, and as soon as he tugged, Attila stopped, attentive, his intelligent eyes questioning. Ryan signaled for him to stay, waiting until the dog was a little calmer. Then they resumed the search, Ryan following a still restive Attila, keeping a tight grip on the leash, through the kitchen, the laundry room, and finally the living room, while Alarcón kept watch at the front door. Attila quickly led him to the packing crates, snuffling between the planks, teeth bared.

Shining his flashlight between the crates at which Attila was pawing, Ryan saw a huddled figure and was immediately plunged into the past again. For a moment he could see two trembling children huddled in a trench—a girl of four or five with a scarf tied around her head, her huge green eyes wide with terror as she clutched a baby. Attila growled and tugged at the leash, jolting Ryan back to the reality, to this moment, this place.

///////////////////

Exhausted from crying, Amanda had fallen asleep inside the packing crate, curled up like a cat in an attempt to keep warm. Attila immediately recognized the familiar scent of the girl and sat back on his hindquarters, waiting for instructions while Ryan woke Amanda. Awkwardly she straightened her cramped body, blinded by the light shining into her eyes, not knowing where she was. It took a few seconds for her to remember what had happened.

"It's me, Ryan," he whispered, helping her out of the crate. "Everything's fine." When she recognized him, she threw her arms around his neck and buried her face in his broad chest while he stroked her back reassuringly, murmuring words of affection that he had never said to anyone, his heart aching as though it were not this spoiled little girl wetting his shirt with her tears but the other girl, the girl with green eyes and her little brother, the children he should have rescued from the dugout, carefully shielding them with his arms so that they would not see what had happened. He wrapped Amanda up in his leather jacket and held her up as they cut through the garden, collecting the backpack she had left under one of the bushes, and headed back to his truck, where they waited for Pedro Alarcón to lock up the house.

Amanda was choked with tears, and with a cold that had been brewing for some days before viciously flaring up that night. Ryan and Alarcón thought she was in no fit state to go back to school, but when she insisted, they stopped by a drugstore, where they bought a cold remedy and rubbing alcohol to remove the fluorescent paint from her arms. They stopped for breakfast at the only café they could find open—linoleum floor, plastic chairs and tables. The room was warm, and the air was filled with the delicious smell of fried bacon. The only other customers were four men wearing overalls and hard hats. A girl with hair gelled into porcupine spikes, blue nail polish, and a sleepy expression took their order, looking as though this was the end of an all-night shift.

While they waited for their food, Amanda made her saviors promise they would not say a word to anyone about what had happened. She, master of Ripper, expert in defeating evildoers and plotting dangerous adventures, had spent the night in a packing crate, a mass of snot and tears. With a couple of aspirin, a cup of hot chocolate, and a stack of pancakes and syrup in front of her, the escapade she recounted to them sounded pathetic, but Ryan and

Alarcón did not make fun or scold her. The former methodically tucked into his eggs and sausage, while the latter buried his nose in a cup of coffee—a poor substitute for maté—to hide his smile.

"Where are you from?" Amanda asked Alarcón.

"From here."

"You sound foreign."

"He's from Uruguay," Ryan interrupted.

"A tiny little country in South America," Alarcón explained.

"This semester I have to do a project on a country for my social justice class. Do you mind if I use yours?"

"I'd be honored, but you'd be better off picking somewhere in Africa or Asia—nothing ever happens in Uruguay."

"That's why I want to use it—it'll be easy. For part of the presentation, I have to interview someone from the country I've chosen, probably on video. Would that be okay?"

They swapped phone numbers and e-mail addresses and agreed to meet up in late February or early March to film the interview. At seven thirty that miserable morning, the two men dropped the girl off in front of the gates of her school. She said good-bye, shyly kissing each of them on the cheek, hiked her backpack onto her shoulder, and walked away, head down, dragging her feet.

Monday, 9

Alan Keller's best-kept secret was that from a young age he had suffered from erectile dysfunction, a constant humiliation that made him avoid intimacy with women he found attractive, for fear of failing, and with prostitutes, because the experience left him depressed and angry. He and his psychoanalyst had spent years discussing the Oedipus complex until they were both thoroughly bored and moved on to other subjects. To compensate, he set himself the task of gaining an exhaustive knowledge of feminine sensuality, the things they should have taught at school if, as he liked to put it, the educational system dealt less with the reproduction of fruit flies and more with human sexuality. He learned ways of making love without having to rely on his erection, skillfully making up for what he lacked in potency. Later, by which time he had already developed a reputation as a ladies' man, Viagra came along, and the problem ceased to torment him. He was on the point of turning fifty when Indiana blew into his life like a spring gale, ready to sweep away any trace of insecurity. He dated her for several weeks, never progressing beyond slow, lingering kisses, laying the groundwork with commendable patience until finally she tired of foreplay, unceremoniously grabbed his hand, and firmly took him to her bed—a four-poster with a preposterous silk canopy hung with little bells.

Indiana lived in an apartment above her father's garage, in an area of Potrero Hill that had never become fashionable, close to the drugstore where, for twenty-nine years, Blake Jackson had earned his living. From here, she could cycle to work by a route that was almost completely level—there was only one hill in between—a major advantage in San Francisco, a city built on hills. At a brisk walking pace, the journey took her an hour; by bike it was just twenty minutes. Her apartment had two separate entrances, a spiral staircase that connected to Blake's house and a door that opened directly onto the street via a steep flight of worn timber steps that were slippery in winter, and which every year her father suggested replacing. The apartment comprised two good-size rooms, a balcony, a half bath, and a tiny kitchenette set into a closet. It was more studio than apartment, and the family called it "the witch's cave," since aside from the bed, the bathroom, and the kitchen, every inch of space was taken up with art and aroma-therapy equipment. The day she took Alan to her bed, they had the place to themselves; Amanda was at boarding school, and Blake was playing squash, as he did every Wednesday night. There was no danger of him coming home early; after a game, he and his buddies would always go out for sauerkraut and beer at some decrepit Bierkeller, where they carried on drinking until they were thrown out at dawn.

After five minutes in bed, Alan, who had not thought to bring a magic blue pill with him, was so intoxicated by the smell of essential oils that he could hardly think. He surrendered to the hands of this youthful, joyous woman, who performed a miracle, managing to get him aroused with no drugs, just a playful tenderness. Gone were his doubts and fears. Amazed, he followed her lead, and at the end of the journey he returned to earth deeply grateful. And Indiana, who had had many lovers and was in a position to judge, was also grateful: this was the first man interested in her pleasure rather than his own. From that moment, it was Indiana who sought out Alan, who called him up, taunting him with her desire and her humor, suggesting they meet up at the Fairmont, flattering and praising him.

Alan never detected any falseness or scheming on her part. Indiana was outspoken. She seemed utterly in love, happy and beguiled. It was easy to love her, yet he did not allow himself to be tied down, considering himself a wayfarer in this world, a traveler who did not take the time to look more deeply into anything except art, which alone seemed to offer permanence. He had had his share of conquests, but no serious lover until he happened on Indiana, the only woman ever to captivate him. He was convinced their relationship worked precisely because they kept it separate from the rest of their lives. Indiana made do with little, and this selflessness suited him, though he considered it somewhat suspect; he believed that all human relationships were a trade-off in which the cleverest came out on top. They had been together for four years and never mentioned the future, and though he had no intention of getting married, it offended Alan that Indiana had not raised the subject. He thought of himself as a good catch—especially for a woman of no means like her. There was still the problem of the difference in their ages, but Alan knew a lot of men in their fifties who dated women twenty years their junior. The only thing Indiana had insisted on from the beginning, from that first unforgettable night spent beneath the Indian silk canopy, was fidelity.

"You make me really happy, Indi," he said in an uncharacteristic surge of honesty, mesmerized by what he had just experienced without recourse to pills. "I hope we can go on seeing each other."

"As a couple?" she asked.

"As lovers."

"Meaning we'd be exclusive. . . ."

"You mean monogamous?" He laughed.

Alan was a social animal; he enjoyed the company of interesting, sophisticated people, particularly of the women who naturally gravitated toward him because he knew how to make them feel special. He was the must-have guest at the parties that appeared in the society pages. He knew everyone, was up-to-date on all the latest gossip, the celebrities and their scandals. Although he deliberately strutted like a playboy to provoke desire among the women and jealousy among the men, he found that sexual relationships merely complicated his life, giving him less pleasure than good conversation or an entertaining show. Indiana Jackson had just proved there were exceptions.

"Let's agree on one thing, Alan," she proposed with unexpected seriousness. "Whatever this is, it has to be mutual—that way neither of us will feel betrayed. When I was married, I was very hurt by my husband's affairs, by his lies—it's something I don't want to go through again."

He readily agreed to monogamy—he had no intention of telling her that sleeping around was the least of his priorities. She agreed, but warned that if he did cheat on her, everything would be over between them.

"And you don't need to worry about me," she added. "When I'm in love, I have no problem being faithful."

"Then I'll have to make sure you stay in love with me."

Lit by the faint glow of candles in the darkened bedroom, Indiana sat naked on the bed, her legs drawn up, her hair tousled, a work of art open to Alan's expert gaze. He thought of *The Rape of the Daughters of Leucippus* in the Alte Pinakothek in Munich—the rounded breasts and pale nipples, the broad hips; the childlike dimples at the elbows and the knees—except that this woman had lips that were swollen with kisses and the unmistakable look of sated desire. *Voluptuous* was the word, he decided, surprised by the reaction of his own body, which had responded with a swiftness and a stiffness he could not remember ever experiencing.

A month later he began to spy on her. He could not believe that in the hedonistic atmosphere of San Francisco, this beautiful young woman would be faithful to him simply because she had given her word. He was so eaten up with jealousy that he hired a private detective, a man named Samuel Hamilton Jr., and instructed him to keep tabs on Indiana and a record of the men she met, including her patients at the Holistic Clinic. Hamilton was a short little man with the innocuous air of a vacuum cleaner salesman, but he had inherited the nose of a bloodhound from his father, a journalist who had solved a number of crimes in San Francisco back in the 1960s and was immortalized in the detective novels of William C. Gordon. The son was the spitting image of his father: short, red-haired, balding, keen-eyed. He was dogged and persistent in his fight against the criminal underworld but, overshadowed by his father's legend, had never managed to truly develop his potential and so scraped by as best he could. Hamilton tailed Indiana for a month without discovering anything of interest, and for a while, Alan was reassured, but his calm was short-lived; soon he would call the detective again, the cycle of mistrust repeating itself with shameful regularity. Fortunately, Indiana knew nothing about these machinations, though she ran into Samuel Hamilton so often, and in such unexpected situations, that after a while they would say hello to one another.

ob Martín arrived at the Ashton residence in Pacific
Heights at 8:55 a.m. that Tuesday morning. At thirty-
six, he was young to be deputy chief of homicide in the Personal
Crimes Division, but no one questioned his competence. Shortly
after he graduated from high school—with great difficulty, having distinguished himself only on the sports field—he had spent
a week partying with his buddies, forgetting that he was recently
married and that his wife had just given birth to a baby girl. So his
mother and grandmother forced him to wash dishes in one of the
family restaurants, working shoulder to shoulder with the poorest
Mexican immigrants—half of them illegals—to teach him what
earning a living was like with no qualifications and no profession.
Four months under the tyrannical regime of these twin matriarchs
had been enough to shake him out of his idleness: he did two years
of college before enrolling in the police academy. Bob Martín had
been born to wear a uniform, to carry a gun, to wield authority. He
learned to be disciplined; he was incorruptible, courageous, and

stubborn, with a physique capable of intimidating any criminal and an absolute loyalty to the department and to his fellow officers.

As he drove to the crime scene, Bob punched the number of his trusty assistant Petra Horr into his cell phone and she gave him the lowdown on the victim. Richard Ashton was a psychiatrist, famous for two books he had written in the 1990s—*Sexual Disorders in Pre-Adolescents* and *Treating the Juvenile Sociopath*—and more recently for his participation at a conference where he demonstrated the advantages of hypnosis in the treatment of autistic children. A video of the conference had gone viral on the Internet, since it co-incided with the news that the incidence of autism had risen at an alarming rate in recent years, and because Ashton's stunt had been worthy of Svengali. To silence the skeptical whisperings from the audience and to prove how susceptible we are to hypnotism, he asked all the delegates to clasp their hands behind their heads. Moments later, though they tugged and twisted, two-thirds of those in the audience were unable to unclasp their hands until Ashton broke the hypnotic trance. Bob could not recall ever having heard of the man, still less his books. To his admirers Ashton was a leading figure in child and adolescent psychiatry, Petra Horr told Bob, and to his detractors he was a neo-Nazi who distorted facts to support his theories and used unlawful methods on underage, mentally challenged patients. The man frequently appeared on television and in the papers to discuss controversial subjects, Petra added, and sent him a link to a video that the deputy chief watched on his cell phone.

"Check it out," said Petra. "It's a video of Ashton's third wife, Ayani."

"Who?"

"Aw, come on, chief, don't tell me you've never heard of Ayani! She's one of the most famous supermodels in the world. She was born in Ethiopia. She's the one who campaigned against female genital mutilation."

On the screen of his smartphone, Bob recognized the woman with the high cheekbones, the languid eyes, the long neck, from the covers of various magazines. He let out a low, admiring whistle.

"Shame I didn't get to meet her before!" he quipped.

"Well, now she's a widow you can try your luck. You're not a bad-looking guy—if you'd just shave off that drug-dealer mustache of yours, you might even be handsome."

"Are you flirting with me, Ms. Horr?"

"Don't sweat it, Chief, you're not my type."

///////////////////

The car drew up outside the Ashton residence, and the deputy chief ended the call. The house was hidden behind a tall, whitewashed wall above which he could see the tops of evergreen trees. From the outside, there was nothing ostentatious about the house, but the Pacific Heights address itself was a clear indication of its owners' elevated social status. The high wrought-iron gates allowing access to cars were locked, but the door for pedestrians was wide open. Bob noticed a fire truck parked on the street and silently cursed the efficiency of the paramedics, who were frequently the first to arrive, blundering in to offer first aid without waiting for police backup. One of the officers led him through an overgrown garden to the house itself, an eyesore composed of concrete and glass cubes jumbled together as though dislodged by an earthquake.

In the garden, a number of police officers and first responders waited for orders, but the deputy chief had eyes only for the ethereal figure coming toward him, a dark-skinned nymph floating on a cloud of blue veils—the woman he had just seen on his cell phone. Ayani was almost as tall as he was, and everything about her was vertical. She had a complexion the color of cherrywood, a body lithe and supple as a bamboo stem, the undulating movements of a giraffe—three similes that immediately sprang to Bob's mind, though he was a man little given to poetic flights of fancy. As he gazed at her, dumbfounded, she glided toward him in bare feet, wearing a silk shift the color of the sky reflected in a lake, and proffered a slim, elegant hand whose fingernails were unvarnished.

"Mrs. Ashton, I presume. . . . I'm Deputy Chief Bob Martín of the Personal Crimes Division."

"You can call me Ayani, Deputy Chief," the model said, sounding remarkably calm. "I called the police."

"Tell me what happened, Ayani."

"Richard didn't come back to the house last night, so early this morning, I went to his study and brought him some coffee—"

"How early?"

"Between eight fifteen and eight twenty-five."

"Why didn't your husband come back to the house to sleep?"

"Richard would often spend the night reading or working in his study. He was a night owl, so I wasn't worried if he didn't come back to the house—sometimes I didn't even notice, since we have separate bedrooms. Today was our anniversary—we've been married one year today—so I wanted to give him a surprise. That's why I brought the coffee to him instead of Galang, who usually takes it."

"Galang?"

"The butler—he's Filipino, he lives on the property. We also have a cook and a maid who work part-time."

"I'll need to talk to all three. Please, carry on."

"It was dark, the curtains were drawn. I turned on the light and . . . and then . . . I saw him. . . ." The beautiful woman's voice quavered, and for a moment her perfect poise faltered, but she quickly composed herself and gestured for Bob to follow her.

The deputy chief told the patrol officers to call for backup and to set up a cordon around the house to keep away rubberneckers and the media, who, given the victim's celebrity, would probably descend on the place very soon. He followed Ayani along one of the side paths to a building adjoining the main house, built in the same ultramodern style. She explained that her husband used the study as a consulting room for his private patients, since it had a separate entrance and there was no connecting door with the house.

"You'll catch cold, Ayani," said Bob. "Go and find something to wrap up warm, and put some shoes on—"

"I grew up with no shoes—I'm used to it."

"Well, then, wait outside, please. There's no need for you to have to see this again."

"Thank you, Deputy Chief."

Bob watched as she glided away across the garden and adjusted his pants, embarrassed by his ill-timed and deeply unprofessional reaction, which unfortunately he experienced quite often. He shook his head to dispel the images provoked by this African goddess and stepped into the annex, which was made up of two large rooms. In the first, the walls were lined with bookshelves and the windows screened by thick linen curtains; there was an armchair, a brown leather sofa, and an antique carved wood table. On top of the wall-to-wall cream carpet lay two well-worn Persian rugs whose quality was evident even to someone as inexperienced in interior design as Bob. Making a mental note of the coverlet and the pillow on the sofa—it must be here that the psychiatrist slept—he scratched his head; why would Ashton rather sleep here than in Ayani's bed? *Now if it were me . . .* He pulled himself out of his daydream and returned his attention to his duties.

On the table rested a tray with a coffeepot and a clean cup; when Ayani set it down, she must not yet have seen her husband. Bob stepped into the other room, which was dominated by a large mahogany desk. He was relieved to see that the first responders had not actually set foot in the studio itself but had assessed the situation at a glance and withdrawn so as not to contaminate the crime scene. He had a few minutes before his forensics team arrived in force. He pulled on a pair of latex gloves and began a preliminary inspection.

Richard Ashton's body lay supine on the floor next to the desk, bound and gagged with duct tape. He was dressed in gray pants and a pale blue shirt; his blue cashmere cardigan was unbuttoned, and he was barefoot. The wild, staring eyes bore a look of sheer terror, but there were no signs that the man had struggled: everything was neat and tidy except that some papers and books were damp. The ink from the documents had run a little, and Bob carefully moved them away from the spilled liquid. He studied the body, careful not to touch it; it had to be photographed and examined by Ingrid Dunn before he was allowed to lay a hand on it. He could see no visible wounds, no blood. He glanced around for a weapon, but since the cause of death was not yet known, it was a superficial glance.

Indiana's peculiar ability to heal by her mere presence and to somatize the ills of others first manifested itself when she was a child, and she bore it like a cross until she finally found a way to put it to practical use. She studied the basics of anatomy, earned a license as a physiotherapist, and four years later opened her consulting rooms at the Holistic Clinic with the help of her father and her ex-husband, who subsidized her rent until she acquired a client base. According to her father, Indiana's instinctive ability to distinguish the precise site and severity of a patient's pain was like the echolocation of a bat. Using this sonar system, she made her diagnosis, decided on a course of treatment, and verified the results, but in healing, what served her best was her kindness and her common sense.

Her ability to somatize was capricious and manifested itself in

different ways; sometimes it worked, sometimes it did not, but
when it didn't she resorted to intuition, which never failed her
when it came to the health of others. Two or three sessions were
enough for her to determine whether a patient was making progress, and if not, she referred them to colleagues at the Holistic
Clinic who practiced acupuncture, homeopathy, herbal medicine,
visualization, reflexology, hypnotherapy, music therapy, dance
therapy, natural nutrition, yoga—and a host of other disciplines
popular in California. Only rarely did she refer patients to a doctor; those who came here had usually exhausted all the possibilities
of traditional medicine.

Indiana began by listening to new patients' histories, thereby
giving them the opportunity to unburden themselves, and sometimes this in itself was enough: an attentive ear can work miracles.
Then she would proceed to the laying on of hands. She believed
that people need to be touched; she had cured patients of loneliness,
of grief, and of regret simply through massage. If an illness is not
fatal, she would say, the body almost always heals itself. Her role
was to give the body time, and facilitate the process; her therapy
was not for those in a hurry. She employed a combination of approaches that she called holistic healing and which her father called
witchcraft—a term that would have frightened off clients even in
a city as easygoing as San Francisco. Indiana relieved symptoms,
bargained with pain, tried to eliminate negative energy and imbue
the patient with new strength. This was what she was currently
doing with Gary Brunswick.

The man lay on his back on the massage table. A sheet was
draped over him, half a dozen powerful magnets were strategi-
cally placed on his torso, his eyes were closed, and he was half dozing, lulled by the restful scent of vetiver and the almost inaudible
murmur of lapping waves, soft breezes, and bird calls. Feeling the
pressure of Indiana's hands on his head, he realized with some sad-

ness that the session was drawing to a close. Today more than ever he needed the healing power of this woman. The previous night had been exhausting. He had woken with the sort of hangover one might get from a bender, though in fact he never touched alcohol, and by the time he arrived in Indiana's consulting room, he had a blinding headache; but her magic touch had managed to relieve it. For an hour, she had visualized a stream of sidereal dust falling from some distant point in the cosmos and passing through her fingers to envelop Gary.

Since the first visit the previous November, Indiana had used a variety of approaches with scant results, and she was beginning to lose heart. He insisted that the sessions with her relieved his pain, yet still she could visualize it with the certainty of an X ray. Believing as she did that wellness depended on a harmonious balance of body, mind, and spirit, and unable to detect anything physically wrong with Gary, she attributed his symptoms to a tormented mind and an imprisoned soul. Gary assured her that he'd had a happy childhood and a normal adolescence, so it was possible that this was related to some past life. Indiana was waiting for the opportunity to delicately broach the idea that he needed to cleanse his karma. She knew a Tibetan who was an expert on the subject.

Indiana realized from the start, before Gary even uttered a word at his first session, that he was a complicated guy. She could sense a metal band pressing in on his skull and a sack of stones on his back: the poor man was carrying around some terrible burden. Chronic migraine, she guessed, and he, astonished by what seemed like clairvoyance, explained that his headaches had grown so bad over the past year that they made it impossible for him to continue his work as a geologist. The profession required him to be in good health, he explained; he had to crawl through caves, climb mountains, and camp out under the stars. At twenty-nine years of age, he had a pleasant face and a puny body, his hair cropped short to disguise his premature baldness and his gray eyes framed by thick black glasses that made him seem insipid. He came to Treatment Room 8 every Tuesday, always arriving punctually, and if he was particularly in need, he would request a second session later in the week.

He always brought Indiana little gifts, flowers or books or poetry. He was convinced that women preferred poetry that rhymed, particularly on the subject of nature—birds, clouds, rivers. This had in fact been true of Indiana before she met Alan, who was ruthless in matters of art and literature. Her lover had introduced her to the Japanese tradition of haiku, particularly the modern variant gendai haiku, though in secret she still enjoyed sentimental verse.

Gary always wore jeans, boots with thick rubber soles, and a metal-studded leather jacket, an outfit that contrasted starkly with his rabbitlike vulnerability. As with all her clients, Indiana had tried to get to know him well so that she could discover the source of his anxiety, but the man was like a blank page. She knew almost nothing about him, and what little she managed to find out, she forgot as soon as he left.

At the end of the session that Tuesday, Indiana handed him a vial of oil of geranium to help him remember his dreams.

"I don't dream," said Gary in his taciturn manner, "but I'd like to dream about you."

"We all dream, but not many people attach any importance to their dreams," she said, ignoring the innuendo. "In some cultures—the Australian aborigines, for example—the dream world is as real as their waking life. Have you ever seen aboriginal art? They paint their dreams—the paintings are amazing. I always keep a notepad on my nightstand, and I jot down my dreams as soon as I wake up."

"What for?"

"So I'll remember them," she explained. "They can guide me, help me in my work, dispel my doubts."

"Have you ever dreamed about me?"

"I dream about all my patients," she said, ignoring the implication once again. "I suggest you write down your dreams, Gary, and do some meditation."

When he first came, Indiana had devoted two whole sessions to teaching Gary about the benefits of meditation, how to empty his mind of thoughts, to breathe deeply, drawing the air into every cell in his body and exhaling his tension. Whenever he felt a migraine coming on, she suggested, he should find a quiet spot and meditate for fifteen minutes to relax, curiously observing his own symptoms rather than fighting them. "Pain, like our other feelings, is a doorway into the soul," she had told him. "Ask yourself what you are feeling and what you are refusing to feel. Listen to your body. If you focus on that, you'll find that the pain changes and opens out inside you, but I should warn you, your mind will not give up without a fight; it will try to distract you with ideas, images, memories, because it's happy in its neurosis, Gary. You have to give yourself time to get to know yourself, learn to be alone, to be quiet, with no TV, no cell phone, no computer. Promise me you'll do that, if only for five minutes every day." But no matter how deeply Gary breathed, no matter how deeply he meditated, he was still a bundle of nerves.

Indiana said good-bye to the man, listened as his boots padded down the corridor toward the stairwell, then slumped into a chair and heaved a sigh, feeling drained by the negative energy that radiated from him, and by his romantic insinuations, which were beginning to seriously irritate her. In her job, compassion was essential, but there were some patients whose necks she longed to wring.

*B*lake Jackson received half a dozen missed calls from his granddaughter while he was running around like a lunatic after a squash ball. After he had finished his game, he caught his breath, showered, and got dressed. By now it was past nine at night, and his buddy was hungry for Alsatian food and beer.

"Amanda? That you?"

"Who were you expecting? You called me!"

"Did you call?"

"You know I called, Grandpa, that's why you're calling me back."

"Okay, jeez!" Blake exploded. "What the hell do you want, you little brat?"

"I want the lowdown on the shrink."

"The shrink? Oh, the psychiatrist who was murdered today."

"It was on the news today, but he was murdered the night before last or early yesterday morning. Find out everything you can."

"How am I supposed to do that?"

"Talk to Dad."

"Why don't you ask him?"

"I will, as soon as I see him, but in the meantime you could get a head start on the investigation. Call me tomorrow with the details."

"I have to work tomorrow, and I can't be calling your dad all the time."

"You want to carry on playing Ripper or not?"

"Uh-huh."

Blake Jackson was not a superstitious man, but he suspected that the spirit of his late wife had somehow managed to pass to Amanda. Before she died, Marianne had told him that she would always watch over him, that she would help him find comfort in his loneliness. He had assumed she was referring to him marrying again, but in fact she was talking about Amanda. Truth be told, he'd had little time to grieve for the wife he loved so much—he spent the first months of widowhood feeding his granddaughter, putting her to bed, changing her diapers, bathing her, rocking her. Even at night he did not have time to miss the warmth of Marianne's body in his bed, since Amanda had colic and was screaming at the top of her lungs. The child's frantic sobbing terrified Indiana, who ended up crying with her while he paced up and down in his pajamas, cradling his granddaughter while reciting chemical formulae he had learned back at pharmacy school. At the time Indiana was a girl herself, barely sixteen years old, inexperienced in her new role as mother, depressed because she was still as fat as a whale and because her husband was worse than useless. No sooner had Amanda stopped suffering from colic than she began cutting her first teeth; then she had chickenpox, with a burning fever and a rash that extended even to her eyelids.

This levelheaded grandfather was surprised to hear himself talking aloud to the ghost of his dead wife, asking what he could do with this impossible creature, and the answer arrived in the form of Elsa Domínguez, a Guatemalan immigrant sent to him by Bob's mother, Doña Encarnación Martín. Elsa already had more than enough work, but she took pity on Blake Jackson, whose house was like a pigsty, whose daughter couldn't cope, whose son-in-law was never there, and whose granddaughter was a spoiled crybaby, and so she gave up her other clients and devoted herself to this family. From Monday to Friday, while Blake Jackson was working at the pharmacy and Indiana was at high school, Elsa would show up in her clapped-out car, wearing sweatpants and carpet slippers, to impose order on the chaos—and she managed to transform the screaming ball of fury that was Amanda into a more or less normal little girl. She talked to the child in Spanish, made sure she cleaned her plate, taught her to take her first steps and, later, to sing, to dance, to use a vacuum cleaner and lay the table. On Amanda's third birthday, when her parents finally separated, Elsa gave her a tabby cat to keep her company and build up her strength. In her village in Guatemala, she said, children grew up with animals, they drank dirty water, but they didn't get sick like Americans, who succumbed to every germ that came along. And her theory proved to be correct; Gina, the cat, cured Amanda of her asthma and her colic.

Friday, 13

*I*ndiana finished with her last patient of the week, an arthritic poodle that broke her heart and that she treated for free because it belonged to one of her daughter's schoolteachers, who was mired in debt, thanks to her gambling-addict husband. Indiana closed Treatment Room 8 at six o'clock and headed for the Café Rossini, where her father and daughter were waiting for her.

Blake Jackson had gone to pick up his granddaughter from school, as he did every Friday. He looked forward all week to the moment he'd have Amanda as a captive audience in his car, and he would eke out the time by choosing routes where the traffic was heaviest. Grandfather and granddaughter were buddies, comrades—partners in crime, as they liked to say. They talked on the phone almost every day the girl spent at the boarding school, and made the most of any spare time to play chess or Ripper. They talked about the tidbits of news that he passed on to her, with the emphasis always on the oddball stories: the two-headed zebra born in a Beijing zoo; the fat guy from Oklahoma suffocated by his own farts; the mentally disabled people who had been kept locked in a basement for years while their captors collected their social security. Recently, their talk had been only about local crimes.

When she got to the café, Indiana noticed with a disapproving glance that Blake and Amanda were sharing a table with Gary Brunswick—the last person she expected to see sitting with her family. Coffeehouse chains had been banned in North Beach to save local businesses from a slow death, to stop the character being sapped from Little Italy—so it was still possible to get excellent coffee at a dozen old-fashioned spots. Neighborhood residents would choose a café and stay loyal to it; it was part of their identity. Gary didn't live in North Beach, but he had stopped by the Café Rossini so often recently that they already thought of him as a regular. He spent much of his spare time hunched over his computer at a table by the window, not talking to anyone except Danny D'Angelo, who—as he admitted to Indiana—flirted shamelessly with Gary just to enjoy the look of terror on his face. He liked watching the guy shrink with embarrassment as Danny put his lips to his ear to ask in a lewd whisper what he could get him.

Danny had noticed that whenever Gary was in the café, Indiana drank her cappuccino standing by the bar and left in a hurry. She didn't want to offend a patient by sitting at another table, but she didn't always have time for a proper conversation. In any case they weren't conversations so much as interrogations, in which Gary bombarded her with inane questions and Indiana answered distractedly: she'd be thirty-four in July; she'd been divorced at nineteen; her ex-husband was a cop; she'd once been to Istanbul and had always wanted to go to India; her daughter Amanda played the violin and wanted to get a new cat because hers had died. Gary would listen with exaggerated interest as Indiana stifled a yawn. This man lived behind a kind of veil, she thought—he was a smudged figure in a washed-out watercolor. And now here he was, having a friendly get-together with her family, playing blindfold chess with Amanda.

It was Danny who had introduced them: Indiana's father and daughter on the one hand, and one of her patients on the other. Gary had figured that grandfather and granddaughter would be waiting at least an hour for Indiana to finish her session with the poodle, and since he knew Amanda liked board games (her mother had told him), he challenged her to a game of chess. Blake timed them with a chess clock he always put in his pocket when he was going out with Amanda. "This girl here can take on multiple opponents at once," he warned Gary.

"So can I," said Gary. And sure enough, he turned out to be a much more astute and aggressive player than his timid appearance suggested.

Folding her arms impatiently, Indiana looked around for another table, but they were all taken. In one corner she saw a man who looked familiar—although she couldn't say from where—with his nose in a book, and asked if she could share his table. The guy got such a fright that he leaped up from his seat and the book fell on the floor. Indiana picked it up: a William C. Gordon detective novel that she had seen among all the books, of variable quality, on her father's shelves. The man, who was now the beetroot color particular to embarrassed redheads, gestured to the empty seat.

"We've seen each other before, right?" said Indiana.

"I haven't had the pleasure of an introduction, but our paths have crossed on a number of occasions. Samuel Hamilton Jr. at your service."

"Indiana Jackson. Sorry, I don't mean to interrupt your reading."

"It's no interruption at all, ma'am."

"Are you sure we don't know each other?"

"Quite sure."

"Do you work around here?"

"From time to time."

They carried on with their small talk while she sipped her coffee and waited for her father and daughter to finish—only a matter of minutes, since Amanda and Gary were playing against the clock. When the game finished, Indiana was shocked to realize that that jerk had beaten her daughter. "You owe me a rematch," Amanda said a little bitterly to Gary as she left—she was not used to losing.

The old Cuore d'Italia restaurant, established in 1886, was famous for its authentic cuisine—and for the gangland massacre that had taken place there in 1926. The local Mafia had met in the large dining room to taste the best pasta in the city, drink good bootleg wine, and cordially divide up California between them; then one gang pulled out their machine guns and blew the others away. In a matter of minutes twenty capos lay dead, and the place was a grisly mess. Though the distasteful incident was soon just a memory, that had never put off the tourists, who flocked there out of morbid curiosity to sample the pasta and take photos of the crime scene, until the Cuore d'Italia burned down and was rebuilt in a new location. A persistent rumor around North Beach had it that the owner had doused it in gasoline and set a match to it to get back at her cheating husband, but the insurance company couldn't prove a thing. The new Cuore d'Italia boasted brand-new furniture but retained the atmosphere of the original, with huge paintings of idyllic Tuscan landscapes, painted terra-cotta vases, and plastic flowers.

By the time Blake, Indiana, and Amanda arrived, Ryan and Pedro Alarcón were already waiting for them. Ryan had invited them all along to celebrate a lucrative new business contract—it was a good excuse for spending time with Indiana, whom he had not seen for some days. He had just come back from Washington,

DC, where he had met with Defense Department officials to discuss the security programs he and Pedro were working on. He did not actually mention his friend's name, though. Thirty-five years ago Pedro had been a guerrilla; for some still stuck in a Cold War mentality, guerrilla was synonymous with Communist, and for those more up-to-date, guerrilla with *terrorist*.

Seeing Indiana dressed in her ridiculous boots, jeans that were threadbare at the knees, a boxy jacket over a tight-fitting blouse that barely contained her breasts, Ryan felt the curious mixture of desire and tenderness she always aroused in him. She was clearly tired, having come straight from work, with no makeup and her hair pulled back into in a ponytail, and still the joy she exuded at simply being alive and comfortable in her own body was so palpable that several men instinctively turned to look her over. It's that sexy walk, thought Ryan, irritated by their primitive male response—only women in Africa have that sort of brazen sensuality. Not for the first time, he wondered how many men must be wandering the world still troubled by memories of Indiana, still secretly loving her; how many still craved her affection, longed for the spells of this good witch to relieve their pain and guilt.

No longer able to bear the doubts, the agony, the sudden bursts of hope that keeping his feelings secret demanded, Ryan had finally confessed everything to Pedro. His friend listened with a look of amusement, then asked Ryan why he had put off telling the only person in the world likely to care about his pathetic crush. This was not just a crush, Ryan insisted; this time it was serious. He had never felt like this about anyone before.

"I thought you and I agreed long ago that love is just an unnecessary risk," said Pedro.

"I know, I know—that's why I've spent three years trying to stamp out my feelings for Indiana—but, well, sometimes Cupid's arrow really hits home."

Pedro shuddered to hear his friend utter such words in a serious tone. He took off his glasses and wiped them with his shirttail.

"You screwed her yet?"

"No!"

"There's your problem."

"You don't get it, Pedro. This isn't about sex—I can get that anywhere. This is about love. Besides, Indiana's already in a relationship—some guy called Keller, they've been together a few years."

"So?"

"So if I try to get her into bed, I'd lose her as a friend. Faithfulness is really important to her—we've talked about it. She's not the kind of woman who dates one guy and flirts with others—actually, that's one of the things I admire about her."

"Jesus, Ryan, you sound like a faggot. Long as she's single, you've got a hunting license. That's the deal. I mean, you and Jennifer Yang aren't exclusive. The moment you take your eye off the ball, some guy who's paying more attention can come in and take her from you. You can do the same to this Keller guy."

Ryan realized that this was probably not the best time to tell his friend that his relationship with Jennifer was over. At least, he hoped it was: she was still perfectly capable of pulling some spiteful stunt. She was a vengeful woman—it was her only flaw as far as he could tell, and in every other respect she stood out as his finest conquest. Jennifer was beautiful, intelligent, a modern woman who didn't have the slightest wish to get married and have kids; she earned a good salary and had a kinky desire to be a sex slave. Strange as it seemed, this young Wells Fargo executive got her kicks from bondage, humiliation, and restraint. Jennifer was a dream for any red-blooded male, but Ryan, a man of simple tastes, had had so much trouble learning the rules and codes that she had to lend him a recent book so he could learn more about it, something with beige in the title—or maybe it was gray, he couldn't remember. It was apparently very popular with women, being the usual vapid love story with a dose of soft porn: the tale of a sadomasochistic relationship between an innocent virgin with bee-stung lips and a handsome, domineering millionaire. In the copy she gave him, Jennifer had underlined the "binding contract" that specified the various forms of abuse that the virgin—as soon as she stopped being a virgin—was obliged to endure: "whippings, floggings, spankings, caning, paddling or any other discipline the Dominant should decide to administer"—as long as he didn't leave any scars or splatter the walls too much. Ryan could not understand what exactly the "Submissive" got out of what—in his eyes—amounted to extreme domestic violence, but Jennifer spelled it out for him: through pain, the ex-virgin could experience guilt-free paroxysms of pleasure.

Things had not worked out with Jennifer as well as they had for the characters in the novel: Ryan could never take his role seriously, and her orgasm would elude her when he beat her with a rolled-up newspaper, doubled over with laughter. Her frustration was understandable, but not the way she clung to him like a drowning woman. A week ago, when he had suggested they take a break—the universally understood euphemism for dumping your lover—Jennifer had thrown a tantrum so dramatic that Ryan had regretted broaching the subject in an elegant tearoom where everybody could hear, including the pastry chef, who came out to see what all the fuss was about.

For once, Ryan's extensive Navy SEAL training failed him. He paid the check as quickly as possible and clumsily manhandled a struggling, sobbing Jennifer out of the tearoom.

"Sadist!" shouted a woman at another table.

Jennifer, still lucid despite being deeply upset, called back over her shoulder, "If only that were true, ma'am!"

Ryan managed to bundle Jennifer into a taxi. As he was running off in the opposite direction, he heard a torrent of threats and
curses through the car window. He thought he caught Indiana
Jackson's name, and wondered how Jennifer even knew of her existence. It must have been by Chinese horoscope, because he had
never mentioned her.

Waiting at the door of the Cuore d'Italia with Ryan and Pedro,
Attila sat, wearing the service dog vest that meant he was admitted everywhere. Ryan had adopted the dog because he was a war
veteran, but he did not need a service dog; he simply liked the company. Indiana was surprised to see her daughter greet the Navy
SEAL and his Uruguayan friend with a kiss on the cheek before
sitting down between them at the table. Attila excitedly took in
Indiana's floral scent, but sat between Ryan and Amanda, who
scratched his scars distractedly while she studied the menu. She
was one of the few people unfazed by Attila's titanium teeth and
his disfigured, wolflike appearance.

Indiana, who had never gotten her figure back since having
Amanda, but who didn't care about carrying a couple of extra
pounds here or there, ordered Caesar salad, gnocchi with osso
buco, and poached pears; Blake ordered a simple seafood linguini.
Ryan, who was sensible about his diet, chose the grilled sole, while
Pedro opted for the biggest filet steak on the menu, even though
he knew it could never be as good as a steak from his own country.
Amanda, who considered meat to be simply a hunk of dead animal
and found vegetables boring, ordered three desserts, a Coke, and
some napkins to blow her nose with, because she still had a terrible
cold.

"You check out that stuff for me, Kabel?" she asked.

"I'm getting there, Amanda, but what do you say we eat before
we chat about corpses?"

"I'm not saying we should talk while we're eating, but you can fill me in between courses."

"Fill you in about what?" asked Indiana.

"The Constante murders, Mom," said Amanda, sneaking Attila a piece of bread under the table.

"Whose murder?"

"I've told you like a thousand times, but you don't listen to me."

"Amanda, don't feed Attila," Ryan warned her. "It's important that he only eats what I give him, so he doesn't get poisoned."

"Who'd wanna poison him? Don't be paranoid, dude."

"Listen to me. The US government spent twenty-six thousand dollars training Attila, so don't go spoiling him. Anyway, what have these murders got to do with you?"

"That's what I was wondering." Indiana sighed. "I don't see why my daughter is researching dead people we didn't know."

"Me and Kabel have been conducting an investigation into the death of Ed Staton, the guy who had a baseball bat shoved up his—"

"Amanda!" her mother cut in.

"What? It's not like it's some secret, it's all over the Internet. Anyway, that was back in October. Now we're doing the Constantes, a couple murdered in November."

"Not to mention the psychiatrist who was killed on Tuesday," Blake added.

"Jesus Christ, Dad!" Indiana objected. "Why are you encouraging her? This obsession is dangerous!"

"There's nothing dangerous about it, it's an experiment," said her father. "Your daughter is single-handedly putting astrology to the test."

"It's not just me," Amanda said. "You're involved in this too, and Esmeralda, Sir Edmond Paddington, and Abatha and Sherlock."

"Who are they?" asked Pedro, who had been savoring his beef with intense concentration, oblivious to the table talk.

"They're the kids from Ripper, the role-playing game," Blake told him. "I'm Kabel, servant to the games master."

"You're not a servant, you're my henchman. You carry out my orders."

"That's what a servant does, Amanda," her grandfather pointed out.

"Counting the Ed Staton murder in October, the Constantes in November, and the psychiatrist on Tuesday, there have only been four deaths that are out of the ordinary since my godmother made her prediction," Amanda explained. "Statistically, it's hardly a bloodbath. We need some more murders."

"How many more, exactly?" Pedro asked.

"At least four or five."

"You're not supposed to take astrology literally, Amanda," said Indiana. "You have to interpret its messages."

"I suppose for Celeste Roko, astrology is an intuitive tool," suggested Pedro, "like a pendulum is for a hypnotist."

"Well, my godmother doesn't see it as a pendulum. To her, astrology is an exact science. But if she's right, it would mean that people born in the same place at the same time—let's say a state hospital in New York or in Calcutta, where lots of babies can be born simultaneously—would all have exactly the same fate."

"Life is a mystery, sweetie," Indiana parried, sopping up olive oil with a piece of bread. "We can't simply dismiss everything we can't explain or control!"

"You're so gullible, Mom. You believe in aromatherapy, and in magnet therapy—you even believe in that homeopathic hogwash your ventriloquist friend practices."

"Veterinarian, not ventriloquist," her mother corrected.

"Whatever. . . . Homeopathy is like dissolving two aspirin in the Pacific and prescribing fifteen drops to a patient. So come on, Kabel, give me details. What do we know about the psychiatrist?"

"Not much yet. I'm still focusing on the Constantes."

While Indiana and Ryan whispered to each other, Amanda interrogated her grandfather—a grilling that Pedro Alarcón, who seemed fascinated by the game Amanda had described, followed closely. More excited now, Blake Jackson pulled the sheaf of notes from his briefcase and laid it out on the table, apologizing for not having made as much progress as he should have. The henchman was a little tied up at the pharmacy—this being flu season—but he had collected almost everything about the Constantes that had so far appeared in the media, and he had to persuade Bob Martín—who still called him his father-in-law, and who couldn't say no to him—to let him comb through the police files, including those that were not publicly available. He handed Amanda a couple of pages outlining the conclusions of the forensics report, and another page summarizing what he had coaxed out of the detectives assigned to the case, two of Bob's fellow officers that he had known for years.

"Neither Staton nor the Constantes defended themselves," he told his granddaughter.

"What about the psychiatrist?"

"Looks like he didn't either. The Constantes were already sedated with Xanax when the heroin was injected," he explained. "Xanax is used to treat anxiety, and depending on the dose, it can cause drowsiness, lethargy, and amnesia."

"So they were asleep?"

"Your father thinks so."

"If the murderer has access to Xanax, it could be a doctor, a nurse—even a pharmacist, like you."

"Not necessarily. Anyone can get hold of a prescription or buy it on the black market. Every time my place has been turned over, it's always to steal medications like Xanax. Some people buy it online. Let's face it, if you can buy a semiautomatic or bomb-making equipment on the Internet, you can sure get yourself some Xanax."

"Are there any suspects?" asked the Uruguayan.

"Michael Constante was a nasty piece of work," Blake explained. "A week before he died, he got into an argument that turned into a brawl with someone called Brian Turner, an electrician from his Alcoholics Anonymous group. The police have Turner in their sights because he's got a checkered past: a lot of petty crime, one felony charge—he did three years inside. He's thirty-two and unemployed."

"Any history of violence?"

"Doesn't look like it. Then again, he attacked Michael Constante with a bottle. It took a couple of people to pull him off."

"Any idea of the reason for the fight?"

"Michael accused Turner of chasing after his wife, Doris. It's pretty hard to credit, since Doris was fourteen years older than Turner and exceptionally ugly."

"No accounting for taste . . . ," muttered Pedro.

"The Constantes' bodies were branded postmortem," Amanda said to him.

"How did they work out that it happened after they were dead?"

"They can tell from the lividity of the skin," explained Blake. "Live flesh reacts differently. It looks like they were burned using the small blowtorch that was found in the bathroom."

"What are those miniature blowtorches used for, anyway?" asked Amanda, shoveling down her third dessert.

"For cooking," replied her grandfather. "Someone probably used one on that crème brûlée you're eating—they use it to caramelize the sugar. You can buy them from kitchen supply stores for between twenty-five and forty dollars. Not that I've ever used one—you know I'm no cook. And it seems weird that the Constantes would have had one. There was nothing in their kitchen except junk food—I can't imagine them eating crème brûlée. The blowtorch was practically new."

"How do you know?" the girl asked.

"Well, the butane canister was nearly empty, but the metal casing looked new. Personally, I don't think it belonged to the Constantes."

"The killer could have brought it with him, like he brought the syringes," said Amanda. "Didn't you say they found some bottle of liquor in the fridge?"

"Yeah. Someone must have given it to the Constantes, though you'd have to be pretty dumb to give liquor to a recovering alcoholic."

"What was it?"

"Vodka or brandy or something from Serbia. You can't buy it here—I asked around, and nobody's heard of it."

At the mention of Serbia, Ryan's ears pricked up. He explained that he and SEAL Team Six had served in the Balkans, and that Serbian *rakija* was more toxic than turpentine.

"What was the brand?" he asked.

"It didn't say in the report. What does it matter?"

"Everything matters, Kabel! Find out," Amanda ordered.

"I guess you want the make of the syringes and the blowtorch, too," said Blake, "and maybe the toilet paper while I'm at it."

"Precisely, Hench. And don't go getting sidetracked."

Sunday, 15

*A*lan Keller came from a family that for more than a century had exerted considerable influence in San Francisco, principally through its wealth, but also through its standing and its social connections—since nowadays the only money that mattered was in the hands of computing and finance billionaires. Historically, the Keller family had been important donors to the Democratic Party at each election, partly out of political conviction, partly as a networking opportunity, giving them access to people without whom it would be very difficult to succeed in this city. Alan was the third child of Philip and Flora Keller, a couple of nonagenarians who regularly appeared in the society pages— two slightly senile old mummies who seemed determined to live forever. Alan's siblings, Mark and Lucille, managed the family's assets, sidelining their younger brother, whom they considered the artist of the family, since he was the only one capable of appreciating abstract art and atonal music.

Alan had never worked a day in his life. He had studied art history, published scholarly articles in specialist magazines, and occasionally acted as an adviser to private collectors and museum curators. He'd had a string of brief affairs but never married, and he had no need to worry about contributing to the planet's overpopulation; since his sperm count was low to the point of nonexistence, he didn't need a vasectomy. Notionally, he preferred breeding horses to breeding children, though he did not do so—as he informed Indiana shortly after they met, it was an expensive hobby. He planned to leave his inheritance to the San Francisco Symphony Orchestra, he added, assuming there would be any money left after he died, since he liked to live life without worrying about how much he spent. This was not quite true, though: Alan was forced to think about his expenses, since they invariably exceeded his income—as his siblings pointed out every time they saw him.

His complete lack of business acumen drew jokes from his friends and criticism from his family. He gambled on unrealistic business ventures, like the vineyard in Napa that he had bought on a whim after taking a hot air balloon ride over Burgundy. He was something of a connoisseur, and the wine business was booming, but he knew nothing about the basics of the industry. What few bottles his winery managed to produce went unnoticed in the small, fiercely competitive world of winemaking. Besides, he was forced to rely on vineyard managers who were not entirely trustworthy.

He was proud of his estate, whose hacienda-style house, ringed with rosebushes, housed his collection of Latin American art, which ranged from Inca figures in terra-cotta and stone, dubiously acquired in Peru, to a couple of medium-size paintings by Fernando Botero. Everything else was stored in the family house in Woodside. Keller was an obsessive collector; he was prepared to travel halfway around the world to get his hands on a unique piece of porcelain or Chinese jade—though he rarely needed to, as he had a network of buyers to do it for him.

He lived in the country mansion his grandfather had built back when Woodside was in the heart of the countryside, long before it became a haven for Silicon Valley billionaires in the 1990s. The villa looked imposing from the outside, but inside it was crumbling into ruin—nobody had bothered to give it a lick of paint or replace the plumbing in more than forty years. Alan was keen to sell, since the land was extremely valuable, but his parents, who actually owned the property, clung to it for reasons he did not understand, given that they never visited. Though Alan wished his parents a long and happy life, he could not help but calculate how much more comfortable his situation would be if Philip and Flora Keller were to die. When the house was eventually sold and he got his share—or when he inherited—he planned to buy a loft apartment in San Francisco, something more convenient for a society bachelor like him than this ramshackle country pile, where he could not even invite people around for cocktails without worrying that a rat might scurry between their feet.

Indiana had not been to the Woodside house or the Napa vineyard; Alan had not thought to take her there, and she was too embarrassed to ask. She assumed that, when the time came, he would take the initiative. Whenever the subject was mentioned, Amanda would say that Alan was obviously ashamed of her mother, and that she hated the idea of having that man as her stepfather. Indiana ignored these comments. Her daughter was too young to appreciate Alan Keller's qualities: his sense of humor, his sophistication, his style. And she was not about to tell her daughter that he was also an expert lover: Amanda still thought her parents were asexual, like amoebas. The girl had to admit that, in spite of his age, Alan was still a good-looking man. He reminded her of that British actor with the perfect hair and the perfect manners who had been caught with a prostitute in a car in Los Angeles, and whose name she could never remember because he hadn't starred in any vampire films.

Thanks to her lover, Indiana had been to Istanbul, and was learning to appreciate fine dining, art, music, and old black-and-white movies. She even watched foreign films—though Alan had to explain them to her because she could never read the subtitles in time. He was funny and charming, he never seemed irritated when people mistook him for her father, and he gave her the freedom, the time, and the space she needed to devote to her family and her work. He opened up new horizons, and he was a wonderfully attentive companion, always eager to please her, to pay her a compliment. Any other woman might have wondered why he did not include her in his social circle and why she had never been introduced to any of the Keller clan; but Indiana, who did not have a malicious bone in her body, put it down to the twenty-two-year age-gap between them. She assumed that Alan, who was always considerate, simply wanted to spare her the tedium of spending time with people much older than she, and that he felt out of place with her younger friends.

"By the time you're sixty, Keller will be an old man of eighty-two with a pacemaker and Alzheimer's," Amanda pointed out. But Indiana trusted to the future: it was just as likely that in his eighties Alan would still be young at heart, and that she would be the one suffering from heart disease and senile dementia. Life was full of little ironies, she thought: better to enjoy what you have than focus on some uncertain future.

Until now, Alan's relationship with Indiana had been spared any serious drama, sheltered as it was from the weight of routine and from the curiosity of others. In recent months, however, there had been complications in his finances, and problems with his health that disrupted his life and this easygoing relationship. He took a certain pride in his incompetence in dealing with money, because it set him apart from the rest of his family, but he could not continue to overlook his poor investments, the losses incurred by his vineyard, the plummeting value of his stocks and shares, and the fact that there was less capital tied up in his art collection than he had imagined. He had just found out that his collection of jade was neither as antique nor as valuable as he had been led to believe. To make matters worse, his annual medical checkup had indicated that he might have prostate cancer, leaving him on tenterhooks for five days until his urologist finally delivered him from his agony by doing a second set of blood tests. The medical lab was eventually forced to admit that they had mixed up his first test results with those of another patient. He had just turned fifty-five, and the worries about his health and his virility that had disappeared when he had met Indiana were coming back to haunt him. He felt depressed. He had achieved nothing in his life that might merit mention in an epitaph. He had frittered away two-thirds of it already, and was counting off the years until he became just like his father. The very thought of his physical and mental decline terrified him.

He had built up crippling debts, and knew that it would be pointless to turn to his siblings, who managed the family fortune as though it was their own and carefully controlled the funds to which he had access, arguing that the only thing he knew how to do was spend. He had begged them to sell the Woodside mansion, a crumbling wreck that was impossible to maintain, only to be told that he was ungrateful—he got to live there rent-free. His elder brother had offered to buy the Napa vineyard, "to help keep you afloat," as he put it, but Alan knew that his motives were far from altruistic: he was simply trying to get the property at a knockdown price. Alan was in bad odor with his bank, which had cut his line of credit, and such things could no longer be sorted out over a round of golf, the way they had been before the economic crisis. A life that until recently had been enviable was beginning to close in on him, and he felt like a fly caught up in a web of difficulties.

His psychiatrist diagnosed him with a transitory existential crisis—something not uncommon in men of his age—and prescribed testosterone and more pills to treat his anxiety. His worries meant he'd been paying less attention to Indiana, and now he was constantly plagued by jealousy—something that was also perfectly normal, his psychiatrist had told him, though Alan had not admitted that he had once again engaged the services of Samuel Hamilton Jr., private detective.

He didn't want to lose Indiana—the very thought of being on his own, of having to start over with another woman, made him weary. He was too old for dating, for subterfuges and skirmishes and concessions in his sex life. His relationship with Indiana was comfortable, and Amanda hated him, luckily, as this absolved him of any responsibility toward her. Amanda would soon be heading off to college, and her mother would be able to devote more time to Alan; but recently Indiana had seemed distracted and distant. She no longer suggested meeting up, and she wasn't always available when he proposed it. Her admiration for him seemed to have palled; these days she often contradicted him, finding any excuse to argue. While the last thing Alan Keller wanted was a submissive partner, something that would have bored him to death, he could not keep walking on eggshells simply to avoid confrontations with his lover. He had arguments enough to deal with from his staff and his family.

Ryan Miller was to blame for the change in Indiana's attitude— there was no other possible explanation, although Alan's private investigator insisted there was no evidence for this. One look at Miller, with his brutish face and his broken nose, and it was obvious he was up to no good. The thought of this warrior in bed with Indiana made Keller feel physically sick. Did his amputated leg limit the things he could do? Who knew, maybe it worked to his advantage: women are curious, they get excited at the weirdest things. He could not raise these suspicions with Indiana. For someone like him, jealousy was unworthy, it was humiliating. He could barely discuss it with his psychiatrist. Indiana claimed that the soldier was her best friend, which in itself was unacceptable— that was Alan's role; and besides, he was convinced that platonic friendship between a man like Miller and a woman like Indiana was impossible. He needed to know exactly what went on when they were alone in Treatment Room 8, on the frequent walks they took in the woods, or in Miller's loft apartment, where Indiana had no business being.

The reports he was getting from Samuel Hamilton Jr. were too vague. Alan no longer trusted the man like he used to, and suspected him of protecting Indiana. Hamilton had even had the nerve to offer advice, to suggest that rather than spying on Indiana, Alan should try to win her back—as though the thought hadn't occurred to him. But how could he do this, with Ryan Miller standing in the way? He needed to find a way to be rid of Miller, to eliminate him—something he mentioned in a moment of weakness to the detective: surely he had some contacts, and for the right price could find some trigger-happy Korean gangsters? But Hamilton was peremptory. "Don't ask me. You want a hit man, go find one yourself." Resolving the matter in a hail of bullets had never been more than a daydream. Alan had no experience of violence, and besides, when it came to guns, Miller was dangerous. Alan wondered what he would do if he came upon irrefutable proof that Indiana had been unfaithful. The question was like a fly buzzing in his ear. It never gave him any peace.

It was like the detective said: he had to win Indiana back. Even the phrase "win her back" made his flesh crawl. It sounded like something out of a soap opera—but something had to be done, he couldn't just stand idly by. He assured his psychiatrist that he could seduce her again, as he had done at the start of their affair, that he had much more to offer her than that gimp, Miller. He knew Indiana better than anyone, knew how to make her happy; not for nothing had he spent the last four years refining her senses and satisfying her as no other man could, certainly not some uncivilized lout like Miller. The psychiatrist listened without saying a word, and with each session Alan began to find his own arguments increasingly hollow.

At six o'clock that Sunday evening, rather than keeping to their routine of meeting at the Fairmont for an intimate dinner, a movie, and a little lovemaking, Alan decided to surprise Indiana. He picked her up at her father's house and took her to the de Young Museum to see *Masters of Venice*—an exhibition of fifty paintings on loan from the Kunsthistorisches Museum in Vienna. Alan had not wanted to brave the crowds to see the exhibition, but, being friends with the director, he managed to get them a private tour while the gallery was closed. The hushed, empty ultramodern building was like a temple in glass, steel, and marble, the vast geometric spaces bathed in light.

The guide they were assigned turned out to be a young man with bad skin, whose memorized spiel Alan soon silenced with his art historian's authority. Indiana was wearing a short, tight blue dress that revealed more than it concealed, her usual sand-colored jacket—which she took off once they were inside—and the battered imitation-snakeskin boots that Keller had tried to persuade her to replace with something more presentable, but which she insisted on wearing because they were comfortable. When he first saw her, the guide's jaw dropped, and he hardly recovered his composure during the rest of their visit. Whenever Indiana asked a question, the guide mumbled something feebly, staring as if hyp-notized into the blue eyes of this gorgeous woman, dizzy from her sinful scent of musk and flowers, excited by the tousled blond curls that made her look as though she had just got out of bed, by the defiant sway of her body.

Had he not been at such a low ebb, Keller might have been amused by the reaction of this guide, whom he had seen a few times in the past. Usually he enjoyed being escorted by a woman other men desired, but tonight he was in no mood for distractions, and he decided to win back Indiana's respect. Irritated, he got between her and the guide and, gripping her arm more forcefully than nec-essary, dragged her from one painting to another. He pontificated about the importance of sixteenth-century Venice—an indepen-dent republic that had been a hub of commerce and culture for a thousand years before these masters painted their works—and pointed out details to demonstrate how the improvements in oil paint had revolutionized art. Indiana was a willing student, happy to soak up all the things he taught her, from the *Kama Sutra* to the correct way to eat an artichoke, and especially art history.

An hour later they were in the final room, standing in front of Tintoretto's *Susanna and the Elders*, a canvas that Alan especially wanted to show her. The piece was hung on its own wall, with a bench in front of it where they could sit and contemplate the work while Alan explained that the story of Susanna had been popular in Renaissance paintings. It had been the pornography of the era, he told her, used to portray male lust and the nude female form. Rich men commissioned paintings to hang in their bedrooms, and—for a tip—the artist might be persuaded to give Susanna the face of the patron's lover.

"According to legend," said Alan, "Susanna is a virtuous mar-ried woman, surprised by two lustful elders while bathing under a tree in her garden. When she refuses their advances, the old men accuse her of having an affair with a young man. At that time, adultery in women was punishable by death."

"Only in women?" Indiana asked.

"Of course. Supposedly it's a Bible story, so obviously it's sexist —though I don't think it appears in the Old Testament."

"So what happened?"

"A judge questioned the old men separately, and when they couldn't agree what kind of tree she had been sitting under—one said it was a larch, and the other, an oak, or something like that—it became obvious they were lying, and the noble Susanna's reputation was restored."

"I hope the old scandalmongers were punished," said Indiana.

"According to the canonical version they were executed, but there is a different version in which they are simply rebuked. Which would you prefer, Indiana?"

"I don't much like either, Alan. I don't agree with the death penalty, but justice has to be done. How about if they were fined, sent to prison, and had to publicly apologize to Susanna and her husband?"

"Too lenient," Keller argued. "Susanna would have been executed if she hadn't been able to prove her innocence. Surely the fairest thing would be if the two horny old perverts suffered the same punishment." He was playing devil's advocate—he too was opposed to the death penalty, except in certain rare cases.

"An eye for an eye, a tooth for a tooth . . . ," Indiana replied, taking up the gauntlet. "If that were the law, we'd all be half blind and using false teeth."

"Well, in the end, the fate of those liars isn't the important thing, is it?" said Keller, turning for the first time toward the guide, who nodded mutely. "The lecherous old men are irrelevant; that's why they're hidden in the shadowy corners of the canvas. The focus of our attention is Susanna, and only her. Just look at the young woman's skin: warm, smooth, gilded by the evening sun. Look at the soft body, the languorous posture. This is no virgin we're looking at: we know she's married, that she's been initiated into the mysteries of sex. Tintoretto has achieved the perfect balance between the innocent girl and the sensual woman; in Susanna they coexist for that fleeting moment before time leaves its mark on her. That moment is magical. Just look at her." Alan spoke directly to the guide. "Don't you think the old men's lust is understandable?"

"I suppose so, sir. . . ."

"Susanna is confident in her beauty, she cherishes her body. She's as perfect as a peach plucked from the bough: all fragrance, color, and taste. There is no sign that the processes of maturity, of aging and death, have already begun. See the gold and copper tones in her hair—look at the graceful lines of her hands, her neck, the expression of abandonment on her face. She has clearly just made love and is basking in the memory. She moves languidly, because she wants to prolong the pleasure of her bathing, of the cool water and the warm breeze blowing through the garden. She's caressing herself; she can feel a faint quivering in her thighs, the moist, throbbing mound between her legs. Do you understand what I'm saying?"

"I suppose so, sir. . . ."

"Tell me, Indiana, who does the Susanna in the painting remind you of?"

"I've no idea," she replied, puzzled by the way Alan was behaving.

"What about you, young man?" Alan asked the guide, his innocent look belied by the sarcasm in his voice.

The mortified teenager's acne scars lit up like craters on his startled face, and he stared at the ground. But Keller was not about to let him off the hook so easily.

"Come on, young man, don't be shy. Take a good look at that painting and tell me who the lovely Susanna reminds you of."

"Really, sir, I couldn't say," the poor boy stammered, ready to bolt.

"You mean you couldn't, or you wouldn't dare? Susanna looks just like my friend Indiana here. You should see her when she's bathing, as naked as Susanna there . . ." Alan slid a possessive arm around his lover's shoulders.

"Alan!" Indiana shouted, pushing him away and stomping out of the room, quickly followed by the terrified guide.

Alan managed to catch up with her at the entrance and take her to his car, pleading and apologetic, as shocked by what he had done as she was. He did not know what had come over him; it had been a moment of insanity. In his right mind he would never do anything so vulgar, so out of character, he said.

It was the painting, he thought—the painting was to blame. The contrast between Susanna's youthful beauty and the disgusting old men ogling her had given him the creeps. He had seen himself as one of those old lechers, infatuated with some woman he couldn't have and didn't deserve, and he tasted bile in his throat. The painting was not new to him; he had been to the museum in Vienna, had seen reproductions in art books—but there in the silence and the light of the deserted museum, it had been like seeing his own skull in a mirror. Tintoretto had reached across five centuries and shown him his deepest fears: decay and death.

Alan and Indiana stood arguing in the parking lot, which was empty by then, until finally he convinced her to come to dinner so they could talk in peace. They found a quiet table in the corner of one of his favorite restaurants, a little place tucked away down an alley off Sacramento Street, which boasted an authentic Italian menu and an excellent wine list. Once her mood had been softened by the first glass of a Piedmont dolcetto, Indiana told him how humiliated she had felt in the museum, paraded like a whore in front of the guide's eyes.

"I didn't realize you could be so cruel, Alan. In all the years we've been together, I've never seen that side of you. I felt like you were punishing me, and I think that poor boy felt the same."

"Don't take it that way, Indi. Why would I want to punish you? On the contrary, I don't know how to thank you for all you give me. I thought you'd be flattered by the comparison with the beautiful Susanna."

"With that whale of a woman?"

Alan started to laugh, and Indiana got the giggles too; suddenly the disastrous scene in the museum weighed on them less. Alan waited until dessert to give her the surprise he had arranged: a two-week trip to India, traveling in whatever style she chose, a concession he was willing to make for the sake of love, despite his recent financial problems and the fact that the unspeakable poverty in India terrified him. They could stay in boutique hotels in the converted palaces of maharajas, he said, sleeping in feather beds with silk sheets, waited on hand and foot—or they could bed down with scorpions on the floor of an ashram. Whatever she wanted. Indiana's spontaneous delight dispelled his fears that the incident at the museum might have ruined the surprise: she kissed him hard, right in front of the amused waiter, who was just then bringing their food. "Are you trying to get me to forgive you for something?" Indiana asked, smiling, little suspecting how prophetic the remark would prove.

Monday, 16

*I*t had been some days since the Ripper players had met up on-line, because Abatha had had a spell in a hospital, tied to the bed, being force-fed through a tube. Her illness was getting worse, and every ounce of body weight she lost took her one step closer to the spirit world, which was where she wanted to dwell anyway. The only thing that distracted her from her determination to die was playing Ripper, and the prospect of solving the San Francisco crimes. Hardly was she out of intensive care and in a private room under twenty-four-hour surveillance than she had asked for her laptop and contacted her only friends—four teenagers and an old man she had never actually met. That night, six computers in various parts of the globe logged in for a new episode, one the games master called the Case of the Electrocuted Man.

Amanda started by giving them the results of the autopsy, which she had found in her father's apartment and photographed on her cell phone.

"Ingrid Dunn's initial examination of the body of Richard Ashton was at 9:10 a.m., and she estimated time of death to be eight to ten hours earlier—which means at about midnight on Monday, though a few minutes either way are unimportant at this point in the investigation. There are still no leads as to the perpetrator or the motive for the crime. My dad's assigned a couple of detectives to the case."

"Let's go over what we know," said Colonel Paddington.

"You have permission to speak, Kabel," Amanda said to her grandfather. "Tell us everything we've got."

"Richard Ashton died of electrocution from a Taser. The autopsy found several puncture marks surrounded by reddened, irritated skin."

"What's a Taser?" asked Esmeralda.

"A weapon police use to control aggressive suspects, or to deter rioters," explained Colonel Paddington, the arms expert. "It's about the size of a large pistol and fires a pair of electrodes connected to conductive wires."

"And it can kill?"

"Depends on how it's used. People have died, but it's rare. The Taser disrupts the nervous system using a powerful electric charge that paralyzes the muscles and knocks the victim out, even at a distance of several meters. You can imagine what effect a number of discharges would have."

"It also depends on the victim," said Amanda. "A Taser can easily kill someone who has a weak heart, but that wasn't true of Richard Ashton."

"Suppose the first electric shock immobilized Ashton, then the murderer tied his hands, covered his mouth with duct tape, and discharged the Taser into him until he died?" Sherlock Holmes suggested.

"Can a Taser be discharged more than once?" asked Esmeralda.

"It needs to recharge," said Colonel Paddington, "which takes about twenty seconds."

"So he used two of them," said Abatha.

"You're right, Abatha!" said Sherlock Holmes. "The killer must

have had more than one Taser, and given Ashton several succes-
sive shocks, without allowing him time to recover, until eventually
his heart failed."

"Electrocuted . . . ," said Abatha. "He was executed, like in the
electric chair."

"Where would someone get hold of a Taser?" asked Esmeralda.

"As well as the ones issued to police, there are civilian models used for self-defense," Paddington explained, "but they don't
come cheap—about five hundred bucks."

"According to my dad's notes, the victim was barefoot," said
Amanda. "A pair of shoes was found under the desk, but no socks."

"He was wandering around with no socks on in the middle of
winter?" said Esmeralda.

"His wife Ayani always goes around barefoot. My dad . . . I
mean, Deputy Chief Martín, says that Ayani has the feet of a princess. Anyway, none of that matters. There was a damp patch on
the rug in Ashton's study, possibly where a glass of water had been
knocked over, although it wasn't close to the desk."

"Elementary, my dear friends," Sherlock reasoned. "Water is an
excellent conductor of electricity. The murderer took the victim's
shoes off and wet his socks to electrocute him."

"I saw something like that in a movie once," said Amanda.
"There was a prisoner being executed by electric chair, they forgot
to put the wet sponge on him, and he was practically cooked alive."

"You shouldn't be watching films like that!" Kabel interjected.

"It was PG rated—there was no sex in it."

"I don't think it would be necessary to wet Ashton's feet," said
Colonel Paddington, "but maybe the killer didn't know that. He
probably took the socks away to confuse the police and gain some
time. Not a bad strategy."

"He needn't have bothered," said Amanda. "The police are
wasting a lot of time investigating other leads. Ashton's study was

full of furniture, rugs, drapes, books, and stuff, and it was only cleaned once a week. The maid was under strict instructions not to touch any of his papers. Forensics found so many prints, hairs, skin cells, and fibers that it'll be almost impossible to tell which ones are relevant."

"We'll have to see what the DNA tests say," said Abatha.

"I talked to my dad about that," Amanda chimed in. "He said DNA tests are used in less than one percent of cases—it's an expensive, complex process, and the department has limited resources. Sometimes an insurance company or the heirs will pay for tests, if there's a good reason."

"Who's Ashton's heir?" asked Esmeralda.

"His wife, Ayani."

"You don't have to look far for a motive in murder cases," said Sherlock Holmes. "Most of the time it's money."

"Permission to speak?" asked Kabel.

"Permission granted."

"Any samples the police take are useless if they have nothing to compare them with. I mean, you have to match samples to the DNA of someone with a police record, someone who's already in the system. Besides, surely the police are already investigating everyone who's been in Ashton's study since the last time it was cleaned."

"Your homework for next week is to come up with theories about the case," the games master said before signing off. "You all know the drill: motive, means, opportunity, suspects, method. And don't forget all the stuff we still have to find out about Ed Staton and the Constantes."

"Okay," the other players replied in unison.

Galang stepped into the parlor with the coffee. The tray he was carrying held a coffeepot with a delicately engraved copper handle, two small cups, and a little glass vial like a perfume bottle. He set the tray down on the table and withdrew.

"Rose water?" Ayani Ashton asked Bob Martín, pouring coffee as thick as crude oil into the cups.

Bob, who had never heard of rose water and was used to drinking diluted coffee in half-pint mugs, did not know what to say. Ayani put a few drops from the vial into the cup and handed it to him, explaining that she had taught Galang to make Arabic coffee the way she liked it: boil the coffee with sugar and cardamom pods three times in the copper pot, then wait for the sediment to settle before serving. Bob sipped the sweet, thick brew, thinking about the dose of caffeine he was ingesting and how badly he would sleep that night. Ayani was wearing a black caftan embroidered with gold thread that fell to her feet, revealing only the slim, elegant hands, the gazelle's neck, and the celebrated face that had haunted Bob's imagination since the moment he first caught sight of her. Her hair was pinned at her neck with two hair sticks; she wore large gold earrings and an ivory bracelet.

"I'm sorry to bother you again, Ayani."

"Not at all, Deputy Chief, it's a pleasure to see you," she said, sitting in one of the armchairs, cradling her cup.

Not for the first time, Bob admired her graceful feet, the toes adorned with silver rings, perfect despite Ayani's habit of wandering around barefoot, something he had noticed the first time he saw her in the garden, that memorable Tuesday of Ashton's death, when she had first stepped into his life. "Stepped into" wasn't the right phrase, though. That still hadn't happened: the woman was a mirage.

"Thank you for coming to the house. I have to admit I felt intimidated at the police station, but I suppose everyone does. I'm surprised you're working today—isn't it a public holiday?"

"Martin Luther King Day, but I don't take holidays. Now, if you don't mind, I'd like to go through a few points in your statement."

"You think I killed Richard."

"I didn't say that. We've only just started the investigation—any assumptions would be premature."

"No need to beat about the bush, Deputy Chief—let's be honest here, the spouse is always the prime suspect, and it makes all the more sense in this case. I suppose you know that I'm Richard's sole heir."

Bob did know. Petra Horr, from whom there were no secrets, had already given him plenty of information about the Ashtons.

Though she still looked twenty-five, Ayani was about to turn forty, and her long career as a model was over; fashion designers and photographers grow tired of seeing the same face all the time. Ayani had lasted longer than most because the public recognized her. As a black woman in a white woman's profession, she was exotic, different. Bob imagined she would still be the most beautiful woman in the world at seventy. For a time Ayani had been one of the world's highest-paid models, the toast of the fashion world, but that had ended five or six years ago. Her income had dried up, and she had no savings; she'd spent her money like it was going out of style, as well as continuing to support her family back in their village in Ethiopia. Before she married Ashton, Ayani had juggled credit cards, taking loans from friends and from banks to keep up appearances. She was still expected to dress as she had when designers had given her their clothes for free, to attend parties and nightclubs with A-list celebrities. She duly showed up in a limousine wherever she could be photographed, but lived modestly in a studio apartment at the unfashionable end of Greenwich Village. She had met Richard Ashton at a gala fund-raiser for the Campaign Against Female Genital Mutilation, at which she gave the opening address. This was something she knew a lot about, and she took every opportunity to expose the true horrors of the practice—she herself had been a victim of it in her childhood. Ashton, like everyone else at the gathering, had been moved by Ayani's beauty, and by her openness in describing her ordeal.

Bob was curious to know what she had seen in Ashton—a boorish, arrogant man with short legs, a potbelly, and the bulging eyes of a toad. The psychiatrist enjoyed a certain sort of fame in his own professional circles, but that was unlikely to impress a woman who rubbed shoulders with real celebrities. Petra Horr thought there was no need to overthink things. The reason was clear: Ashton was as rich as he was ugly.

"I understand that you and your husband met in New York in December 2010 and married a month later. It was his third marriage, and your first. What moved you to take such a step with a man you barely knew?" asked Bob.

"His intellect. He was a brilliant man, Deputy Chief, as anyone will tell you. He invited me to dinner the day after we met, and we spent four hours in deep conversation. He suggested we write a book together."

"What sort of book?"

"About female genital mutilation. My role was to tell my experience and conduct a series of interviews with victims, mostly in Africa. He would investigate the physical and psychological consequences of the practice, which affects forty million women worldwide, scars them for life."

"Did you ever write it?"

"No," Ayani replied. "We were still planning the book and assembling material when . . . when Richard died."

"I understand. Dr. Ashton must have had other qualities for you to fall in love with him, aside from the book project," Bob suggested.

"Fall in love? Let's be serious, Deputy Chief, I'm not the type of woman who's a slave to her emotions. Romance and passion are things that happen in movies, not in the life of someone like me. I was born in a village of mud huts, and I spent my childhood carrying water and tending goats. When I was eight, a filthy old woman cut me, and I almost died of hemorrhage and infection. When I was ten, my father started looking for a husband for me among other men of his age. I only escaped a life of backbreaking work and poverty because an American photographer spotted me and paid my father to let me come to the United States. I'm a practical woman: I have no illusions about the world, about humanity, or about my own fate. Still less about love. I married Richard for his money."

Her frank declaration hit Bob like a punch in the gut. He didn't want to admit Petra Horr was right.

"And I'll say it again, Deputy Chief: I married Richard so I could live comfortably and securely."

"When did Dr. Ashton make his will?"

"The day before the wedding. I made it a condition, on my lawyer's advice. Our prenup stipulated that in the event of his death, I'd inherit everything, but that if we divorced, I'd only get fifty thousand dollars. Richard would practically tip that amount in a restaurant."

In his pocket the deputy chief had a list of Ashton's assets, given to him by Petra: the Pacific Heights mansion, a Paris apartment, a five-bedroom ski chalet in Colorado, three cars, a fifty-five-foot yacht, several million dollars' worth of investments, and the rights to various books that brought in a modest but steady income, being required reading in the world of psychiatry. In addition, there was a life-insurance policy for a million dollars in Ayani's name. Richard Ashton's children from his previous marriages were to receive a token sum of a thousand dollars apiece, and nothing at all if they disputed the terms. Logically, of course, this clause would be invalid if they could prove Ayani responsible for their father's death.

"I'll be straight with you, Deputy Chief: becoming a widow was the best thing that could happen to me," Ayani said finally. "But I didn't kill my husband. As you know, I won't see a cent of my inheritance until you find the killer."

Friday, 20

Blake Jackson arranged his hours at the drugstore so that he could be free on Friday afternoons to fetch his grand-daughter from school when class finished, at three o'clock. He took her either to his own house or to Bob Martín's, and since it was his turn this weekend, he was looking forward to two whole days of indolence and companionship—more than enough time to play Ripper. He saw Amanda step out of the school among the gaggle of girls, trailing her backpack, her hair a mess, looking around for him with the nervous expression he always found so touching. When Amanda was a little girl, Blake would hide just to see the enormous smile of relief on the girl's face when she found him. He preferred not to think about what life would be like when she flew the nest. Amanda kissed him hello, and together they heaved her backpack, a bag of dirty laundry, her books, and her violin into the trunk of the car.

"I have an idea for your book," she said.

"Really?"

"A detective novel. You just choose one of the crimes we're investigating. All you have to do is elaborate a bit, make it really gruesome, throw in some sex, loads of torture, and a few car chases. I'll help you."

"It would need a hero. Who would the detective be?"

"Me."

Back at the house they found Elsa Domínguez—who had brought a chicken casserole—and Indiana, who was laundering sheets and towels from her clinic in her father's rickety old washing machine, rather than taking them to the laundromat in the basement of the Holistic Clinic like the other tenants in the building. Four years earlier, when Amanda went to boarding school, Elsa had decided to cut her working hours and now only came to clean twice a month, but she still visited Blake often. She would discreetly leave plastic tubs of his favorite dishes in the refrigerator and phone to remind him to cut his hair, take out the trash, or change his sheets—little details that would not occur to Indiana or Amanda.

Whenever Celeste Roko stopped by, Blake would shut himself in the bathroom, phone Elsa, and ask her to come and rescue him. He was terrified at the thought of being left alone with the soothsayer, who, shortly after he was widowed, had informed him that, given that their astral charts were uniquely compatible, and both were single and available, it might not be a bad idea for them to get together. Elsa always came straight away, served tea, and sat in the living room, keeping Blake company until Celeste admitted defeat and left, slamming the door behind her.

At forty-six, Elsa looked sixty. She suffered from chronic back pain, arthritis, and varicose veins, none of which stopped her being cheerful and singing hymns to herself wherever she went. Nobody had ever seen her wear anything but a blouse or a long-sleeved top, because she was ashamed of the machete scars she'd suffered in the attack when soldiers killed her husband and two of her brothers. She had arrived in California at the age of twenty-three, alone, having left four young children in the care of relatives in a border town in Guatemala; she worked around the clock to send money to support them, then brought them to California one by one— riding on train roofs at night, crossing Mexico in trucks, and risking their lives to get over the border along secret roads. She was convinced that if life as an illegal immigrant was hell, staying in her own country was worse. Her oldest son had joined the military in hopes of making a career and getting American citizenship. He was now on his third tour in Iraq and Afghanistan, and had not seen his family in two years, but in the brief phone calls he was allowed, he sounded content. Her two daughters, Alicia and Noemí, had an entrepreneurial streak and had managed to get themselves work permits; Elsa was sure that they would keep making progress, and that if the future was bright and there was an amnesty for immigrants, they would become permanent residents. The two girls ran a cohort of undocumented Latino women who wore pink uniforms and cleaned houses. They drove their employees to work in trucks just as pink, with "Atomic Cinderellas" emblazoned on the bodywork.

Amanda set her bags down in the hallway and kissed her mother and then Elsa—who called her "my angel" and had spoiled the girl to compensate for every moment she had not been able to spend spoiling her own children when they were young. While Elsa and Indiana took clothes from the dryer and folded them, Amanda began calling out moves from the kitchen in a blindfold chess game with her grandfather, who was seated in front of the chessboard in the living room.

"A nightshirt and some bras and panties have disappeared from my wardrobe," Indiana announced.

"Don't look at me, Mom," Amanda shot back. "I'm a size two, and you barely squeeze into a ten. Anyway I'd rather die than wear lace, it's so itchy."

"I'm not accusing you, honey. But somebody's stolen my underwear."

"Maybe you lost it," Elsa suggested.

"Where, Elsa? I only take my underwear off in the house." That wasn't strictly true, but if she had left it in a room at the Fairmont, she would have realized before she got to the elevator. "I'm missing a pink bra and a black one, two pairs of pink panties, and a sheer nightshirt I never even managed to wear—I was saving it for a special occasion."

"*¡Qué raro, niña!* Your apartment's always locked."

"Somebody has been in here, I just know it. And whoever it was moved my aromatherapy bottles, too, but I don't think they took any."

"Did they reorganize them?" asked Amanda, suddenly interested.

"They lined them up in alphabetical order, and now I can't find anything. I've got my own order."

"So they had time to rummage around in your drawers, take some clothes they wanted, and line up your bottles. Did they take anything else? Did you check the locks, Mom?"

"I don't think they took anything else. The locks are fine."

"Who's got keys to your place?"

"A couple people: Elsa, my dad, and you," Indiana replied.

"And Alan Keller, although he's hardly going to steal back the ridiculous lingerie he bought you," muttered Amanda.

"Alan? No, he doesn't have a key—he never comes around here."

Blake called out to Amanda from the living room that he had moved a knight. She'd have him in checkmate in three moves, she called back.

"Dad has a key too," she reminded Indiana.

"Bob? Why would he have one? I don't have a key to his place!"

"You gave it to him so he could fix the TV when you went to Turkey with Keller."

"Amanda, how you even think of suspecting your father?" Elsa Domínguez cut in. "Jesus, *hija*. Your papa ain't no thief, he's a policeman."

Indiana agreed with her in principle, but she had her doubts; Bob could be unpredictable. He often caused her grief—mostly because he routinely broke his promises to Amanda—but in general he treated her with the considerateness and affection of an older brother. He would sometimes surprise her with a grand gesture—like on her last birthday, when he had sent a cake for her to the Holistic Clinic. Her colleagues, led by Matheus Pereira, all came along with champagne and paper cups to toast her and share the cake. As she was cutting the cake with a paper knife, Indiana found a small plastic bag inside containing five hundred-dollar bills, a not insignificant sum for her ex-husband, whose only income was his police salary, and a huge amount for her. But the same man who'd had a cake made for her with hidden treasure in it was also capable of entering her apartment without her permission.

In the three years they were married and living together under Blake Jackson's roof, Bob had controlled her like a maniac, and after the divorce it took him some time to accept that he needed to keep his distance and respect her privacy. He had matured a little, but he still had the dominant, aggressive character of the jock he had always been, which had served him well in his career in the police department. When he was younger he used to suffer fits of rage, destroying anything he laid his hands on. At moments like that Indiana would hold her daughter close and flee to a neighbor's house until her father came, having been called urgently at the pharmacy. Bob would calm down the moment his father-in-law came in, proof that he hadn't in fact lost his mind. The two men developed a strong bond that survived Bob and Indiana's divorce. Blake continued to be a kindly father to Bob, who acted like a good, obedient son in return. They went out to football games and action movies, and sometimes had a few beers at the Camelot, their favorite bar.

Until she met Ryan Miller, her ex-husband had been the only person aside from her father that Indiana turned to in times of need. She could be sure that Bob would solve the problem, even if he lectured and criticized her as he did so. She admired his good qualities and loved him very much, but it wasn't beyond Bob to play a joke on her: he could have stolen her underwear just to prove how easy it was to rob her. For a while now he had been nagging her to change her locks and get an intruder alarm.

"You know you promised to get me a cat, right?" Amanda asked, interrupting her mother's ruminations.

"You're going to college at the end of August, sweetie. Who's going to look after a cat after you leave?"

"Grandpa. We already talked about it—he's cool with it."

"It'll be good for Mr. Jackson to have a pet." Elsa sighed. "He's gonna be real lonely without his granddaughter."

*S*unday, 22

*B*ob Martin's apartment was on the fifteenth floor of one of the blocks that in recent years had sprouted like mushrooms south of Market Street. A few years earlier, the area had been a squalid harbor district full of sheds and warehouses. Now it stretched the length of the Embarcadero and was one of the most affluent neighborhoods in the city, with restaurants, art galleries, nightclubs, luxury hotels, and apartment buildings, all within a few blocks of the financial district and Union Square. The deputy chief had bought his apartment early, before prices skyrocketed, with a mortgage that would keep him in debt for the rest of his days. The imposing tower was a bad investment, Celeste Roko had pointed out, since it was going to collapse in the next earthquake. The planets, however, couldn't tell her exactly when that might be. From the living room, Bob could look right out across the bay, speckled with sailboats, all the way to the Bay Bridge.

Amanda, feathers threaded through her hair, had on yellow-striped socks, and the cardigan of her grandfather's she always wore, which had holes at the elbows. She and her father were sitting on high stools at his black granite kitchen table, eating. One of Bob's ex-girlfriends, a landscape gardener, had decorated his apartment for him with uncomfortable ultramodern furniture and a small forest of houseplants that had died of melancholy the moment she left. Without the plants, the place was about as welcoming as a hospital, except for Amanda's room, which was stuffed full of junk and had walls plastered with posters of bands, as well as her personal heroes: Tchaikovsky, Stephen Hawking, and Brian Greene.

"Is the Pole coming today?" the girl asked her father. She was used to his flings, which were brief, and—aside from the occasional collection of dead potted plants—left no trace.

"She's got a name, and you know it perfectly well: Karla. She's not coming today, she's just had her wisdom teeth out."

"Well, that's good, and I'm not talking about the wisdom teeth. What's that woman want from you, Dad? A green card?"

Bob slammed a fist on the granite and launched into a tirade about filial respect, rubbing his bruised hand as he spoke. Amanda, unfazed, went right on eating.

"You're always declaring war on my girlfriends!"

"Don't exaggerate, Dad. I mostly put up with them, but this one gives me the creeps—she's got a laugh like a hyena and a heart of stone. But I don't want to fight about it. How long you been with her? Month and a half, I make it. Give it a couple weeks and she'll be gone, then I'll stop harping on it. I just don't want this woman taking advantage of you."

Bob couldn't help smiling. He loved his daughter more than anything in the world—more than life itself. He ruffled her Indian feathers and got up to serve dessert. He admired Amanda's judgment when it came to his love affairs: it had proved a lot more reliable than his own. Though he was not about to tell her, his relationship with Karla was already on its last legs. He fetched coconut ice cream from the refrigerator and served it in the black sundae glasses that the landscape gardener had picked out, while his daughter rinsed the pizza plates.

"I'm waiting, Dad."

"What for?"

"Come on, don't play dumb," she demanded, drowning her ice cream in chocolate syrup. "I need the details of the psychiatrist's death."

"Richard Ashton? He died on Tuesday, the tenth."

"You sure?"

"Of course I'm sure, Amanda. I've got the records on my desk."

"But you can never determine the precise time of death—there's always a margin of a few hours. I read about it in a book about corpses—it's called *Stiff* or something."

"Jesus, girl, what kind of books are you reading?"

"Worse ones than you can even imagine, Dad. The psychiatrist has got to be important—you always keep the best cases for yourself. You wouldn't waste your time on some garden variety murder."

The deputy chief sighed dramatically. "If you're this cynical when you're seventeen, I dread to think what you'll be like when you're thirty."

"Cold and calculating, like your Polish friend. So tell me more."

Bob gave in and took her to his computer. He showed her photographs from the crime scene, along with some shots of the body, and let her read his notes, which included details about the victim's clothes and the medical report she had photocopied on her last visit.

"His wife found him in the morning. You should see her, Amanda, she's incredible—the most beautiful woman I've seen in my life."

"You mean Ayani, the model. She's been on TV more than

the victim. Her photo's everywhere. She goes around wearing a mourning veil like those old widows—it's ridiculous!"

"There's nothing ridiculous about it. Maybe that's the custom in her country."

"Well, if I was her, I'd be pretty glad to be the widow of such a horrible guy and end up rich. What did you think of Ayani? Her personality, I mean."

"Apart from being a wonderful woman, she's got a lot of control over her emotions. She was very composed on the day I met her."

"Composed, or relieved? Where was she when her husband was murdered?" Amanda was thinking of the information the Ripper players would want to know.

"Ingrid Dunn estimated he'd been dead about eight or ten hours, but we still haven't gotten the results from the autopsy. His wife was asleep in the house."

"How convenient."

"The housekeeper, Galang, said she takes sleeping pills and tranquilizers. I guess that's why she was so calm the next day— that and the shock, obviously."

"You can't be sure Ayani took a sleeping pill that night."

"Galang took it to her with a cup of hot chocolate, as usual. But he didn't see her swallow it, if that's what you're saying."

"She's the prime suspect."

"In a cop show, maybe, but in real life it's my experience that guides me; and I got a sixth sense for these things, that's why I'm a good policeman. There's not a shred of evidence against Ayani, and my sixth sense tells me—"

"You shouldn't let the prime suspect's supermodel figure inter-fere with this sixth sense of yours, Dad. But you're right, we need to be open to other possibilities. If Ayani was planning to murder her husband, she'd have made sure she had a better alibi than a sleeping pill."

Wednesday, 25

hen she got back to her father's house that night, Indiana sifted through the mail. Among the bills and political pamphlets, she found a glossy magazine she sometimes saw in dentists' waiting rooms, sent by subscription to the holders of some of the more distinguished credit cards. The house was silent: it was the night her father played squash and hung out at the Bierkeller. She took the magazine to the kitchen with the other letters, put the kettle on, and sat down to leaf through it distractedly. A page was marked with a paperclip, she noticed idly; she turned to it. It was then she saw the article that would turn her life upside down.

The photo accompanying the article showed Alan Keller greeting guests at his vineyard. Hanging on his arm was a blond woman—Geneviève van Houte, according to the caption, a Belgian baroness and agent to a handful of European fashion designers. Indiana read with mild curiosity up to the third paragraph, where she discovered that though Geneviève currently lived in Paris, it was rumored that she would soon be moving to San Francisco—as Alan Keller's wife. The article described the lavish party given at the vineyard in honor of the conductor of the San Francisco Symphony, and quoted the opinions of various guests regarding the forthcoming marriage—which the couple didn't deny—and the pedigree of the van Houtes, a family whose aristocratic title dated back to the seventeenth century. On the following page were four photographs of Alan and the same woman in different places: at a Los Angeles club, on a cruise in Alaska, at a gala party, and walking hand in hand down a street in Rome.

Dumbfounded, with shaking hands and a drumming in her temples, Indiana nonetheless noticed that Geneviève's hair was short in some of the pictures and long in others, and that in the Alaska shot, Alan was wearing the beige cashmere sweater Indiana loved so much that he had given it to her. Since that was just a few weeks after they'd met, the only possible conclusion was that her lover and this baroness of his shared a long history. She reread the article and scanned the photographs again, searching for some clue that would expose it all as a lie, but she couldn't find one. Setting the magazine down on top of the envelope stuffed with travel brochures for India, she sat staring at the dishwasher as the kettle on the stove let out its soft whistle.

It had been fifteen years since she'd felt the sting of betrayal. When married to Bob Martín, she had put up with his irresponsible, adolescent behavior: the beer cans on the carpet, him and his puerile friends sprawled in front of the TV, his violent outbursts; she only made up her mind to divorce him when she could no longer ignore his cheating. Three years after the divorce, Bob was still asking her for a second chance, but she couldn't trust him. In the years since then, all her relationships had ended amicably; none of the men had deceived or left her. If the spark went out, she found a discreet way to distance herself. Alan Keller might not be the ideal partner—as her daughter, her ex-husband, and Ryan Miller all liked to remind her—but until now she had not once doubted his fidelity, which for her was the cornerstone of their relationship. That glossy magazine spread proved her wrong.

In order to heal others, Indiana had learned to listen to her own body very closely, and she could tune in to herself just as intuitively as she could with her patients. Alan said she related to the world through her senses and her emotions; she lived in a magical universe that existed in an age before the telephone, trusting in people's basic goodness. He agreed with Celeste Roko, who claimed that in a previous incarnation Indiana had been a dolphin, and would return to the sea in the next—she wasn't made for dry land, lacking the gene that made other people mistrustful. She had also spent a number of years treading a spiritual path that led her to become detached from material things, and liberated in her mind and heart. But none of these defenses helped when she saw Alan Keller and Geneviève van Houte in the magazine.

She went upstairs to her apartment, turned the heat on, and stretched out on her bed to commune with her feelings in the darkness, breathe mindfully and summon her chi—the cosmic energy she channeled into her patients—as well as *prana*, the life force and one of the many powers of Shakti, her guardian goddess. She felt a painful wrench in her chest. She cried for a long while, until at last, sometime after midnight, tiredness overcame her, and she fell into a few hours' troubled sleep.

Thursday, 26

*I*ndiana woke up early, after turbulent dreams she couldn't remember. She rubbed a few drops of neroli—orange flower essence—onto her wrists to calm herself, and went down to her father's kitchen to make herself some chamomile tea with honey and put ice cubes on her puffy eyelids. Her whole body ached, but after the herb tea and twenty minutes of meditation her mind had cleared a little, and she was able to view the situation with some detachment. Knowing this Zen-like state would be short-lived, she decided to act before her emotions overtook her again. She called Alan to suggest they meet at one o'clock that afternoon at their usual spot, a favorite bench in Presidio Park. After an uneventful morning absorbed in her work, she closed the treatment room, stopped by Danny D'Angelo's for a cappuccino, then cycled to the park. She arrived ten minutes early and sat waiting, the magazine in her lap. The calming effects of the neroli and the chamomile tea were long gone.

Alan arrived right on time, all smiles at the fact that she had called him, just like in the early days of their affair, when the heat of passion had swept aside her shyness. Convinced that his trick of surprising her with the trip to India had worked, he sat down beside her and playfully tried to hug her, but she pulled away and thrust the magazine into his hands. Keller didn't need to open it—he knew what was in there. Until now it hadn't worried him; the possibility of it falling into Indiana's hands had seemed so slight.

"Surely you don't believe gossip like that, Indi," he said breezily. "I thought you were an intelligent woman—don't disappoint me."

It was the worst tactic he could have chosen.

He spent the next half hour trying to convince her that Geneviève van Houte was simply a friend, that they'd met while he was doing his doctorate in Brussels, and that he'd stayed in touch because it was mutually convenient: he introduced her to elite social circles, while she encouraged and advised him on his investments. They had never thought of getting married—the very idea was absurd, nothing but scurrilous rumors. Then he went on to detail his recent financial problems. Indiana listened in stony silence: while her life could be calculated dollar by dollar, Alan lived his by the hundred thousand.

The year before, walking hand in hand through Istanbul, the topic of money and how to spend it had come up. During their stay, Indiana had not felt the slightest bit tempted by the junk on offer at the bazaar, and later, in the spice market, though she smelled everything on offer, in the end she bought just a quarter ounce of turmeric. Keller, on the other hand, spent the week haggling over antique rugs and Ottoman vases, only to complain later about the cost. That day Indiana finally asked him how much was enough. When would he be satisfied? Why did he feel the need to accumulate things? And where did he get all his money, if he never did any work? "Darling, no one gets rich working," he'd replied, amused, and proceeded to give her a lecture on the distribution of wealth, and how governments and religions joined forces to protect the goods and privileges of the rich. That was too bad for the poor— the system, he admitted, was extremely unfair—but luckily, he was one of the chosen few.

Indiana thought back to that speech as they sat on the park bench, and Keller explained to her how much he owed in taxes, credit card bills, and other debts; how his latest investments had failed; how he could not keep his creditors at bay much longer with promises and his prestigious family name.

Keller sighed at length. "You don't know how horrible it is being rich and not having any money."

"A hell of a lot worse than being dirt-poor, I'll bet. But we're not here to talk about that—we're here to talk about us. I can see you've never loved me like I love you, Alan."

She picked up the magazine, gave him back the brochures about the trip to India, strapped on her helmet, and cycled off, leaving Alan sitting there shocked and angry. What he had told Indiana was a half-truth, he admitted quietly to himself. While it was true he had no intention of marrying Geneviève, he had neglected to mention that they had had an *amitié amoureuse* for the past sixteen years.

Alan and the Belgian baroness did not see each other often, because she was always traveling between Europe and the United States, but they met up whenever they were in the same city. Geneviève was educated and witty—they could spend all night playing sophisticated intellectual games laced with irony and malice—and if she so desired, he could satisfy her in bed and not get tired, with the help of a few battery-operated devices she always packed when she traveled abroad. They understood one other, belonging as they did to that stateless social class whose members recognize each other wherever they are in the world, and are at ease in luxurious settings, their natural habitat. They were both devoted music lovers; Geneviève had given him half of all the music he owned, and they would sometimes hook up in Milan, New York, or London for the concert season. There was a stark contrast between this woman, whom Plácido Domingo and Renée Fleming personally invited to their concerts, and Indiana Jackson, who had never seen an opera until Alan took her to *Tosca*. Indiana had not been much impressed with the music, but by the end the tragedy had her sobbing on his shoulder.

Keller angrily decided that he had broken no agreement with Indiana. What he and Geneviève shared was not love; besides, he was sick to death of misunderstandings, of feeling guilty about such petty issues. It was about time he ended the relationship; it had already dragged on too long. Even so, as he watched her cycle off into the distance, he wondered how he would react if their roles were reversed, if Indiana and Miller had been having the affair. "Go to hell, you stupid bitch," he muttered, disgusted with himself. He didn't plan to see her ever again—creating a scene like that had been tasteless, something Geneviève would never have done. Wipe Indiana from his mind and forget all about her, that was what he would do—and in fact, he'd already started to forget her. He dried his eyes with the back of his hand and trudged grouchily over to his car.

That night, he stayed up shuffling around the Woodside mansion, his overcoat and gloves pulled over his pajamas—what little warmth the central heating provided was swept away by drafts that slipped through the cracks in the floorboards with an eerie whistle. He finished his best bottle of wine as he chewed over a number of reasons to dump Indiana for good: what had happened that day only proved once again how narrow-minded and vulgar she was. What the hell did she want, anyway? For him to cut himself off

from his friends, from his social circle? His little romps with Geneviève meant nothing—only someone as naive as Indiana could
kick up a fuss over something so trivial. He didn't even remember
promising he would be faithful. When had that happened? It must
have been in some moment of confusion—if he had done so, it
was more of a formality than a promise. He and Indiana were not
compatible, he had known it from the start; his mistake had been
to give her false hope.

The wine hit him hard. He woke up with a sour taste in his
mouth and a pounding headache, but after a few aspirin and a gulp
of Pepto-Bismol he soon felt better, ate some toast and jam and
gathered enough strength for a cursory glance at the paper. He had
plans for the day, and he was not about to change them. He took a
long shower to scrub off the effects of the bad night, and thought
he had recovered his usual composure, but when he went to shave,
a grizzled old man from a Tintoretto painting stared back at him
from the mirror. He had aged ten years overnight, he realized. He
sat on the edge of the bathtub, naked, studying the blue veins in his
feet, muttering Indiana's name and cursing her.

Saturday, 28

The San Francisco Bay met the dawn swathed in its usual milky fog, its outline blurred to the world. Mist crept down over the tops of the hills like a slow-moving avalanche of cotton, dulling the water's steely glint. It was a typical day, with several degrees' difference between the two ends of the Golden Gate Bridge: winter in San Francisco, autumn sun a few miles north. For Ryan Miller, the temperate climate was the best thing about this place—it allowed him to train outdoors all year round. He had competed in four Ironman triathlons: a 2.4-mile swim, a 112-mile bicycle ride, and a 26.2-mile marathon run with no break. He usually averaged fourteen hours—which was passable—but every time the press had hailed it a "triumph over adversity," which made him angry; being an amputee was so common among war vets it was hardly worth mentioning. At least his prosthetic leg was top-of-the-line—that gave him an edge over other amputees, who had to make do with standard gear. His limp was so slight he could have danced the tango if he had had more of a sense of rhythm and less fear of looking like an idiot; but he had never been a dancer. To Ryan, Dick Hoyt was a genuine example of triumph over adversity: here was a father who did the triathlon carrying a disabled adult son who weighed as much as he did. Hoyt swam pulling a rubber dinghy with his son inside, cycled with his son strapped into a backseat, and pushed him in his wheelchair during the marathon. Every time Ryan saw him compete, this father's unswerving love—a stark contrast to his own father's brutality—moved him to tears.

As always, Ryan had started his day at five with Qigong exercises. This centered him for the rest of the day, and helped him to focus his awareness. In a book about the samurai, he had once read a quote that had become his motto: "A warrior without a spiritual practice is nothing but a killer." He prepared breakfast—a thick green smoothie with enough protein, fiber, and carbohydrates to get a guy through a day in the Arctic—then took Attila out for a run so he wouldn't get lazy. The dog still had boundless energy, but at eight years old he was not getting any younger, and after his service in the war there was a risk he would get bored with his sedentary life in San Francisco. Attila had been trained to defend and attack, to sniff out mines and terrorists, ward off enemies, parachute, swim through icy waters, and a variety of things that were not much use in civilian life. Though deaf, and blind in one eye, Attila compensated with a sense of smell remarkable even in a dog. Ryan communicated with him using hand signals, and the dog obeyed if the command seemed relevant; if it didn't, he took refuge in his deafness and ignored it.

By the time they got back after an hour's run, man and dog were puffing and panting. Attila slumped in a corner while Ryan subjected himself to exercise machines laid out like macabre sculptures in his apartment, along with the king-size bed, a TV, a stereo, and a bench that served as dining table, office, and workshop. A huge bank of computers connected him directly to the government agencies he worked with. There were no photographs to be seen, no diplomas, no medals; there was nothing personal, as though he had just arrived or was just about to move out, although the walls were hung with a collection of weapons that he would disassemble and clean to pass the time.

His apartment wasn't exactly comfortable but had enough space for his restless soul, and boasted a huge garage and an industrial elevator—an iron cage that could lift a tank if need be. He had chosen the loft for its size, and because he liked to be alone. He was the only tenant in the building, and after six o'clock and on weekends, the streets of the industrial district were deserted.

Ryan swam in an Olympic pool or in the bay, alternating days. Arriving at Aquatic Park that Saturday, he headed for the Dolphin Club with Attila. It was cold out, and at that early hour there was no one around except a few joggers, who would suddenly appear like ghosts out of the thick fog. He put a muzzle and leash on Attila, just to be safe; the dog could still run at thirty miles an hour and rip through a bulletproof jacket with his teeth, and when his jaws locked around his prey, there was no way to make him let go. Ryan had spent a year acclimatizing the dog to the city, but he worried that, if provoked or taken by surprise, Attila might still attack, and if that happened, there would be no choice but to have him put down. It was something Ryan had accepted when he took Attila in, but the idea of having his battle comrade and best buddy put to sleep was more than he could bear. He owed that dog his life. In the explosion in Iraq that had cost him his leg in 2007, Ryan had barely managed to apply a tourniquet before passing out, and would have died had it not been for Attila, who dragged him a hundred yards through sustained machine-gun fire and then lay on top of his master as a shield until help arrived. As he was being airlifted out, Ryan called the dog's name in the helicopter, and he was still repeating it on the plane that took him to the American hospital in Germany.

Months later, during his long convalescence, Ryan got a letter telling him that Attila had been assigned a new handler and was serving with another Navy SEAL team in a zone held by al-Qaeda. There was a photo, but in it Attila was unrecognizable: his coat had been shaved, leaving only a strip on his back like a Mohawk, which made him look even more threatening. Ryan kept up with his progress through friends in SEAL Team Six, who periodically sent news.

By November 2008 Attila had been involved in countless assaults and rescue operations, saved numerous lives, and was fast becoming a legend among the SEALs. One day, while he was traveling in a convoy with his handler and some other SEALs, a bomb exploded by the road, destroying a number of vehicles and leaving two men dead and five injured, as well as Attila. The dog had been in such a bad way that no one expected him to survive, but they took him to safety with the rest of them because you never leave a fallen comrade behind—it's a sacred rule. Attila survived his injuries thanks to medical intervention—although he would not serve in battle again—and was decorated for his bravery. Ryan still had a photo of the ceremony, and kept Attila's medal in a case with his own.

When he found out that Attila had been retired from active service, Ryan began the long process of getting him repatriated to the United States and adopting him, something that required him to overcome a number of bureaucratic hurdles. When at last the day came and Ryan went to pick the dog up from the military base, Attila immediately recognized him. He leaped on him, and they rolled around on the ground, playing the way they always had.

The Dolphin Club had been around since 1877, from which date it had kept up a healthy rivalry with the club next door, the South End Rowing Club. They operated out of the same ramshackle old wooden building, the two separated only by a thin wall and a door with no lock. At a discreet signal, Attila sneaked stealthily into the changing rooms and hid next to the yellow sign that read No Dogs, while Ryan went upstairs to a viewing gallery, a little circular room with a couple of threadbare armchairs and a rocking chair. There he found Frank Rinaldi, the caretaker, who at the ripe old age of eighty was always the first to arrive, already settled in his rocking chair to enjoy the city's greatest spectacle: the Golden Gate Bridge lit by the morning sun.

"I need volunteers to clean the bathrooms," he said by way of greeting. "Put your name down on the list, kid."

"Sure. You swimming today, Frank?"

"What do you think?" grumbled the old man. "That I'm going to sit here by the goddamn gas heater the rest of the day?"

Frank was not the only octogenarian to brave the icy waters of the bay. A recently deceased club member—a man who, on his sixtieth birthday, had swum across from Alcatraz with shackles on his ankles, pulling a boat behind him—had still been swimming there at ninety-six. Rinaldi, like Ryan and Pedro Alarcón, belonged to the Polar Bear Club, a group whose members were required to swim at least forty miles over the course of the winter. Each member entered his total for the day on a piece of graph paper tacked to the wall. To calculate the distance covered, there was a map of Aquatic Park and a piece of knotted string, a rudimentary system that nobody saw any need to change. Like everything else at the club, calculating mileage was subject to an honor code that had worked perfectly for a hundred and thirty-five years.

In the locker room, Ryan changed into his swim trunks. Before heading down to the beach he patted Attila on the back, and the dog settled down to wait for him, huddled in a corner, nose between his front paws, trying not to be seen. On the beach Ryan met Pedro, who had arrived before him but decided not to brave the water because he had the flu. He had a rowboat ready to take out, and was wrapped up in a heavy coat, woolly hat, and scarf, his maté gourd in one hand and a thermos of hot water tucked under his arm. The two men greeted each other with an almost imperceptible nod.

Pedro gave the boat a push, nimbly hopped into it, and vanished into the fog. Ryan, meanwhile, pulled on his orange swim cap and his goggles, unstrapped his prosthetic leg—he tossed it onto the sand, sure nobody would touch it—and dived into the waves. The cold was like a sudden blow, but soon he was feeling the heady euphoria of a swimmer. At moments like this—feeling weightless as he defied the treacherous currents, withstanding the near-freezing temperatures that made his bones creak, propelling himself with the powerful muscles in his arms and his back—he was once again the man he used to be. After a few strokes he no longer felt the cold, and could focus on his breathing, his speed, and his direction, orienting himself by the buoys that he could just pick out through his goggles and the fog.

The two men trained for an hour and arrived back on the shore at the same time. Pedro dragged the boat up onto the sand and handed Ryan his prosthesis.

"I'm in bad shape," muttered Ryan, heading for the club, leaning on Pedro's shoulder and limping from stiffness and the pain in his stump.

"Legs only give you ten percent of your power in the water. You've got thighs like a horse, my man. Don't waste 'em swimming. In the triathlon you need to save your leg power for the cycle and the run." They were interrupted by Frank Rinaldi, whistling from the top of the steps to tell them they had a visitor. Standing next to him, holding two paper cups, was Indiana Jackson, her nose red and her eyes watering, having just hopped off her bike— her usual form of transport.

"I brought you the most decadent thing I could find," she said. "Sea salt caramel hot chocolate from Ghirardelli."

"Something wrong?" asked Ryan, alarmed to see her at the club, where she had never set foot before.

"Oh, it's nothing urgent—"

"Then let Miller get in the sauna a while," Rinaldi told her. "Bunch of reckless guys have died of hypothermia from that water."

"And a bunch more were eaten by sharks," Ryan joked.

"Is that true?" she said.

Rinaldi explained to Indiana that no sharks had been seen there in a long time, but years ago a marauding sea lion had managed to get into Aquatic Park Lagoon, bitten fourteen people on the leg, and chased another ten who narrowly escaped unharmed out of the lagoon. Experts said he was protecting his harem of mates, but Rinaldi was still convinced the animal had brain damage from toxic algae.

"How many times I tell you not to bring your dog to the club, Miller?"

"Lot of times, Frank, and every time I've told you that Attila's a service animal, like a guide dog."

"I'd like to know what kind of service you get out of a mutt like that!"

"He calms my nerves."

"Club members are complaining, Miller. That dog could bite somebody."

"How the hell is he going to bite someone with a muzzle on, Frank? Besides, he only attacks if I order him to."

Ryan took a quick shower and dressed hurriedly. He was surprised that Indiana remembered he trained at the club at the same time every Saturday—he assumed she had her head in the clouds most of the time. Indiana was a little kooky—everyday details passed her by. She regularly got lost walking through the streets, could never keep track of what she spent, continually lost her cell phone and her purse; yet in her work she was inexplicably punctual and organized. When she tied her hair back with a scrunchie and put on the white smock she wore for therapy, she was transformed into the straitlaced sister of the woman he knew—the one with the tousled mane of hair and the too-tight clothes. Ryan loved them both. He loved the distracted, scatterbrained friend who brightened his existence and aroused his protective side, the woman who danced drunk on salsa and piña colada in the Latino club Matheus Pereira took them to, while Ryan watched her from his seat; and he also loved the serious, sober healer who soothed his muscle pains, the high priestess of ethereal essences, of magnets for aligning the forces of the universe, of crystals, pendants, and candles. Neither woman knew anything about the love he felt for her, this feeling like the tendrils of a creeper he could feel encircling him.

Ryan signaled Attila to stay in his corner while he went up to the viewing gallery to join Indiana, waiting on her own now that Pedro and Rinaldi had gone. They sat down in the battered armchairs in front of the picture windows, where a flurry of seagulls greeted them, looking out at the opalescent landscape as the towers of the Golden Gate Bridge rose above the dwindling fog.

"To what do I owe the pleasure?" asked Ryan, forcing himself to drink the near-cold hot chocolate she had brought, though the cream had curdled and started to form a paste.

"I take it you know it's over between Alan and me?"

"Really?" Ryan exclaimed, not bothering to hide his satisfaction. "How did that happen?"

"How can you ask me that? It was all your doing—you're the one who sent me that magazine. I was so convinced of Alan's love. . . . How could I have been so wrong about him? When I saw those photos, I felt like I'd been punched in the gut, Ryan. Why did you do it?"

"I didn't send you anything, Indi, but if whatever it was persuaded you to dump that old fool, well, it was about time."

"He's not old, he's fifty-five, and he looks fantastic. Not that I care—he's not in my life anymore," she announced, blowing her nose.

"Tell me what happened."

"First, you have to swear it wasn't you who sent the magazine."

"It's like you hardly know me!" Ryan protested, annoyed now. "I don't do backstabbing. What you see is what you get. I've never given you any reason to doubt my honesty, Indiana."

"I know, Ryan. I'm sorry, I'm just really confused right now. I found this in the mail," she said, passing him a few pages folded in half, which he read quickly and handed back to her.

"This Baroness van Houte looks just like you," was Ryan's tactless response.

"Sure, we're identical! Except she's twenty years older, twenty-five pounds lighter, and wears Chanel."

"You're much more beautiful."

"I can't deal with disloyalty, Ryan. I just can't."

"A second ago you were accusing me of betraying you."

"No, it's just the opposite—I thought you'd sent me the article out of loyalty. As a favor, to open my eyes to the truth."

"I'd be a coward if I didn't say it to your face, Indiana."

"You're right, of course. I need to know who did this, Ryan. It didn't come with the mail—there was no stamp. Someone took the trouble to put it in my mailbox."

"It could have been any of your admirers, Indi, acting with the best intentions: so you'd know what kind of a guy Alan Keller is."

"Well, whoever it was left it at my house, not the clinic, so whoever it was knows where I live, knows about my private life. Did I tell you I'm missing some underwear? I'm sure someone's been in my apartment, more than once even, but there's no way to be certain. It's easy to get to my place without being seen from the street—the staircase is at the side of the house, hidden behind a big pine tree. Anyway, Amanda said something to Bob, and you know how possessive he is: he showed up with a locksmith without even telling me and had the locks changed on my dad's house and my apartment. Nothing has gone missing since, but sometimes I feel like someone's been there. I can't explain it, there's a presence in the air, like a ghost. I think somebody's spying on me, Ryan."

Monday, 30

In the three years Denise West had been attending the Holistic
Clinic, she had become a favorite patient of a number of the
therapists. Rain or shine, she devoted every Monday afternoon
to her health and her art: she visited Indiana Jackson for Reiki,
lymphatic drainage, and aromatherapy, then Yumiko Sato for acupuncture; David McKee supplied her with his gentle homeopathic
remedies; and to round off her afternoon, she took art lessons with
Matheus Pereira. She never missed a session, although it took her
an hour and a half to drive there in the same beat-up truck she
used to deliver products from her garden to farmers' markets. She
would set out early, since parking the truck on North Beach was
quite a chore, and always brought some treat from her garden—
lemons, lettuces, onions, a spray of narcissus, fresh eggs—to give
to the people she called her "soul doctors."

Denise was sixty years old, and insisted that she was only alive
thanks to the Holistic Clinic, which had restored her health and her
optimism after an accident that left her with a cerebral contusion

and six broken bones. At the Holistic Clinic, she could vent her political and social frustrations—Denise was an anarchist—and absorb enough positive energy to fight the good fight for the rest of the week. Her "soul doctors" were enormously fond of her, as was Matheus Pereira, though Denise's artistic style made him nervous. Pereira's own paintings were vast canvases of tortured souls in broad sweeps of primary colors, while Denise painted chickens and lambs. Her subject matter could only be explained by the fact that she farmed and raised animals, since it was deeply at odds with her Amazonian temperament. Despite these divergent artistic approaches, the atmosphere in their classes was good-natured. Denise was scrupulous in paying Pereira fifty dollars a lesson, which he accepted guiltily, since the only thing she had learned in three years was how to prime a canvas and wash her brushes. At Christmas, the woman would give gifts of her artwork to her friends, including the soul doctors; Indiana had a collection of chickens and lambs in her father's garage, while Yumiko invariably received her gift with both hands, bowing deeply, in accordance with the etiquette of her country, before discreetly making it disappear. Only David McKee appreciated the oil paintings, and hung them in his office. He was a veterinarian by profession, but his homeopathic remedies had become so renowned that all his clients now were human except for the arthritic poodle, who was also a patient of Indiana's.

It was Ryan Miller and Pedro Alarcón who had first brought Denise West to the Holistic Clinic and entrusted her to Indiana's care, hoping she might be able to help. Denise and Pedro were old friends—in fact they had been lovers for a short time, though neither ever mentioned the fact, pretending to have forgotten all about it. Denise's bones had been reset during a series of complex operations, leaving her with a weakness in her knees and hips and the unpleasant sensation of having a spike jammed into her spine.

The pain, which she kept at bay with fistfuls of aspirin and swigs of gin, did not limit her activities. She was exhausted and angry at the world when she first arrived at the clinic, but the combined efforts of her "soul doctors" and the distraction of the art classes had worked wonders in bringing back the joyfulness that had seduced Pedro Alarcón years before.

That Monday, at the end of her session with Indiana, Denise got down from the massage table with a contented sigh. She pulled on corduroy trousers, a lumberjack shirt, and the work boots she wore every day, then waited for Ryan Miller, who had his appointment with Indiana after hers. Thanks to her holistic treatments, she could make it to the second floor, clutching the art-deco balustrade as she went. But she had never been able to climb the ship's ladder that led to the flat roof, so her painting classes took place in treatment room 3, which had been empty for some years. The Chinese businessman who owned the building could not lease it, because two previous tenants had committed suicide there; the first had discreetly hanged himself, but the second had blown his brains out, creating a shocking scene of blood and brain matter. More than one alternative practitioner had expressed interest in the unit—the location was good, and benefited from the prestigious reputation of the Holistic Clinic—only to walk away when they heard the story. It was rumored in North Beach that treatment room 3 was haunted by the suicide victims, but Pereira, who lived in the building, had never seen anything out of the ordinary.

After his Monday sessions with Indiana, Ryan would often stop by to collect Denise from her painting class and help her back to her truck. He too was lucky enough to receive the farmyard-themed oil paintings for Christmas. He took them to the annual auction at a shelter for battered women, where they were gratefully received.

Ryan emerged from Indiana's treatment room at peace with himself and with the world, taking with him an image of her and the physical sensation of her hands on his body. In the hallway he ran into Carol Underwater, whom he saw from time to time at the clinic.

"How are you, ma'am?" he asked out of courtesy, knowing the response, which was always much the same.

"Well, I still got cancer, but I'm hanging in, as you can see."

After her session with Ryan, the tranquillity that filled Indiana while she worked, intent on her healing, melted away, and she once more found herself overwhelmed with sadness at her failed relationship, and the vague, unshakable fear that she was being watched. A few hours after splitting up with Alan in the park, her anger had faded, replaced by the grief of losing him; never had she cried so much over love. She wondered how she had missed the signs that something was wrong. Alan had not seemed to be there in spirit; he had been distracted and withdrawn, and they had grown apart. Instead of probing, she had chosen to give him time and space, little suspecting that another woman was behind it all. Now she gathered up the sheets and towels, tidied the treatment room, and jotted down some notes about the general state of health of Denise West and Ryan Miller, as she did with every patient.

That day it was Carol Underwater who consoled Indiana—something of a novelty in their relationship, in which Carol had assumed the role of the victim. Carol heard what had happened with Alan on Sunday, when she phoned Indiana to invite her to the movies. Sensing that Indiana was upset, she had persuaded her to get it off her chest. Indiana saw her arrive with a basket on her arm and, moved by the kindness of this woman who might well die soon and had more serious reasons than she to give in to despair, regretted all the times she had been impatient with Carol. Seeing her patient sitting in reception in her thick skirt and her mud-colored jacket, a scarf tied around her head, the basket in her lap, she decided that once Carol finished radiation and had recovered a little, she would take her to her favorite thrift stores and buy her some clothes that were a bit younger, a bit more feminine. Indiana thought of herself as an expert in secondhand clothes; she had a good eye, and would frequently discover priceless treasures amid the piles of old rags—like the snakeskin boots she considered the height of elegance, and which she could wear with a clear conscience, since no reptile had been skinned for them. They were plastic: made in Taiwan.

"I'm so sorry, Indi," Carol said. "I know you're hurting, but you'll soon see that this is a blessing. You deserve someone better than Alan Keller."

She spoke in a halting, broken voice, in fitful whispers, as though breathless or bewildered. "The voice of a vacuous blonde movie star in the body of a Balkan peasant," Alan had described it, on the one occasion when the three of them met at Café Rossini. Indiana, who had to strain to hear Carol, could scarcely hide how irritated she was by this way of talking, but she attributed it to Carol's illness, thinking maybe her vocal cords were damaged.

"Listen to me, Indiana—Keller was no good for you."

"Nobody goes into a relationship thinking about what's good for them, Carol. Alan and I were together four years, and we were happy—at least, I thought we were."

"That's a long time. When did you plan to get married?"

"We never talked about it."

"Why on earth not? You're both single."

"We were in no hurry. I thought I'd wait till Amanda went off to college."

"Why? Didn't she get along with him?"

"Amanda never gets along with anyone who goes out with me or her father. She's a jealous girl."

"Don't cry, Indiana. Soon you'll have men lining up around the block, and I hope this time you'll be a bit more selective. Keller is a thing of the past, it's like he was dead, don't think about him any-more. Look, I brought a gift for Amanda. . . . What do you think?"

She set the basket on the table and lifted off the cloth covering it. Inside, curled up in a nest improvised from a woolly scarf, was a little animal, fast asleep.

"It's a kitten," she said.

"Oh, Carol!"

"You said your daughter wanted a cat. . . ."

"What a wonderful gift! Amanda will be so pleased."

"It didn't cost a thing—I got her from the Humane Society. She's six weeks old, in good health, and she's had all her shots. She's good as gold. Can I give her to your daughter myself? I'd like to meet her."

Tuesday, 31

T he deputy chief was in his office, sitting in his ergonomic desk chair—an extravagant gift from his subordinates to mark his fifteenth anniversary with the department—his feet up on the desk, his hands clasped behind his head. Petra Horr came in without bothering to knock, as always, carrying a paper bag and a cup of coffee. Before he got to know her, Bob had felt that her powerful name did not suit this little woman and her childlike face, but he soon changed his mind. Petra was thirty; she was short and slender and had a heart-shaped face with a wide forehead and a pointy little chin, a freckled complexion, and short hair, which was teased into spikes with gel and dyed black at the roots, orange in the middle, and yellow at the tips, like fox fur. From a distance—and indeed from close up—she looked like a girl, but the minute she opened her mouth, any impression of weakness disappeared. She set the bag down on the desk and handed the coffee to Bob.

"How long since you had something to eat, boss? You'll end up with hypoglycemia. Organic chicken sandwich on whole wheat. Very healthy. Eat."

"I'm thinking."

"Well, that's new! About who?"

"About the case of the psychiatrist."

"About Ayani, you mean." Petra sighed theatrically. "Now you mention it, boss, I meant to say, you've got a visitor."

"Is it her?" asked the deputy chief, taking his feet down off the desk and straightening out his shirt.

"No. Some really hot guy. The butler who works for the Ashtons."

"Galang. Send him in."

"No. Eat first, the gigolo can wait."

"The gigolo?" the deputy chief asked through a mouthful of the sandwich.

"Oh, boss," Petra called out as she left. "You're such an innocent!"

Ten minutes later Galang found himself sitting across the desk from the deputy chief. Bob had interviewed him a couple of times at the Ashton house, where the young Filipino wore black trousers and a long-sleeved white shirt: a tasteful uniform that, together with his inscrutable expression and his slinky feline movements, made him all but invisible. There was nothing invisible, however, about the man who presented himself at the police department that day: he was slim and athletic, his black hair tied up in a little ponytail at the back of his neck like a bullfighter's. He had carefully manicured hands and an easy, dazzling smile. He took off his navy-blue raincoat, and Bob recognized the classic beige-and-black lining of Burberry, which Galang could never afford on his salary. He wondered how much this man earned and whether somebody bought his clothes for him. With his elegant appearance and exotic face, Galang could pose in an advertisement for men's cologne—some sensual and mysterious fragrance, Bob thought. Petra would have corrected him: for that, he would pose nude and without shaving.

Bob leafed through the available information again: Galang Tolosa, thirty-four, born in the Philippines, immigrated to the States in '95, one year of college, worked at a Club Med, a few gyms, and the Institute of Conscious BodyWork. He asked Petra what the hell this last one was, and she explained that it was an approach to massage therapy that used the power of conscious attention and intention as a powerful tool to bring about change in cell tissue. Witchcraft, just like Indiana's, thought Bob, whose idea of a massage was a sleazy parlor full of topless Asian girls in hot pants and latex gloves.

"Sorry to take up your time, Deputy Chief. I was passing and thought I'd come and talk to you," said the Filipino with a smile.

"About what, may I ask?"

"I'll be frank with you, Deputy Chief. I've got a resident's visa, and I'm applying for American citizenship. I can't afford to get mixed up in a police investigation. I'm worried that this business with Dr. Ashton might cause problems."

"Are you referring to the murder of Dr. Ashton? You've every reason to worry, my friend. You were at the house, you had access to the study, you have no alibi—and if we dig around, I'm sure we'll find a motive. Would you like to add something to your previous statement?" The policeman's affable tone was in stark contrast to the implied threat of his words.

"Yes, well . . . ," Galang ground to a halt. "It's about what you just mentioned: a motive. Dr. Ashton was a difficult man, and I had some altercations with him." His smile had disappeared.

"Explain."

"The doctor could be violent, especially when he drank. During their divorce hearings, both his first and second wives accused him of abuse—you can check it out, Deputy Chief."

"Was he ever violent toward you?"

"Yes, three times, but only because I tried to protect Mrs. Ashton."

The deputy chief curbed his curiosity and waited for the other man to continue at his own pace, carefully observing his facial expressions, his gestures, the almost imperceptible tics. Bob was no stranger to lies and half-truths, and had long since resigned himself to the fact that almost everybody lies: some out of vanity, to present themselves in a favorable light, others out of fear, and the majority out of sheer habit. Everyone gets nervous in a police interview, even the innocent; it was Bob's job to interpret their responses, detect any false notes, intuit the omissions. He knew from experience that people who are anxious to please, like Galang, cannot stand an awkward silence, and, given the right encouragement, will talk much more than they should.

He did not have to wait long. Thirty seconds later, the Filipino began a speech that he may have prepared, but stumbled off course in his desperate need to be convincing. He had first met Ayani in New York a decade ago, he said, and they had been friends when she was at the peak of her career. They were more like brother and sister than friends, though: they helped each other out, saw each other almost every day. Both had struggled to find work when the economic crisis hit, and by late 2010, when she met Ashton, their situation was getting desperate. As soon as Ashton and Ayani were married, she had brought Galang to San Francisco as a butler, a job far beneath his qualifications, but he had wanted to get away from New York, where he had problems with money and other things. The salary was meager, but Ayani made up for it by giving him money behind her husband's back.

It had been awful for Galang to watch his friend suffer—Ashton treated her like a queen when they were in public and like trash when they were at home. At first he had tortured her psychologically—he was a master at that—and then he had begun hitting her. Galang noticed bruises on Ayani a number of times, which she tried to conceal using makeup. Galang tried his best to help her, but despite the trust between them, this was an aspect of her marriage that she would not talk about—it made her ashamed, as though her husband's brutality was her fault.

"They fought a lot, Deputy Chief," he concluded.

"Why did they fight?"

"Trivial things: a meal she'd cooked him that he didn't like, the phone calls she made to her family in Ethiopia. Dr. Ashton was infuriated that she was recognized wherever she went, while he was ignored. On the one hand, he liked to be seen with Ayani on his arm, and on the other he wanted to keep her locked away. So that's what they fought over."

"And did they also fight over you, Mr. Tolosa?"

The question took Galang by surprise. He opened his mouth to deny it, thought better of it, and nodded silently, looking pained and rubbing his forehead. Richard Ashton could not stand his friendship with Ayani, Galang said; he suspected her of buying him things and giving him money. Ashton knew that she trusted Galang with her secrets—from her spending sprees and evenings out to the friends she continued to see, even though Ashton forbade it. The psychiatrist would test them, humiliating Galang in front of Ayani, or mistreating Ayani until Galang could bear it no longer and had to confront him.

"Look, Deputy Chief, I'll admit that sometimes my blood would boil. It was all I could do not to punch him. I lost count of the times I had to intervene to pull him off his wife—to shove him or hold him down like a spoiled child. Once, when he went after Mrs. Ashton with a kitchen knife, I had to lock him in the bathroom until he calmed down."

"When was this?"

"Last month. Recently things had gotten better—they were going through a good phase; they were happy together and started talking about the book they were planning to write. Ayani—Mrs. Ashton—was happy."

"Anything else?"

"That's everything, Deputy Chief. I wanted to explain the situation to you before the housemaids give you their version. I suppose this makes me a suspect, but you have to believe me, I had nothing to do with Dr. Ashton's death."

"Do you have a weapon?"

"No, sir. I wouldn't know how to use one."

"And would you know how to use a scalpel?"

"A scalpel? No, of course not."

After Galang Tolosa left his office, the deputy chief called his assistant.

"Did you catch much of that, Petra? What did you think?"

"That Mrs. Ashton had more than enough of a motive for getting rid of her husband, and the butler for helping her."

"Do you think Ayani's the kind of woman who could electrocute her husband with a Taser?"

"No. She'd probably put an Ethiopian viper in his bed. But I think there's one detail Galang Tolosa forgot to mention."

"What?"

"He and Ayani are lovers. Hang on, boss, don't interrupt. There are a lot of aspects to their relationship: they're accomplices and confidants, she protects him, and he must be the only man who knows every inch of her body and can satisfy her sexually."

"Jesus! You dream up some perverted things, Petra!"

"I don't dream them much, but I bet you Galang's got an extensive repertoire. If you like, I'll tell you exactly what kind of genital mutilation Ayani suffered when she was eight: excision of the labia and clitoris. It's no secret—she has talked about it publicly. I could show you a video, so you can see what they do to young girls with a blunt knife or a rusty razor blade, no anesthetic."

"Thanks, Petra, but that won't be necessary." Bob sighed.

*f*ebruary

*B*lake Jackson's *numerous responsibilities now* included Save-the-Tuna, the cat Carol Underwater had given his granddaughter. The kitten was a lot of trouble, but he had to admit that the little animal turned out to be good company, just as Elsa Domínguez had predicted. Amanda had named her after her imaginary friend from childhood; no one in the family saw the irony in the cat being fed canned tuna.

"How's Save-the-Tuna, Grandpa?" Amanda asked. "I really miss her."

"Clawing the upholstery to bits."

"That doesn't matter, the furniture's all old. What's happening with your book?"

"Nothing yet. I've been mulling over your idea of a crime novel."

"I was thinking about that today," his granddaughter replied. "We're studying *autos sacramentales*. Do you know what they are?"

"No idea."

"They were morality plays in Renaissance Spain, similar to those of medieval England—allegories about the struggle between Good and Evil. Good always triumphed, but Evil always had the most interesting role—no one would go to see an *auto sacramental* that didn't have a load of vice, sin, or cruelty in it."

"What's that got to do with my book?"

"The formula for crime thrillers is pretty much the same. Evil is personified by a criminal who challenges Justice, and loses, and gets his punishment, and then Good triumphs, and everyone is happy. Got it?"

"I think so."

"Listen, old man, you stick to the formula and you got nothing to lose. I'll give you more advice later—the next session of Ripper is about to start. You ready?"

"Ready. See you online in a minute," said her grandfather, and hung up.

Minutes later, all the players were sitting at their computers, and the games master opened the proceedings.

"We're going to set aside the cases of Ed Staton and the Constantes for a moment and focus on Richard Ashton. Kabel's got some news for us. Go ahead, Hench."

"The night of his death, a swastika was carved into Richard Ashton's chest. The equilateral cross is a symbol that has been used by many cultures throughout the ages, from the Aztecs to the Celts and the Buddhists—but most of all it's associated with the Nazis."

"We know all that, Kabel," his granddaughter interrupted.

"I read it in Ingrid Dunn's report. Amanda's father, I mean Deputy Chief Martín, gave me written authorization to go through the department's files on Ed Staton and the Constantes, so, using the same letter, I asked to see Richard Ashton's file, and they gave it to me. According to Ingrid Dunn, the swastika was carved using a number-eleven scalpel with a triangular blade and a sharp point. It's a common tool, easy to get hold of, used to make precision cuts and right angles. The swastika was so clear-cut, it's possible the killer used a stencil."

"I didn't see anything about this in the media," said Sir Edmond Paddington.

"The deputy chief kept that piece of information under wraps. It's the ace up his sleeve that might help identify the killer—so it would be a bad idea to reveal it now. When the body was taken away, no one noticed the swastika because Ashton was wearing a T-shirt, a shirt, and a cardigan; it was only discovered when they undressed him at the morgue."

"Wasn't there blood on his clothes?" asked Esmeralda.

"The incision was relatively shallow, and it was made postmortem. Corpses don't bleed."

"Where exactly did they cut the swastika?"

"In the photo it's up high, above the sternum," said Amanda.

"The killer would have to have taken off his cardigan and shirt," mused Sherlock Holmes. "Otherwise it would have been impossible to take Ashton's arms out of his T-shirt and hitch it all the way up to his neck to cut the symbol into the upper part of his chest. He'd have had to dress him again after."

"The swastika is a message," said Abatha.

"Who knew Ashton's habits, that he often slept in the study?" Esmeralda asked.

"Only his wife and the butler," said Amanda.

"Ayani wouldn't have cut a swastika into her husband's body, even if he was dead," offered Abatha.

"Why not?" said Esmeralda. "She could have done it to throw people off the scent. That's what I would have done."

"You're a gypsy, there's nothing you wouldn't do," argued Paddington, maintaining the racist and sexist attitudes of his character.

"But a lady would never commit such a repugnant act—and what's more, she wouldn't be strong enough to manhandle the body. It has to be the butler."

Everyone laughed at the classic solution—the butler did it—and then they explored the possibility that the crime was ideologically motivated, since Ashton had been accused of being a Nazi. Sherlock Holmes pointed out a parallel with Jack the Ripper, who had also mutilated his victims with a scalpel.

"One theory has it that Jack the Ripper had some medical training," he reminded them.

"That's not much of a basis for speculation," said Paddington. "You don't need to be a doctor to cut a symbol with a scalpel and a stencil. It's easy—even a woman could do it."

"I'm not sure. . . . I have an image in my mind, like a vision or a premonition," said Abatha, who had gone so long without eating that she was starting to hallucinate. "I think the three cases we're investigating are somehow related."

Time was running short, so Amanda closed the session with instructions to look for possible connections between the cases, as Abatha had suggested. What they were dealing with might not be the simple bloodbath Celeste Roko had predicted, but something a lot more interesting: a serial killer.

Saturday, 4

ob Martín kept odd hours, sometimes working two days straight without sleeping. For him there were no public holidays, no vacations, but he did spend as much time with his daughter as possible on the weekends when she stayed with him. Every other Friday, Blake Jackson would drop the girl off at Bob's apartment or at his office after she had had dinner with her mother, then pick her up again on Sunday and drive her back to the boarding school if Bob wasn't free. In the fifteen years since his divorce, Bob had dragged his daughter along to so many crime scenes, for lack of a babysitter, that the whole San Francisco Police Department knew her. The closest the girl had to a female friend was Petra Horr, from whom she wheedled the information her father tried to keep from her. According to Indiana, Bob was to blame for Amanda's morbid fascination with crime; Bob, on the other hand, had been convinced that from the moment she was born, crime was Amanda's true calling: she would end up a lawyer, a detective, a policewoman, or, if worse came to worst, a criminal. She would succeed on either side of the law. That Saturday he had let her sleep in while he went to the gym and stopped by the office, before picking her up at midday and taking her to her favorite eatery, the Café Rossini, where she could gorge on sugar and carbohydrates. This was another point of contention with Indiana.

Amanda was waiting for him, wearing sandals and a sarong she had wrapped around herself in a not-so-traditional way. When he pointed out that it was raining, she put on a scarf and a woolen Bolivian cap that covered her ears, tied under her chin by two multicolored braids. The girl settled Save-the-Tuna into her basket, a gift Elsa Domínguez had brought back from Guatemala. The little animal could be remarkably unobtrusive, curling up in the basket for hours without a sound in places where pets were forbidden. Everyone at the Rossini knew what was in the basket, but Danny D'Angelo had made it clear that anyone who complained about the cat would have to answer to him.

Danny greeted them in his usual flamboyant manner. He did not need to take their order, as they always had the same thing: cheese omelet and a coffee for the deputy chief, a selection of cakes and a mug of hot chocolate with whipped cream for his daughter. He brought their food and apologized for not being able to stay and chat; the place was full, as usual on weekends, and there were people on the sidewalk waiting for a table.

"Grandpa saw Richard Ashton's autopsy report, Dad. You didn't tell me about the swastika. Anything else about the case you haven't told me?"

"For your peace of mind, honey, I can promise you that Ayani's beauty hasn't interfered with my policeman's instinct the way you thought it would. Ayani's at the top of our list of suspects. We interrogated her, and the servants too. The big surprise is that the missing socks turned up."

"You're kidding!"

"No, and it was completely weird. Get this—Mrs. Ashton got a package in the mail with a book and her husband's socks. The package went through a lot of hands in the postal service, but the contents have no fingerprints—they were handled with gloves or else meticulously cleaned."

"What kind of book?" asked the girl.

"A novel. *Steppenwolf*, by a Swiss German writer named Herman Hesse, a classic published in 1929 before the rise of Nazism. One of the psychologists at the department is studying the copy, looking for some sort of message there must be one, or why send it to Ayani?"

"Do you think one person could have committed all three crimes?"

"Which crimes?"

"The only interesting ones we've got, Dad—Ed Staton, the Constantes, and Ashton."

"What are you talking about? They have nothing in common."

"They were all committed in San Francisco."

"That doesn't mean anything. Serial killers usually target the same type of victim, the motive is usually sexual, and they work to a kind of pattern. The victims in these crimes are completely different, the MO is different, even the weapon isn't the same. I have the whole department looking into them."

"Separately? Someone needs to look at them together."

"That someone is me. But the cases aren't linked, Amanda."

"Listen to me, Dad—don't dismiss the possibility that they might be the work of a serial killer. This kind of crime is really rare."

"You're right about that. Most of the murders we deal with are gang-related—they come from turf wars, fights, or drugs. The last serial killer round here was Joseph Nasso, who was accused of murdering a series of women between 1977 and 1994. He's seventy-eight now, and about to go on trial in Marin County."

"I know, it's all in my file," said Amanda. "Nasso refused a lawyer—he's planning to defend himself. He expressed no remorse, he's proud of what he did. But if these murders were committed by the same person, I think he's proud too. I think he's leaving signs or clues to mark his territory."

"Is that what it says in the serial killer handbook?" teased the deputy chief.

"Wait, I've got it here," she said, scrolling through the notes on her cell phone. "Listen to this: most serial killers in the United States are white males between the ages twenty-five and thirty-five, though other races are also represented; they tend to be lower- or middle-class; they act alone, motivated by psychological gratification; they have typically suffered from neglect or sexual or emotional abuse in childhood, and they've been on the wrong side of the law, through robbery or vandalism. They're arsonists and sadists, and they torture animals. They suffer from low self-esteem, and a total lack of empathy for their victims—in other words, they're psychopaths. Some are insane and suffer hallucinations, believing that God or the devil has sent them to wipe out gay men, or prostitutes, or people of other races or religions. The sexual motive you referred to will often lead them to torture or mutilate their victims for pleasure. For example, Jeffrey Dahmer tried to turn the young men he killed into zombies, drilling holes in their skulls and injecting acid into their brains; he even practiced cannibalism to—"

"Amanda, that's enough!" Bob was livid.

"One more thing, Dad—"

"No, Amanda! I know all this, we studied it at the academy. But it's not something you should be filling your head with."

"Please, listen! Something's not right. Most serial killers have a low IQ and limited education. But in this case, I think the guy is really smart."

"You do realize it could be a woman," said Bob. "Although I admit it's not common."

"Absolutely. It could be my godmother."

"Celeste?" asked her father, surprised.

"To make sure her prediction comes true, to prove the stars are never wrong," argued the girl, with a wink.

///////////////////

The deputy chief fervently hoped his daughter's fascination with crime would soon pass, just as her obsessions with dungeons, dragons, and vampires had. This was what he had been assured by Florence Levy, the psychologist Amanda had seen as a child and whom Bob had just consulted on the phone. According to Ms. Levy, it was simply another manifestation of the girl's insatiable curiosity, another intellectual game. As a father, Bob was worried by Amanda's new hobby, but as a detective he understood better than anyone why a person might have a fascination with crime and justice.

Indiana liked to claim there was no such thing as good or evil; that evil was simply a distortion of natural kindness, the expression of a sick soul. For her, the prison system was a form of collective vengeance used by society to punish those who transgressed, locking them up and throwing away the key and making no attempt to rehabilitate them—although she reluctantly admitted that there were some irredeemable criminals who had to be incarcerated so they didn't harm others. Bob found his ex-wife's naïveté maddening. Ordinarily, the drivel she came out with didn't bother him, but she planted these ridiculous notions in Amanda's head; she failed to protect her, not taking even the minimal precautions any normal mother would. Indiana was still the same idealistic girl who had fallen in love with him at the age of fifteen. They had both been kids when Amanda was born, but he had grown up since, he had toughened up, become experienced; he had become "an admirable man in some respects," as Petra Horr put it after a beer too many. Meanwhile, Indiana was stuck in an endless puberty.

In my line of work, he thought, I've seen too many horrors to harbor any illusions about human beings: they're capable of the worst atrocities. There aren't many decent people in this screwed-up world—there's a reason the prisons are full to bursting. Okay, so prisons are full of the poor, of drug addicts, of alcoholics, of petty criminals, while gangsters, rogue traders, and corrupt politicians—the people who commit crime on a large scale—rarely get caught. I know that, but I've still got a job to do. There are crimes that turn my stomach, that make me want to take the law into my own hands: pedophilia, child prostitution, human trafficking, and don't get me started on domestic violence. How many women have I seen murdered by husbands or lovers? How many children who have been beaten up, raped, abandoned? And the streets of San Francisco are getting more dangerous all the time. Prisons are the most profitable business in California, and the crime rate is still rising. As far as Indiana is concerned, that's proof that the system doesn't work, but what's the alternative? Without law and order, society would be ruled by terror. By fear. Fear is the root of all violence. I suppose there are people, like the Dalai Lama, who achieve a heightened state of consciousness and are not afraid of anything, but I've never met them. As far as I'm concerned, to live without fear is ridiculous, it's sheer stupidity. Not that I'm saying the Dalai Lama is stupid, obviously—the guy must have some reason to go around smiling all the time—but I'm a cop, and a father, and I know all about violence, perversion, and depravity. And I need to prepare my daughter for that. But how do I do that without destroying her innocence? Hell, let's be realistic, he concluded. What innocence? Amanda's seventeen, and she's studying gruesome murders in detail. It's like she's planning to commit one herself.

*R*yan *Miller went to pick* up Indiana from the house on Potrero Hill at 9:00 a.m., as agreed, ignoring the depressing TV weather forecast, still optimistically planning for the two of them to take their bikes and head out to the woods and hills of West Marin. The water on the bay was choppy, the sky the color of lead, and the chill wind would have discouraged anyone less single-minded and in love than Ryan. He was getting ready to win Indiana's heart with the same fierce determination that had served him in battle, but he knew that meant a steady advance. He could not storm in; he might frighten her, which could cost him the extraordinary friendship the two of them had forged. He needed to give her time to get over Keller, but he wasn't planning to give her too much time. He had already been very understanding, and as Pedro Alarcón pointed out, someone smarter might turn up and sweep her off her feet. Better not to think about that eventuality, since it meant he would have to kill the guy, he thought with a certain excitement, disappointed that the rules of war did not apply in such cases—how much easier it would be to just do away with a rival, no questions asked. Though it had only been three years, he felt he had been part of Indiana's life for all eternity, that he knew her better than he knew himself. But now that the opportunity had finally presented itself, she seemed depressed, not open to a new relationship. She went on working, but even Ryan, who considered himself the least perceptive of her patients—being incapable of appreciating the subtleties of Reiki or magnets—could tell that she lacked her usual vitality.

Indiana was waiting for him with freshly made coffee, which they drank standing up in the kitchen. She had little desire to go out, with a storm threatening to break, but she didn't want to disappoint Ryan, who had been looking forward to this trip all week—or Attila, who was crouching by the door with an expectant look. She rinsed the cups, left her father a note saying she would be back that evening and wanted to see Amanda before he drove her back to school, then pulled on her jacket and helped Ryan load her bike into the truck. She climbed into the seat between him and Attila, who never gave up his window seat for anyone.

The wind whistled in the cables of the bridge and buffeted the few cars that were out at such an hour. There were none of the usual Sunday sailboats, no tourists crossing the Golden Gate Bridge on foot. Their hope that the skies might have cleared a little on the far side of the bay, as often happened, quickly dissipated, but still Ryan ignored Indiana's suggestion that they postpone the day trip. He carried right on up Route 101 up to Sir Francis Drake Boulevard, and from there toward the Samuel P. Taylor State Park, where they had met.

Over the next forty minutes the storm raged. Great black clouds crackled with electricity, and trees, bent double by the wind, looked like ghosts in the white flashes of lightning. Twice they had to stop because the downpour made it impossible to see farther than the windscreen, but no sooner had the storm abated than Ryan would drive on, skidding round bends and slaloming past branches ripped from trees, at the risk of crashing or being charred to death by lightning. Finally admitting defeat, Ryan pulled over and switched off the engine. Burying his face in his arms, he slumped over the wheel and cursed like a soldier, while Attila surveyed the calamity from his pink cushion with a look of such disappointment that Indiana laughed. The sound was so infectious that Ryan quickly joined in, and soon the two of them were laughing uncontrollably at the preposterous situation, tears streaming down their faces, much to the bewilderment of the dog, who saw nothing funny about being trapped in a van when he could be running around in the forest.

Later, when each was alone with the memory of having just made love, neither could say quite how it had started—whether it had been the howl of the storm that seemed to shake the whole world, the relief of the laughter they had shared, or the cramped conditions of the truck's cabin: or whether it had been inevitable because they were both ready. They moved as one, staring at each other, revealing themselves as they had never done before, and in Ryan's eyes Indiana saw a love so true, it awoke in her desires that she had repressed and sublimated for years.

Indiana knew this man better than anyone else: she knew every inch of his body from his head to his only foot; she knew the reddened, shiny scar tissue of his stump, his powerful thighs, slashed with scars, his stiff waist; she knew every vertebra in the curve of his spine, the strong muscles in his back, chest, and arms; she knew every finger of his elegant hands, that neck that was solid as wood, the nape always tense, and the sensitive ears she never touched when she massaged him to spare him the embarrassment of an erection. Blindfolded, she could recognize his scent—a mixture of soap and sweat—the texture of his close-cropped hair, the timbre of his voice. She loved the way he moved, the way he drove one-handed, played with Attila like a little boy; the way he held his cutlery, took off his shirt, or strapped on his prosthetic leg. She knew that he cried at sentimental movies and that his favorite ice cream was pistachio; that when he was with her, he never looked at other women, and that he missed his life as a soldier; that he was a wounded soul, and that he never, ever complained. In their countless healing sessions, she had worked every inch of this man's body, which looked much younger than his forty years, admiring the robust masculinity, the coiled strength. At times she could not help but compare him to Alan Keller, her slim, handsome lover, who was sophisticated, sensitive, ironic—the polar opposite of Ryan Miller. But at that moment, in the cabin of the pickup truck, Alan did not exist, had never existed; the only thing that was real was the overwhelming desire she felt for this man who was suddenly a stranger.

In that lingering look, they said everything they needed to say. Ryan slipped his arm around her and pulled her toward him. She lifted her face, and they kissed as though this were not the first time, kissed with a passion that had burned inside him for three years, and one that she had thought she would never feel again, having settled for the placid love of Alan Keller. Indiana had taken real pleasure in the leisurely erotic games she and Alan played, but it was nothing compared to the wild desire with which she clung to Ryan now, holding him down with both hands and kissing him until he gasped for breath—surprised at the softness of his lips, the taste of his saliva, the intimacy of his tongue, frantically trying to take off her jacket, sweater, and blouse without breaking the kiss, to squeeze past the steering wheel and straddle him in that cramped cabin. She might have managed it had Attila not interrupted them with his long, horrified howl. They had completely forgotten about him. Thanks to the moment of clarity the dog had afforded them, they were able to break off for a short while and decide what to do about this reluctant witness. Since they couldn't throw him out into the storm, they decided on the most obvious solution: looking for a hotel.

Ryan drove blindly, recklessly, through the rain while Indiana stroked and kissed him wherever she could, drawing offended looks from Attila. The first lights they spotted were those of the pretentious boutique hotel where she and Alan sometimes came on Sundays to breakfast on the best French toast with crème fraîche in the area. Given the weather, the staff were not expecting guests, but they offered Indiana and Ryan the best room in the place: a riot of floral wallpaper, claw-foot furniture, and tasseled curtains, with a wide, sturdy bed capable of withstanding their strenuous love-making. Attila was forced to wait in the truck for several hours, until Ryan remembered he existed.

Tuesday, 7

At 8:15 p.m., *Judge Rachel* Rosen parked her Volvo in the garage of the building where she lived. From the trunk she took the heavy briefcase stuffed with the files she intended to read that evening and a grocery bag containing tonight's dinner and tomorrow's lunch: a salmon fillet, broccoli, a couple of tomatoes, and an avocado. She had grown up in a frugal home and considered any unnecessary expenditure an insult to the memory of her parents—survivors of a concentration camp in Poland who had come to America with nothing and worked hard to build a comfortable life. Judge Rosen bought exactly what she needed each day, and wasted nothing: leftovers from dinner she would have for lunch the following day, taking them in a Tupperware box to juvenile court so she could eat alone in her chambers. She lived well, but allowed herself few luxuries and hoarded like a magpie in the hope that she could retire at sixty-five and live off her savings. She had inherited the family furniture and her mother's modest jewelry, which was only of sentimental value; her sole possessions were her penthouse apartment, a portfolio of shares in Johnson & Johnson, Apple, and Chevron, and a savings account. She planned to spend every last cent before she died—she did not want her son and daughter-in-law enjoying the fruits of her work. They did not deserve it.

She hurried out of that dank parking garage, the most perilous place in the building; she had heard stories about such places, stories about assaults on solitary women, on elderly women—on women like her. For a while now she had been feeling vulnerable and threatened; she was no longer the tough, decisive woman she had been, the woman who could make vicious gangsters quake in their boots, who was respected by the police and by her colleagues. Now those same people whispered behind her back. They had a nickname for her—the Butcher, or something like that—though obviously they did not say it to her face. She was tired, or rather tired of living; she could no longer run, could barely stroll around the park. It was time to retire: there were only a few months left before she could enjoy a well-earned rest.

She took the elevator straight up to her apartment without going into the lobby to pick up her mail, since the doorman finished at seven and locked up behind him. It took a minute or two to open the double lock on her apartment door, and as she stepped inside, she realized she had forgotten to activate the alarm when she left that morning. It was an unforgivably careless mistake, one she had never made before. She would have liked to attribute it to the fact that in recent weeks she had been overworked, to being distracted and in a hurry; but a small voice in her head, one that had become more insistent, more needling, told her she was losing her memory. Suddenly, she felt sure that someone had been in her apartment. She had heard that no alarm was really safe, that electronic gadgets could be used to disable them.

Rachel Rosen did not much like her home. It had been her husband's idea to buy this bleak, dated, high-ceilinged apartment. They had never got round to refurbishing it as they had once dreamed they would, and it was exactly as it had been thirty years ago, permeated with the chill breath of a mausoleum. As soon as she retired, she planned to sell, to move somewhere sunnier, like Florida, where no one needed central heating. Exhausted from a long day arguing with lawyers and juvenile delinquents, she turned on the hall light, set the briefcase on the dining table, and groped along the dark corridor to the kitchen, where she dropped the bag of groceries on the counter, then went to her room to take off her work clothes and change into something more comfortable. Fifteen minutes later she was in the kitchen, making dinner, wearing pajamas, a flannel dressing gown, and sheepskin-lined slippers. She never did empty the grocery bag.

She sensed something behind her, a shadowy presence like a bad memory; she stood motionless, engulfed by the same fear she had felt in the garage. She tried to control her imagination—she did not want to end up like her mother, who had spent her last years locked in her apartment, never going out, convinced the Gestapo was waiting on the other side of the door. Old people get scared, she thought, but I'm not like my mother. She thought she heard a rustling of paper or plastic and turned toward the kitchen door. She could make out a shadow in the doorway, a blurred, bloated, faceless figure, moving slowly and awkwardly like an astronaut on the moon. A hoarse, terrible howl came from the pit of her stomach, surging up through her chest like a blazing fire. She saw the fearsome creature advance toward her. A second scream stuck in her throat, and she ran out of air.

Rachel Rosen stepped backward, bumped into the table, and fell sideways, shielding her head with her arms. She lay on the floor, begging in a whisper for him not to hurt her, offering money and anything else of value in the house. Trembling, she crawled under the table and curled up, pleading and weeping, for the three never-ending minutes she was still conscious. She did not even feel the pinprick in her thigh.

Friday, 10

It was unusual for Bob Martín to still be in bed at seven thirty on a Friday morning, as he usually got up at dawn. He was lying on his back, his arms behind his head—the most comfortable position for him—watching the wan daylight streaming through the white window blind and fighting the urge for a cigarette. He had quit seven months ago, and now wore nicotine patches and went around with an acupuncture needle in his earlobe, given him by Yumiko Sato. But still he felt a craving for tobacco. During one of the meetings that had gone from being interrogations to friendly conversations, Ayani had suggested he try hypnotism—one of the psychological techniques that had made her husband famous—but Bob didn't like the idea. He thought hypnotism was open to abuse, like in that movie where a magician hypnotizes Woody Allen and forces him to steal jewels.

Bob had just made love to Karla for the third time in five hours—hardly an athletic feat, since it had taken him only twenty-three minutes in total. Now, while she was in the kitchen making coffee, he was thinking about Ayani, remembering the sweet scent of her skin (or rather imagining it, since he had never been close enough to her to catch it), her long neck, those honey-colored eyes with their sleepy eyelids, and the deep, lilting voice like a river's roar or the motor of a tumble dryer. It had been a month since Ashton's death now, and Bob was still finding excuses to visit the widow almost every day. This prompted sarcastic comments from Petra: she was losing respect for him, getting sassy. He needed to put her in her place.

Rolling around in bed in the dark with Karla, he would imagine he was with Ayani. Both women were tall and slim, with a long face and high cheekbones; but the spell was broken every time Karla opened her mouth to utter a string of obscenities in the thick Polish accent that had once excited him but which he had quickly tired of. He felt sure that Ayani made love in silence—or perhaps purred like Save-the-Tuna, but there would be no outburst of Ethiopian obscenities. He did not want to imagine Ayani sleeping with Galang, as Petra suggested, still less about the mutilation she had suffered as a child. Bob had never seen a creature as extraordinary as Ayani. Just as the aroma of coffee reached his nostrils, the phone rang.

"Bob, it's Blake, can you come over to my place? It's urgent."

"Has something happen to Amanda? To Indiana?" shouted the deputy chief, jumping out of bed.

"No, but it's serious."

"I'll be right over."

Blake Jackson was not easily agitated; so there had to be a good reason for his call. Two minutes later, having splashed cold water on his face and pulled on what clothes he could find, Bob raced to his car without saying good-bye, leaving Karla standing naked in the kitchen with a coffee cup in each hand.

Arriving at Potrero Hill, Martín found the pink Atomic Cin-

derellas van parked outside. Blake Jackson was in the kitchen with
Elsa Domínguez and her daughters, Noemí and Alicia. They were
young, with pretty faces and strong, muscular bodies, but with
none of their mother's innocence and gentleness. The girls had
started cleaning houses while still in high school, to help out with
the family finances, and a few years later they were successful
businesswomen. They found the clients, negotiated the contracts,
and sent other women to do the cleaning; they did the end-of-
month invoices, paid wages, and bought cleaning products. The
women who worked for them ran no risk of being exploited by
heartless bosses, and the clients did not need to worry about the
legal status of their employees or translating their instructions into
Spanish: they worked directly with Noemí and Alicia, who took
responsibility for both the quality of the work and the integrity of
their staff.

Atomic Cinderellas had expanded in recent years, and now covered a wide area of the city; there was a waiting list for their services. A team of two or three cleaners generally visited a client's
house once a week, working so diligently that within hours the
place was spotless. This was a service they had provided for Rachel Rosen at her home on Church Street. Until Friday morning,
when they found her hanging from a ceiling fan.

Alicia and Noemí told the deputy chief that Rachel Rosen had de-
vised so many excuses not to pay on time that, tired of the monthly
wrangling, they decided to withhold their services. They had
gone that morning to collect outstanding checks for December
and January and to tell her the Cinderellas would not be coming
back. They had arrived at 7:00 a.m., before the doorman came on
duty—his shift started at eight—but they knew the entry code
and had a key to their client's apartment. The heating was switched
off, so the apartment was cold when they went in. They found it

strange that the place was so quiet. Rosen was an early riser, and by this time she would usually be drinking tea, catching the morning news, dressed in a tracksuit and sneakers, ready for her morning walk in Dolores Park. Her route never changed: she crossed the footbridge at Church Street, power-walking for a half hour, stopping off at La Tartine on the corner of Guerrero and Eighteenth Street for a couple of rolls before heading home to take a shower and dress for court.

Alicia and Noemí had wandered through the living room, the study, the dining room, and the kitchen, calling the judge's name, then knocked on the door of her bedroom. When there was no reply, they plucked up the courage to go in.

"She was hanging from the ceiling," whispered Alicia, as though she was afraid of being heard.

"Suicide?" the deputy chief asked.

"That's what we thought at first," said Noemí nervously, "and we checked to see if she was still alive so we could cut her down, but it looked like she'd been murdered. I mean if you're going to commit suicide, you don't put duct tape over your mouth, right? So then we got scared. Alicia said we should get out. Then we remembered about fingerprints and stuff, so we wiped the door handles and everything else we'd touched."

"You contaminated a crime scene!"

"Excuse me, but we didn't contaminate nothing. We cleaned it all with damp tissues. You know, the disposable kind with disinfectant, we always have them with us."

"Then we called Mamá from the van," her sister chipped in, nodding to Elsa, who was sobbing quietly in her seat, clutching Blake's hand.

"I told them to come to Mr. Jackson's house immediately," said Elsa. "What else could they do?"

"Oh, I don't know," Bob suggested, "call nine-one-one, maybe?"

"The girls don't want trouble with immigration, Bob," explained Blake. "They have work permits, but most of their workers are undocumented."

"As long as they're legal, they've got nothing to worry about."

"That's what you think. You're not an immigrant with a Hispanic accent," his ex-father-in-law replied. "Rachel Rosen was really suspicious. Nobody ever visited her, even her son didn't have a key to her apartment—only Alicia and Noemí, who dropped off the cleaners every week. They're bound to be treated as suspects."

"Judge Rosen's things never went missing," explained Alicia. "That's why she finally trusted us with a key. In the beginning, she'd stay to keep an eye on us, she'd count the cutlery and each piece of clothing that went into the machine—but later she relaxed a little."

"I still don't understand why you didn't call the police," said Bob, reaching for his cell phone. Blake stopped him.

"Bob, wait!"

"We been working in this country for many years, we're decent people," sobbed Elsa Domínguez. "Please, señor, you know us—what if they blame my girls for this lady's death."

"Don't worry, Elsa, it'll all be cleared up quickly," Bob reassured her.

"Elsa's worried about Hugo, her youngest," Blake cut in. "The kid's had run-ins with the police, as you know—you've helped him yourself a couple of times, remember? He did some time for violence and robbery. Hugo has access to the key for that apartment."

"What do you mean?" asked the deputy chief.

"My brother lives with me," Noemí explained. "We keep the keys to the houses where we work in a cabinet in my room with the clients' names next to them. Hugo's a bonehead, he gets mixed up in all kinds of stuff, but he wouldn't hurt a fly."

"Your brother might have gone to Rosen's apartment to rob her . . . ," the deputy chief speculated.

"And you think he was going to string that woman up? For God's sake, Bob!" pleaded Blake. "Help us out here, we got to keep the boy out of this."

"I'm afraid that's not possible. We have to interrogate anyone who had contact with the victim, and Hugo's name is bound to come up in the investigation. I'll try and give him a couple of days. I'm heading back to the office. In ten minutes, make an anonymous nine-one-one call from a phone booth and report the crime. You don't have to give your names, just Rosen's address."

The deputy chief stopped at a gas station to fill up, and just as he expected, within minutes his cell phone rang: Petra Horr, telling him that a body had been found on Church Street. He drove toward the address while his assistant, with her usual military efficiency, filled him in with the basic information on the victim: Rachel Rosen, born 1948, graduated from Hastings, worked as a lawyer for a private firm, then as a district attorney, finally as a judge in the juvenile court, a post she held until her death.

"She was sixty-four, ready to retire next year," Petra added. "Married David Rosen, separated, not divorced, one son, Ismael, who lives in San Francisco and seems to work in a liquor store, but I still need to confirm that. He hasn't been informed yet. I know what you're thinking, boss—the husband is always the prime suspect—but David Rosen's got a rock-solid alibi."

"Which is?"

"Died of a heart attack, 1998."

"Just our luck, Petra. Anything else?"

"Rosen never got on with her daughter-in-law, so she grew apart from her son and three grandchildren. As for the rest of her family, she's got a couple brothers in Brooklyn, apparently hasn't seen them in years. Sounds like she was a bitter, twisted woman. Not exactly friendly. She had a vicious reputation at the court— her sentences were feared."

"Money?"

"That I don't know, but I'm looking into it. Want to know what I think, boss? She was a spiteful old bitch who deserved to burn in hell."

By the time Bob got to Church Street, opposite Dolores Park, half the block had already been taped off, and police were diverting traffic. An officer escorted him to the building, where the porter on duty, a Hispanic guy named Manuel Valenzuela, about fifty years old and wearing a dark suit and a necktie, explained that he had not made the 911 call. He only realized what had happened when two cops showed up and ordered him to open Rachel Rosen's apartment with his master key. He said he'd seen the lady for the last time on Monday, when she last picked up her mail, but she hadn't done that Tuesday, Wednesday, or Thursday—so he figured she was out of town. Sometimes she would go away for a few days at a time; it was part of her work. That morning he called up to her apartment just after eight, when his shift had hardly started, to ask if she wanted him to bring her all the mail that had stacked up, plus a package that had arrived the afternoon of the day before—but nobody picked up the phone. Valenzuela assumed that if she was back from her trip, she was probably in the park. Before he had time to start worrying, the police, a fire crew, and an ambulance arrived, making enough noise that the whole neighborhood knew about it.

Bob ordered the doorman to stay at his desk and give the minimum of information to the other tenants in the building to avoid any panic. Then he took the mail and the package and walked up to Rachel Rosen's apartment. Sergeant Joseph Deseve, the first officer to respond to the 911 call, was waiting. The deputy chief was glad to see him: he was a sensible guy with years of experience, and he knew how to handle a situation like this one. "I restricted access to the apartment," the sergeant told him. "I'm the only one who's entered the crime scene. We had to use force to stop some reporter coming in who'd managed to get all the way up here. Beats me how the press finds out before we do."

The victim's penthouse had windows overlooking the park, but net curtains and thick drapes blocked out the view and any daylight, giving the place a funereal atmosphere. Its owner had decorated it with dilapidated antique furniture, imitation Persian rugs, gilt-framed paintings of bucolic landscapes in pastel colors, plastic plants, and a sideboard with glass doors where a whole menagerie of Swarovski glass animals was on display. The deputy chief saw it out of the corner of his eye as he went into the bedroom.

The officer blocking the entrance stepped aside when he saw them. Joseph Deseve stayed in the doorway while the deputy chief went in with his little Dictaphone to record his first impressions—they were often the most accurate. The judge was barefoot and wearing her pajamas, just as Alicia and Noemí had said, hanging from the fan in the middle of the room, and gagged with duct tape. Bob noticed immediately that her feet were touching the bed, which meant that it might have taken her hours to die as she fought instinctively to hold herself up before fatigue won out, or she fainted and was strangled by her bodyweight.

He crouched down and examined the carpet, confirming that the bed had not moved from its usual place, then stood up to look at the fan. He stopped short of climbing onto a chair or the table, since the forensics team would need to take fingerprints first. It was strange, he thought, that the fan had not come away from the ceiling during the victim's desperate struggle.

The process of decomposition was well under way: Judge Rosen's body was swollen, her face distorted, her eyes bulging.

The skin was streaked black and green like marble. From the look of the body, Bob deduced death had probably occurred some thirty-six hours before, but he would rather wait for Ingrid Dunn to arrive than speculate.

He took off his latex gloves and face mask, and stepped out of the bedroom, giving orders for it to be locked and guarded. He called Petra so she could notify the medical examiner and the various crime scene officers who would need to examine and inventory the contents of the room, and photograph and film the body before it was removed. He shivered as he zipped up his jacket, realizing that he was hungry, and hadn't had his usual morning coffee. In a flash, he saw Karla standing naked, holding two cups of coffee—her long-limbed body like a heron, all protruding hips and collarbones, and the generous breasts she'd saved up for three years to buy—a strange, exotic creature from another planet who had appeared in his kitchen by accident.

While Sergeant Deseve headed down the street to corral the press and the rubberneckers, Bob Martín drew up a list of the people he needed to question and then sifted through what had arrived in the mail for Rachel Rosen—a few bills, a couple of catalogs, three magazines, and an envelope marked "Bank of America," as well as the package, which contained another crystal animal. Bob called down to the lobby, and the doorman explained that Miss Rosen had received one every month for years.

Shortly afterward, the forensics team showed up en masse, led by Ingrid Dunn and accompanied by Petra Horr, who had no reason to be here and as a pretext had brought the deputy chief a supersize latte, as though she could read his mind. "Sorry, boss," she explained, "but I couldn't stand it, I had to see her with my own eyes." Bob remembered the story Petra had told him on a night of celebrations that had begun with mojitos and beers at the

Camelot—the old Powell Street bar where cops and detectives often went after work—and ended in tears and confidences in Petra's apartment. They had gone out with some fellow officers to celebrate O. J. Simpson's conviction in Las Vegas—thirty-three years for kidnapping and armed robbery—which they welcomed as irrefutable evidence of divine justice. The admiration they all used to feel for the man's talents as a football player had turned to frustration thirteen years earlier, when he was acquitted of the murders of his ex-wife and her friend despite overwhelming evidence against him. Police officers across the country felt they had been mocked.

That memorable evening in the Camelot had been in December 2008, at which point Petra had already been with the department for some time. Toting up the years they had been working together, Bob was astonished to realize that she had not aged a single day—she was still the little imp she had always been, the one who after three mojitos had become sentimental and dragged him back to her bare rented room. At that time Petra was living like a penniless student, paying off the debts left by an itinerant husband who had hopped off to Australia. Petra longed for some human warmth, and both she and Bob were unattached, so, taking the initiative, she began to fondle him. Bob could hold his drink a little better than she could, though, and with what little clearheadedness he still possessed, he decided to let her down gently. If he didn't, he was sure they would both regret it in the morning. It was not worth risking their excellent working relationship for a few drunken kisses.

They lay down fully clothed on the bed, and she laid her head on his shoulder and recounted all the troubles she had known in her short life while he half-listened, fighting off sleep. At sixteen, Petra had been sentenced to two years in prison for possession of marijuana, partly because of the incompetence of her public defender, but mostly because of the legendary strictness of Judge Rachel Rosen. Those two years had turned into four when another young prisoner ended up in the infirmary after an altercation with her. According to Petra, the other girl had slipped and hit her head on a concrete pillar, but Rosen had considered it aggravated assault.

Half an hour later, when they had taken down Rachel Rosen's body from the fan and laid it on a gurney, Ingrid Dunn reported her initial impressions to the deputy chief.

"At first glance, I figure time of death was at least two, maybe three days ago. Decomposition may have been slowed because the apartment's like a fridge. There no heating in this building?"

"According to the doorman, residents are responsible for regulating and paying for their own heating. Rachel Rosen was not exactly short of funds, but she suffered the cold. Cause of death seems obvious."

"She died of asphyxia," said Ingrid, "but not from the rope around her neck."

"No?"

The medical examiner pointed out a thin blue line, different from the marks left by the rope, and explained that the injury must have been sustained while the judge was still alive, since it had caused bleeding from ruptured blood vessels. The groove marks caused by the rope supporting the weight of the body showed no sign of bruising because they had been made postmortem.

"The woman was strangled and then hanged at least ten or fifteen minutes later, by which time a body no longer bruises."

"That explains why the fan didn't come loose from the ceiling," said Bob.

"I don't follow."

"If the woman had been standing on tiptoe, struggling for her life, as we thought at first, the fan would never have withstood the pulling and jerking."

"If she was already dead, why hang her?" asked the ME.

"You tell me. I assumed the tape was put over her mouth to stop her screaming—I mean, while she was still alive."

"We'll know for certain when I remove the duct tape at the autopsy, but I can see no reason why they would gag her after she was dead."

"For the same reason they hanged a corpse."

After the body had been taken away, the deputy chief left the forensics team to get on with their work and invited Ingrid Dunn and Petra Horr to breakfast. This would be their one moment of peace before they plunged into the maelstrom of a new investigation.

"Do you believe in astrology?" he asked his companions.

"In what?" said the ME.

"Astrology."

"Absolutely," said Petra. "You won't catch me missing Celeste Roko's horoscopes."

"I don't believe any of that drivel," said Ingrid. "What about you, Bob?"

"If you asked yesterday, I would have said no." The deputy chief heaved a sigh. "Today I'm not so sure."

Saturday, 11

Out of consideration for Elsa, who had helped raise his daughter and had been with the family for seventeen years, the deputy chief arranged to meet Hugo Domínguez at the home of his sister Noemí, in the Canal area of San Rafael, rather than questioning him down at the precinct as per standard procedure. He brought Petra Horr along so that she could record the statement. As they drove, she explained to him that 70 percent of the residents of the Canal area were low-income families from Mexico and Central America, many of them undocumented, and that several families would often share a house just so they could make the rent. "Have you ever heard of hotbeds, Chief?" said Petra. "It's when two or more people take turns using the same bed at different times." They passed "the stop," where, even at three o'clock in the afternoon, a dozen men were waiting for a truck to pick them up and give them a couple of hours' work. The neighborhood had an unmistakable Latino feel, with taco stands, markets selling products from south of the border, and signboards in Spanish.

The block where Noemí lived, one of several identical buildings, turned out to be a concrete hulk painted the color of mayonnaise, with tiny windows, outside stairwells, and doors that opened onto narrow covered walkways where adults gathered to chat and children to play. From the open doorways came the sound of radios and televisions tuned to Spanish stations. They climbed two flights of stairs under the hostile gaze of the tenants, who were clearly suspicious of strangers and could sniff out a cop at fifty paces, even those in plainclothes like Petra and the deputy chief.

The inhabitants of the apartment—two rooms and a bathroom—were waiting for them: Noemí and her three children, a teenage niece whose belly was as swollen as a watermelon, and Elsa's youngest son Hugo, aged twenty. The father of Noemí's children had vanished into thin air shortly after the birth of the youngest child, who had just turned five, and Noemí had a new partner, a Nicaraguan immigrant who theoretically lived with them whenever he happened to be in the Bay Area, but, being a trucker, was away most of the time. "I've been lucky," as Noemí put it; "I found myself a good man, and he has a job." A refrigerator, a television, and a sofa jostled for space in the living room.

The pregnant teenager appeared from the kitchen carrying a tray laden with glasses of chilled horchata, nacho chips, and guacamole. As her boss had told her not to refuse anything she was offered so as not to seem rude, Petra made an effort and tasted the pale, dubious-looking concoction, which, as it turned out, was delicious. "It's my mother's recipe," explained Alicia, who appeared just at that moment. "We make it with ground almonds and rice water." She lived with her husband and two children a block away, in an apartment very similar to her sister's, but more spacious because they were the only family living there.

Six months earlier, Bob had been seconded to the Marin County Sheriff's Office to advise on gang-related crime, so he was not about to be fooled by Hugo Domínguez's appearance. He assumed the boy's sisters had convinced him to wear a long-sleeved shirt and a pair of chinos instead of the vest and low-slung baggy jeans—precariously belted below the navel, crotch hanging down to the knees—that gangbangers always wore. The long-sleeved shirt concealed his tattoos and the bling around his neck, but his haircut, which was cropped at the sides and long at the back, as well as the piercings in his face and ears, and most of all the attitude of arrogant contempt, clearly marked him as a gangbanger.

The deputy chief had known the boy all his life, and he felt sorry for him; he had grown up under the thumb of a family of strong women, just as Bob Martín had been raised by a grandmother, mother, and sisters who all had temperaments of steel. Hugo was on file as being a deadbeat and a fool, but Bob did not think the boy was bad by nature, and with a little help he might avoid ending up in prison. The deputy chief had no wish to see Elsa's son behind bars, to see him join the 2.2 million convicts in America—a higher number than in any other country, including the worst dictatorships, making up 25 percent of the world's prison population: a nation imprisoned within a nation. He found it difficult to imagine Hugo committing premeditated murder, but he'd had a lot of surprises in this job, so he was prepared for the worst. Hugo had dropped out during his freshman year in high school, had had run-ins with the police, and was now a young man with no self-esteem, no papers, no work, and no future. Like so many others in his circumstances, he had gravitated toward the violent culture of the streets because he had no alternative.

The police had spent decades fighting Latino street gangs in the Bay Area. There were the Norteños, by far the most numerous, whose gang color was red and who had the letter *N* tattooed on their arms; the Sureños—of which Hugo Domínguez was a member—who favored blue and had the letter *M*; the Border Brothers, mercenary killers who wore black; and the fearsome Mafia Mexicana—*La eMe*—who trafficked in drugs, prostitution, and guns from behind bars. The Latino gangs fought turf wars among themselves and with black and Asian gangs; they robbed, raped, dealt drugs, terrified the local populace, and openly defied authority in a never-ending war. For an alarming number of young men, the gangs became a substitute family that offered protection and a sense of identity, and they were the only means of survival in jail, where prisoners divided along ethnic lines. Having served their sentence, gang members were deported back to the countries they had come from, where they would join other gangs with links to the United States, and so, over time, the trade in drugs and guns had become a business with no borders.

Hugo Domínguez had undergone the necessary initiation to become a member of the Sureños, a brutal "beat in" that had left him with several broken ribs. He had a scar on his back from a knife wound and another from a superficial bullet wound on one arm. He had been arrested several times, and was sent to a juvenile detention center at fifteen; when he was seventeen, Bob had managed to save him from being sent to an adult prison, where he would have had ample opportunity to refine his criminal skills.

Despite his record, the deputy chief doubted Hugo was capable of a crime as contrived and as far from his turf as the murder of Rachel Rosen. He could not dismiss the possibility, though: the judge was notorious for handing down long prison sentences to the juvenile gang members who appeared before her. More than one of those sentenced by her had threatened revenge, and it was possible that Hugo had been entrusted with the task as part of his initiation.

Keenly aware of the strategic value of making a suspect wait, Bob did not even glance at Hugo when he came in, but focused on the chips and guacamole and talked to the women as though this

were a social occasion. He asked the teenage girl when the baby
was due, who the father was, and whether she had been going to
prenatal classes, then chatted about the past with Noemí and Alicia, told a couple of stories, and drank another glass of horchata
while the three children, standing in the doorway of the kitchen,
watched him with the steady gazes of old men and Petra tried to
hurry him along with impatient glances. Hugo Domínguez pretended to be reading text messages on his cell phone, but beads of
sweat were rolling down his face.

Finally the deputy chief broached the subject everyone wanted
to hear about. Noemí told him she had known Rachel Rosen for
eight years, and that in the early days she had cleaned the judge's
apartment. Later, after Noemí and her sister had set up the company
Atomic Cinderellas, the judge had canceled the service because she
was not prepared to allow strangers into her house. Noemí had forgotten all about her, but then suddenly Rachel Rosen called.

"I am very organized when it comes to my clients," Noemí
said. "I wrote down the exact date when we started cleaning for
her again. Señora Rosen haggled over the price, but eventually we
came to an agreement. It was more than a year before she was prepared to give us a key and go out of the apartment when the Cinderellas came to clean. She was fussy, and really suspicious, so we
always sent the same women, who knew about the judge's quirks."

"But they didn't go to her apartment last Friday—it was you
and your sister," said Bob.

"Because she was two months behind with her payments. Invoices are issued twice a month, and she'd owed us since the beginning of December," said Alicia. "We went to tell her that we
couldn't go to work there any more because, besides being late on
her payments, she treated the staff badly."

"In what way?"

"Well, she wouldn't allow them to open her fridge, for example, or use the toilets in the apartment—she thought she might catch some disease. Before she sent a check, she would call to complain that there were dust balls under the bed, rust in the dishwasher, a stain on the rug—she was always finding fault. One time a small cup got broken, and she claimed it was an antique and charged us a hundred bucks. She collected little glass figurines we weren't allowed to touch."

"One arrived for her on Wednesday," said the deputy chief.

"It must have been a special delivery. Sometimes she'd get them from the Internet or from antique dealers, but the ones from her subscription always came at the end of the month in a box printed with the name of the company."

"Swarovski?" suggested Bob.

"That's it."

While Petra recorded and took notes, Noemí and Alicia showed Bob their client list, their accounts, and the office where they kept the keys to the various houses they cleaned, keys that they gave only to their oldest and most trusted employees.

"We have the only key to Señora Rosen's place," said Alicia.

"But everyone has access to that office."

"I never touched those keys!" Hugo Domínguez exploded, unable to contain himself any longer.

"I see you're a member of the Sureños," said Bob, looking him up and down and noting the blue bandanna around his neck. His sisters, it seemed, had not succeeded in persuading him to remove it. "Everyone respects you now, Hugo, though not exactly for your fucking accomplishments. No one dares to disrespect you now, right? Wrong! I dare!"

"What do you want with me, you fucking pig?"

"You can thank your mother that I didn't drag you down to the precinct to question you, because my guys don't exactly go easy on jerks like you. You're going to give me a minute-by-minute account of what you did from last Tuesday afternoon until noon on Wednesday."

"This is about that old bitch, right, the one who got merked? I don't know her name, and I had nothing to do with it."

"Answer my question!"

"I was in Santa Rosa."

"It's true," Noemí interrupted. "He didn't come home that night."

"Anyone see you in Santa Rosa? What were you doing there?"

"How do I know if anyone saw me? I don't take no notice of that shit. I went for a walk."

"You need to come up with a better alibi than that, Hugo," the deputy chief warned, "unless you want to land a murder charge."

Monday, 13

*P*etra Horr cropped her hair short like a boy, never used makeup and always wore the same clothes: boots, black trousers, and a white cotton shirt, and in winter a thick sweatshirt with some rock band logo on the back. Her two concessions to fashion were her hair, dyed so it looked like a foxtail, and the lurid nail polish she wore on her fingernails and toenails, which she kept clipped short because she practiced martial arts. She was in her cubicle painting her nails fluorescent yellow when Elsa Domínguez showed up, dressed in a pair of high heels and an antique fur necklet as though on her way to mass, asking for the deputy chief. Suppressing a sigh of boredom, Petra explained that the boss was out on a case and would probably not be back that afternoon.

More than ever in recent weeks, Petra's job seemed to her to consist of covering up for Bob, who would disappear while on duty, offering only the most implausible of excuses. But for him to do it on a Monday, thought Petra, really was the limit. She could not keep count of the number of women Bob had been infatuated with in the time she had known him—it would have been a tedious, pointless task—but she reckoned it must be between twelve and fifteen a year. That made one woman every twenty-eight days, if her arithmetic was correct. He was not particularly discriminating in such matters, and any woman who winked at him could turn his head, but before Ayani appeared on the scene he had not yet counted murder suspects among his girlfriends, and certainly no one capable of distracting him from his work. Though he may have had serious flaws as a lover, thought Petra, as a cop Bob had always been above reproach: not for nothing had he risen through the ranks so quickly.

The young assistant saw Ayani the way one might an iguana—exotic, fascinating, dangerous. She could see how some people might be taken in by the woman, but for the deputy chief of the homicide detail of the Personal Crimes Division—who had not only reason enough to be suspicious of her but enough evidence to arrest her—it was unforgivable. And right now, while Elsa Domínguez sat in her office crumpling a sheet of paper, the deputy chief was with Ayani, probably in the very bed that, a month ago, she had shared with her late husband. Petra assumed Bob did not keep secrets from her, partly because he was careless, and partly because he was vain: he liked her to know about his conquests. But if this was an attempt to make her jealous, Petra thought, blowing on her fingernails, he was wasting his time.

"Is there anything I can do to help, Elsa?"

"It's about Hugo, my son. You met him the other day—"

"Sure, I remember. What's the matter with him?"

"Hugo has had his problems in the past, señorita, I won't deny it," admitted Elsa. "But he has never been violent. This attitude he puts on, with the gold chains and the tattoos, it's a fad, nothing more. Why do they think he's a suspect?" She brushed away a tear.

"Among other reasons, because he's a member of a gang with

a vicious reputation, he had access to the key to Rachel Rosen's place, and he has no alibi."

"No what?"

"No alibi. Your son can't prove that he was in Santa Rosa on the night of the murder."

"But he wasn't there—that's why he can't prove he was."

Petra Horr put the bottle of nail polish in a desk drawer and picked up a notepad and pencil.

"Where was he? A convincing alibi could keep your son out of prison, Elsa."

"Better he should go to prison than that they kill him, I think."

"Who's going to kill him? Tell me what Hugo's got himself mixed up in, Elsa. He selling drugs?"

"No, no . . . well, only marijuana and some of that crystal stuff. Hugo was involved in something else on Tuesday, but he can't say anything about that. You know what these people would do to a snitch?"

"I have an idea."

"You don't realize what these people are capable of!"

"Calm down, Elsa, let's try to help your son."

"Hugo won't say anything, señorita, but I will. But no one can know that this information came from me, otherwise they won't just kill my Hugo, they'll kill our whole family."

The assistant showed Elsa into Bob's office, where they would have a little more privacy, then went to the vending machine down the corridor, returning with two coffees, and sat down to listen to the woman's confession. Twenty minutes later, when Elsa Domínguez had left, she called Bob on his cell phone.

"Sorry to interrupt the crucial interrogation of a suspect, chief," she announced, "but I think maybe you should throw some clothes on and get back here now. I've got news."

Tuesday, 14

*A*lan Keller fell ill within twenty-four hours of breaking up with Indiana, and spent the next two weeks with his stomach in knots, suffering a crippling bout of diarrhea like one that had hit him years earlier, after a trip to Peru—when he thought he had been cursed by the Incas for buying pre-Columbian artifacts on the black market and smuggling them out of the country. He canceled all his social engagements, and he was unable either to write his review of the exhibition at the Legion of Honor—*The Cult of Beauty in the Victorian Era*—or to say his good-byes to Geneviève van Houte before she headed off to Milan for Fashion Week. He lost nine pounds, and now he looked emaciated rather than just thin. The only things his stomach could tolerate were chicken soup and Jell-O. He could barely walk, and his nights were plagued by insomnia if he did not take sleeping tablets, and by hideous nightmares if he did.

The pills left him in a deathlike state: he imagined himself imprisoned in Hieronymus Bosch's triptych *The Garden of Earthly*

Delights, which he had seen in the Museo del Prado in Madrid. The painting had fascinated him as a boy, and he knew it in minute detail, as it had been the subject of one of his finest articles for *American Art*. He saw himself surrounded by the fantastical creatures conjured up by the Dutch painter, copulating with animals under the cruel gaze of Indiana, tortured with tridents by his banker, slowly devoured by his siblings, pitilessly mocked by Geneviève, foundering in excrement and spitting scorpions. Even when the sleeping pills wore off and he managed to wake up, images from the dream would haunt him all day. He had no trouble interpreting them—their meaning was obvious—but understanding them did not free him from their clutches.

A hundred times he found himself clutching the phone, on the point of calling Indiana, knowing she would rush to help him—not because she had forgiven him or because she loved him, but simply out of her compulsion to help anyone in need. He resisted the temptation. He was no longer sure of anything, not even that he had loved her. This physical pain he accepted as a purge, an expiation, utterly disgusted with himself, with his aversion to taking risks, his emotional detachment, and his egotism. Alone and unable to consult his therapist—who was on a pilgrimage to the ancient Zen monasteries of Japan—Keller did much soul-searching, and came to the conclusion that he had squandered fifty-five years of his life on trivialities, never truly committing himself to anything or anyone. He had frittered away his youth without developing any emotional maturity, and even now he was navel-gazing like a petulant child when already his body had begun inexorably to sag. How much time did he have left? He had already burned up his best years, and even if there were thirty more to come, they would inevitably trace a slow decline.

Eventually, the combination of antidepressants, tranquilizers, painkillers, antibiotics, and chicken soup had its effect, and he began to recover. He was still unsteady on his feet and had a permanent aftertaste like rotten eggs in his mouth when he found himself summoned by his family "to make decisions," as they put it, a message that boded ill, since his family never consulted him about anything. It coincided with Valentine's Day, a day that, for the past four years, he had spent with Indiana; now he found that he had no one to share it with. The summons, he assumed, concerned his recent debts, rumors of which had probably reached his family. Although he had done it in secret, his brother knew that Alan had sent the Botero paintings to the Marlborough Gallery in New York to sell. He needed money; this was why he had had his jade pieces valued, only to discover that they were worth much less than he had paid for them. About his ill-gotten Inca artifacts, meanwhile, there was nothing to be said: it would be too dangerous to try and sell them.

The family meeting took place in his brother Mark's office, on the top floor of a building in the heart of the financial district. With its sweeping views of the bay, the office was a sanctuary, its sturdy furniture, shaggy area rugs, and framed engravings of Greek columns symbolizing the marmoreal solidity of this law practice, which charged $1,000 an hour. His family sat around an ostentatiously polished mahogany table: his father, Philip Keller, a shadow of the dictatorial patriarch he had once been, shriveled and unsteady but dressed like the captain of a yacht, his skin a map of liver spots; his mother, Flora, her gold bracelets tinkling interminably, wearing a look of perpetual surprise fashioned by plastic surgery, a pair of patent leather trousers, and an Hermès scarf to disguise her wrinkled neck; his sister, Lucille, elegant and slender, her face as gaunt as an Afghan hound's, accompanied by her husband, a lugubrious imbecile who only ever opened his mouth to agree; and finally Mark, upon whose hippopotamine shoulders rested the heavy burden of the Keller dynasty.

Alan knew perfectly well that his elder brother despised him: Alan was tall and handsome, with a luxuriant head of hair streaked with gray; he was charming and sophisticated, attractive to women, while the unfortunate Mark had been cursed with the ghastly genes of some remote ancestor. For all these reasons Mark hated his brother, but above all because while he had spent his whole life working like a dog to add to the family patrimony, the only thing Alan had ever done—as Mark was wont to accuse him on occasion—was bleed the family white.

The vast office was filled with the smell of pine air freshener mingled with the lingering scent of Madame Keller's Prada perfume, a combination that made Alan, who was still convalescing, faintly queasy. To quell any doubts about his status in the family, Mark occupied a high-backed chair at the head of the table, various folders laid out in front of him, while everyone else sat on rather less imposing chairs on either side. It occurred to Alan that time, money, and power had only served to heighten his brother's simian traits, something that no tailor, however talented, could disguise. Mark was the natural heir to many generations of men blessed with financial acuity and emotional myopia, whose ruthlessness and lack of scruples were etched onto their faces in permanent expressions of ill-tempered arrogance.

As a boy, when he had trembled before his father and still admired his big brother, Alan had wanted to be like them, but this desire had faded in his teens as soon as he realized he was of a different—and more noble—mettle. Some years ago, during a lavish party to celebrate Flora Keller's seventieth birthday, taking advantage of the fact that his mother had drunk more than she should, Alan had dared to ask her whether Philip Keller really was his father. "I can say for certain that you're not adopted," his mother had replied between hiccups and stifled giggles, "but I can't remember who your real father is."

Before the family meeting, sick and tired of supporting their younger brother's feckless ways, Mark and Lucille had agreed to put the screws on Alan—their parents had been invited along simply to make up numbers—but their resolve faded when they saw his sorry state. He was pale, unkempt, and with bags under his eyes worthy of Dracula.

///////////////////

"What the hell is the matter with you?" Mark barked at him. "Are you sick?"

"I've got hepatitis," said Alan, for something to say, and because he felt terrible.

"Great!" said his sister, throwing up her hands. "That's all we need!"

But Alan's brother and sister were not utterly heartless, and had only to glance at one other, raising an eyebrow—a Keller family tic—to agree to tone down their strategy a little. The conclave was humiliating for Alan; it could hardly have been otherwise. Mark began by venting his feelings, accusing his brother of being a parasite, a playboy, a freeloader living on handouts, with no work ethic and no dignity, and went on to warn him that the family had come to the end of their patience and their resources. "We've had enough," he said peremptorily, and with a meaningful slap on the folders laid out in front of him. His recriminations, interspersed here and there with comments from Lucille, had lasted twenty minutes, during which time Alan realized that in the files was an account of every cent squandered, every loan received, every disastrous business deal in his name, laid out in chronological order and duly notarized. For decades Alan had been signing promissory notes, assuming that this was mere formality and Mark would forget about them as easily as Alan wiped them from his own memory. He had underestimated his brother.

In the second part of the meeting, Mark Keller laid out the mod-
ified conditions he and Lucille had silently agreed on, one eyebrow
raised. Rather than insisting that Alan sell his vineyard to pay off
his creditors, as they had originally planned, he conceded that the
value of the property had plummeted drastically since the crash of
2008 and consequently this was the worst possible time to sell. On
the other hand, he insisted the vineyard become collateral should
they bail Alan out this last time. The most important thing, he
said, was that Alan pay off his debts to the IRS, which might otherwise land him in jail, a scandal which the Keller family was not
prepared to tolerate. Then Mark announced his intention to sell the
Woodside property, something that so shocked Philip and Flora
Keller that they could not protest. Mark explained that a finance
company was keen to build two apartment blocks on the site, and
given the disastrous state of the housing market, they could not afford to reject such a generous offer. Alan, who had tried for years
to offload the decrepit old mansion so he could pocket his share,
stood by the window listening, staring at the panoramic views of
the bay with studied indifference.

The black sheep of the family could clearly feel the contempt and
deep-seated resentment his siblings felt for him, and also the extent
of his punishment: in a novel and unexpected development, he was
to be excluded from the family. He was to be stripped of his position and his financial security, his connections and his privileges;
with a forceful shove they were relegating him to the lower rungs
of the social hierarchy. That morning, in less than an hour and
without the intervention of some catastrophe—a world war, or a
meteor collision—he had lost what he considered to be his birth-
right.

Alan was surprised to note that, rather than being furious with
his siblings or worried about his future, he felt only a certain curi-

osity. What would it be like to join the teeming multitudes of what Geneviève van Houte referred to as "ugly people"? He remembered a quote he had used in one of his articles to describe an aspiring artist with vaulting ambition but little talent: "At some point everyone stoops to his own particular level of incompetence." It occurred to him as he left his brother's office that from now on he would have to manage on his own; he would land facedown in his own incompetence.

In short, he was ruined. The sale of Woodside might take a little while, but it hardly mattered, since he would not see a penny—his family would set his share against the monies they had given him in the course of his life, what he had called "advances on his inheritance," but what the rest of the Keller family considered loans. He had never kept track of these debts, but they were immortalized in the files that even now Mark was squashing with his fat, pasty hand. He assumed he could survive for a while on the sale of his artworks, though it was difficult to know for how long, since he never kept track of his expenses either. With a bit of luck he might make a million and a half on the Boteros after the gallery took its commission—Latin American painters were fashionable just now—but it was never a good idea to be in a hurry to sell, as he was. He owed a lot of money to banks—the vineyard had been an expensive whim—and to other minor creditors, from his dentist to a couple of antiquarians, to say nothing of his credit cards. How much did it all come to? He had no idea. Mark made it clear that he would have to vacate Woodside immediately, and the house, which an hour ago Alan had cordially loathed, now inspired in him a certain nostalgia. Wearily, he thought that at least he would not have to ask others for a place to live; he could move to the vineyard in Napa for a couple of months until Mark seized that too.

Alan kissed his mother and his sister Lucille on the cheek and clapped his father and his brother on the shoulder. Stepping from the lift and out into the street, Keller saw that at this turning point in his life, winter had fled, and San Francisco glittered in sunshine come from distant climes. He headed to the Clock Bar at the Westin St. Francis for a whiskey, the first since he had fallen ill, and which just then he craved; the shot lifted his spirits, dispelled his doubts and fears. He ran his fingers through his curls, happy to have such a good head of hair, straightened up, and felt a great weight lifted from his shoulders. He no longer depended on his siblings; he was done with juggling credit cards, with the obsessive need to keep up appearances and the duty to uphold the honor of the family name. His house of cards had collapsed, and he lay among the ruins—but he was free. He felt euphoric, weightless, years younger. The only thing he missed was Indiana, but she too belonged to the past; she too had been carried off by the wind.

Thursday, 16

*S*ometime around midmorning, *Blake Jackson* got a call at the drugstore from his granddaughter. He set aside what he was doing—counting pills for a prescription; the tone of Amanda's voice was worrying.

"Shouldn't you be in class right now?" he asked with some concern.

"I'm calling from the restroom," she said, and he could tell she was making a valiant effort not to cry. "It's about Bradley. . . ."

"What's up?"

"Oh, Pops, he's got a girlfriend!" She began to sob.

"Oh, honey, I'm so sorry. . . . How did you find out?"

"He posted it on Facebook. Bad enough that he betrays me, he has to mock me publicly. He posted a photo of her—she looks like she's captain of the swim team just like him, shoulders like a guy and an evil face. Oh, Pops, what am I going to do?"

"I don't know, Amanda."

"I guess nothing like this ever happened to you?"

"I don't remember. It's the kind of thing people forget—"

"Forget! I'll never forgive Bradley! I sent a message to remind him that we were going to get married, but he never replied." Amanda was crying now. "He's probably trying to think up some excuse to palm me off. Guys are all cheats, just like my dad and Alan Keller. You can't trust any of them."

"I'm not like that, Amanda."

"Yeah, but you're old!"

"Of course there are guys you can trust—most of us are decent men. Your father is a free agent—I mean, he's divorced, he's not being unfaithful to anyone."

"Are you trying to tell me that Bradley is a free agent, that he didn't have to be faithful to me, even though we were supposed to get married?"

"This whole thing about you guys getting married . . . I don't think it was ever settled. Maybe Bradley didn't know that you were thinking of marrying him."

"I'm not talking about the past, I'm talking about now. Just wait till I go to MIT, I'll wipe that girl off the face of the earth."

"That's the spirit, Amanda."

His granddaughter went on crying for a minute or two, while he held the phone, not knowing how to console her.

Finally he heard her blow her nose noisily.

"I should get back to class." Amanda sighed.

"I guess this isn't a good time to talk about autopsies," said Blake. "I'll call you tonight."

"What autopsy?"

"Rachel Rosen. The ME believes she was drugged, using a syringe. She found a small puncture mark on the left thigh. She was muzzled, then strangled—actually, it would be more accurate to say she was garroted, using fishing wire and a tourniquet—and only afterward strung up from the ceiling fan."

"It all sounds kind of convoluted, Kabel, don't you think?"

"I sure do. The tox screen identified the drug, something called Versed—it has a lot of medical uses, including sedating a patient before an operation. Given the dose, Rosen would have been unconscious in a matter of minutes."

"That's interesting," said Amanda, sounding somewhat recovered from her broken heart.

"Get back to class, honey. D'you love me?"

"No."

"Me neither."

Friday, 17

For her penultimate patient of the week, Indiana had prepared by dabbing a drop of oil of lemon on her wrists—which helped focus her mind—and lighting a stick of incense to the goddess Shakti in a prayer for patience. It had been one of those weeks when Gary Brunswick needed two sessions, and she'd had to reschedule other patients to fit in with his timetable. Once upon a time she could cheer herself up after a difficult session with two or three dark chocolate truffles, but since she'd finished with Alan Keller, the truffles had lost their restorative powers, and life's irritations—like Gary—left her feeling helpless. She needed something stronger than chocolate.

Gary had not come to her consulting room that first time with any ulterior motive, unlike the men who turned up with imaginary ailments, hoping to try their luck with her. Indiana had had her share of jokers who strutted around naked, hoping to impress her, until she found some way to get rid of them before they could become a threat; from time to time she'd had to ask Matheus Pereira for help. The artist had rigged up an alarm button under the massage table so that she could call him whenever things got out of hand. Now and again these jerks would come back shamefaced and ask her for a second chance, but she always refused; in order to heal, she had to concentrate, which was difficult when the patient had a boner under the sheet. Gary wasn't like that; he'd been referred to her by Yumiko Sato, who trusted her miraculous acupuncture needles to treat almost any complaint but, having failed to cure Brunswick of his persistent migraines, sent him down the hall to Treatment Room 8.

Gary had never seen Indiana, so he was surprised when she opened the door and he found himself staring at a Valkyrie dressed as a nurse, not at all what he had been expecting. In fact, he had not even expected a woman, assuming Indiana to be a man's name, like in the Indiana Jones movies he'd seen as a teenager. Even before their first session was over, he was overcome by a surge of new feelings he found difficult to deal with. He prided himself on being a dispassionate man completely in control of his actions, but Indiana's warm, caring, feminine presence, along with the pressure of her firm hands and the heady mixture of scents in the treatment room, disarmed him, and during that hour-long session he felt like he was in heaven. This was why he came back, like a supplicant, not so much to be cured of his migraines as simply to see her, hoping to reexperience the same bliss; but he never recaptured the intensity of that first session. Like an addict, he needed a stronger dose every time.

His shyness and awkwardness made it impossible for him to declare his feelings to Indiana, but his hints had dangerously increased in frequency. Indiana would have sent any other man packing without a second thought, but Gary seemed so fragile, despite his combat boots and his macho jacket, that she was afraid she might fatally wound him. She had mentioned this to Ryan, who had seen Gary once or twice. "Why don't you just ditch the pathetic little weasel?" was his reaction. But this was precisely why she couldn't. He was pathetic.

The session went better than she had expected. Indiana noticed that Gary was nervous at first, but he relaxed as soon as she began the massage and dozed off during the twenty minutes of Reiki. When she finished, she had to shake him gently to wake him up. She left him to put his clothes on and waited in the little reception area. The stick of incense had burned away by now, though the room still smelled like a Hindu temple. She opened the door to the hallway to let in a breath of air just as Matheus Pereira showed up, spattered with paint, carrying a pot plant as a gift for her. Matheus spent his days between long marijuana-induced siestas and bursts of artistic creativity, which in no way affected his powers of observation: nothing that happened in North Beach escaped his attention, especially at the Holistic Clinic, which he considered his home. Originally, his contract with the Chinese owner of the building had consisted of keeping him informed of the tenants' comings and goings in exchange for a small stipend and the chance to live rent-free in the attic, but since nothing much of note ever happened, the agreement had lapsed somewhat. Through his routine of making the rounds of the building, putting letters into mailboxes, dealing with complaints, and overhearing secrets, he had eventually built friendships with the tenants—his only family—and especially with Indiana and Yumiko, who treated his sciatica with massage and acupuncture.

Matheus noticed that the Japanese florist no longer came by on Mondays to deliver the ikebana arrangement, and assumed something had happened between Indiana and her lover. A real shame, he thought, since Keller was a sophisticated guy who knew a lot about art; any day now he might have bought one of Pereira's canvases, maybe one of the big ones, like the painting of the slaughterhouse inspired by Chaim Soutine's animal carcasses, which Matheus considered his masterpiece. Of course, on the other hand, if Keller was out of the picture, he could invite Indiana up to his attic once in a while to smoke a little weed, make a little love—that wouldn't compromise his creativity as long as it didn't become a habit. Frankly, platonic love was boring. Indiana thanked him for the plant with a chaste peck on the cheek and quickly sent him on his way; her patient, now fully clothed, had suddenly appeared.

Matheus shuffled down the hall while Gary paid for the two sessions he'd had that week—in cash, as always, and without accepting a receipt.

"You should keep that plant away from your clients, Indiana—that's a grass plant. Does that guy work here? I've seen him around a couple of times."

"He's an artist, he lives up on the top floor. The paintings in the lobby are by him."

"They're pretty creepy, if you ask me, but I don't know much about art," said Gary. Then, staring down at his shoes, he stammered, "Hey, at Café Rossini tomorrow they're making *cinghiale*. . . . I thought, I don't know, maybe we could go. I mean, if you like. . . ."

Cinghiale never appeared on the menu of the Café Rossini. From time to time, the owner of Café Rossini went hunting up in Monterey and came back with a wild boar carcass. He would butcher it in his own kitchen—a grisly process—to create, among other delicacies, the finest wild boar sausages in the world, the crucial ingredient in his *cinghiale*. The dish was served only to those regular customers who were in on the secret. That this now included Gary was proof of his persistence: he had already managed to become accepted in North Beach, an acceptance that sometimes took others decades to win.

Some weeks earlier Indiana had made the mistake of agreeing to have dinner with Gary and had spent two seemingly interminable hours struggling to stay awake while he lectured her on the geological formations of the San Andreas fault. She had no intention of repeating the experience.

"Thanks, Gary, but no. I'll be spending the weekend with my family—we have a lot to celebrate. Amanda's been accepted to MIT, and they've offered her a scholarship to cover half the tuition."

"Must be a genius, your daughter."

"She is, but you still beat her at chess," said Indiana kindly.

"She's beaten me often enough."

"You mean you've seen her again?" Indiana said, alarmed.

"We play online sometimes. She's going to teach me how to play Go—it's harder than chess. It's this two-thousand-year-old Chinese game—"

"I know what Go is, Gary," Indiana interrupted, making no attempt to hide her annoyance. The man was becoming a nuisance.

"You sound angry. Is something wrong?"

"I don't allow my daughter to have anything to do with my patients. I'd be grateful if you didn't get in touch with her again."

"Why? I'm not some pervert!"

"I never said you were, Gary." Indiana retreated, startled to see this timid little man raising his voice.

"I understand that, as a mother, you have to protect your daughter, but you don't have to be afraid of me."

"Of course not, but all the same—"

"I can't just stop seeing Amanda with no explanation," Gary interrupted. "I've got to at least talk to her. Actually, if it's okay with you I'd like to do something for her. Didn't you tell me she's always wanted a cat?"

"That's very sweet, Gary, but Amanda already has a kitten. It's called Save-the-Tuna. She was given it by a friend of mine, Carol Underwater—you've probably seen her around."

"Then I'll have to think of something else to give Amanda."

"No, Gary, I can't allow it. From now on our relationship has to be confined to the four walls of this consulting room. Please don't be offended—it's nothing personal."

"It couldn't be more personal, Indiana," Gary blurted out, flushed with embarrassment, looking heartbroken. "Don't tell me you don't know how I feel about you."

"But we hardly know each other, Gary."

"If you want to know more, you only have to ask, Indiana—I'm an open book. I'm single, I have no kids, I'm organized, hardworking, a good citizen, and a decent guy. Maybe it's a bit premature to tell you about my finances, but I can say they're in pretty good shape. A lot of people lost everything they had in the crisis, but I've managed to stay afloat, I've even made a profit because I understand the stock market. I've been trading for years, and—"

"None of this is any of my business, Gary."

"I just want you to think about what I've said, Indiana. I'll wait as long as it takes."

"I'd rather you didn't. In fact, I think you should look for another healer—I can't go on treating you. It's not simply because of what you've just said, it's because the treatments haven't done much good."

"Don't do this to me! You're the only one who can heal me, Indiana, I've been much better thanks to you. I promise I'll never mention my feelings for you again."

He looked so desolate that Indiana could not bring herself to insist, and when Gary saw her hesitate, he made the most of it. Pretending he hadn't registered anything she had told him, he said he would see her next Tuesday, and hurried off.

Indiana closed the door and turned the key in the lock, feeling she had been manipulated like a little girl. She washed her face and hands, hoping to wash away her anger, nostalgically thinking about the jacuzzi at the Fairmont Hotel. Ah, the perfumed water, the vast cotton towels, the perfectly chilled wine, the exquisite food, the loving caresses, Alan Keller's wit and affection. Once, after they had watched *Cleopatra* on television—three hours of Egyptian decadence, heavily made-up eyes and boorish Romans with wonderful legs—she mentioned that the best thing in the movie was Cleopatra bathing in milk. Alan had leaped out of bed, left the room without a word, and reappeared half an hour later, just as she was about to doze off, carrying three boxes of powdered milk that he emptied into the jacuzzi so that she could bathe like a Hollywood pharaoh. The memory made her laugh, and she felt an ache in her chest as she wondered whether she could live without this man who had given her so much pleasure, and whether she would ever come to love Ryan as she had loved Alan.

The physical attraction she felt for the ex-soldier was so intense that it reminded her of what she had felt for Bob Martín back in high school. It was like a fever, a smoldering heat. She wondered how she had managed to ignore it, to resist this overwhelming desire that had surely been welling in her for some time. The only possible answer was that her love for Alan had been stronger. She knew her own temperament; she knew that when she was truly in love, she couldn't casually sleep with someone else; but now, after that first night spent with Ryan in that little room lashed by the storm, she felt she understood anyone who surrendered to the madness of desire.

Twelve days had passed since then, and she had spent every night with Ryan, except for Saturday and Sunday, which she spent with Amanda. At this very moment, though she still had one patient left to see, she was already longing to take him in her arms, to be with him in his loft, where Attila, resigned, no longer howled miserably. She thought with pleasure about the pared-back simplicity of the apartment, the rough towels, the bitter cold that forced them to make love wearing sweaters and thick woolen socks. She loved his powerful masculinity, the strength he exuded, the warrior air about him, which in her arms changed to helplessness. In a way, she liked the fact that he made love like a bewildered boy, something she put down to the fact that Ryan had never really had a serious lover, someone who had taken the trouble to teach him how to pleasure a woman. This, she decided, would change once the thrill of being newly in love passed, and they had time to slowly explore each other. It was a pleasant thought. Ryan was a surprising man, gentler and more sentimental than she had imagined, but they had no shared history, and all relationships need some. There would be ample time for them to get to know each other, and for her to forget about Alan.

She tidied up the massage room, gathered away the sheets and towels, and got ready for her last session of the week: the poodle, her favorite patient and the most affectionate, an old, crippled, coffee-colored little dog that submitted to her treatments with obvious gratitude. Since she had a few minutes to spare, she looked up Gary Brunswick's file, which did not give his exact time of birth, unfortunately, since that would have been useful for preparing an astrological chart. Then she called Celeste Roko to ask her for the number of the Tibetan who cleared negative karma.

Saturday, 18

At 8:30 p.m. sharp on Saturday, Pedro Alarcón and Ryan Miller, with Attila at his heels, rang Indiana's doorbell. They were quickly followed by Matheus Pereira, Yumiko Sato, and her life partner Nana Sasaki. Indiana, having invited them on behalf of Danny D'Angelo, greeted her guests wearing a slim black silk dress and heels—gifts from Alan Keller back when he had been trying to turn her into a lady—which drew wolf whistles from the men. They had never seen her look so elegant—in fact they'd never seen her wear black, a color she believed attracted negative energy and hence avoided. Attila delightedly sniffed the combination of essential oils that pervaded the apartment. The dog hated artificial smells but was a sucker for natural aromas, which explained his fondness for Indiana, whom she cherished among human beings. Ryan grabbed Indiana and kissed her full on the lips, while the other guests pretended not to notice. Then the hostess uncorked a bottle of Primus, a delicate blend of carménère and cabernet grapes—another gift from Alan, who knew that Indiana could not afford to buy a bottle of wine that cost more than her winter coat—and poured Ryan a glass of his favorite soda. There had been a time when the Navy SEAL prided himself on being a wine buff, but after he gave up alcohol he became a connoisseur of Coca-Cola: he preferred it served in small bottles, never cans, and liked his Coke imported from Mexico—where they added more sugar—and always without ice.

The day before, Danny had invited Indiana to his Saturday performance. It was a special occasion, since it was his birthday, and the owner of the club, as a tribute to his years on the stage, had given him a starring role that Danny had carefully rehearsed. "What's the point of being the star of the show if no one cares? Come watch me, Indi, and bring your friends—I could do with an ovation." Since Danny hadn't given her much notice, Indiana didn't have time to rally the sort of crowd he would have liked and had to make do with these five loyal friends. They all dressed up for the occasion—even Matheus, who, over his usual paint-splattered jeans, was wearing a striped, neatly pressed shirt and a bandanna around his neck. There was a general consensus in North Beach that Matheus Pereira was the most handsome man in the area, and he knew it. Tall and slim, his face chiseled with deep lines, he had the yellow-green eyes of a cat, full, sensual lips, and wore his hair in dreadlocks. He was so striking that people would often stop to have their picture taken with him, as though he were a tourist attraction.

Yumiko and Nana had known each other as children in the Iwate Prefecture back in Japan, and emigrated together to the United States; they lived together, worked together, even dressed alike. That evening, they were wearing their going-out uniform: black pantsuits with white silk Mao-collar blouses. They had married on June 16, 2008—the day same-sex marriage was legalized in California—and that night held a wedding reception of sushi and sake at the Hairy Caterpillar gallery, with all the therapists from the Holistic Clinic in attendance.

Matheus helped Indiana with dinner—takeout ordered from the local Thai restaurant, served on paper plates with chopsticks. The friends sat on the floor to eat, since Indiana used the only table in the apartment as an aromatherapy lab. The conversation drifted back and forth—as all conversations did at that time—between whether Obama would lose the election and whether *Midnight in Paris* would win an Oscar. They finished the wine, and for dessert they had green tea ice cream that Yumiko and Nana had brought. Then everyone piled into Yumiko's car and Ryan's van—with Attila riding shotgun, since no one dared commandeer his seat.

They parked on Castro Street and, leaving Attila in Ryan's truck, where, with Buddhist patience, the dog would wait for hours, walked two blocks to the Narcissus Club. At that time of night the neighborhood was teeming with young people, a few insomniac tourists, and the gay men who crammed the bars and the cabarets. Outside, the place where Danny was performing was simply a doorway and a blue neon sign; it would have gone unnoticed but for the people waiting in line to go in, and the groups of men smoking and chatting. Pedro and Ryan made a couple of ironic remarks about the kind of club it was but meekly followed Indiana, who greeted the burly bouncer working the door and introduced her friends as Danny D'Angelo's special guests. Inside, the club was much bigger than they had expected. The air was stifling, the place crowded, and the audience almost entirely male. In dark corners shadowy figures were making out or slow-dancing, oblivious to everyone else, but the rest of the audience moved around, talking at the tops of their voices or crowding around the bar for beer and Mexican tacos.

Beneath the flickering lights of the dance floor—which also served as a stage—four go-go dancers gyrated to the pulsing rhythm of the music, wearing only bikinis and crowned with plumes of white feathers. They might have been mistaken for quadruplets: all four were the same height and wearing identical wigs, jewelry, and makeup. They had shapely legs, toned buttocks, arms sheathed in long satin evening gloves, and breasts that spilled out of their bejeweled bras. Only close up and in bright daylight would it have been possible to tell that they were not women.

Danny's friends elbowed their way through the noisy crowd, and a busboy led them to a ringside table reserved in Indiana's name. Pedro, Yumiko, and Nana headed for the bar to get drinks and a Coke for Ryan, who, oblivious to the fact that he and Matheus were attracting attention, assumed that the regulars were all staring at Indiana.

Shortly afterward the plumed go-go dancers finished their routine and the houselights went down, the club plunged into a darkness greeted by catcalls and whistles. A whole minute passed, and then, when the hecklers had calmed down, the crystal-clear voice of Whitney Houston filled the room with a slow, mournful lament that sent shivers down the spine of everyone present. Suddenly the beam of a yellow spotlight picked out the ghost of the singer, who had died a week before, standing in the center of the stage, her head bowed, one hand clutching a microphone, the other pressed to her heart. Her hair was short, her eyes closed, and she was wearing a long backless dress that emphasized her breasts. This sudden apparition took the audience's breath away. Slowly, Whitney Houston raised her head, brought the microphone to her face, and from somewhere in the depths of the earth came the haunting phrase "I Will Always Love You." The crowd erupted in a spontaneous ovation, followed by an awed silence as the voice sang its farewell, a torrent of affection, of promises and regrets. That unmistakable face, those tremulous hands, the gestures, the passion, the grace: it was her. Five minutes later, the last notes of the song quivered in the air amid a thunder of applause. The illusion was so perfect that it didn't occur to Indiana and her friends that this diva, returned to life by some magical spell, might be Danny D'Angelo, the scruffy waiter from Café Rossini—until the lights went up, and Whitney Houston bowed and pulled off her wig.

////////////////////////

Ryan had been to places like the Narcissus Club in other countries with his comrades in arms, who made tasteless jokes to disguise the fact that they enjoyed drag shows. Ryan found drag queens entertaining: to him they were outlandish, innocuous creatures from some different species. He considered himself the sort of broadminded man who has seen the world and can no longer be shocked by anything, tolerant of other people's sexual preferences so long as they do not involve children or animals. He did not approve of gays in the armed forces, fearing that, like women, they would be a distraction and generate hostility. Not that he doubted their bravery, he insisted, but battle is a test of manliness and loyalty, war is fought with testosterone; every soldier has to depend on his comrades, and he would not feel comfortable putting his life in the hands of a gay man or a woman. That night in the Narcissus Club, without the support of his fellow Navy SEALs, his tolerance was put to the test.

The confined space, the atmosphere of sex and seduction, the crowd of men's bodies brushing past him, the smell of sweat and beer and aftershave: all of it made him tense and uneasy. He wondered how his father would have reacted in these circumstances, and—as always happened when he thought about his father—he saw the man standing to attention next to him, his uniform immaculate, a row of medals pinned to his chest, his jaw clenched, glowering in disapproval at everything Ryan was, at everything he'd done. What is a son of mine doing in this sordid dive with a

gaggle of preening faggots? his father, in that way he had always
had, snarled through clenched teeth without moving his lips.

Ryan barely noticed Danny's performance; by then he had realized that the meaningful stares were intended not for Indiana
but for him. He felt violated by this throbbing masculine energy,
at once fascinating, dangerous, and seductive—it both attracted
and repulsed him. Without thinking, he grabbed Pedro's glass of
whiskey and drained it. He had not touched alcohol in years, and
the liquid burned his throat, coursing through his veins in a wave
of heat and energy that obliterated all thoughts, all memories and
qualms. There was nothing in the world like this magical liquid,
this wonderful, smoldering, molten gold, this nectar of the gods
that thrilled through him, invigorated and inflamed him. There
was nothing in the world like whiskey—he couldn't understand
how or why he had given it up, what a fool he had been. The image
of his father retreated, and was swallowed up by the crowd. Ryan
turned back to Indiana, leaning in to find her lips, but the kiss died
in midair, and instead he grabbed her beer. Indiana, mesmerized
by the vision of Whitney Houston, didn't notice a thing.

Ryan never knew at what point he got up from the table and
angrily elbowed his way to the bar; he never knew how the show
ended or how many drinks he'd had when he completely lost control. He never knew where the blinding, incandescent fury came
from when a young man put a hand on his shoulder and whispered
something, his lips brushing against Ryan's ear; he never knew at
precisely what point reality began to blur and he felt himself swell,
his body straining inside his skin, about to explode. He never knew
how the scuffle started, nor how many people he lashed out at, fists
flailing; he never knew why Indiana and Pedro were screaming at
him, or how he came to end up handcuffed in the back of a police
car with swollen knuckles and blood on his shirt.

Pedro picked Ryan's jacket up off the floor, found the keys to the van, and followed the car that was ferrying his friend to the police station. He parked nearby and went inside, where he had to wait for an hour and a half before an officer could speak to him. He explained what had happened, playing down Ryan's role in the events while the officer listened distractedly, staring at his computer.

"He'll have time enough to argue his case in front of a judge on Monday," the cop said in a friendly tone. "In the meantime, there's a cell here where he can sober up and calm down."

Pedro explained to the officer that Ryan was not drunk but medicated, having suffered brain damage during the Iraq War, in which he had also lost a leg; that he suffered from bouts of erratic behavior but was not dangerous.

"Not dangerous? Try telling that to the three guys he put in the emergency room!"

"What happened in the Narcissus Club was a one-off—he's never done anything like that before. He was provoked."

"How do you mean, provoked?"

"Some guy tried to touch him up."

"You don't say," the officer said sarcastically. "In a club like that? You learn something new every day."

At this point, Pedro played the trump card he used only as a last resort: he told the officer that Ryan worked with the government and was currently on a confidential mission. If the officer didn't believe him, he added, he had only to check the prisoner's wallet, and he would find the relevant ID, and if that was not enough, Pedro would give him a code so he could check directly with CIA headquarters in Washington, DC.

"As I'm sure you can understand," Pedro stressed, "we can't afford a scandal."

The policeman, who by now had shut down the computer and was listening skeptically, told him to go back to his seat and wait.

It was another hour before they could get Washington to cor-
roborate Pedro's story, and yet another before they released Ryan,
after getting him to sign a statement. During this time, Ryan had
sobered up a little, though he still stumbled as he walked. They
finally left the police station at about five in the morning, Pedro
desperate for his first maté of the day, Ryan with a pounding
headache—and the unfortunate Attila, who had spent the whole
night in the van, desperate to cock his leg at the nearest available
tree.

"Attaboy, Miller, you ruined Whitney Houston's comeback,"
said Pedro back in the loft apartment as he helped his friend out of
his clothes, not before giving the dog some water and letting him
out to pee.

"I feel like my brain's about to explode."

"Serves you right. I'll make some coffee."

Sitting on the edge of the bed, his face buried in his hands with
Attila nuzzling his knee, Ryan tried in vain to reconstruct the
events of the night. He felt a crippling shame; his head seemed to
be full of sand; his lip was split, his knuckles and his eyelids swollen, and his ribs so bruised it hurt to breathe. This was the only
time he'd fallen off the wagon; he had managed three years and
one month of total abstinence, with no alcohol and no drugs except
the odd toke on a joint from time to time. He had gone cold turkey,
without any of the psychiatric help he was entitled to as a navy vet,
nothing but antidepressants. Given that in battle he was capable of
coping with more pressure and more pain than any other human
being—that was how he had been trained—he wasn't about to be
beaten by a glass of beer. He could not work out what had happened, did not even remember when he had taken that first sip of
alcohol. He felt himself tumbling into the abyss.

"I've got to call Indi," he said to Pedro. "Pass me the phone."

"It's five forty on a Sunday morning, bro," said Pedro. "This is no time to be calling people. Here, drink this and get some shut-eye. I'll take Attila for a walk."

Ryan just managed to swallow the strong coffee and a couple of aspirin before racing to the bathroom to throw up, while his buddy tried in vain to persuade Attila to let him put on the muzzle and the leash. Having no intention of leaving Ryan in such a state, the dog sat in front of the bathroom door, whimpering, his one ear cocked, his one good eye alert, awaiting orders from his companion in misery. Ryan turned on the shower, holding his head under the freezing water for a few minutes, and then emerged from the bathroom in his boxer shorts, dripping wet, hopping on his one leg and gesturing for the dog to go with Pedro. Then he pitched forward onto his bed.

Out in the street, Pedro's ringtone blared, a brass band playing the military strains of the Uruguayan national anthem. Struggling with the dog's leash, he fished his cell phone from the bottom of his pocket and answered to hear Indiana's voice, asking for Ryan. She had last seen him being dragged by two burly cops into a waiting police car while two other officers, with the help of the gorilla who worked the door, tried to calm down a number of drunken, emotional revelers who were still throwing punches while the go-go dancers shrieked, still wearing their feathered finery. As he cowered behind the bar, Danny D'Angelo had watched the upheaval, a nylon stocking still covering his hair, his Whitney Houston wig in one hand and his eyeliner streaming down his tear-streaked face.

In his laconic manner, Pedro brought Indiana up to speed.

"I'm coming right over," she said. "Could you pay for the cab?"

Thirty-five minutes later Indiana appeared in the loft apartment, wearing her snakeskin boots, a raincoat thrown over the black dress she'd been wearing the night before—and with a black eye. She kissed Pedro and Attila and went over to the bed where Ryan was snoring, covered with a blanket Pedro had thrown over him. She shook him until he took his head out from under the pillow and sat up, blinking and trying to focus.

"What happened to your eye?" he asked Indiana.

"I tried to restrain you and got a smack in the face."

"I hit you?" Ryan was wide awake now.

"It was an accident. It doesn't matter."

"How could I have sunk so low, Indi?"

"We all make mistakes from time to time, Ryan—we fall flat on our faces, then pick ourselves up again. Now get dressed."

"I can't move."

"Aw . . . the poor little Navy SEAL! Get up! You're coming with me."

"Where are we going?"

"You'll see."

"*Hi, my name's Ryan and* I'm an alcoholic, and I've been sober for six hours."

This was how he introduced himself, repeating the formula used by the people dotted around this windowless room who had gone before him. His words were greeted with sincere applause. A few moments earlier, Pedro had driven Ryan and Indiana to a building with a tall spire on the corner of Taylor and Ellis in the heart of the Tenderloin.

"What the hell kind of place is this?" Ryan had asked as Indiana took him by the arm and pulled him toward the entrance.

"It's Glide Memorial Church. How can you have lived here for years and not known about it?"

"I'm an agnostic. Why are we here, Indiana?"

The soul of Glide Memorial Church, Indiana told Ryan, was the African-American pastor Cecil Williams, now retired. In the 1960s he'd been assigned to this failing Methodist church and transformed it into the spiritual heart of San Francisco. He had the

crucifix removed from the sanctuary, saying that it was a symbol
of death and that this congregation should celebrate life.

"That's why we are here, Ryan: to celebrate your life."

She explained to him that Glide attracted tourists because of the
irresistible music of its gospel choir and its open-door policy. Everyone was welcome here regardless of race or creed or sexual ori-
entation: Christians of any denomination, Muslims and Jews, drug
addicts and beggars, Silicon Valley millionaires, drag queens,
movie stars and criminals. No one was turned away; Glide had
hundreds of aid programs to house, clothe, educate, protect, and
rehabilitate the poor and the desperate.

They elbowed their way through the people patiently waiting
in line for a free breakfast. Indiana spent several hours a week here
helping with the seven-to-nine morning shift, the only time she
could spare, she told Ryan; the church offered three free meals every day of the year to thousands of people in need, something that
required seventy-five thousand hours of voluntary work.

"I only do about a hundred hours," she said, "but they've got so
many volunteers there's a waiting list."

At such an early hour, the crowds had not yet begun to arrive
for the Sunday service. Indiana clearly knew her way around, and
led Ryan directly to a small room where the first Alcoholics Anonymous group of the day was meeting. Only half a dozen people
were standing around the side table, which was laid out with pots
of coffee and plates of cookies, but more arrived over the next ten
minutes. Everyone took a seat on the plastic chairs arranged in a
circle. There were people of all colors, races, and ages, and most
of them were men; almost all of them were worn down as a result
of their addiction, and some—like Ryan—bore the scars of a recent brawl. With her healthy glow and cheerful manner, Indiana
looked as though she had wandered in by mistake. Ryan had been
expecting a class or a lecture, but a short, skinny man wearing

thick glasses began the meeting. "Hi, I'm Benny Ephron, and I'm an alcoholic," he introduced himself. "I see a couple of new faces here this morning. Welcome, friends." Then they went around the circle, with everyone in turn giving his or her name.

Coaxed by comments or questions from Benny, some of them talked about their experiences, how they had started drinking, lost their jobs, their families, their friends, their health, and how through AA they were trying to turn their lives around. One man proudly held up a chip with the number 18—the number of months he had been sober—and everyone applauded. One of the four women in the group, a smelly, disheveled wreck with rotting teeth and a restless stare, confessed that she had lost hope because she had relapsed so often, and the group applauded her for having the courage to face them that morning. Ephron told her that she was on the right path, that the first step was to admit you were powerless over your life, adding that hope returns when you entrust your life to a higher power. "I don't believe in God," she said defiantly. "Neither do I," said the scrawny, bespectacled man, "but I believe in the higher power that is love; the love we are able to give and the love that we receive."

"Nobody loves me. Nobody's ever loved me," said the woman, blundering to her feet to leave, only to be stopped by Indiana, who put her arms around her. The woman struggled for a moment, trying to break free, then collapsed sobbing against this young woman who held her with the firm tenderness of a mother. They hugged each other tightly for a moment that seemed to Ryan to be interminable, unbearable, until the woman calmed down and they both returned to their seats.

Ryan spoke only to introduce himself, and listened to the revelations of the others with his head drawn into his shoulders, his elbows resting on his knees, fighting back the waves of nausea and the throbbing pain in his temples. He had more in common with these people than even he would have suspected the night before, when in a moment of distraction or rage he had grabbed the nearest drink and, for a while, become the thuggish brute of his adolescent fantasies again. Like all the men and women around him, he too was a prisoner of his addictions, terrified of the enemy lurking inside, waiting for the moment to destroy him—an enemy so stealthy he had all but forgotten it. He thought about the golden glow of the whiskey, its sunlight sparkle, the delicious tinkle of the ice cubes in the glass; he thought about the pungent smell of the beer, the gentle effervescence, the delicate froth.

He wondered what had gone wrong: he had spent his whole life in training to be the best, learning to be disciplined, developing his self-control, keeping his weaknesses in check. And now, when he least expected it, the enemy had come out from its lair and ambushed him. Once upon a time—when he had been lonely, when he had given up hope of finding love—he would have had every excuse to crawl into a bottle for a while, but he had stayed sober. He couldn't understand why he had given in to temptation now, when he finally had everything he'd longed for. For the past two weeks, he'd felt happy and fulfilled. That blessed Sunday when he had finally taken Indiana in his arms, his life had changed. He had surrendered completely to the wonder of loving her, to the consummation of desire, to the miracle of being loved, being needed, to the dream that he had been redeemed, healed forever of all his wounds. "My name is Ryan Miller, and I'm an alcoholic," he said to himself over and over, feeling his eyes prickle with unshed tears, feeling a desperate urge to run away from this place, but held there by Indiana's hand on his shoulder. When they finally left forty-five minutes later, one or two people clapped him on the back, called him by his name. He didn't answer.

At midday, Indiana and Ryan went on a picnic to the same park with the redwood trees where two weeks earlier a freak thunderstorm had given them an excuse to make love. The weather was changeable, with moments of light drizzle and others when the clouds parted and the sun shyly revealed itself. Ryan brought an uncooked chicken, lemonade, charcoal, and a bone for Attila; Indiana took care of the bread and the fruit. Indiana was carrying an old hamper lined with red-and-white gingham, one of the few things she had inherited from her mother, and ideal for picnics. There wasn't a soul in the park—it would be thronged with people by summer—and they were able to sit in their favorite spot, a stone's throw from the river. Sitting on a thick tree trunk, wearing ponchos against the chill air, they waited for the charcoal to heat up while Attila raced around after the squirrels.

Ryan's face looked like a battered pumpkin, and his body was a map of deep purple bruises—but he was thankful: according to the primitive justice his father had taught him with his belt, punishment absolves guilt. During his childhood, the rules had been clear: evil deeds and reckless actions must be punished. It was one of the inescapable laws of nature. If Ryan got up to mischief without his father finding out, the exhilaration of getting away unpunished was short-lived; he was quickly overwhelmed by feelings of terror and the conviction that the universe would avenge itself. In the end, it was always easier to atone for his sins with a few lashes of his father's belt than to live in dread, waiting for some nameless retribution. Evil deeds and reckless actions . . . He wondered how many he had committed during his forty years, deciding that there must have been many.

In the years he had been a soldier—young, strong, in the thrill of adventure or the heat of battle, surrounded by comrades and protected by powerful weapons—he had never questioned his actions, just as he had never doubted his impunity. In war, it was acceptable to play dirty: he didn't have to justify himself to anyone. He honorably fulfilled his duty to defend his country; he was a Navy SEAL, a member of the elite troop of mythic warriors. Only later did he begin to question things. During the months in the hospital and in rehabilitation, when he was pissing blood and learning to walk with irons strapped to his stump, he decided that if he was guilty of anything, he had more than paid for it with the loss of his leg, his comrades, and his military career. The price had been so high—exchanging a hero's life for a life of tedium—that he wound up feeling cheated. He took spurious comfort from alcohol and hard drugs, staving off the loneliness and the self-loathing as he languished in a bleak condo in Bethesda.

And then, just when the temptation of suicide was almost irresistible, Attila saved his life a second time. Attila had been seriously wounded by a land mine ten miles outside Baghdad: Ryan had a new mission. Fourteen months after being airlifted out of Iraq, strapped to a gurney and doped up on morphine, he was jolted out of his depression and back on his feet.

To Maggie, his neighbor in Bethesda, a widow in her seventies with whom he became friendly over games of poker, he owed the second motto that governed his life: Those who seek help will always find it. A tough old bird who cursed like a longshoreman, Maggie'd done twenty years for killing her husband after he broke almost every bone in her body. This hulking woman, feared by everyone in the neighborhood, was the one person Ryan could bear to spend time with during this dismal period. Maggie treated him with her usual crudeness but also with surprising kindness. In the beginning, before he could fend for himself, she cooked his meals and drove him to his medical appointments; later she scraped him off the floor when she found him drunk or high on drugs and kept him busy playing cards or watching action movies. When they heard what had happened to Attila, Maggie announced that the only way Ryan would get custody of the dog—assuming it survived—was to sort his head out, since no one would entrust a heroic animal to this wreck of a human being.

Ryan had refused to have anything to do with the military hospital's addiction programs, just as he had refused to see a psychologist specializing in PTSD. Maggie agreed that addiction programs and therapy were for faggots, insisting there were quicker and more effective ways of dealing with things. She emptied his pill bottles down the sink or into the toilet, then made him strip and took away his clothes, his laptop, his cell phone, and his prosthetic leg. As she left, she gave him a thumbs-up, then locked him in his apartment, crippled and butt-naked. Ryan was forced to go through the hell of those first days cold turkey: shivering, hallucinating, half-crazed with nausea, paranoia, and pain. He tried to break the door down with his fists, without success; he knotted bedsheets together to try and escape by the window, but he was on the tenth floor. He pounded on the wall separating his apartment from Maggie's until he fractured his knuckles, and his teeth chattered so hard one of them broke. On the third day he collapsed, exhausted.

Maggie came by that night to visit and found him curled up on the floor, whimpering softly and more or less calm. She made him take a shower, gave him a bowl of hot soup, put him to bed, and sat there keeping an eye on him while she pretended to watch TV.

So began Ryan Miller's new life. He focused on staying sober, on the campaign to get custody of Attila, who by now had recovered from his injuries and been awarded a medal. The red tape he had to negotiate to adopt the dog would have put off anyone not motivated by Ryan's steadfast gratitude. Helped by Maggie, he wrote hundreds of requests to the authorities, made five separate trips to Washington to plead his case, and managed to get a private audience with the secretary of defense, thanks to a letter signed by his brothers from SEAL Team Six. He left the secretary's office with the promise that Attila would be flown back home and, after

the standard quarantine period, Ryan would be allowed to adopt
him. During these months of bureaucratic wrangling he moved
to Texas, prepared to spend all his savings on the best prostheses
in the world. There, he began to train as a triathlete and finally
thought of a way to put the skills he had learned in the navy to
good use. He was an expert in security and communications; he
had contacts high up the chain of command, an impeccable military record, and four decorations to attest to his good character.
He called Pedro Alarcón in San Francisco.

Ryan had been friends with Pedro since the age of twenty. After
high school, he had applied to join the Navy SEALs—both to
prove to his father he was as much of a man as he was, and because
he felt he didn't have the skills to go on to college, being dyslexic
and suffering from ADHD. In high school, he hadn't shown the
slightest interest in studying, but he had been a star athlete. He
was a mass of hard muscle, and felt he had the endurance and the
stamina for any physical task. Even so he found himself eliminated from the Navy SEALs during Hell Week: a hundred and
twenty punishing hours designed to test each candidate's ability
to achieve the goal at any cost. It was there that he learned that
the strongest muscle is the heart. Shortly after he started, when
he knew he had reached the limits of his ability to withstand the
pain and exhaustion, he found it could give more and more—but
not enough. His humiliation at having failed was compounded
by the sneering contempt of his father when he heard the news.
For this man—coming from a long line of military men and having retired with the rank of rear admiral—the fact that Ryan
had been rejected simply served to reinforce his low opinion of
his son. Neither Ryan nor his father ever mentioned the subject,
each retreating into a sullen silence that would separate them for
almost a decade.

Over the next four years, Ryan studied computing while putting himself though rigorous training so he could reapply to the Navy SEALs. This was no longer about vying with his father, it was a vocation; he knew now what it meant and wanted to devote his life to it. If Ryan had succeeded at college, it was because one of his professors had taken a personal interest in his case, had helped him to manage his dyslexia and his ADHD and overcome the mental block he had about studying. The same professor had convinced him of his intellectual ability and persuaded him to graduate before enlisting in the navy. That man had been Pedro Alarcón.

In 1995, when Ryan finally achieved his ambition of becoming a Navy SEAL and the deputy chief pinned the Special Warfare insignia—the SEAL Trident pin—on his chest, the first person he called was his former professor. He had survived Hell Week; and in the endless months of brutal training that followed over sea, land, and air—weeks during which he endured extreme temperatures, was deprived of sleep, was molded by hardship and physical suffering, and strengthened by the unbreakable bonds of brotherhood—he had pledged to live and die like a hero. In the sixteen years that followed, until he was wounded and given a medical discharge, he saw little of Pedro, but they kept in touch. While he was off on secret missions in some of the most dangerous places on earth, Pedro had been hired as professor of artificial intelligence at Stanford University. This was how Ryan discovered that his old friend was something of a genius.

Enthusiastic about Ryan's scheme for supplying complex security systems for the military, Pedro had suggested that, to succeed, he would need one foot in Washington and the other in Silicon Valley, the only place such technology could be developed. Ryan rented an office a ten-minute drive from the Pentagon, which would serve as his head office, packed his scant belongings, and moved with Attila to California. The Uruguayan was waiting for them at the San Francisco airport, prepared to help Ryan—but from the shadows, as his political past was suspect.

Indiana knew some of Ryan's story; he'd told her how he had been reconciled with his father before his death. But of the mission to Afghanistan, which haunted his nightmares, she knew nothing. There amid the redwood trees of the park, as he watched the chicken cook slowly in the sultry heat, Ryan told her the story of that night. In modern warfare, he explained, most killing is done from a distance; it's an abstraction, a video game involving no risks, no feelings, in which the victims are faceless. But fighting on the ground is a test of every soldier's courage and humanity. The all-too-real possibility of dying or sustaining horrific wounds has profound psychological and spiritual consequences—a unique experience, impossible to put into words, something understood only by those who have known that intoxicating combination of fear and elation. "Why do men fight? Because it's a primal urge as powerful as the survival instinct," said Ryan. There was nothing to compare to war: once he'd experienced it, everything in civilian life seemed bland. Violence affects not only its victims but those who inflict it. Ryan had been trained to face pain and death, and he had also been trained to kill: he had done it for years, never keeping count, feeling no remorse. He could torture a man, if it was necessary to obtain information—though it made him sick to his stomach, and he preferred to leave that job to others. To kill in the heat of battle or to avenge a friend was one thing: at such moments a soldier does not think, he acts blindly, spurred on by overpowering hatred; his enemy is no longer human. But to look civilians in the eye and kill them, to kill women, children . . . that was a different matter.

In early 2006 intelligence reports had Osama bin Laden hiding in a mountain range on the border with Pakistan, where some al-Qaeda units had regrouped after the American invasion. The region was too vast to search: it was an endless hive of caves, natural tunnels, and barren hills, its tribal peoples united by their faith and a common hatred of Americans. The Navy SEAL teams had already carried out missions in this harsh, dry landscape and suffered significant losses when the enemy combatants used their better knowledge of the terrain to lay ambushes.

How many of these humble goatherds, whose lives had scarcely changed since the time of their biblical ancestors, might in fact be enemy combatants? Which of the mud-colored huts were secret weapons caches? What might these women be hiding beneath their black robes? How much did the children know? Convinced that bin Laden was within reach, the Navy SEALs had been sent on a secret mission to kill him on sight and, if they couldn't find him, to gather information and prevent the local population from helping him. As always in war, the end justified the means. Why this particular village? Ryan's job was not to ask why but to follow orders; the legitimacy of the attack was not his concern.

He remembered every detail—he dreamed about it, relived it relentlessly. The SEALs and their dog were advancing stealthily, jaws clenched, each man carrying a hundred pounds of body armor and equipment, including ammunition, water, two days' food, batteries, bandages, and morphine—to say nothing of his weapons, his helmet equipped with flashlight, camera, and headphones. They were wearing gloves and night-vision goggles. They were the chosen ones, those sent on the most delicate and dangerous missions. They parachuted from helicopters two miles outside the village. Though they could call on air support and troops, right now they were alone. Attila, muzzled and strapped into a harness, had also parachuted, rigid with fear. That jump into thin air was the only thing that terrified him, but the moment he landed he was ready for action.

The enemy could be anywhere: hidden in one of those mud huts, in the mountain caves, or sneaking up behind them. And death could come in many forms—a land mine, a sniper, a suicide bomber with an explosives belt. This was the irony of a war in which the most highly trained army in the world, the devastating might of the most powerful empire in history, was pitted against fundamentalist tribesmen prepared to defend their territory by any means necessary—with stones, if they ran out of bullets. It was David against Goliath. Goliath's invincible weapons and technology weighed him down like a pack animal, while his enemy was nimble, cunning, and knew the terrain. This was a war of occupation, unsustainable in the long term—it is impossible to subjugate a rebellious population forever. The war on the ground might be won by gunfire, but on a human level it was bound to fail, and both sides knew it. It was just a matter of time. The Americans did their best to avoid collateral damage, because it came at a cost: every civilian death, every ruined house, simply increased the number of enemy combatants and fueled the anger of the local people. The enemy was elusive, invisible, melting into the villages, blending in with shepherds and farmers, driven by a maniacal courage—and Navy SEALs respect courage, even in the enemy.

Ryan moves in front, flanked by Attila. The dog is kitted out with a bulletproof jacket, goggles, headphones for receiving orders, and a camera mounted on his head, streaming images back to base. Attila is still a frisky pup—but when his service harness is strapped on, he becomes an armor-plated, almost mythical beast. He does not panic at gunfire or exploding grenades; he can distinguish between the sound of American weapons and those of the enemy, between the engine of a friendly truck and that of a rescue helicopter. He is trained to detect mines and traps. Attila never strays from Ryan's side; when the dog senses danger, he presses against the man's leg as a warning, and if Ryan should fall, Attila will protect him at the cost of his own life. He is one of twenty-eight hundred U.S. military service dogs in the Middle East. Ryan knows that he should not allow himself to be fond of the pup—Attila is a weapon, part of his equipment, but also, and above all, his companion. They can read each other's minds; they eat together, sleep together. Ryan silently blesses the dog and pats him on the head.

All the muscles in Attila's body tense—his hackles rise, his snout goes up, and he bares his jagged teeth. He is cannon fodder: he'll be the first to cross the threshold. He advances cautiously but decisively; the only thing that will stop him now is Ryan's voice in his headset. Crouching silent and invisible in the shadows, Ryan follows him, hugging his M4 assault rifle, the most versatile close-combat weapon there is. He stops thinking now—he's poised, his attention focused on the target but still aware of his surroundings. His comrades, he knows, have fanned out around the village for a simultaneous assault. The enemy will hardly know what's hit them. It must be a lightning raid.

The first house to the south is Ryan's. He can just make it out in the pale glow of the waning moon: a squat, square hut, mud and stone that merges with the terrain as though it's grown up out of the ground. A goat bleats somewhere, breaking the silence of the night a second time. Ryan twitches. He thinks he can hear a baby crying, stops ten yards from the door, but silence falls again. He wonders how many terrorists are hiding in this shepherd's hut. He takes a deep breath, filling his lungs, then signals to the dog, who has been watching attentively, and the two race toward the hut. At exactly the same moment his comrades burst into the village—there are shouts, curses, explosions. Ryan fires a burst at the door and kicks it down. Attila goes in first and waits for instructions, ready to attack. Ryan follows behind, analyzes the situation through his night-vision goggles, gauging the space, the distance between the walls, the ceiling so low he has to crouch. He registers the dirt floor, the brazier, the cooking pots hanging above an unlit stove, three or four wooden stools. It is a one-room hut, and at first glance it seems empty. He shouts in English that nobody should move; at his side Attila growls. Then everything happens so fast that later he will not be able to piece together the events. At unexpected moments, disparate images will flash into his mind with the force of body blows; over and over he will relive this night in hideous dreams. He will never be able to master it, to come to terms with it.

He shouts again, hears something move behind him, turns, and fires—a burst of gunfire, and a body slumps with a strangled cry. A sudden silence follows the noise, an agonizing pause in which Ryan pulls his goggles onto his forehead and flicks on his flashlight, the beam sweeping the room and coming to rest on the figure on the floor. Attila leaps forward; his jaws snap shut. Ryan moves closer and has to repeat his command before the dog lets go of his prey. He kicks the body, turning it over to make sure it's dead. A bundle of black rags; the weather-beaten face of an old woman. A grandmother.

Ryan swears under his breath. Collateral damage, he thinks, but he's not sure: something went wrong. He is about to leave when, out the corner of his eye, he sees something at the other end of the room, hidden in the shadows. He whips round, and in the torchlight sees somebody cowering against the wall. They face each other, just a few feet apart. Ryan barks an order not to move, but the figure jumps up, making a sound a little like a sob, and Ryan catches a glimpse of something, a weapon. He doesn't stop to think, he pulls the trigger, and his face is spattered with blood as the spray of bullets lifts the enemy off the ground. Ryan stands, waiting, feeling as though he is watching the whole scene in a movie somewhere far away, detached. Then suddenly he is overcome with exhaustion and feels the sweat and the tingling in his skin that comes after an adrenaline rush.

At last, deciding the danger has passed, the Navy SEAL walks over. It is a woman. The bullets missed her face, and he can see she is a young, very beautiful girl, with a mane of dark, undulating hair. Her huge, pale eyes are wide, emphasized by thick black brows and lashes. She is barefoot, wearing a light robe like a nightshirt; next to her hand lies an ordinary kitchen knife. Beneath the bloody robe he sees that her belly is swollen; she is pregnant. The woman looks Ryan in the eye; he can tell she has just moments to live, that there is nothing he can do for her. Her bright eyes mist over. He feels his throat heave, and doubles over, trying not to retch.

It's barely three minutes since Ryan kicked down the door. He needs to keep moving, to search the rest of the village—but first he has to make sure there's nobody else in the hut. He hears Attila growl, searches for him with the flashlight, and sees the dog behind the stove, where a little opening leads into a windowless alcove with straw on the ground, a pantry of some kind. There are sides of smoked meat hanging from hooks, a sack of grain—rice or wheat—and a couple of jugs of oil, and some jars of preserved peaches—contraband, probably, as they look like the ones from the mess hall at the American base.

Attila looks ready to pounce, and Ryan orders him to keep back while he scans the rough dirt walls with his flashlight, then scuffs some of the straw away with his foot, realizing that, unlike the rest of the hut, the floor here is not dirt but wooden planks. There could be anything underneath them, he knows, from a weapons cache to a terrorist hideout; he knows he should call for backup before investigating further. But Ryan is nervous, and without quite knowing what he is doing, he gets down on one knee and pries the boards loose with his hand. He doesn't need to force it, as three planks come away together: a trapdoor.

He jumps to his feet and points his gun down into the hole, convinced there is someone hiding in there, shouts in English for them to get out—there is no response. He moves the beam of light around, finger still on the trigger. And then he sees them. First the girl, with a scarf tied round her head, squeezed tightly into a trench, gazing at him with her mother's eyes; then the baby she's holding, maybe one or two years old, sucking on a pacifier. *Fuck, fuck, fuck,* the soldier murmurs as though praying, and kneels down next to the hole, his chest so tight he can hardly breathe. He can guess that the mother hid her children, telling them to stay still, to keep quiet, while she prepared to defend them all with a blunt kitchen knife.

The Navy SEAL stays on his knees, unable to turn away from the hypnotic gaze of the solemn girl, cradling her brother to her body, protecting him. Ryan has heard all kinds of stories: the enemy is callous; they turn women into suicide bombers; they use children as human shields. By rights he should check to see whether the girl and her brother are blocking the entrance to a tunnel or a weapons store. He should make them climb out of their hideout, but he cannot. Finally he stands up, brings a gloved finger to his lips to tell the girl to keep quiet, closes the trapdoor, covers it with straw again, and, trembling, walks out.

///////////////////////

The operation in the Afghan village was a failure, though aside from the American soldiers and the Afghan survivors, nobody ever knew. If that dusty corner of the world had ever harbored a terrorist cell, somebody had warned them in time, and they had managed to dismantle their systems and disappear without a trace. No weapons or explosives were found—but the fact that only el-

derly people, women, and children were there was considered suf-
ficient to justify the CIA's suspicions. The attack left four Afghans
injured, one seriously, and two dead women in the first hut. Officially, the operation never took place: there was no investigation,
and if anybody had asked, the brotherhood of the SEALs would
have given a consistent version of events. But nobody did ask.
Ryan would have to shoulder the burden of his actions alone. His
navy buddies did not need him to explain; they took it for granted
he had done what was right in the circumstances, had fired only in
self-defense or as a precaution.

"The other men in the unit managed to take the village with
a minimum of collateral damage," Ryan confessed to Indiana. "I
was the only one who lost control."

He knew that war was chaos, that the risks were enormous,
that at any moment he could be left wounded, crippled, brain-
damaged, that he could die in combat, or be captured, tortured,
and executed. He had no illusions about war. He had not joined the
navy for the uniform, the weapons, or the glory; it was a vocation.
He was prepared to kill or be killed, was proud to serve the most
glorious nation in history; his loyalty had never wavered, nor had
he ever questioned the orders he'd received or the means employed
to secure victory. There was always the risk he might kill civilians:
that was inevitable. Half the collateral damage caused in the wars
in Iraq and Afghanistan came from terrorist attacks, the other half
from American fire. Even so, until now the missions assigned to
his team had never involved engaging with unarmed women and
children.

Ryan had no time to brood about what had happened that night
in the village, since his unit was immediately redeployed, this time
in Iraq. He pushed the events into the deepest, darkest recesses of
his mind and carried on with his life. The girl with the green eyes
did not come back to haunt him until a year later, when he came

around from the fog of anesthesia in a hospital in Germany and saw her sitting, solemn and silent, cradling her little brother, in a metal chair a few feet from his bed.

Indiana shivered under her poncho as she listened to Ryan in the chill damp of the woods that day. She did not need to ask any questions. As he told the story, she had slipped into the hut behind Ryan and Attila; after they'd left, she had crept into the hole beneath the wooden boards and stayed with the children, hugging them close until the attack was over and the women in the village came and took away the bodies of their mother and their grandmother, until they came and found them and took them from this hideout so they could begin the long process of mourning their dead. Everything happens simultaneously, she thought to herself; time does not exist, there are no limits in space, we are part of the spiritual whole that embraces all the souls of previous incarnations, the spirits of the past and of the future. We are tiny drops in one great ocean, she thought, as she often did during her meditations. She turned toward Ryan, who was sitting on a tree stump next to her and hanging his head, and saw that his cheeks were wet with the rain, or perhaps with tears. She reached out to dry them in a gesture so sad, so tender, that he heaved a mournful sigh.

"I'm fucked up, Indi, my body and my mind. I don't deserve anybody's love, much less yours."

"If that's what you believe, then you're more fucked up than you think, because the only thing that can heal you is love—but you have to let it in. You're your own worst enemy, Ryan. You need to start by forgiving yourself. If you don't do that, you'll always be trapped in the past, hounded by your memories—which are subjective."

"What I did wasn't subjective—it was real."

"You can't change the things that happened, but you can change the way you see them," Indiana said.

"I love you so much it hurts, Indi. Hurts me here, right in the center of my body, like I've got a gravestone crushing my chest."

"Love doesn't hurt, Ryan. What's crushing you are war wounds, guilt, remorse—all those things you've seen and the things you've had to do. Nobody comes through something like that unscathed."

"So what do we do now?"

"Well, first off, we're going to leave the crows to eat this chicken—it's as raw now as when we started—and then we're going to go to bed, and we're going to make love. That's always a good idea. I'm freezing, and it's starting to rain—I need to be in your arms. And then you're going to stop running, Ryan, because there are some memories you can't escape: they'll always catch up with you. You need to make peace with yourself and with the girl with green eyes. Call to her so she can come and listen to your story, ask her to forgive you."

"Call to her? How?"

"With your mind. And while you're there, you can call her mother and grandmother too, who must be wandering close by, floating among the sequoias. We don't know what that girl's called, but it would be easier to talk to her if she had a name. Let's call her Sharbat, like the girl with green eyes on the famous *National Geographic* cover."

"What can I say to her? She only exists in my head, Indi. I can't forget her."

"She can't forget you either, Ryan; that's why she comes to visit you. Imagine what that night must have been like for her, huddled in that little hole, shaking with fear before this huge alien and his rabid dog, both of them ready to kill her. Afterward she saw her mother and grandmother lying in a pool of their own blood. She'll never be able to exorcise those horrible images without your help, Ryan."

"But how can I help her?" he protested. "It happened years ago, on the other side of the world."

"Everything in the universe is connected. Forget about distances, about time, and realize that everything takes place in an unending present, in this very forest, in your memory, in your heart. Speak with Sharbat, ask her forgiveness, explain to her that you'll go and look for her and her little brother and that you'll try and help them. Tell them that if you don't find them, you'll try and help other children like them."

"I might not be able to keep a promise like that, Indi."

"If you can't, I'll go for you," she replied, and, taking his face in her hands, she kissed him on the mouth.

To evade the police, the dogfights were held in various different locations. Elsa Domínguez had alerted the deputy chief there was a fight scheduled on Presidents' Day, but she could not tell him where, so Bob Martín got one of his informants to find out, then called the San Rafael Police Department to let them know what was happening and to offer his support. The San Rafael force had enough trouble dealing with crimes committed by the gangs in the Canal district; they were not interested—though they knew the dogfighting events were hotbeds of gambling, drunken brawls, prostitution, and drug trafficking—until Bob pointed out that something like this might make the news. People cared more about animals than they did about kids. He could contact a photographer and a reporter at the local paper to go with them to the raid—an idea that came from Petra Horr, who knew the journalist and thought she might be interested to find out what went on a few blocks from her house.

Not all those who owned fighting dogs were hardened criminals. Many were black kids or unemployed Latino and Asian immigrants, trying to make a living with their champions. To register an animal, you had to pay three hundred dollars up front, but once the dog had won a few bouts, the owner could charge to enter him into fights, and make money on the betting too. The "sport," as they called this illegal activity, was so gory that the reporter struggled not to vomit when Petra showed her a video of a dogfight and photographs of animals lying dead, their entrails ripped out.

Hugo Domínguez and another boy his age had a promising rottweiler-mastiff cross weighing ninety-five pounds they had raised on raw meat with no contact with other dogs and no affection from its owners. They forced the animal to run for hours until his legs gave way, goaded him to attack, maddened him by feeding him drugs and putting chili in his rectum. The more the creature suffered, the more savage he became. His owners would trawl the poorest neighborhoods of Oakland and Richmond for strays. They would find a bitch in heat, tie her to a tree, and wait for dogs to be attracted by the smell, then catch them in a net, throw them in the trunk of their car, and take them home for the rottweiler to practice on.

That Monday, George Washington—and by extension every other US president—was celebrated with discounts in the stores, flags, at fairgrounds in the parks, and a whole day of patriotic TV programs. Being a cloudy day, it got dark early, and by seven thirty, when Bob met the San Rafael officers to prepare for the raid, it was night. Petra Horr and her reporter friend followed the convoy of five cars—three from the San Rafael department, two from San Francisco—and they drove silently, their headlights off, toward the deserted industrial district.

Bob knew his informant had been right when he saw a row of vehicles parked by a construction warehouse that looked as if it had been derelict for years. He owed most of the successes in his career to his informants—his job would be impossible without them—so he protected them and treated them well. He dispatched two officers to take the license plates of the cars—they could identify them later. The others surrounded the warehouse, covering all possible exits, with Bob leading the unit. They had hoped to spring a surprise attack, but the organizers had posted a lookout.

There were warning shouts in Spanish, and suddenly the men stampeded toward the exits, easily outnumbering the police, followed by a few screaming women, who kicked and clawed at the officers. A few seconds later, the lights of the patrol cars bathed the scene. There was an explosion of orders, insults, police batons, and even a few warning shots fired into the air. They succeeded in arresting a dozen men and five women; the rest got away.

The building was a sort of hangar, with piles of bricks and twisted metal lying around in the corners. The air was thick with cigarette smoke and sweat, with barking, blood, and excrement. A homemade "ring," about three yards wide, was surrounded with a barrier of wooden planks about four feet high, to separate the audience from the enraged animals. An ordinary rug laid on the floor of the ring to stop the dogs' feet from slipping was as blood-spattered as the wooden barrier. Several dogs that had not yet fought that night were caged or chained up, and in a corner of the warehouse, two badly injured animals lay dying. Bob phoned the Humane Society, who had a car with two veterinarians waiting nearby.

Hugo, as though he knew his luck had run out, made no attempt to escape. He'd sensed something was up when his mother and sisters begged him to stay home that night. I've got a bad feeling about it, his mother had said. But from her tone and the way she avoided his eyes, he knew it was more than a bad feeling—it was a betrayal. How much did the women in his family know? Enough to bring him down, he was sure of that. They knew about the rottweiler, and they'd found the bag with his syringes and other gear.

Assuming it was drug paraphernalia, they'd been so shocked that he had to explain that it was first aid equipment. Those who owned fighting dogs couldn't take an injured animal to a vet, who would recognize the bite marks, so they had to learn to bandage or stitch wounds, inject medications, and give antibiotics. Having invested time and money in their dogs, they did everything they could to save them. A dog that couldn't be saved was thrown into the canal or tossed onto the highway, so it would look as though it had been run over. Nobody investigated the death of a dog, even if it looked like it had been mauled to death. What his mother and sisters did not know was that in turning him over to the police, they were condemning him—and themselves—to death, if the Sureños or the crazy Koreans who ran the dogfight circuit ever found him. And the circuit bosses found out about everything.

The deputy chief found Hugo Domínguez crouching in a corner behind a sack of gravel, waiting. He had decided that the best way to divert suspicion from himself and his family was to let himself be arrested. Prison was safer than the street: he could blend in with the other Latinos in San Quentin. He wouldn't be the first Sureño to be banged up there. A deportation order would be waiting for him after he did his time. And what could he do in a hostile, unfamiliar country like Guatemala? Join another gang, of course: what else?

"Which one's your dog, Hugo?" Bob asked, dazzling the boy with the beam of his flashlight.

The kid pointed to one of the chained dogs, a stocky, battle-scarred animal with a snout that looked as if it had been burned.

"The black one?"

"Yeah."

"Two weeks ago, on Tuesday, February seventh, this dog won a big fight. You and the Sureños each pocketed two thousand dollars, after the Koreans took their cut."

"Don't know nothing about that."

"I don't need you to confess. Dogfighting is a disgusting practice, Hugo, but in your case it also gives you an alibi that gets you out of the frame for something much more serious: the murder of Rachel Rosen. Turn around and hold out your hands." Bob had the handcuffs ready.

"Tell my mom I'm never going to forgive her," the kid said, crying tears of rage.

"Your mother had nothing to do with this, you little thug. When she finds out, it's going to break the poor woman's heart."

Friday, 24

*C*eleste Roko's house was one of Haight-Ashbury's "Painted Ladies," the 48,000 Victorian and Edwardian houses that sprouted up in San Francisco between 1849 and 1915, some brought from England and assembled like jigsaw puzzles. Hers was a relic: more than a hundred years old, it had been built shortly after the 1906 earthquake and had seen various stages of glory and decline. During both world wars it had suffered the indignity of being painted battleship gray with navy-surplus paint. But in 1970 it had been renovated, the foundations reinforced with concrete, and painted in four colors: Prussian blue background, sky blue and turquoise decorative reliefs, and white window and door frames. The house—which was dark and cramped inside, a veritable labyrinth of tiny rooms and steep staircases—had recently been valued at $2 million, as it was part of the city's heritage and a tourist attraction. Celeste had bought it for much less than that, on the strength of a few well-placed Wall–Street investments based on astrological predictions.

Indiana climbed the fifteen steps and rang the bell, an interminable peal of Viennese bells, and her daughter's godmother quickly came to the door. Celeste had been chosen as Amanda's godmother because of her friendship with Encarnación Martín, which stretched back many years, and because she was still a practicing Catholic, even though the Vatican condemned divination. Celeste's Croatian grandparents had met and married on the ship that brought them to Ellis Island in late the 1800s. The couple settled in Chicago, rightly called Croatia's second capital because of the large number of emigrants from that country who lived there. The family started out working on construction sites and in clothes factories, and soon spread to other states. Each branch of the family prospered— especially the one that went to California and made its fortune in grocery stores. Celeste's father had been the first in the family to go to college. She followed him, getting a degree in psychology and working in that field for a short time before she discovered that astrology was a faster and more effective way of helping clients. The combination of her astrological and psychological knowledge made her so successful that clients, prepared to wait months for a consultation, soon besieged her. It was then that she had the idea of the TV show that had now been on air for fifteen years. Later, with the help of a young team, she started to advertise her services on the Internet. She would appear onscreen in an impeccably tailored dark-blue skirt, a silk blouse, a necklace of pearls the size of turtle's eggs, her blond hair tied in an elegant bun at her neck, and wearing cat's-eye glasses that had not been seen since the 1950s. In public she dressed like a faintly old-fashioned Jungian analyst, but at home she wore kimonos she bought in Berkeley. The robes, with their T shape and baggy sleeves, did little to flatter her Croatian body, but she wore them with a certain flair.

Indiana followed Celeste up a flight of stairs to a hexagonal room and sat waiting for the tea that her hostess had insisted on bringing.

She found the atmosphere of the creaking old house, with its porcelain lamps and yellow parchment screens, oppressive; the heating was too high, and it smelled of damp rugs and wilting flowers. She had a faint sense that the ghosts of previous inhabitants might appear through the walls, or eavesdrop on conversations.

A few minutes later Celeste came back from the kitchen, kimono sleeves fluttering like flags in the wind, bearing a tray laden with two china cups and a black iron teapot. She lifted the lid of the teapot so Indiana could take in the aroma of her French Marco Polo tea—a blend of fruit and flowers, one of the luxuries that compensated for her life as a single woman. She served the brew, then settled in one of the armchairs, crossing her legs like a fakir.

Indiana blew on the hot tea and confessed her worries. Their conversations were based on years of friendship and astral readings, and Indiana did not need to go into much detail; Celeste was already aware of what had happened with Alan Keller. Indiana had called on the phone the day after she got the magazine that was to end four happy, loving years. Worried about Indiana ending up single in her mid-thirties, Celeste had downplayed the incident at the time, thinking that her own life would be happier with Blake Jackson in it; it was a shame that the man seemed determined to remain a widower. Youth passes quickly, she said, and there is nothing as tedious as growing old alone. But for Indiana, infidelity was more than enough of a reason to break up with her partner.

At Indiana's request, Celeste had now drawn up Ryan's astral chart, though she had never met the man.

"This Miller's the masculine type, right?"

"Right."

"And yet eight of his planets are in the feminine quadrants."

"You're not saying he's gay!" Indiana exclaimed.

Celeste explained that astrology could not predict a person's sexual preference, only his destiny and character—and Ryan's character showed strong feminine traits. He was caring, loving, and protective—you could almost say maternal—all of which made an ideal grounding for a doctor or a teacher; but he was cursed with a "hero complex," and there were serious anomalies in his astral chart. This was why he had gone against the dictates not only of the stars but of his own nature, and was forever torn between emotions and actions. Celeste spoke at length about his overbearing father and depressive mother; his need to prove his manliness and his courage; his ability to surround himself with fiercely loyal friends; his tendency toward addiction and impulsive behavior. She even pointed out on the chart a decisive moment in his life around 2006. She did not mention that he had been a soldier, nor that he had lost a leg and almost died.

"You're in love with him," Celeste concluded. Indiana laughed.

"Is that what the planets say?"

"It's what I say."

"I don't know about 'in love,' but I find him very attractive. He's a great friend—but it's better not to think about love, it gets way too complicated. And the truth is, Celeste, I'm complicated too."

"If you're clinging to him just to forget about Alan Keller, you're going to break the poor man's heart in two."

"He's had a lot of bad stuff happen to him—he's a ball of regrets, blame, aggression . . . and bad memories and nightmares. Ryan isn't at home in his own body."

"What's he like in bed?"

"Good, but he could be much better, and compared to Alan he comes up short."

"Short, huh?" asked Madame Roko.

"Hey, don't be crude! What I mean is, Alan knows me, he knows how to treat me—he's romantic, imaginative, and refined."

"A person can learn all that. This Miller, he got a sense of humor?"

"Kind of."

"What a shame, Indiana. That can't be learned."

They drank a few more cups of tea, and agreed that a comparison of Indiana's and Ryan's star charts would probably clear a few things up. Before seeing her out, Celeste gave Indiana the address of the karma-cleansing monk.

*O*nce a year, *Amanda would* venture into the kitchen with a nobler mission than making her usual cup of hot chocolate in the microwave: she would set about making a traditional *dulce de leche* cake for her grandmother Encarnación's birthday. The recipe—a veritable time bomb of cholesterol—was her only culinary achievement, although much of the hard work— the kneading and baking of the thin layers of puff pastry—fell to Elsa Domínguez. All Amanda had to do was boil four cups of condensed milk on the stove to make the *dulce de leche*, stick the cake layers together, and poke little candles into the finished product.

Encarnación Martín, who still wore bright red lipstick and dyed her hair jet black, had been turning fifty-five every year for the past decade. This meant she had given birth to her first child at the age of nine, but nobody was cruel enough to keep a precise count. The age of Encarnación's mother was something else that no one could calculate: as sturdy as an oak tree, with her hair in a tight bun and eagle eyes that could see into the future, Amanda's great-grandmother was impervious to the passage of time. Encarnación always celebrated her birthday the last weekend of February, with a party at the Loco Latino, a salsa and samba dance hall that would close to the public to make room for the Martín family's guests. The party always climaxed with the arrival of a group of ancient mariachis, who long ago had played with Encarnación's late husband, José Manuel Martín. Encarnación would dance until there was not a single man left standing, while the great-grandmother surveyed the scene from a sort of raised throne, making sure that nobody, however drunk, behaved indecently. And the family certainly owed her their respect: it was thanks to the tortilla factory she had founded in 1972 that they had prospered, and that generations of immigrant workers from Mexico and Central America had survived.

The almost indestructible, bulletproof caramel cake weighed four kilos (not counting the tray) and was large enough to feed ninety people, cut into paper-thin strips. Frozen, it would last several months. Even though she didn't eat sweet things, Encarnación would gush with gratitude because the cake was a gift from her favorite grandchild—the apple of her eye, her little angel, the jewel of her twilight years, as she called Amanda in her more inspired moments. While she forgot her grandsons' names, she had collected Amanda's baby teeth, or locks of her hair. Nothing made the matriarch happier than to see her seven grandchildren all together with her sons and daughters and their partners. She also invited Blake Jackson, for whom she had a soft spot. He was the only man who might have taken José Manuel Martín's place in her widow's heart, but sadly he was an in-law. Was that incest, or simply sin? She couldn't say. She had forbidden Bob to bring any of those bimbos he dated, because in the eyes of God he was still married to Indiana, and he would remain so until he got an annulment from the Vatican.

"So you didn't bring the Pole?" Amanda whispered to her father as they arrived at Loco Latino.

The succession of Mexican dishes—uncontaminated by any North-American influence—began arriving early, and guests were still eating and dancing at midnight. Amanda, who by now was bored with talking to her cousins, whom she considered philistines, dragged her father off the dance floor, got her grandfather up from his table, and took them to one side.

"We're making real progress in Ripper, Dad, investigating the crimes."

"What nonsense have you come up with now, Amanda?"

"It's not nonsense. Ripper's inspired by one of the great puzzles in the history of crime: Jack the Ripper, the legendary murderer who terrorized London neighborhoods in 1888. There are more than a hundred theories about the Ripper's identity—including one that he was a member of the royal family."

"What has any of this got to do with me?" her father asked her, sweating from all the tequila and dancing.

"Nothing—I'm not talking about Jack the Ripper, I'm talking about the San Francisco Ripper. Me and the other players have been piecing together the facts. What do you think?"

"I think it's a terrible idea, Amanda, as I've told you before. Why don't you just leave things to the Personal Crimes Division?"

"Because your department is doing nothing about it, Dad! I'm convinced these murders are the work of a serial killer," Amanda insisted. She'd spent her midterm break going through her files with a fine-tooth comb and messaging with the other players.

"So what evidence have you come up with, Little Miss Ripper?"

"Just look at the coincidences. Five victims: Ed Staton, Michael and Doris Constante, Richard Ashton, and Rachel Rosen. All murdered in San Francisco; none of the bodies showed signs of struggle; in each case the killer entered without forcing any locks, which means he had easy access, knew how to pick locks, and possibly knew the victims themselves—he certainly knew their habits. He gave himself enough time to plan and execute each murder perfectly. Each time, he had brought the murder weapon with him: a pistol, a baseball bat, two syringes of heroin, a Taser—possibly two—and a length of fishing wire."

"How did you know about the fishing wire?"

"From Ruth Rosen's preliminary autopsy report, which Kabel read. He also looked through Ingrid Dunn's report on Ed Staton, the guard they shot in the school—remember him?"

"Of course I do."

"D'you know why he didn't defend himself and why he was on his knees before the coup de grâce was delivered?"

"No, but I'll bet you do."

"The Ripper players think the killer used the Taser he killed Richard Ashton with to stun Ed Staton, and before he could get up, the killer shot him."

"That's not bad, sweetheart," the deputy chief admitted.

"How long does a Taser paralyze someone for?" Amanda asked.

"Depends. A guy Staton's size . . . could be three or four minutes."

"More than enough time to kill him. Would Staton have been conscious at that point?"

"Sure, but pretty confused. Why?"

"Nothing. . . . Just, Abatha, the psychic in Ripper, says the killer always leaves enough time so he can talk to his victims. She thinks he's got something important to tell them. What do you think, Dad?"

"It's possible. None of the victims was killed from behind or taken by surprise."

"And shoving the handle of the baseball bat up his . . . you know what I mean—he did that after Staton died. That's important,

Dad, because it's something else all the murders have in common. The killer didn't torture the victims while they were alive, he desecrated their bodies: Staton with the baseball bat, the Constantes branded like cattle, Ashton with the swastika carved into him, and Rosen strung up like a convict."

"Listen, don't get ahead of yourself. The Rosen autopsy isn't finished."

"Okay, so there are details still to come, but that much we already know. There are differences between the crimes, but the similarities point to a single killer. It was Kabel who spotted that the victims were being desecrated postmortem." Amanda emphasized the technical term she had recently learned from a detective novel.

"That's true," Blake said. "It's like Amanda says: the killer didn't want to brutalize the victims, he wanted to leave a message.

"Do you know Rachel Rosen's time of death?" Amanda asked her father.

"The body had been hanging there for a couple of days. We know she died on Tuesday night, but we don't know exactly what time."

"So it looks like all the crimes took place around midnight. The Ripper players are looking for similar cases over the past ten years."

"Why ten years?" asked the deputy chief.

"You got to set some kind of cutoff, Dad. Sherlock Holmes—the kid I play Ripper with, I mean, not the Conan Doyle character—anyway, he says studying old cases would be a waste of time. Because if it's a serial killer, like we think it is, and he fits the usual profile, he's less than thirty-five years old."

"Well, we can't be certain it is a serial killer, and if it is, he's not your typical case," the deputy chief replied. "There are no common factors linking the victims."

"I'm convinced there have to be. Instead of investigating the cases separately, look for something they all have in common, Dad. Then we'll find the motive. The motive's the first stage of any investigation, and in this case it's not money, like it usually is."

"Thanks, Amanda. Just what would the homicide detail do without your valuable help?"

"Laugh if you want to, but I'm telling you we're taking it all pretty seriously in Ripper. You're going to be embarrassed as hell when we solve the crimes before you do."

Tuesday, 28

*A*lan Keller's life had changed on the day he had been summoned to his brother's office and stripped of his privileges. Mark and Lucille Keller took over his debts to the IRS and began the process of selling the Woodside house. There was no need to throw him out of the tumbledown mansion. He couldn't wait to leave: for years he had felt like a prisoner there. In less than three days he had taken his clothes, his books, his CDs, a few pieces of antique furniture, and his art collection and moved to the Napa vineyard. He thought of it as a temporary solution; Mark had had his eye on the vineyard for some time and would take it from him sooner or later—unless something very unexpected happened, like Philip and Flora Keller both dying at once, for example, but that was only the remotest possibility. Keller's parents were not about to do anybody the favor of dying, much less Alan. He resolved to enjoy his stay at the vineyard while he could, without worrying too much about the future. Unlike the paintings, the jades, the porcelains, and the smuggled Inca treasures, it was the one possession that he really wanted to keep.

That week in February it was fifteen degrees warmer in Napa than in San Francisco. The days were balmy and the nights chilly; magnificent clouds glided across a watercolor sky. The air smelled of the soft, sleeping earth, where the vines were getting ready to burst with spring buds, and the fields were streaked with the bright yellow of wild mustard. Keller knew nothing about farming or winemaking, but he had the passion of a landowner: he loved his estate, and would stroll between the neat rows of vines, study the shrubbery, gather bunches of wildflowers. He would survey the contents of his little cellar, count the cases and the bottles, and then count them again. He talked to the few workers who were out pruning, itinerant Mexican laborers who had lived off the land for generations; their movements were quick, precise, and graceful. They knew exactly what to prune and what to let grow.

Alan would have given his all to save this blessed place, but the money he'd raise from the sale of his artworks and antiques would scarcely cover his credit-card debts, the interest on which had sky-rocketed. It would be impossible to keep the vineyard from his brother's greedy clutches: when Mark got an idea into his head, he pursued it with a frightening determination. When she realized the dire straits he was in, Geneviève van Houte offered to find some venture capitalists who could turn the vineyard into a profitable business, but Mark preferred to relinquish it to his brother, at least it would stay in the family and not fall into the hands of strangers. He wondered what he would do after he lost the place, where he would live. He was sick of San Francisco: the same endless round of parties, the same faces, the same caustic gossip and banal con-versations. There was nothing to tie him to that city anymore ex-cept its cultural life, something he was not about to give up. He fantasized about living in a modest house in one of the quiet towns in Napa Valley, like St. Helena, and working—although the idea of looking for his first job at fifty-five was laughable. What kind of work would he do, exactly? His education and sophistication might be praised in the salons, but they would be of little use when it came to making a living. He was utterly incapable of keeping to a timetable or taking orders: he had an "authority issue," as he would say in passing when the topic came up.

"Marry me, Alan," Geneviève said on the phone one day. "At my age, having a husband looks a hell of a lot better than a series of gigolos," she added, chuckling.

"Would this be an open marriage, or monogamous?" Alan asked, thinking about Indiana.

"Polygamous, obviously!"

It was as quiet as a convent at Alan's country retreat, with its thick, pumpkin-colored walls and tiled floors. Here, he could sleep without the need for pills; he had time to turn ideas over slowly, instead of being trapped in a winding, chaotic maze of thoughts. Sitting in a wicker armchair on the covered veranda, staring out over the hills and the vineyards that stretched into the distance, a drink in one hand and María, the maid's dog, at his feet, Alan made the most important decision of his life. It was the one that for weeks on end had plagued him when he was awake, and that he had dreamed of while he slept, his intellect waging war with his emotions. He dialed Indiana's number a few times and got no answer: he thought she must have lost her cell phone for the third time in six months. He finished his drink and told María he was going into the city.

An hour and twenty minutes later, Alan was parking his Lexus in the garage under Union Square and walking the half block to the Bulgari store. He didn't know what people saw in expensive jewelry: it had to be kept locked in a safe, and wearing it made any woman look ten years older. Geneviève van Houte bought jewelry as an investment, believing that when the next global crisis came, gold and diamonds would be the only thing to retain their value. But she never wore them: they were locked away in a Swiss bank vault, while she wore paste copies. Once he had gone with her to the Bulgari store on Fifth Avenue in Manhattan and admired the designs, the audacious combinations of stones, and the quality of the craftsmanship; but he had never been into the San Francisco branch. The security guard—obviously an expert in determining a customer's social class—ushered him in, not batting an eye at Alan's disheveled clothes and boots encrusted with dried mud. A woman dressed in black, with white hair and professional makeup, was there to serve him.

"I need a memorable ring," he told her, without so much as glancing at the display cases.

"Diamonds?"

"No diamonds. This woman thinks they're bought with African blood."

"All our jewels are of certified provenance."

"Try explaining that to her."

Just as the security guard had done before her, the sales adviser quickly divined her client's particular brand of sophistication. She asked him to wait a moment and disappeared, returning a few moments later with a black tray lined in white silk. On it was a ring with an oval stone, a beautifully understated piece that reminded him of the simple jewels of the Roman Empire.

"This is from an antique collection—you won't find anything like it in contemporary ranges. It's a Brazilian aquamarine—a cabochon, which is very unusual for the stone, set in twenty-four-karat mat gold. As you can imagine, sir, we have more expensive gems than this one, but it's the most striking item I can show you today."

Alan could feel himself about to take the plunge and give in to the sort of extravagance that his brother Mark would crucify him for; but once his collector's eye had fallen on the exquisite piece, he did not need to look at any others. One of his Boteros was about to be sold in New York, and though he knew the money should go to shoring up his debt, he decided that "the heart has its reasons."

"You're right, it is . . . extraordinary. I'll take it, although it's probably too expensive for a washed-up playboy like me and too sophisticated for a woman who wouldn't know if it came from a jeweler's or a joke shop."

"If you wish, sir, you can pay in installments——"

"I need it right now," Alan interrupted. "That's what credit cards are for, right?" He smiled his warmest smile.

As he had time to spare and there were no taxis in sight, he walked to North Beach, a cool breeze in his face and a spring in his step. He prayed that Danny D'Angelo would not be working when he went into the Café Rossini, but there he was, coming out to greet him with effusive enthusiasm and once again apologizing for vomiting in his Lexus.

"Forget about it, Danny, that was last year," said Alan, trying to wriggle out of the man's embrace.

"Order whatever you like, Mr. Keller, it's on me," Danny declared, almost shouting. "How can I ever repay what you've done for me?"

"You can start right now, Danny, by ducking out of here a few minutes and going over to see Indiana. I think she lost her cell phone again. Tell her somebody's asking for her, but don't tell her it's me."

Danny was not a man to harbor a grudge: he had forgiven Indiana for the furor at the Narcissus Club because two days afterward she had showed up, Ryan Miller in tow, to apologize for ruining his celebration. He forgave the Navy SEAL, too, but couldn't resist an opportunity to needle him with the fact that homophobia usually masks our fear of finding homosexuality in ourselves, and that military camaraderie is riddled with homoerotic overtones. They live together, Danny teased, they're always horsing around, they're united by loyalty, by love, and they champion masculinity to the exclusion of women. On any other day Ryan would have punched the man for casting doubt on his manhood, but this time —still bruised from the fight in the club and humbled by the Alcoholics Anonymous meeting—he accepted the telling-off.

Danny gave Alan a conspiratorial wink and slipped off to the Holistic Clinic. He soon returned, reporting that Indiana would be along as soon as she could finish with her last patient. He served Alan an Irish coffee and a giant sandwich that he hadn't ordered but that he attacked hungrily. Twenty minutes later, when Alan saw Indiana cross the street, her hair tied up and wearing her work smock and clogs, he was so overcome with feeling that he was rooted to the seat. She was so much more beautiful than he had remembered—flushed and radiant, like an early breath of spring. When she came in and saw him, she hesitated, ready to leave again, but Danny reeled her in and steered her toward Alan, who by then had managed to get to his feet. Danny persuaded Indiana to sit down, and then retreated far enough to give them a feeling of privacy, but not so far that he couldn't hear what they were saying.

"How you doing, Alan? You look thin," she said neutrally by way of greeting.

"I've been sick, but now I feel better than ever."

Just then Gary, Indiana's last patient on a Tuesday, trailed in after her, hoping to buy her dinner. Seeing her with another man, he hung back, disconcerted. Danny made the most of this hesitation to steer him toward another table, whispering that he should leave them alone; this had "date" written all over it.

"What can I do for you, Alan?" Indiana asked.

"A lot. Like change my life. You can transform me, turn me inside out like an old sock."

She gave him a distrustful sideways glance while he dug around for the Bulgari box, which seemed to have become lost in his pocket. He found it eventually and presented it to her with all the awkwardness of a schoolboy.

"Will you marry a poor old man, Indi?" he asked her, not recognizing his own voice. Then he told her everything that had happened recently, talking up a storm and taking big gulps of air as he spoke. He was happy to have lost everything—perhaps "everything" was an exaggeration, he still had enough, he was not about to go hungry, but he was living through the most serious crisis of his life. He remembered the Chinese saying, "Crisis = Danger + Opportunity"; well, this was his big opportunity to start over, and to do it with her, his one true love. How had he not realized that the moment he met her? He was a fool, and he couldn't carry on like this. He was sick to death of his life, of himself, his selfishness and his wariness, and he was determined to change—he promised her that—but he needed her help, he couldn't do it alone; they had both invested four years in their relationship, they could hardly let it fall apart over some misunderstanding. He talked about the house he planned to buy in St. Helena, near the Calistoga springs: it would be an ideal place for her aromatherapy work. They would lead an idyllic existence and breed dogs—which made a lot more sense than breeding horses. And he went on unburdening himself to her, trying to tempt her with all the things they could do together, begging for her forgiveness, and imploring her to marry him tomorrow.

Overwhelmed by it all, Indiana reached across the table and put a finger on Alan's lips.

"Are you sure, Alan?"

"I've never been so sure of anything in my life!"

"Well, I'm not. A month ago I would've said yes straight away, but now I've got serious doubts. Things have happened to me that—"

"Me too!" he interrupted. "Something's opened up inside me, in my heart. Some huge, crazy force has taken over. It's impossible to explain how I feel—I'm full of energy, I can overcome any obstacle. I'm going to start straight away, and come out of this strong. I feel more alive than ever! And I can't go back now, Indi. This is the first day of my new life."

"I can never tell when you're being serious, Alan."

"I couldn't be more serious. For once I'm not being ironic, Indi: I might be talking like a cheap romance novel, but that's how I feel. I adore you, did you know that? There's no other love in my life. Geneviève means nothing to me, I swear to you."

"This isn't about her, it's about us. What do we have in common, Alan?"

"Love, what else!"

"I'm going to need some time."

"How much? I haven't got a whole lot: I'm fifty-five. But if that's what you want, I can wait. Will a day do it? Two days? Please, just give me another chance. You won't regret it. We can go to Napa—it's still mine, though not for much longer. Close your treatment room for a few days and come with me."

"And what about my patients?"

"For God's sake, Indi, nobody's going to die for lack of a magnet or two and a bit of pollen!" he replied. "I'm sorry. I didn't mean to insult you, I know your work's very important. But can't you even take a couple days' vacation? I'm going to make you fall in love with me so hard, Indi, that you're going to be begging me to marry you." Alan smiled.

"Well, if we get that far, you can give this to me then," Indiana said, handing him back the Bulgari box without opening it.

March

Friday, 2

*A*manda *sat waiting for her* father in the little cubicle that
belonged to his assistant. The walls were plastered with
photos of Petra Horr in her white *keikogi* and black belt at martial
arts tournaments. Petra was five feet tall and weighed 105 pounds,
but she could lift and throw a man twice her size. This particular skill had not been of much use to her since she started working in homicide, but it had been essential for defending herself in
the prison yard, where the fights were as violent as they were in
the men's jails. When she was twenty, after finishing the sentence
handed to her by Rachel Rosen, she spent the next thirty months
traveling the country on a motorcycle. It was on those interminable roads that she gave up trying to rescue some dream from
her childhood of neglect and her adolescence spent running with
gangs. The only consistent thing in her itinerant life was martial
arts, which she used to protect herself and to earn her bread.

Whenever she arrived in a town, Petra would look for a bar—
there would always be one, no matter how remote and run-down the

place—and sit at the counter, nursing a single beer. Soon enough, men would approach her with only one thing on their minds, and—unless they were truly irresistible, which was rare—she would brush them off, telling them she was a lesbian, then challenge the biggest of them to a bare-knuckle fight. She was clear that there was only one rule: anything was permitted, except weapons of any kind. The guys would take bets, go out into a yard or some quiet alleyway, and form a circle; with the sound of their booming laughter in her ears, Petra would flex her little girl's arms and legs and tell the man he could have the first punch. The man would smile and make a few friendly, harmless feints before realizing that Petra was slipping out of his grasp like a weasel at every turn, and making a fool of him. Then, goaded by the jeering of the crowd, he would go for her, ready to destroy her with a single punch. As Petra wanted to give a good, honest show and not let her audience down, she liked to play the toreador and taunt her opponent for a while, dodging his blows, wearing him down, until eventually, when she had him panting with rage, she would use the man's weight and momentum to get him in one of her holds and pin him to the ground. To gasps of respectful admiration, she would collect her winnings, pull on her jacket and her helmet, and speed off on her motorcycle before her opponent could recover from the humiliation and decide to come after her. She could earn two or three hundred dollars from a single fight, enough to last her a few weeks.

She finally arrived back in San Francisco with a brand-new, sweet-natured, handsome drug addict of a husband on the back of her motorbike. They moved into a seedy hostel, and Petra took whatever work she could find, while her husband spent her earnings and played guitar in the park. She was twenty-four when he left her, and twenty-five when she got a secretarial job in the police department by using the technique she'd perfected on the road.

At the Camelot, where guys from the department liked to relax over a couple of drinks after work, the regulars were so regular that a stranger was instantly the center of attention—especially a stranger like Petra Horr, who strode in as though she owned the place. The barman thought she was underage, and asked to see ID before serving her a beer. Petra took her drink and went to face Bob and the others, who were sizing her up. "What y'all lookin' at? Have I got something you want to buy?" she said, and found herself challenging the strongest of them to a fight. By general consensus, that turned out to be Bob Martín. On this occasion she thought it best that the policemen not risk their badges by placing illegal bets, so she gave her little demonstration out of pure sporting spirit. Instead of resenting his defeat and the jeers of his colleagues, Bob got up off the ground, brushed himself off, straightened his hair, congratulated the girl with a sincere handshake, and offered her a job. And so began Petra Horr's life in an office chair.

"Is Dad dating Ayani?" Amanda asked Petra.

"What do I know? Ask him."

"He says no, but I've seen the way his eyes twinkle when he mentions her. I like Ayani a lot more than the Polish woman, though I don't think she'd make much of a stepmother. Have you met her?"

"She came in once to give her first statement. She's pretty, that's for sure, but I don't know what your dad would want with her. Ayani's a complicated woman with expensive tastes. Your dad needs someone straightforward who loves him and doesn't give him any trouble."

"Like you?"

"Don't be sassy. My relationship with the deputy chief is purely professional."

"Well, that sucks! I wouldn't mind having you as a stepmother, Petra. Anyway, did you talk to Ingrid Dunn yet?"

"Yeah, but no dice—your dad would kill her if she allowed you to watch an autopsy."

"Who says he needs to find out?"

"Don't drag me into this, girl. Why don't you talk to Ingrid yourself?"

"Well, you could at least get me copies of the Ashton and Rosen autopsy reports."

"Your grandpa's already seen them."

"He misses all the important stuff! I'd really rather look over them myself. Do you know if they're going to run DNA tests?"

"Only on Ashton. If their kids can prove that Ayani offed her husband, they could claim the inheritance. As for Judge Rosen, turns out she had three hundred thousand dollars in savings, and she's leaving it to the Guardian Angels, not her only son."

"Seems pretty normal a judge would want to support a crime-prevention group," Amanda mused.

"Maybe, but the son was pretty disappointed. Losing his inheritance has hit him harder than losing his mother. He's got an alibi—we already checked it out—he spent the week away on a business trip."

"Maybe he hired a hit man to get rid of her. They got on badly, right?"

"That kind of thing might happen in Italy, honey, but here in California people don't put a hit on their mom just because they don't get along. By the way, the blowtorch marks on the Constantes? They didn't look like anything at first, but in the photos you can see that there are some letters."

"Which letters?"

"*F* and *A*. We still don't know what they mean."

"Well, it's got to mean something, Petra. With every murder, the killer's left some kind of sign or message. I said this to my dad like ten days ago, but he never listens to me: we're dealing with a serial killer."

"Oh, he listens to you, babe. Right now he's got the whole department looking for anything to connect the crimes."

Sunday, 4

On the first Sunday of every month—even if it was a weekend she was supposed to spend with her father—Amanda would spend an hour dealing with her mother's crude accounting. Indiana's laptop was six years old, and badly in need of being replaced, but she saw it as a talisman and intended to carry on using it until it died of natural causes—even though it had done some disturbing things lately. At random moments, images of violent sex —a lot of bare flesh, struggling, and pain—would suddenly flash up on her screen. Indiana would immediately close the disturbing images, but they reappeared so often that she ended up giving a name to the pervert that lived in her hard drive, or who crawled through the window and tampered with her computer. She called him the Marquis de Sade.

Amanda, who had been managing Indiana's accounts with a bank manager's precision since the age of twelve, was the first to realize that her mother's income was scarcely enough to keep a nun. Helping and healing others was a slow process that drained Indiana's energy and resources, but she would not change her job for the world. In fact, she saw it less as a job than as a sort of spiritual mission. Her focus was on the well-being of her patients, not her salary. She could live on very little; she'd never been materialistic. She measured happiness using a simple equation: one good day plus another good day equals a good life. Her daughter had given up telling her she should jack up her prices—an illegal immigrant picking oranges earned more per hour than she did—when she finally understood that her mother had received a divine mandate to heal the suffering of others and had to obey it. In practical terms, this meant she would always be poor—unless she found a benefactor or married someone rich, like Keller. Amanda preferred the idea of a life of poverty.

Although she did not believe in prayer as an effective solution to practical problems, Amanda had appealed to her grandmother Encarnación—who was in direct contact with Saint Jude—to get Keller out of her mother's life. Saint Jude worked miracles for a reasonable price, payable in cash at the shrine on Bush Street or by a check in the mail. Scarcely had Doña Encarnación made the request when the magazine article that was to cause Indiana so much heartache appeared. Amanda thought she was rid of the man for good, that he would be replaced by Ryan Miller, but her hopes had been dashed; Indiana had gone off to Napa with her old lover. Her grandmother would have to restart negotiations with the saint.

To Doña Encarnación's mind, divorce was a sin, and in the case of Indiana and her son Bob, an unnecessary one, since with a little goodwill they could live together as God intended. They must surely love each other deep down, since neither had remarried; she hoped they would soon accept this clear evidence and get back together. She did not like the fact that Bob had girlfriends of dubious virtue—men are imperfect creatures—but she would not tolerate Indiana risking her reputation, and her place in heaven, with extramarital affairs. For years Indiana had conspired to hide Alan Keller's existence from Encarnación, until Amanda, in a fit of unwarranted honesty, told her all about it. Encarnación had sulked for several weeks, until finally her heart won out over her Catholic scruples and she welcomed Indiana back into the fold—as she pointed out, to err is human, to forgive divine. She was fond of her daughter-in-law, even though many areas of this young woman's life showed room for improvement: not simply her manner of raising Amanda, her clothes, and her hairstyle, but also her work, which Encarnación considered little more than pagan ritual.

Even Indiana's taste in interior decor was suspect. Instead of tasteful furniture, Indiana had filled her apartment with enormous tables, shelves, and cupboards lined with test tubes, weights, funnels, droppers, and hundreds of glass bottles of different sizes in which she kept all manner of strange substances, some from dangerous countries like Iran and China. Her home looked for all the world like one of those secret laboratories where they make drugs you see on television. On more than one occasion the police had come knocking on Indiana's door, alarmed by the perfumed miasma that drifted from the apartment as though it were a shrine. Amanda asked the ever obliging Blake Jackson to put rails on all the shelves so that, in the event of an earthquake, the bottles of essential oils would not spill everywhere, poisoning her mother and probably several of the neighbors. The girl had just read a book of erotic stories in which a fifteenth-century Japanese courtesan poisoned an unfaithful lover using perfume. Doña Encarnación thought somebody should keep a closer eye on her granddaughter's reading habits.

Amanda was thankful that the gift of healing was not hereditary. She had other plans for her future. She wanted to study nuclear physics, or something like that, to have a successful career, live a charmed life, and along the way fulfill her moral duty by taking care of her mother and grandfather, who, according to her calculations, would by then be a couple of geriatrics of forty and seventy.

Her mother spent little, traveled everywhere by bicycle, cut her own hair twice a year with kitchen scissors, and wore secondhand clothes, because, as she said, nobody noticed what she wore, although that wasn't true—Alan Keller noticed, and it mattered to him. Despite her thriftiness, Indiana struggled to make her money last the month, and often had to ask her father or her ex-husband to bail her out. Since they were family, Amanda considered this normal, but she was shocked to discover that Ryan Miller had also come to Indiana's rescue a number of times. Miller, but never Keller: her mother said that a lover, however generous, would always end up calling in the debt with favors.

The only remotely profitable part of Indiana's business was aromatherapy. She had made a name for herself with the essential oils, which she bought in bulk and poured out into small, lovingly labeled bottles to sell in California and elsewhere. Amanda helped her package them, and promoted them online. For Indiana, aromatherapy was a fine art that had to be practiced with care, studying the individual patient's needs to determine the best combination of oils in each case; but Amanda had explained to her that, from an economic point of view, such attention to detail was unsustainable. It had been Amanda's idea to make some money from the aromatherapy in hotels and luxury spas to help fund the expensive raw materials. Those establishments would buy the most popular oils and apply them at random, a drop here and a drop there, as though they were perfume, without taking the slightest precautions or reading the instructions, despite Indiana's warnings that they could be harmful if used wrongly—if an epileptic were exposed to fennel and aniseed, for example, or a nymphomaniac to sandalwood and jasmine. Her daughter told her she had nothing to worry about: epileptics and nymphomaniacs made up a negligible percentage of the population.

Amanda could name all of her mother's essential oils, but their properties didn't interest her: aromatherapy was an esoteric art form, and she preferred an exact science. The way she saw it, there was no proof that patchouli stoked romantic feelings or that geranium oil sparked creativity—as certain ancient Oriental texts, of dubious authenticity, claimed. Neroli did not soothe her father's anger, nor lavender oil enhance her mother's common sense, as they were supposed to. Amanda had used lemon balm for her shyness, with no noticeable effect, and sage oil for her period pains, which was only effective in combination with painkillers from her grandfather's pharmacy. Amanda liked to live in a structured world with clearly defined rules, and aromatherapy, like all her mother's treatments, only made it more baffling and mysterious.

She had finished checking the accounts and was packing to go back to school when Indiana arrived home with a small bag of dirty laundry and a slight tan from the pale but constant sunshine of Napa Valley in winter. Amanda greeted her mother with a long face.

"What kind of time do you call this, Mom!"

"I'm sorry, honey, I wanted to be here when you arrived, but we got held up in traffic. I was exhausted—I needed a couple days' vacation. How are the accounts looking? I bet you've got bad news for me, as usual. . . . Let's go to the kitchen and talk awhile—I'm going to make some tea. It's still early—your grandpa won't be taking you to school till five."

She tried to kiss Amanda, but the girl dodged her and sat down on the floor to call her grandfather's cell phone and tell him to hurry and come home. Indiana sat down beside her, waited for her to finish speaking, and took her face in both hands.

"Look at me, Amanda. You can't go back to school angry with

me—we need to talk. I called you on Wednesday to tell you that Alan and I had made up, and we were going to spend a few days in Napa. This didn't come as a surprise to you."

"If you're going to marry Keller, I don't wanna know about it!"

"We don't know if we're going to get married yet, but if I decide to do that, you'll be the first to know—whether you want to or not. You're the most important thing in my life, Amanda, I'm never going to abandon you."

"I bet you didn't tell Keller about Ryan! You think I don't know you slept with him? You should be more careful with your e-mails, you know."

"You read my private correspondence!"

"Nothing of yours is private—I can read whatever I want to on your laptop. That's why I've got your password: Shakti. You gave it to me yourself, same as you gave it to Grandpa, to Dad, to half of California. I know what you did with Ryan, and I read your stupid love letters. You're such a liar! You got his hopes up, and then you ran off with Keller. What kind of a person are you? You can't be trusted! And don't tell me I'm just a kid and I don't know anything about anything—I know exactly what I'm talking about!"

For the first time in her life Indiana felt the impulse to slap Amanda, but she didn't so much as raise her hand. Instinctively, she tried to reinterpret her daughter's message, since the words might have distorted it. When she saw how angry the girl was, she blushed with shame. For someone who valued loyalty as much as she did, what she had done to Ryan was inexcusable. She should have given him an explanation before going off with Alan, but she'd just disappeared, ignoring the plans they had made together for the weekend. If she loved Ryan, as she'd led him to believe she did, or at least if she respected him as he deserved, she would not have treated him this way. She should have been open with him and given him her reasons. She hadn't dared confront him, and had justified this by arguing that she needed time to decide between the two men; in fact she had gone to Napa because she had already chosen Alan, to whom she felt connected by something more than just four years of love. She had gone with the intention of sorting her head out and had come back with a ring in her purse—she had taken it off her finger as she stepped out of Alan's car, so her daughter would not see it.

"You're right, Amanda," she admitted, hanging her head.

There was a long silence. Mother and daughter sat on the floor, close yet not touching, and then Amanda reached up and wiped the tears from her mother's face. Indiana's horror at the idea of marrying somebody her daughter detested was growing by the minute, while Amanda was beginning to think that if Keller was going to be her stepfather, she would have to make some effort and be polite to him.

Their thoughts were interrupted when Amanda's cell phone chirped into life: Carol Underwater, trying to find Indiana, whom she hadn't had contact with since Thursday. Indiana took the phone from her daughter and explained that she had spent a few days in Napa. In her usual plaintive tone, Carol said she was pleased for Indiana that she had so much going for her: love, holidays, and health, most of all health, and she hoped that Indiana never lacked it, because without health life wasn't worth living, she could tell her from experience. Radiotherapy was her last hope. She wanted to hear all the details about Indiana's little break in Napa, about how Alan had persuaded her to take him back—after all, a betrayal like his was impossible to forget. Indiana ended up giving her an explanation, as though she owed it to Carol, and they agreed to meet at the Rossini at six thirty on Wednesday.

"Carol called me a bunch of times, asking about you," said

Amanda, "and she flipped when I told her you were back with Keller. You must be her only friend."

"How come she has your phone number?"

"She calls to ask about Save-the-Tuna. Actually, she's come by to visit her a couple times. Carol loves cats—didn't Grandpa tell you?"

Monday, 5

*E*smeralda *played the next session* of Ripper from a hospital bed in Auckland. The boy was undergoing embryonic stem cell treatment, another stage in his mission to walk again. Amanda, in her role as games master, had drawn up a list of all the key data relating to the five murders they had been puzzling over since January. Each player had a copy, and having studied the facts through the magnifying glass of his unassailable logic, Sherlock Holmes had arrived at conclusions that were very different from those of Abatha, who had approached the same facts via her meandering, mysterious pathways, or from those of Colonel Paddington, whose approach was dictated by strict military criteria, and from those of Esmeralda—a gypsy waif who saw no need for anyone to rack their brains, since things would become clear in their own time, one only needed to ask the right questions. The kids all agreed, however, that they were faced with a criminal as enthralling as Jack the Ripper.

"Let's start with the Case of the Misplaced Baseball Bat," began the games master. "Go ahead, Kabel."

"Ed Staton was briefly married in his youth, but had no relations with women after that, and paid male escorts and watched gay pornography. Neither the jacket or the cap of his uniform were found in the school or his jeep, but the students who were in the parking lot saw him leave and recognized him by his uniform."

"Who were the escorts?" asked Esmeralda.

"Two Puerto Rican guys, but neither of them had a date with him that night, and their alibis are solid. The witnesses from the parking lot didn't see anyone else in the car he left in."

"Why didn't Staton use his own vehicle?"

"Because the person they saw wasn't Ed Staton," Sherlock inferred. "It was the killer, who put on the guard's jacket and cap and calmly left the school in plain view of the three witnesses, to whom he waved before getting into the same car he had arrived in. The guard never left the school, because by that time he was lying dead in the gymnasium. The killer arrived at the school when the parking lot was full of cars, and nobody noticed his—he went in the main gate without a problem, hid inside, and waited for everybody to leave."

"He attacked Staton in the gymnasium when Staton was doing his rounds, closing up and putting the alarm on," Colonel Paddington continued. "The surprise attack: a common strategy. He paralyzed the victim with a Taser and then executed him with a bullet in the head."

"Have we found the link between Ed Staton and Arkansas State University?" Esmeralda asked.

"No. Deputy Chief Martín looked into that. Nobody at that university or on its sports team, the Red Wolves, knew Staton."

"The Red Wolves? Maybe there isn't a connection, but it's some kind of code or message," suggested Abatha.

"The red wolf—Canis rufus—is one of the two North American species of wolf," said Kabel, who had studied the topic the year before, when his granddaughter had developed an obsession with werewolves. "The other species, the gray wolf, is larger. In 1980 they declared the red species extinct in the wild, but they mated the few animals they had in captivity and managed to set up a breeding program. Now there are estimated to be about two hundred in the wild."

"That's of no use to us at all," the colonel replied.

"Everything is of use," Sherlock corrected him.

The games master suggested moving on to the Case of Branding by Blowtorch, and Kabel shared with them the photograph he had gotten hold of, showing the burns on the victims' buttocks: an *F* on Michael Constante, an *A* on Doris. He also presented them with photos of the syringes, the blowtorch, and the bottle of liquor, explaining that the Xanax the killer had used to put the Constantes to sleep was dissolved in a carton of milk.

"For a cup to have the necessary effect, the murderer had to dissolve at least ten or fifteen tablets in the liter of milk."

"It would be irrational to dissolve the drug in milk: it's a drink for children, not adults," the colonel cut in.

"The kids were on a trip to Lake Tahoe," Kabel explained. "For dinner, the couple would always have ham or cheese sandwiches and a cup of instant coffee made with milk. Henrietta Post, the neighbor who discovered the bodies, told me that. The coffee masked the taste of the Xanax."

"So the killer knew the couple's habits," Sherlock mused.

"How did that liquor get into the Constantes' refrigerator?" Esmeralda asked.

"*Rakija* can't be found in this country," the games master explained. "The bottle was totally clean of prints."

"Or it was handled with gloves," said Sherlock, "like the syringes and the blowtorch, which means the killer put it there deliberately."

"Another message," Abatha said, interrupting.

"Exactly."

"A message from one reformed alcoholic to another?" asked Esmeralda. "From Brian Turner to Michael Constante?"

"Who?" asked Paddington.

"Turner was the guy who had the fight with Constante, remember?"

"Brian Turner's a crude guy—that would be way too subtle for him," said Kabel. "If he'd wanted to send a message, he would have tipped a couple bottles of beer over the bodies, not gone looking for a rare Serbian liquor to put in the refrigerator."

"Do you think the killer is Serbian?"

"No, Esmeralda," said the colonel, irritably. "But in each case I think the killer left a clue for us to identify him with. He's arrogant enough that he thinks he can afford to play games with us."

"Play games with the police, you mean—he doesn't know we exist," said Amanda.

"That's what I mean. I think you get the point."

"Nothing has been found to link the suspect, Brian Turner, who had had a fight with Michael Constante, with the other victims," said Amanda. "The night the psychiatrist died, Turner was being held in jail in Petaluma for another fight. That proves his poor character, and it also proves he's not our suspect."

"The night of their death . . . ," Abatha stammered, but, dizzy with hunger and medication, she could not even finish her sentence.

The games master explained that in the Case of the Electrocuted Man, the prime suspects were still Ayani and Galang. Her father had questioned everybody who had contact with the psychiatrist in the two weeks leading up to his death, above all anyone who had been in his study. He was investigating the possibility that a Taser had been lost by the police or someone else authorized to use one, and looking for anybody who had bought one or more in California in the last three months, even though the killer could have gotten hold of one in many other ways. The criminal psychologist who had been studying *Steppenwolf*—the novel that Ayani was sent in the mail along with her husband's socks—found a dozen or so leads to follow, but they all turned out to be dead ends; it was a complex book, open to endless interpretations. More than sixty distinct types of DNA were found in Ashton's study, and only Galang's matched a registered sample, as he had spent six months in jail in Florida in 2006 for possession of narcotics; but as Galang worked in the Ashton house, it was only natural that he had left traces everywhere.

"And finally, we've got the definitive autopsy report for the Case of the Executioner Executed," said the games master. "The woman was garroted."

"The garrote is a time-honored torture method," Paddington informed the players. "It involves strangling the victim slowly to prolong their agony. Generally the instrument has been a chair with a post at the back that they tied the convict to. The rope, wire, or a metal cinch around the neck would then be tightened from behind with a tourniquet. Sometimes it had a knot at the front that pressed down on the larynx."

"They used something like that on Rosen—nylon fishing line with a little ball on it, possibly of wood," the games master said.

"Once it's set up, the garrote makes easy work for the executioner; you just have to turn the tourniquet," continued Paddington, always keen to show his knowledge in this area. "There's no strength or dexterity needed. And Rosen was drugged—she couldn't defend herself. A little old woman could strangle a giant with a garrote."

"A woman . . . It could have been a woman, why not?" suggested Abatha.

"A woman could have killed Staton, Ashton, and the Constantes, but it would take strength to overpower Rosen, lift her body, and hang it from the fan," the games master pointed out.

"It depends," said Paddington. "Once Rosen was on the bed, it would just have been a question of hoisting her up bit by bit."

"And the woman was sedated when they garrotted her—that's why she didn't defend herself."

"Hmm, the garrote . . . It's an exotic weapon," mused Sherlock. "The victims were all executed. In each of these cases the killer chose a different method of capital punishment: Staton was given the mercy shot; the Constantes, lethal injection; Ashton was electrocuted; and it was the garrote, or else the noose, for Rosen."

"Do you think these people deserved particular types of execution?" asked Esmeralda.

"We'll know that when we have the motive and the connection between the victims," Sherlock replied.

Friday, 9

edro Alarcón got to Ryan's loft shortly after ten in the evening, having tried unsuccessfully to reach him on the phone. He'd had a call from Indiana sometime around noon to say she was very worried about Ryan, having told him the night before that she was going to marry Alan Keller.

"I thought you loved Ryan," Pedro said.

"I do, I do love him. But Alan and I have been together four years, and we have something in common that I don't have with Ryan."

"And what's that, exactly?"

"That's not the point, Pedro. Besides, Ryan has a lot of stuff to deal with from his past—he's not ready for a serious relationship."

"You were his first love—that's what he told me. He was going to marry you. Typical Miller, coming to a decision like that without actually talking to the person in question."

"He did talk to me, Pedro. This whole thing is my fault, I wasn't clear with him. I guess I was in a pretty bad way after Alan and

I broke up, and I clung to Ryan—he was like a lifeline. We spent a couple of wonderful weeks together, but even while I was with Ryan, I was thinking about Alan—it was inevitable."

"Comparing them?"

"Maybe . . . I don't know."

"I find it hard to believe that Keller came off better."

"It's not as simple as that, Pedro. There's another reason, but you can't tell Alan, because it's got nothing to do with him. Ryan got mad, accused Alan of controlling me, of manipulating me—he told me I wasn't capable of making a rational decision, said he was going to protect me, to stop me doing something stupid. He was screaming and threatening to sort things out his way. He changed, Pedro. He was like a lunatic, just like that night at the club with Danny D'Angelo, except that last night he hadn't been drinking. Ryan's like a volcano—he'll suddenly explode and spew red-hot lava everywhere."

"What do you want me to do, Indiana?"

"Go see him, talk to him, try to make him see sense. He won't listen to me, and now he won't even take my calls."

Pedro was the only other person with a key to Ryan's apartment, mostly so that he could take care of Attila when Ryan was traveling. If it was only for a couple of nights, Pedro would stay in the loft with the dog; if it was an extended trip, he took Attila back to his apartment. Pedro pushed the buzzer a few times, but when he got no answer, he punched in the key code, opened the door to the old printworks, and rode the huge industrial elevator up to the only floor in the building that was occupied. He used the key Ryan had given him to unlock the heavy metal doors and stepped straight into the vast, empty space his friend called home.

Everything was dark. He couldn't hear Attila barking, and no one answered when he called out. He groped along the wall for a switch, turned on the light, and hurried to turn off the alarm, the security system designed to electrocute potential intruders, and the CCTV cameras, which would be activated by the slightest movement—all of which Ryan turned on whenever he went out. The bed was made; there wasn't so much as a single dirty glass in the dishwasher, the place was as neat and pristine as a monk's cell. Pedro sat down and read one of Ryan's computer manuals while he waited.

An hour later, having tried several times to call his friend on his cell, Pedro drove back to his place to pick up some maté and the Latin American novel he'd been reading and took them back to the loft. He popped a couple of slices of bread in the toaster, boiled some water for the maté, and sat down in the armchair again to read. This time he took a pillow and Ryan's electric blanket, as the loft was freezing and he still hadn't managed to shake the cold that had been bothering him since January. At midnight, feeling tired, he turned out the light and fell asleep.

At 6:25 a.m., Pedro woke with a start to feel the barrel of a gun pressed against his forehead. "I nearly killed you, you knucklehead!" The faint glow of a misty dawn spilling through the curtainless windows made Ryan's imposing figure seem gigantic. His pistol was gripped in both hands, his body coiled and ready to attack; his face bore the blank, single-minded expression of a killer. The impression lasted only a moment before Ryan straightened up and slipped the weapon back into the holster under his leather jacket, but still the image was burned onto Alarcón's mind like a revelation. Attila—still panting in the elevator, where Ryan had probably told him to wait—watched the scene.

"Where you been, dude?" asked Pedro, pretending to be calm, though his heart was in his mouth.

"Don't ever come in here again without warning me! The alarm and the electrics were disconnected—I was expecting the worst."

"A Russian gangster or an al-Qaeda terrorist? Sorry to disappoint."

"I'm serious, Pedro. You know I've got classified information in here. Don't ever scare me like that again."

"I called and called. So did Indiana. I came because she asked me to. So I'll ask you again, where have you been?"

"I went to talk to Keller."

"You went strapped? Great idea. I suppose you killed the guy."

"I just shook him up a little. What the hell does Indi see in that poser? The guy's old enough to be her father."

"Sure. The point is, he's not her father."

Ryan explained that he'd gone down to the Napa Valley vineyard, planning to have it out with Keller, man to man. For four years he had watched this man treat Indiana like some part-time, almost secret lover—one of many, since he dated other women, including the Belgian baroness everyone said he was planning to marry. When Indiana finally worked out what was going on and dumped him, Keller had let weeks pass without getting in touch, proving how little the relationship meant to him.

"But as soon as he hears she was with me, he shows up with a ring and proposes—another of his little tactics to buy himself time. Well, if he marries her, it'll be over my dead body! I'm going to protect my woman whatever it takes."

"You know, I kinda think the Navy SEAL approach isn't going to work out in this case," said Pedro.

"You got a better idea?"

"Yeah, spend your time convincing Indiana instead of threatening Keller. I'm going to make myself another maté and head off to the university. You want some coffee?"

"No, I've already had breakfast. I'm going to do my Qigong and take Attila out for a run."

///////////////////

An hour later Pedro was headed into Palo Alto, driving at a leisurely pace down I-280, listening to the sultry voice of Cesária Évora and enjoying the landscape of rolling green hills, as he had done every day for some years now, and always with the same soothing effect on his soul. He had no classes that Friday, but he needed to go in to meet two researchers he was working on a project with, a couple of whiz kids who, with fearlessness and imagination, would often rapidly arrive at the same conclusions that he only reached with considerable effort and research. As a discipline, AI belonged to the younger generation, who had technology wired into their DNA, Pedro thought with a sigh—not to some guy like him, who should be thinking about his retirement. He had spent a rough night on Ryan's sofa and had only had a couple of matés to keep him going. He'd get some breakfast as soon as he reached Stanford, he decided, where he could eat like a king in any of the cafeterias. His cell phone blared out the Uruguayan national anthem, and he answered using the car's hands-free system.

"Indiana? I was just about to call to fill you in on Ryan. It's all cool—"

"Pedro! Alan's dead!" Indiana interrupted, sobbing so hard that she couldn't continue.

Deputy Chief Martín came on the line and told Pedro that they were phoning from his car, explaining that twenty minutes earlier Indiana had had a call from the Napa Police Department, informing her that Alan Keller had been found dead at his vineyard. They refused to give any details other than that they were treating it as a suspicious death. They'd asked her to come and identify the body—although this had already been done by the servants—and offered to send a car to pick her up, but Bob had decided to drive her there himself; he didn't want Indiana to have to deal with this alone. His tone was clipped and precise, and he hung up before Pedro could find out any more.

That morning, Indiana had only just stepped out of the shower and was still naked, her hair wet, when the call came from the

Napa Police Department. She stood paralyzed for thirty seconds, then, wrapping a towel around herself, raced down to her father's house, screaming his name. Blake Jackson had grabbed the phone and called the one person he could think of in his state: his former son-in-law. In the time it took Indiana and her father to dress and make coffee, Bob Martín had already shown up, along with another officer in a patrol car. He and Indiana took off at top speed, sirens wailing, heading straight up Route 101.

As he drove, Bob called one of his colleagues at Napa Police, Lieutenant McLaughlin, who had no doubt that they were dealing with a murder; the cause of death ruled out both accident and suicide. He explained that they had received the 911 call at 7:17 a.m. from one María Pescadero, who described herself as a maid working in the house. He had been the first officer to arrive and had made a cursory examination of the scene before sealing it off and interviewing the two Mexican workers—María and Luis Pescadero, legal immigrants who had worked at the vineyard for eleven years, initially for the previous owner and more recently for the victim. They spoke little English, but McLaughlin explained that a Spanish-speaking officer was on his way and would help out with the interview. Bob offered to act as interpreter and asked that the whole property, not just the house, be cordoned off, then asked who would be taking away the body. The lieutenant replied that it was a pretty peaceful county, which rarely had to deal with cases like this, and they did not have a pathologist or a medical examiner, so usually a local doctor would sign the death certificate. If there were any doubts as to cause of death, and an autopsy was required, they called on someone in Sacramento.

"We'll do everything we can to help," Bob told the lieutenant. "The San Francisco Personal Crimes Division is at your disposal. We have all the necessary resources. Alan Keller belonged to an important family in San Francisco and was temporarily residing at the vineyard. If you like, I can give orders to have my forensics team come and collect the body and gather evidence. Has the Keller family been notified of the death?"

"We're doing that now. We found Indiana Jackson's name and phone number stuck to the fridge with a magnet. The Pescaderos had instructions to call her in case of an emergency."

"I'm just turning onto Route Twenty-Nine, Lieutenant—I'll be there soon."

"I'll be here, Deputy Chief."

Indiana explained that Alan was always worried about his health, took his blood pressure every day, and was convinced that at his age he could have a heart attack at any moment; he'd also had a recent health scare because of some lab error, which was why he had her phone number in his wallet and on his fridge.

"Fat lot of good it would have been, given that your cell phone is always lost or the battery is dead," Bob remarked, but realized he ought to go easier on Indiana, who'd been crying since they set off. His ex-wife clearly loved Keller more than the guy deserved, he concluded.

At the vineyard they were met by Lieutenant McLaughlin, a man of about fifty who looked Irish, with gray hair, the red nose of a dedicated drinker, and a paunch that hung over his belt. He moved like a seal out of water, but he had a quick mind and twenty-six years' experience on the force. With much patience and little glory, he had risen through the ranks to the position he now held in Napa, where he could lazily work out the rest of his time until retirement. The presence of the deputy chief of San Francisco's Personal Crimes Division did not intimidate him. For his part, Bob, eager to avoid problems, treated him with some deference.

McLaughlin had already cordoned off the house and stationed police cars around the perimeter of the vineyard to stop anyone coming in. He had left Luis Pescadero in the dining room and his wife in the kitchen, so they had no opportunity to agree on their stories before they were interviewed. He allowed only Bob to come with him to the room in which the body had been found, preferring to "spare the little lady from having to see such things," as he put it, forgetting that this was the same woman he had asked to identify the body. They would have to wait for the forensics team sent by Petra Horr, which was already on its way.

Alan Keller was slouched in a comfortable, tobacco-colored armchair, head lolling against the chair back like someone caught taking a nap. Only his face—the split lip, the traces of blood—and the arrow buried in his chest betrayed that he had died a violent death. Bob studied the body and the rest of the scene, dictating his initial observations into a pocket recorder while McLaughlin watched from the doorway, his arms folded over his belly. The arrow had penetrated deeply, pinning the corpse to the back of the armchair, indicating that the shooter was either an expert archer or had fired from close range. The bloodstains on the shirt cuff had come from Keller's nose, Bob thought; he was surprised at how little the arrow wound had bled, but he could not inspect the body until the forensics team arrived.

In the kitchen María had made coffee for everyone, and sat alternately stroking a white Labrador and Indiana's hand. For her part, Indiana could barely open her eyes, they were so swollen from crying. She was convinced she'd been the last person—aside from his killer—to see Alan Keller alive. After an early dinner in San Francisco, he'd dropped her off at home, and they'd made plans to meet up on Sunday after Amanda went back to school. Keller had headed back to the vineyard, a trip he was happy to make, since there was little traffic at night and he listened to audiobooks as he drove.

Bob Martín and Lieutenant McLaughlin interviewed María Pescadero in the library, where Keller's collections of artifacts and jade were kept locked in plate-glass display cabinets set into the walls. María had turned off the alarm in the library so that McLaughlin could make his initial inspection of the scene, but warned the officer not to touch the display cases or the collection, which were protected by a separate alarm system. Keller constantly got his security codes mixed up, and often an alarm would go off because he couldn't work out how to switch it off. This was why he had nothing to do with the house alarm, only the one in the library, where he also had motion sensors and CCTV cameras installed. McLaughlin had already viewed the tapes for the previous night, which showed nothing unusual; no one had come into this room before María opened it for the police.

The woman turned out to be one of those perfect witnesses who simply answers questions and does not speculate: excellent memory, no imagination. She told Bob that she and her husband lived in a little cottage on the grounds, ten minutes' walk from the main house. She managed the kitchen and the other household chores while her husband took care of repairs and acted as caretaker, gardener, and chauffeur. They got on well with Keller: he was a generous boss who paid no attention to detail. The dog belonged to her and her husband and had lived here all its life; it had never been much of a guard dog, however, and now, at the age of ten, was finding it difficult to walk. The dog spent most of its time sleeping—on the porch in summer, in its kennel in winter—so there was no way of knowing when the killer had entered the house. At around seven the previous evening, María's husband had brought in the logs and stacked them next to the fireplaces in the living room and in Keller's bedroom; then they had locked up the house without setting the alarm and left, taking the dog with them.

"And did you notice anything unusual last night?"

"From our cottage, you can't see this house or the entrance to the vineyard. But yesterday afternoon, just before Luis brought in the logs, some man showed up, wanting to talk to Señor Keller. I told him the master was not here. He didn't give his name—he left."

"Did you recognize him?"

"I've never seen him before."

María explained that this morning, she had arrived at the big house at 6:45, as usual, to make a breakfast of coffee and toast for her boss. She stayed in the kitchen, but opened the door to the hall because Keller liked to be woken up by the dog, who clambered arthritically onto the bed and slumped down on top of him. A moment later, María had heard the Labrador howling.

"I went to see what was going on, and I found the master in the armchair in the living room. I felt sorry for him, sleeping there like that with no blanket and the fire out, he must have been freezing. . . . Then when I came closer I saw . . . I saw . . . and I went back to the kitchen, called Luis on his cell, and then I dialed nine-one-one."

*W*hile *Alan Keller's body was* lying in the morgue waiting to be examined by Ingrid Dunn, the dead man's
siblings, Mark and Lucille, were doing everything in their power
to hush up this shocking incident that smacked of gangsters, underworld connections, and God knows what else the "artist" of
the family was mixed up in. Indiana, calmer now after her dose of
aromatherapy, cinnamon tea, and meditation, had started planning
a memorial service for this man who had played such an important
role in her life—since there would be no funeral in the immediate
future. After being misdiagnosed with prostate cancer, Keller had
written an advance directive making it clear that he did not wish to
be kept alive by artificial means, that he wanted to be cremated and
have his ashes scattered over the Pacific. He had made no provi-
sion, however, for the humiliating process of an autopsy, or lying
frozen in a morgue for months on end until the circumstances of
his death had been definitively established.

The forensics team that Deputy Chief Martín had put at Lieutenant McLaughlin's disposal arrived in Napa en masse, and collected an uncommon amount of evidence from the crime scene and the surrounding areas. On the soft, damp earth of the patio and the garden they found tire tracks and footprints, and there were animal hairs in the doorway that did not match the Pescaderos' Labrador; on the doorbell, the door, and in the living room, they discovered fingerprints that, once those living on the property had been eliminated, might be used to identify any intruders. The tiled floor showed tracks from muddy shoes—based on the prints, they seemed to be well-worn combat boots of the kind that could be bought in any army surplus store and that were popular with young people. There were no signs of forced entry, so Bob assumed that Keller had known his killer, invited him in. The stains on his shirt indicated that most of the blood had come from his nose, as the deputy chief had thought, and had got there by simple force of gravity while the victim was still alive.

In her preliminary report, Ingrid Dunn pointed out that Keller must have been dead for some time when he was shot with the arrow, since there was no blood spatter. The arrow had been fired straight on, from a distance of about five feet, using a small crossbow of the kind used in sports and hunting—small by comparison with other models but, given the shape, difficult to conceal. Had the victim been alive when the shot was fired, he would have bled profusely.

María Pescadero's description of the person who had come asking for Keller on the afternoon of the shooting was as recognizable as if she had shown Bob a photo of Ryan Miller, a man for whom he had little respect, but one who clearly loved Indiana. María's account mentioned a black high-suspension van with oversize tires, a weird dog covered with scars and bald patches, a tall, heavyset man with a military buzz cut and a limp. It all fitted.

Indiana was incredulous at the suggestion that Ryan had been to Keller's house, but she had to accept the evidence; there was nothing she could do to stop her ex-husband getting a search warrant for the loft apartment and sending half his department out to look for the suspect, who had now disappeared. According to Pedro Alarcón and the various members of the Dolphin Club who had been interviewed, Ryan frequently traveled for his work—but they could not explain where he had left his dog and his van.

When she heard the news, Elsa Domínguez moved into the Jackson house to take care of the family, cook comfort food, and be there through the long litany of visits from people offering Indiana their condolences—everyone from her colleagues at the Holistic Clinic to Carol Underwater, who arrived with an apple pie and only stayed five minutes. Feeling that Indiana was in no fit state to go back to work the following day, Carol offered to telephone her patients and let them know. Everyone agreed, and Matheus Pereira said he'd put a note on the door of Treatment Room 8, explaining that it was closed as the result of a bereavement and would reopen the following week.

Blake Jackson had spent the past two days with his former son-in-law and had more than enough material to feed the morbid curiosity of the Ripper players; his granddaughter, meanwhile, was plagued by guilt. More than once she had imagined a long, slow death for her mother's lover and called on the mystical powers of Saint Jude to eliminate him, never suspecting the saint would take her prayers literally. She was waiting for Keller's ghost to come to her in the night, looking for revenge. She felt all the more guilty because of the excitement this new crime stirred in her: here was another challenge for Ripper. By now, grandfather and granddaughter both accepted that they had been bested by astrology: Celeste Roko's predicted bloodbath had become an indisputable fact.

*A*s soon as the house was quiet again and her mother—who had taken on the role of a grief-stricken widow, without having had the time to get married—had finally stopped crying, Amanda convened a session of Ripper. The least that they could do to appease the ghost of the unfortunate Keller—who was coming for her with an arrow planted in his chest—was to find out who had fired the shot. Alan Keller had been the love of her mother's life, as Indiana had put it between sobs, and his tragic death was an affront to the whole family. Amanda told her buddies everything she knew about the Case of the Killer Crossbow, and asked them to help her find the real culprit as a personal favor to her, and to stop Ryan Miller having to pay for a crime he hadn't committed.

Sherlock Holmes suggested they go through all the available information. After a detailed examination of the crime scene photos obtained by Kabel, which he had enlarged on his computer, he announced that he had discovered something important.

"The bottle of liquor in the fridge of the former alcoholic Michael Constante was labeled CHER BYK, which means 'Snow Wolf' in Serbian," explained Sherlock. "Wolves are mentioned in the book that Richard Ashton's wife got in the mail two days before he was murdered. Criminal psychologists looked for clues in the novel, but I think the clue is the title itself: *Steppenwolf.* The logo on the baseball bat in the Ed Staton murder shows the Red Wolves of Arkansas State University."

"Abatha said it had to be a message of some sort," Amanda reminded them.

"It's not a message or a clue—it's the killer's signature," said Colonel Paddington. "The signature means something only to him."

"But surely in that case he'd have left his signature at all the crime scenes," Esmeralda interrupted. "Why not do it in the case of the Rosens or with Keller?"

"Hang on a second," said Amanda. "Kabel, call my dad and ask him about the crystal figurine the judge received in the mail after the murder."

While the kids carried on speculating, Blake Jackson phoned his ex-son-in-law, who would take a call from Blake any time except when he was in the bathroom or in bed with a woman. Bob told him that the Swarovski figurine was a dog. "Could it have been a wolf?" asked Jackson. Bob agreed it could have been: it had looked like a German shepherd with its head raised, as though howling at the moon. It was one of a series that had been discontinued in 1998, making it more valuable. Judge Rosen had probably bought it on the Internet, though the deputy chief could find no trace of the transaction.

"If it is a wolf," said Amanda, "we've identified the killer's signature in each of the murders except Alan Keller's."

"Though at first glance they look very different, all of the crimes have a similar MO," said Esmeralda. "Again, with the exception of Keller—why?"

"There's no wolf at the Keller crime scene, and the murder took place some distance outside San Francisco—the area mentioned in Celeste Roko's prediction, which the killer has stayed within until now," said Amanda. "There's something else, too: Keller's the only victim who was beaten before being killed, although, like the others, he didn't defend himself."

"I've got a hunch that the killer may be the same," said Abatha. "But the motive may be different."

"But we don't have a motive for any of the murders," interrupted Colonel Paddington.

"Even so, we should listen to Abatha," Amanda interjected. "Her instincts are almost always right."

"It's because I receive messages from the Beyond," murmured Abatha. "I communicate with angels and spirits. The living and the dead are with us constantly, we are as one substance—"

"Well, if I lived on nothing but fresh air, I'd probably see visions and hear voices too," Esmeralda interrupted, worried that Abatha would lead them down some esoteric path and derail the investigation.

"So why don't you?" asked the psychic, who was convinced that the human race would evolve to a higher state if everyone stopped eating.

"That's enough," the games master said, calling them to order. "May I remind you that sarcastic comments are forbidden in the rules of Ripper."

"Intuitions aren't facts," grumbled Colonel Paddington.

"Our killer vented his rage on his victims, like Jack the Ripper and other famous murderers we've studied," said Sherlock, "but he did so after he'd killed them. There's a message there. He left not only a signature but a message."

"You think so?"

"Elementary, my dear Esmeralda. The ways in which the victims were executed is also a message; the killer isn't choosing a means of death at random. What we're dealing with is a highly organized, ritualistic killer."

"He plans every step of the crime, including his getaway," the colonel mused admiringly. "I suspect he will have had military training. He's a formidable strategist, and would make a first-class general."

"But he's not," said Amanda. "He's a cold-blooded murderer."

"It might not be a man," interrupted Abatha. "I dreamed we were dealing with a woman."

Kabel requested permission to speak, and once it was granted, he brought the players up-to-date on the Alan Keller investigation. From the angle of the blow to the face, forensics determined Keller had been struck by a closed fist, punched by a powerful, left-handed attacker somewhere between five-eleven and six-two, which corresponded to the size of the boot prints found on the tiled floor; this ruled out the possibility of the killer being a woman. The autopsy revealed that death occurred at least half an hour before the arrow was fired into the body. From the bright pink tinge of Keller's skin, cause of death was initially assumed to be cyanide, something later confirmed by the toxicology screening.

"Could you explain that, Kabel?" Amanda asked.

"It's a little complicated, but I'll simplify. Cyanide is an efficient, fast-acting metabolic poison that stops cells from absorbing oxygen. It's as though all the air was suddenly sucked out of the body. The victim can't breathe, experiences dizziness, nausea, vomiting, and loss of consciousness, and may suffer seizures before dying."

"But why does the skin become pink?"

"It's a chemical reaction produced when cyanide binds to hemoglobin—to red blood cells. The blood in the veins turns a vivid red, like paint."

"So the blood on Keller's shirt cuff was bright red?" asked Esmeralda.

"Not exactly. The nosebleed clearly occurred before Keller ingested the poison. There is evidence of some bleeding after the cyanide poisoning, but very little. There was no bleeding from the arrow wound, because by then he was dead."

"Do we know how the poison was administered?" asked Sherlock.

"Traces of cyanide were found in a water glass next to the victim and also in a glass on the nightstand in his bedroom. The killer put a pinch of white powder, barely visible to the naked eye, at the bottom of the glasses to be sure that if Alan Keller didn't ingest the poison with his usual nightcap of whiskey, he would do so during the night."

"Cyanide is particularly toxic," Sherlock Holmes explained. "The slightest trace can cause death within a matter of minutes. It can be absorbed through the skin, even by inhalation—so the killer would have had to be very careful."

"I've seen movies where spies have cyanide capsules so they can commit suicide if they're about to be tortured," said Esmeralda. "How would someone get their hands on it?"

"It's easy. It's used in metalworking, in mining silver and gold, and in the electroplating process for silver, gold, copper, or platinum. The killer could have bought it online or from any chemical supplies store."

"Poison is a woman's weapon. It's the coward's method. Men don't use poison. When we kill, we do it face-to-face." This observation by Colonel Paddington was greeted with a roar of laughter, but the colonel insisted. "A strapping, six-foot-two woman in army boots? She must be built like an Olympic weightlifter. A woman like that wouldn't need to use poison, she could have smashed the victim's head in with another punch."

"What if the person who punched Keller isn't the same person who killed him?" suggested Abatha.

"Too far-fetched, too many coincidences," said the colonel. "I don't like it."

"It's possible," Sherlock interrupted, "but we'd need to reexamine the evidence, bearing in mind what Abatha has just said."

///////////////////////

Eight days earlier, the two young whiz kids at Stanford's Artificial Intelligence Lab had waited in vain for Professor Alarcón to show up for their scheduled meeting. As soon as he got the call from Indiana letting him know Alan Keller was dead, Pedro did a U-turn and drove straight back to San Francisco. On the way, he made several attempts to reach Ryan. He arrived at the loft just as Ryan stepped out of the shower and was getting dressed, having earlier taken Attila out for a run and had a conference call with a general at the Pentagon. As soon as the metal grille on the elevator opened, before Ryan could ask why he'd come back, Pedro blurted out the news.

"What d'you mean, Keller's dead? How? When?"

"Indiana called an hour ago, but she couldn't talk long. Her ex-husband, the cop, came on the line, so I didn't find out any more. All I know is that they're treating the death as suspicious. I'm sure she phoned me so I'd tell you. What the hell's wrong with your cell phone?"

"It got wet—I need a new one."

"If this is murder, Ryan, then you're in it up to your neck. You were with Keller last night—you went down to Napa with a gun and, if I may quote you, 'shook him up a little.' This puts you in the enviable role of prime suspect. So where were you all night?"

"You accusing me of something?" Ryan growled.

"I'm here to help, man. I wanted to get here before the police."

Ryan tried to control the rage welling inside him. The death of his rival came at the perfect time, and he certainly wasn't sorry Keller was dead, but Pedro was right: he was in deep shit. He had motive and opportunity. He explained to his friend that he'd arrived at the vineyard in Napa around sunset the previous day—probably some time around six thirty, though he hadn't checked his watch. He had driven through the front gate, which was open, then about three hundred yards down a driveway until he came to a house with a circular fountain outside. He parked outside the door and got out, taking Attila on a leash because the dog needed to pee. He'd knocked on the door about three times before finally a Latina woman opened it and, wiping her hands on her apron, told him Alan Keller was not home. The conversation ground to a halt then because a white Labrador showed up, wagging its tail, and the moment it saw Attila, started barking. Attila anxiously began tugging on the leash, and the woman closed the door in Ryan's face. He went and put Attila in the van, then came back and rang the doorbell, which was answered almost immediately, and through the narrow crack the woman said in broken English that Señor Keller would not be back until the evening and asked if he wanted to leave his name. Ryan simply said he would phone later. Meanwhile, both dogs were still yowling, one inside the house, the other in the truck. He'd decided to wait for Keller, but clearly he could not do so here; the woman was not about to invite him in, and he thought it would look strange if he simply waited in the van, so he drove back out onto the street.

Ryan found a nearby parking spot where he could clearly see the gates to the vineyard, lit by two old-fashioned lanterns.

"The gates were still wide open," he told Pedro. "Keller was just asking to be burgled—I mean, he didn't take any security precautions, even though apparently he has a bunch of art and other valuable stuff."

"Go on," said Pedro.

"I did a quick reconnoiter. There's thirty feet of brick wall either side of the gates, more for decoration than security, and other than that the property's only protected by rosebushes. I noticed they were already in bloom, even though it's only the beginning of March."

"What time did Keller get back?"

"I waited for two hours. His Lexus pulled up outside the gates, and Keller got out to collect mail from the mailbox, then got back in the car, drove in, and closed the gates behind him, using a remote. As you can imagine, I wasn't about to give up when I ran into a bunch of rosebushes. I left Attila in the van because I didn't want to scare Keller, and I walked right up the driveway to the house—I didn't try to hide, to get the jump on him, nothing like that. I rang the doorbell, and Keller himself opened. And—you're not going to believe this, Pedro—you know what he said? He said, 'Good evening, Mr. Miller, I've been expecting you.'"

"The maid obviously told him a punk matching your description had been asking after him. You're hard to miss, Miller, especially when you've got Attila with you. Keller knew you. Anyway, maybe Indiana had warned him you'd threatened to take matters into your own hands."

"In that case, he wouldn't have opened the door—he'd have called the police."

"You see? He wasn't such a wimp after all."

Ryan briefly explained that he had followed the man into the living room, refused to sit down, declined the whiskey offered him, and told Keller what he thought of him, told him that he'd fucked up his chance with Indiana, that she was with him now, and that Keller had better back off or he would regret it. If Keller was scared, he hid it well, calmly replying that it was up to Indiana to choose. "May the best man win," he said mockingly, gesturing to the door, and when Ryan didn't move, Keller reached out to grab his arm. Bad idea.

"It was reflex, Pedro. I didn't even think, I just whacked him in the face."

"You punched him?"

"Not hard. He staggered a bit and he got a nosebleed, but I didn't knock him down. I felt terrible. What the hell's happening to me, Pedro? The tiniest thing these days, and I completely lose it. I didn't used to be like that."

"Had you been drinking?"

"Not a fucking drop, man, I swear."

"What did you do afterward?"

"I apologized—I helped him to an armchair and poured him a glass of water. There was a jug of water and a bottle of whiskey on the sideboard."

Keller wiped his bloody nose on his shirtsleeve, took the glass of water, and set it on a table by the chair, gestured again for Ryan to leave, and told him there was no reason to say anything to Indiana about the whole unseemly episode. According to Ryan, that was all there was to it. He went back to his van and headed for San Francisco. He was tired and, when it started to rain, blinded by the reflection of the streetlights on the road, since he wasn't wearing his contact lenses. He thought it best to park and sleep in the van for a while.

"I don't know what's wrong with me, Pedro. I used to be able to keep a cool head under machine-gun fire, and now a five-minute spat leaves me with a blinding headache."

He pulled off the road, he explained, stopped the van, climbed into the backseat, and fell asleep almost immediately. He woke up toward dawn, just as the overcast sky began to pale, with Attila pawing at him gently, desperate to get out. He opened the door of the van so the dog could get out and relieve himself, then drove to the nearest McDonald's he could find open, bought a burger for

Attila and ate breakfast and came back to the loft where Alarcón had been waiting for him.

"I didn't kill him, Pedro."

"If I thought you did, I wouldn't be here. But you left a nice trail of evidence, including your fingerprints on the doorbell, the glass, the water bottle, and God knows where else."

"Why the hell wouldn't I have left prints? I had nothing to hide. Apart from a bloody nose, Keller was fine when I left."

"You'll have a job convincing the cops."

"I'm not planning to try. Bob Martín hates my guts, and the feeling is mutual. Nothing would give him greater pleasure than to arrest me for Keller's death—and maybe for all those other murders recently, if he can make it stick. He knows Indi and I are friends, and he's got a suspicion we used to be together. Whenever we see each other, you could cut the atmosphere with a knife. Sometimes we run into each other at the shooting range, and he'll get pissed because I'm a much better shot than he is, but what he really can't handle is the fact that his daughter loves me. Amanda, who's always hated her mother's boyfriends, was happy when she found out we were together, and Bob Martín can't forgive me for that."

"So what are you going to do?"

"I'll settle it my own way, like I always do. I'll find out who killed Keller before Martín locks me up and closes the case. I need to disappear."

"Are you nuts? Running away will just make you look guilty. We'd be better off finding you a good attorney."

"I'm not planning to go far. I'll need your help, though. We've got a couple of hours before they identify my prints and come looking for me. I need to copy everything on my computers to a flash drive and then wipe the hard drives, because that's the first thing they'll seize, and there's a lot of confidential information there. It's going to take a while."

In the meantime he asked Pedro to get him a boat with a single berth and a decent engine, but not from a dealer, who might be suspicious about him paying cash and call the police: it needed to be secondhand, but in good condition. He would also need enough fuel in jerry cans to last several days and two prepaid cell phones so they could keep in touch, since his cell wasn't working and Pedro would need one just to talk to him.

Ryan opened a hidden wall safe and took out several wads of bills, credit cards, and driver's licenses. He gave Alarcón $15,000 in stacks of hundreds, fastened with elastic bands.

"Jesus!" said Pedro with a whistle of admiration. "I always suspected you were a spy."

"They pay me well, and I don't spend much."

"The CIA or the United Arab Emirates?"

"Both."

"You rich?" Alarcón asked.

"No. And I don't want to be. What's in this safe is pretty much every cent I have. I've never been interested in money, Pedro—that's one thing Indiana and I have in common. The only thing I'll worry about if we do get together is us not winding up as a pair of hoboes."

"So what are you interested in?"

"Adventure. I want you to take everything that's in the wall safe here before the police impound it. We're likely to have a few expenses. If anything happens to me, give the rest to Indiana, okay?"

"No dice. I plan on keeping the lot—and no one's ever going to find out, because all this money has to be illegal or counterfeit, right?"

"Thanks, Pedro, I knew I could rely on you."

"If anything does happen to you, Ryan, it'll be because of that arrogance of yours. You've no sense of reality—you think you're Superman. Aha! I see you've got five different passports here, all with your mug shot on them—"

"You never know when they might come in useful. And yeah, I might be arrogant, but I'm very careful. It's like guns, Pedro. I don't like to use them, but I feel safer just having one."

"If you hadn't been a soldier, you'd have been a gangster."

"Probably. I'll be on the quay at Tiburon in three hours, and I'll wait there until two p.m. You need to be careful not to leave a paper trail when you're buying the boat. Oh, and I'm gonna need you to make my pickup truck disappear too. All this shit you're doing for me makes you an accessory. You got a problem with that?"

"Nope."

Monday, 19

Two weeks later, when the fearful hand of Celeste Roko's grisly prophecy finally gripped his family, Deputy Chief Martín would kick himself for not heeding his daughter's repeated warnings earlier. Until now, as Amanda kept him informed of the discoveries she and the other Ripper players had made, her father had simply dismissed this as five kids and an old man playing online games, until finally—reluctantly—he had to agree that they were right. The bloody murders plaguing San Francisco were the work of a serial killer. Until the death of Alan Keller, the work of the homicide detail had consisted of analyzing evidence and trying to make a connection between the killings. This was different from their usual approach, which began with looking for a motive—but it had been impossible to guess what had provoked the murderer to choose such an array of victims.

After Keller's death, though, the investigation took a new turn. They were no longer blindly following clues in an attempt to find a killer—instead they were determined to track down a suspect and prove him guilty. That suspect was Ryan Miller.

Since Bob Martín followed the legal requirements to the letter—to ensure that any evidence found would be admissible at
trial—it took several days to get a search warrant for the old printworks where Miller lived. Few judges were prepared to sign such a
sweeping search warrant. The suspect was a former Navy SEAL,
a decorated war hero who apparently worked on secret projects for
the government and the Pentagon; the slightest misstep could have
grave consequences, but hindering the arrest of a suspected murderer would be even worse. Finally, the judge bowed to the deputy
chief's pressure. The moment he had the warrant, Bob personally
led the ten-strong team that stormed Miller's loft, using the most
technologically sophisticated equipment.

The deputy chief was determined to match the evidence in his
possession with what they found in the loft apartment. He had María
Pescadero's descriptions of the man with the dog, which fitted Ryan
Miller and that hideous creature that usually trotted around after
him. At the crime scene, they had found animal hairs that identified
the dog as being a Belgian Malinois, bootprints in the hallway and
on the tiled floor, fingerprints on the doorframe, the bell, the water
bottle, and the glass, synthetic fibers identified as being pink nylon
fleece, and—most importantly—traces of skin and hair, left when
the attacker had punched Keller in the face, from which they could
extract DNA. In Miller's apartment they found the same dog hairs,
the same pink fibers, the same boot prints on the floor; they also
discovered bottles of Xanax and lorazepam, firearms, and a crossbow that employed a series of levers and pulleys, of the sort used
in archery competitions. The ammunition found in the apartment
was not the same caliber as the bullet recovered from the head of Ed
Staton, and the arrows were also different from that retrieved from
Keller's body, but the existence of the bow proved that the owner
was familiar with the weapon.

The team seized Miller's computers and sent them to a lab, but before the forensic technicians could open them, an order arrived from Washington, insisting that they be sealed until a decision could be made. In all probability Miller had installed a self-destruct program, but if he had not, only the proper authority would be permitted to access the contents.

During his interrogation, Pedro Alarcón explained that his friend worked with a number of security companies in Dubai, and it was not unusual for him to go away for a couple of weeks. But no one carrying Ryan Miller's passport had left the country.

"Ryan didn't do this, Dad," Amanda said when Petra Horr told her about the search. "Does he look like a serial killer to you?"

"He looks like a suspect in Alan Keller's murder."

"But why would he kill Alan?"

"Because he was in love with your mother," said Bob.

"People haven't murdered out of jealousy since Shakespeare's day, Dad."

"You're wrong—it's the most common motive for murder among couples."

"Okay, maybe Ryan did have a motive to kill Keller, but why would he have been involved in the other murders? I mean, they were all committed by the same person."

"He was trained to wage war, trained to kill. Now I'm not saying that all soldiers are potential murderers, nothing like that, but sometimes mentally unbalanced men join the army and are given medals for the very actions that in civilian life would land them in jail or in a nuthouse. And there are also men driven mad by war."

"Ryan's not crazy, Dad."

"You're hardly an expert in psychology, Amanda. I really don't get what you like about this guy. He's dangerous."

"The only reason you don't like him is because he's friends with Mom."

"Your mother and I are divorced, Amanda—her friends are

none of my business. But Miller has a history of physical and emotional problems, depression, drug and alcohol addiction, and violence. He's taking anxiolytics and sleeping pills—the same pills used to drug the Constantes."

"Gramps says lots of people take those drugs."

"Why are you defending him?"

"It's common sense, Dad. In every single earlier murder the killer was careful not to leave any evidence—he was probably wearing plastic coveralls, he made sure he left no fingerprints, even on the stuff he sent by mail, like Ashton's book and Judge Rosen's glass wolf. Do you really think a guy who wiped his prints off the arrow in Keller's body would have left them all over his house, including on the poisoned glass? It doesn't add up."

"There are cases where a suspect's life spins out of control and he starts leaving clues, because deep down he wants to be caught."

"I guess one of your criminal psychologists told you that? Ryan Miller would split his sides if he heard that theory. To handle cyanide, the killer would have to wear latex gloves. You really think Ryan put on gloves to tip the powder in, then took them off to pick up the glass? He'd have to be an idiot!"

"I don't know precisely what happened yet, but you have to promise me that you'll let me know if Miller tries to get in touch with your mother."

"Please don't ask me that, Dad. This could end with an innocent man being sentenced to death."

"I'm not kidding, Amanda. Miller will have a chance to prove his innocence, but right now we have to assume he's very dangerous. Even if he did not commit the other murders, in the Keller case, all the evidence points to him. Am I making myself clear?"

"Yes, Dad."

"Promise?"

"I promise."

"What?"

"That I'll tell you if I find out Ryan Miller has been in touch with Mom."

"Have you got your fingers crossed behind your back?"

"No, Dad, it's not a trick."

///////////////////

Though she promised her father she would rat out Ryan, Amanda had no intention of keeping her word—a broken promise would weigh less heavily on her conscience than ruining the life of a friend. She had to choose the lesser of two evils, but to ensure the situation did not arise in the first place, she asked her mother not to tell her if Ryan made another appearance on her patient list or in her love life. Indiana must have seen something in her daughter's face, because she asked no questions, only nodded.

Indiana knew that the police had a warrant out to arrest Ryan as the only suspect in Alan Keller's murder, but like Amanda, she did not believe he was capable of cold-blooded murder. No one was more desperate to see Alan's killer caught than Indiana, but she felt certain that her friend, her one-time lover, this man she felt she understood, whose body she had caressed with the hands of a healer and the lips of a lover, was not guilty. She would have found herself in a difficult situation if asked why she was so convinced of the innocence of an ex-soldier prone to fits of violence, a man who had shot civilians, including women and children, and tortured prisoners in order to secure confessions. But no one did ask; no one, aside from Pedro Alarcón, knew about Ryan's past. Indiana's belief in Ryan's innocence was based on intuition as well as on the wisdom of the planets, and under these circumstances she trusted it more than she did the judgment of her ex-husband. Bob had had problems with all the men Indiana had dated since their divorce, but he had taken a particular dislike to Ryan. Amanda was quick to explain it: just like orangutans, as alpha males, they were incapable of sharing the same territory. Indiana, on the other hand, was happy about her ex-husband's dating, convinced that among his many conquests he would find the perfect stepmother for Amanda and settle down.

In the end, Indiana didn't need to keep secrets from her daughter—who in turn did not need to lie to her father—because Ryan did not contact Indiana. Instead he got in touch with Amanda indirectly. Pedro Alarcón showed up at her boarding school just as class got out, waited for the buses and cars to leave, and then went in and asked if he might speak to Amanda Martín about a video. He was greeted by Sister Cecile, who looked after the boarders—a tall, powerful Scottish woman who looked younger than her sixty-six years, and whose piercing blue eyes could detect sins in her pupils before they had committed them. When he explained Amanda's project about Uruguay, she led him into the Silent Room, as they called the small annex off the chapel. Since the school's ecumenical policy was considered more important than its Catholic heritage, this room was provided for girls of other denominations and for agnostics. Here they could worship in their own fashion, or simply sit in silence. The room had a polished wooden floor and tranquil blue-gray walls; there was no furniture except a few cushions for meditations and some rolled-up prayer mats for the two Muslim girls at the school. At this hour the room was empty and almost dark, lit faintly by slim shafts of evening light that filtered through the two narrow windows. Outside, the slender branches of the larch trees were silhouetted against the glass, and the only sound to be heard was a distant piano. Pedro felt a lump in his throat as he suddenly found himself transported to another time, another place, to the distant country of his childhood before guerrilla warfare put an end to his innocence. He was once again in his grandmother's little chapel in the familiar surroundings of Paysandú, a cattle-farming region where sweeping pastures rolled away toward a boundless turquoise horizon.

Sister Cecile brought in two folding chairs, offered the visitor a bottle of water, went to fetch her pupil, and left the two alone. The door remained ajar, however, and she made it clear she would be close by, since Alarcón was not on the list of the girl's authorized visitors.

As they'd agreed in their e-mails, Amanda showed up with a video camera that she set up on a tripod before opening her note-pad. They talked about Uruguay for fifteen minutes before spending a further ten minutes talking in whispers about the fugitive. In January, when he heard the Ripper kids had started investigating the San Francisco murders, Alarcón had been immediately interested—not simply because he was intrigued by the idea of five shy, reclusive, gifted brats taking on the vast apparatus of a police investigation, but because the function of the human brain was his specialty. Artificial intelligence, as he liked to say to his students on the first day of class, is the theory and development of computer systems capable of accomplishing tasks that ordinarily require human intelligence. Is there a difference between human and artificial intelligence? Is it possible for a machine to create, to feel emotions, to imagine, to have consciousness? Or can it merely imitate and perfect certain human abilities? From these questions came the academic discipline that most fascinated Professor Alarcón: cognitive science, which—like artificial intelligence—posits that human thought can be understood in terms of computational procedures. The objective of the cognitive sciences is to reveal the workings of the most complex device we know: the human brain. When Alarcón announced that the number of distinct states of the human mind is probably greater than the number of atoms in the universe, any preconceived idea his students had about artificial intelligence crumbled. The kids who played Ripper reasoned using logic, something a machine could do with unbelievably greater power, but they also had something unique to human beings: imagination. They enjoyed complete freedom in the game, playing simply for the fun of it, and could therefore access inner spaces that, for the moment, artificial intelligence could not reach. Pedro Alarcón dreamed of the possibility of harvesting this elusive feature of the human mind and applying it to a computer.

Amanda knew nothing about any of this. She had kept Alarcón up to speed about the progress of Ripper simply because he was a friend of Ryan's, and because he and her grandfather were the only adults who had shown any interest in the game.

"Where's Ryan?" Amanda asked.

"He's on the move. A moving target is harder to hit. Listen, Amanda, Ryan's no Jack the Ripper."

"I know. What can I do to help?"

"You can find out who the real killer is, and fast. You and the kids playing Ripper can be the brains of this operation, and Ryan can be the executive arm."

"You mean like James Bond?"

"Yeah, but without the gadgets. No death-ray-shooting fountain pens or shoes with jet engines in the soles. All he's got is Attila and his Navy SEAL gear."

"What does that consist of?"

"I don't know—a pair of swim trunks so he doesn't have to go skinny-dipping, probably, a knife in case he gets attacked by a shark."

"He's living on a boat?"

"That's confidential information."

"There's a hundred acres of park and unspoiled forest right here in the school grounds, and it's teeming with coyotes, deer, raccoons, skunks, and probably a couple of polecats—but no people.

It would be a good place to hide out, and I could bring food from the canteen. The food's good here."

"Thanks, I'll bear that in mind. For the time being, Ryan can't get in touch with you or anyone else—I'm the only link. I'll give you a number. If you need me, call, let it ring three times, then hang up. Don't leave a message. I'll find you. I need to be careful, I've got people watching me."

"Who?"

"Your dad. I mean, the cops. But don't worry about them, Amanda, I can shake a police tail—I spent half my youth dodging the cops back in Montevideo."

"Why?"

"I used to be an idealist, but I got over that a long time ago."

"It was easier to shake off the cops in the old days than it is now, Pedro."

"Oh, it's still easy, don't you worry."

"You know how to hack into people's computers?"

"No."

"I thought you were some kind of computer genius, worked in artificial intelligence or something."

"Computers are to artificial intelligence what telescopes are to astronomy," said Alarcón. "What do you need a hacker for?"

"It'd be useful to have in my line of investigation. We could use a hacker for Ripper."

"When the time comes, I can find you one."

"We'll use my henchman as a messenger. Kabel and I have a code. Kabel's my grandfather."

"I know that. Can we trust him?"

Amanda answered with an icy stare.

They said their good-byes at the front door of the school, closely watched by Sister Cecile. The nun was particularly fond of Amanda Martín because she shared her taste for brutal Scandinavian crime novels and because, in a moment of weakness she later regretted, the girl had told her she was investigating the bloodbath predicted by Celeste Roko. She regretted it because ever since, Sister Cecile, who would have given her right arm to play the game if the kids would allow her, had insisted on following every detail of the investigation, and Amanda found it difficult to keep anything from her.

"A charming gentleman, your Uruguayan friend," she said in a tone that immediately put Amanda on the alert. "How do you know him?"

"He's a friend of a friend of the family."

"Does he have anything to do with Ripper?"

"That's ridiculous, Sister. He only came to help me out with my social justice project."

"Then why were you whispering? I thought I sensed a certain complicity   "

"Occupational hazard, Sister. After all, it's your job to be suspicious, isn't it?"

"No, Amanda." The Scottish woman smiled, flashing teeth as big as dominos. "My job is to serve God and to educate young women."

Saturday, 24

Ryan spent the first week of his new life as a fugitive from justice sailing around San Francisco Bay in the boat Pedro had managed to find, a half-cabin sixteen-foot Bell Boy with a Yamaha outboard motor, registered under a false name. At night he moored in small inlets and sometimes went ashore with Attila so they could run a few miles in the darkness, the only exercise he could take aside from swimming, and that only if he was very careful. He could have gone on bobbing on the bay for years without ever having to show his permit or being intercepted as long as he did not dock in any of the popular marinas, since Coast Guard vessels could not navigate in shallow water.

His knowledge of the bay, where he had often gone out rowing, sailing, or fishing for sturgeon and sea bass with Pedro, made life as an outlaw easier. He knew he was safe in places like Toothless Creek—the nickname given to a tiny port full of clapped-out boats and floating houses whose few residents had lots of tattoos but very few teeth; they barely spoke to each other and would not even look a stranger in the eyes. He was also safe in some of the ramshackle villages near the mouths of the creeks, where locals grew weed or cooked meth and no one was in a hurry to attract the attention of the police. Even so, the cramped boat quickly became unbearable for both man and dog, so they began hiding out on land, camping in the woods. Ryan had had very little time to prepare before he ran, but he had brought the essentials: his laptops, various ID cards, a bag containing cash that was waterproof and fire-resistant, and some of his Navy SEAL equipment—more for sentimental reasons than because he thought he might use it.

He and Attila holed up for three days in Wingo, a ghost town in Sonoma with a disused bridge eaten away by rust, boardwalks bleached by the sun, and tumbledown cabins. They would have stayed longer among the ducks, the rodents, the deer, and the silent presence of the ghosts that gave Wingo its reputation, but Ryan was afraid, with spring fast approaching, that the place would attract fishermen, hunters, and tourists. At night, huddled in his sleeping bag, with the wind whistling between the timbers and the warmth of Attila's body beside him, he imagined Indiana lying next to him, her head on his shoulder, one arm slung across his chest, her curly hair brushing against his lips.

It was on their third night in the abandoned village that Ryan dared summon the image of Sharbat for the first time. It took a while to come, but when it did, she was not the faint, blood-drenched figure of his nightmares but the little girl he remembered—unhurt, a surprised look on her face, wearing a flowered headscarf and carrying her little brother. He was able to ask her forgiveness, to promise that he would go halfway around the world to find her, and in an unstoppable torrent of words, he told her all the things he could tell to no one but her: no one wants to know the truth about war, only the heroic account stripped of all horror; no one wants to listen to a soldier talking about his pain. He could tell her how, after World War II, when it was discovered that only one in four soldiers was prepared to shoot to kill, military training had been developed to eliminate this instinctive aversion and replace it with an automatic reflex to fire at the slightest stimulus—a reflex burned so well into soldiers' muscle memory that 95 percent of soldiers now killed without even thinking. But the army still had not found a way to silence the tolling bell of conscience that rang out later, after the fighting, when soldiers rejoined the ordinary world and had time to think; when they were plagued with nightmares and with shame that even booze and drugs could not blot out; when they had nowhere to vent the rage welling inside them, forcing some to pick fights in bars and others to beat their wives and children.

He told Sharbat that he belonged to a group of elite soldiers, the best in the world. Each was a deadly weapon, violence and death their profession, but sometimes conscience can prevail over military training, and over all the noble justifications for war—duty, honor, country. And when this happens, some men see the devastation caused wherever they go to fight. They see their comrades bleed to death from an enemy grenade; they see the bodies of the old, the women, and the children caught up in the conflict, and they begin to wonder why they are fighting, begin to question the reasons for this war, for this occupation of a foreign land, for the suffering of people just like them. They ask themselves how they would feel if enemy tanks invaded their neighborhood and razed their houses, if the bodies trampled underfoot were those of their children or their wives; they ask themselves if they really owe greater loyalty to their country than they do to God and to their own sense of good and evil; they ask themselves why they carry on with this murderous rampage, and how they will live with the monsters they have become.

The girl with the green eyes listened quietly and attentively, as though she understood the language Ryan spoke, as though she knew why he was weeping, and she stayed with him until, exhausted, he finally dozed off, one arm thrown over the dog that watched him as he slept.

When Ryan's photo was circulated to the media in an appeal for information on his whereabouts, Pedro contacted Denise West, a friend whose discretion he trusted absolutely. He needed her help, he told her, in aiding a suspect in a case of first-degree murder—as he jokingly put it—though he did not downplay the risks involved. Denise West was enthusiastic about hiding this man, not only because she was Pedro's friend and Ryan did not look like a killer, but also because she operated on the assumption that the government, the judicial system in general, and the police in particular were corrupt. She welcomed the Navy SEAL into her home, which Pedro had chosen because it was located in a farmland area and close to the estuary of the Napa River where it flowed into San Pablo Bay, the northern extension of San Francisco Bay.

Denise had a four-acre property that included a kitchen garden where she grew vegetables and flowers for herself, a horse sanctuary that took in animals whose owners would otherwise have sent them to the slaughterhouse, and a small agribusiness selling fruit, chickens, and eggs at farmers' markets and to organic grocery stores. She had lived there for forty years, surrounded by neighbors who, like her, were not particularly sociable but devoted themselves to their land and their animals. Into this humble haven she had created, protected from the bustle and vulgarity of the world, she welcomed Ryan and Attila, who would have to adapt to rural life—the house had no television, no domestic appliances, though it did have a good Internet connection—among pampered pets and retired horses. Neither had ever shared a home with a woman, and both were surprised that it was not as bad as they had feared. From the start, Attila showed his military discipline by stoically refraining from devouring the chickens foraging in the yard or attacking the cats that goaded him with obvious contempt.

Besides giving him somewhere to hide out, Denise offered to play Ryan's character on Ripper, since he could not show his face. Amanda needed him in the game and quickly created the character of Jezebel, a particularly talented private investigator. The only people who knew Jezebel's true identity were the games master and her loyal henchman Kabel, but even they did not know where the Navy SEAL was hiding out, nor did they know the identity of the middle-aged woman with long gray hair who played the role for him. The other kids playing Ripper had not been consulted about Jezebel because, as the crimes had become more complicated, Amanda had become more autocratic; but those who objected in principle quickly realized the new player was worth her weight in gold.

"I've been going over the police files for the cases," said the games master.

"How did you get those?" asked Esmeralda.

"My henchman has access to police records, and I'm friends with the deputy chief's assistant Petra Horr, who keeps me up-to-date. We've given copies of the files to Jezebel."

"Not fair! No one should have an advantage over the other players!" protested Colonel Paddington.

"I agree. I'm sorry, it won't happen again. Let's see what Jezebel has to say."

"I've found a connection between all the victims except Alan Keller. All five of the early victims worked with children. Ed Staton worked at a juvenile detention center in Arizona, the Constantes ran a home looking after children sent to them by Child Protective Services, Richard Ashton was a pediatric psychiatrist, and Rachel Rosen was a juvenile court judge. Now, it could be a coincidence, but I don't think so. Keller, on the other hand, never worked with children—in fact, he didn't even want kids."

"That's an interesting clue," said Sherlock. "If the motive has to do with children, then we can assume our killer didn't murder Keller."

"Or that he was killed for some other reason," interrupted Abatha, who had already suggested this possibility.

"These won't have been ordinary kids," said Colonel Paddington. "We're talking about orphans, children with behavioral problems, children at risk. That limits our options."

"The next step is to work out whether the victims knew each other, and if so, how," said Amanda. "I'm guessing there must be one or more children that link these cases."

Monday, 26

T he crimes that had Bob Martín on tenterhooks gained a certain amount of notoriety in the San Francisco media, but the population was not particularly alarmed, since the news that a serial killer was at large did not leave the Major Crimes Division. The press treated the murders as unrelated, and the rest of the country was oblivious to what was happening. While the American public could occasionally be moved by a white supremacist or a student armed for the Apocalypse going rogue and massacring innocents, they were utterly uninterested in six bodies in California. The only person to mention the crimes was a famous right-wing radio host who claimed they were divine retribution for San Francisco's policies on homosexuality, feminism, and the environment.

Bob was hoping that national indifference would mean he could get on with his job without federal agencies getting involved, and so it proved until two weeks after suspicion had fallen on Ryan Miller, when two FBI agents showed up at his office, cloaked in so much mystery that he had to wonder whether they were impostors. Unfortunately their badges turned out to be genuine, and he received orders from the chief of police to give them all possible assistance, something he did only reluctantly.

The San Francisco Police Department, founded in 1849 at the time of the gold rush, was, according to a commentator at the time, "largely made up of ex-bandits, and naturally the members are interested above all in saving their old friends from punishment. Policemen here are quite as much to be feared as the robbers. . . . The city is in a hopeless chaos, and many years must pass before order can be established." In the end, the police force sorted itself out much more quickly than that particular writer had anticipated, and Bob was proud to be part of the SFPD. His department had a reputation for being tough on crime but lenient when it came to minor offenses, and could certainly not have been accused of brutality, corruption, and incompetence, like other forces. Though it received an inordinate number of complaints alleging misconduct, very few of the allegations had any foundation. The problem, Bob believed, lay not with the police but with the tendency of the citizens of San Francisco to defy authority. He trusted his team completely, which was precisely why he was sorry to see the FBI turn up. They would only hinder the investigation.

The agents in the deputy chief's office introduced themselves as Napoleon Fournier III, an African American from Louisiana who had worked for narcotics, immigration, and customs enforcement before being transferred to the Secret Service, and Lorraine Barcott, from Virginia, who was something of a celebrity in the agency, having shown outstanding bravery during an antiterrorist operation. Barcott, with her black hair, dark eyes, and long lashes, turned out to be much more attractive in person than in her photos. As they shook hands, Bob thought he might charm her with the widest smile he could manage, but he stopped when Barcott almost crushed his fingers; here was a woman on a mission, not about to be distracted by pleasantries. His Mexican upbringing had taught him to be gallant, so he pulled out a chair for her; she sat else-where. Petra Horr, watching this scene from the doorway, cleared her throat to suppress a laugh.

The deputy chief showed the visitors the case files for the six murders and brought them up-to-date on the investigation, as well as his own thoughts on the matter, without mentioning the con-tributions of his daughter Amanda and his ex-father-in-law Blake Jackson, for fear that the agents might take these for nepotism. This was how Alan Keller had described the convoluted relation-ships in Indiana's family; before hearing it from Keller's lips and looking it up in the dictionary, Bob had never heard the word.

The first order of business for Barcott and Fournier was to make sure no one had touched Ryan Miller's computers, which were safely stored in the department's secure evidence locker. This done, they hunkered down to review the evidence in search of some detail that might reveal a conspiracy by the usual enemies of the United States. They informed Bob Martín only that the Navy SEAL worked for a private security company that had contracts with the US government in the Middle East; this was the official line, and they could not reveal any further details. Miller's work was confidential, and spanned a number of gray areas where it was necessary to work outside normal agreements in order to be effec-tive. Given the complexities of the situation in the Middle East, it was important to weigh the duty to protect American interests in the region against international treaties that unreasonably limited their ability to act. The government and the armed forces could not be seen to be involved in activities forbidden by the Constitu-tion or which the public found distasteful, and so they employed private military contractors. It was obvious that Miller worked for the CIA; since the agency did not have jurisdiction on home territory, however, the case fell to the FBI. The agents had no interest whatsoever in the six murder victims; their brief was to retrieve the information in Ryan Miller's possession before it fell into enemy hands, find the Navy SEAL so he could answer a number of questions, and then take him out of circulation.

"So Miller's been involved in crimes on an international scale?" said Bob, thunderstruck.

"Missions," said Fournier III, "not crimes."

"And here I was, thinking he was just some workaday serial killer!"

"You have no evidence to substantiate such an allegation, Deputy Chief Martín," spat Barcott, "and I don't appreciate the sarcasm."

"The evidence against him in Keller's case file is convincing enough," said the deputy chief.

"Evidence that he visited Mr. Keller, not that he killed him."

"Then why did he run away?"

"Has it occurred to you that he may have been kidnapped?" asked the woman.

"No," said Bob, barely able to suppress a smile. "I can honestly say it hasn't."

"Ryan Miller would be of great value to the enemy."

"Which enemy are we talking about?"

"I'm afraid we cannot discuss that."

FBI headquarters in Washington also sent an expert in computer forensics to examine the machines seized from Miller's apartment. Deputy Chief Martín had suggested they use his forensics team, but was informed that the content of the hard drives was classified. Everything was classified.

Barely twenty-four hours had passed since the federal agents had arrived, and already Bob was at the end of his rope. Fournier turned out to be obsessive, incapable of delegating, and so intent on understanding every minor detail that he held up work for everyone else. The deputy chief had got off to a bad start with Lorraine Barcott and his later attempts to ingratiate himself with her were unsuccessful; the woman was immune to his charms, even to simple camaraderie.

"Don't take it to heart, boss," Petra Horr consoled him. "Maybe you haven't noticed, but Barcott's a lesbian."

The computer forensics expert spent his time analyzing the hard drives, doing his best to salvage something, though he assumed that Miller knew exactly how to safely erase everything on there. In the meantime, Bob gave Fournier and Barcott an account of the twelve-day manhunt to track down Miller. Initially they had put out feelers to the other police forces around the Bay Area and to their usual informants, but after the first week they issued a photo and a description of Miller to the media and published it online. Since then, they had received dozens of calls from people who had seen a cripple with a face like a gorilla hobbling around with some savage beast on a leash, but none of the reports had led to anything. On a handful of occasions one or the other tramp and his dog had been mistakenly arrested and then immediately released. A Gulf War vet tried to turn himself in at Richmond Police Station, claiming to be Ryan Miller, but no one took him seriously—his dog was not only a Jack Russell but a bitch.

They had interviewed people who had dealings with the fugitive—Frank Rinaldi, the owner of the Dolphin Club, where Miller regularly went swimming; the superintendent of the building where he lived; a couple of underprivileged kids he was teaching to swim; Danny D'Angelo at the Café Rossini; the people at the Holistic Clinic, and, most particularly, his closest friend, Pedro Alarcón. Bob had talked to Indiana but, determined not to bring his own family to the agency's attention, casually implied to the FBI agents that she was just another therapist working at the Holistic Clinic. He knew that Indiana had had a brief affair with Miller, which for reasons he didn't understand bothered him more than the four years she had been with Alan Keller. He could not help but wonder what Miller had that appealed to Indiana. She had probably slept with him out of pity, he decided; given her compassionate nature, Indiana could not have rejected an amputee. He couldn't believe how dumb she could be. What would it be like, making love to someone with a missing leg? It was a circus act; the possibilities were limited, and it was better not to imagine. His determination to apprehend the fugitive was sheer professional zeal; it had nothing to do with whatever filthy things the man had done with the mother of his child.

"This Alarcón, he a Communist?" said Lorraine Barcott, after finding his file in the FBI database via her cell phone in under a minute.

"No, he's a professor at Stanford University."

"That doesn't preclude his being a Communist," she snapped.

"So there's still a few commies out there, huh? I thought they'd gone out of fashion. We have Alarcón's cell wiretapped, and we're keeping a tail on him. So far, we've found nothing linking him to the Kremlin, and nothing illegal or suspicious in his daily routine."

The FBI agents pointed out that the fugitive was a Navy SEAL trained to survive in the most inhospitable conditions—to hide, evade the enemy, or fight him to the death. It would be difficult to track him down, and the only thing achieved by alerting the public would be to spread panic. The police would be better off, they suggested, saying nothing to the media and quietly carrying on the investigation with the invaluable help the FBI could provide. It was imperative, they insisted, that nothing be revealed about Ryan Miller's activities or the international security firm.

"My job isn't to keep secrets for the FBI," said Bob, "it is to lead this investigation, solve the six open cases, and ensure no further crimes are committed."

"Of course, Deputy Chief," said Napoleon Fournier III. "We wouldn't dream of interfering in your work, but I think it best to warn you that Ryan Miller is a possibly unbalanced individual who may have committed the murders he is accused of while in an altered mental state. One way or another, as far as we're concerned, he's got himself burned."

"What you mean is, he's no use to you anymore, he's a problem, and you don't know what to do with him. Miller is dispensable, Agent Fournier—is that what you're telling me?"

"Your words, not mine."

"May I remind you that Miller is violent and heavily armed," Lorraine Barcott interrupted. "He's been a soldier all his life, used to shooting first and asking questions later—I strongly advise you do likewise: think about the safety of your officers and of civilians."

"It wouldn't do for Miller to be captured and start talking, would it?"

"We seem to understand each other, Deputy Chief."

"I don't think we understand each other at all, Agent Barcott," snapped Bob, piqued. "I realize the agency's methods are rather different from those of the police, but Ryan Miller is innocent until proven otherwise. It's our intention to arrest him and question him as a suspect, and in doing so to cause as little harm to him and to any bystanders as possible. Is that clear?"

As he came out of the meeting, Petra Horr, who had been eavesdropping from her cubicle as usual, grabbed the deputy chief's sleeve, pushed him behind the door, and stood on tiptoe to kiss him on the mouth.

"You told 'em! I'm so proud of you, boss!"

Bob was so stunned that he could think of no response before his assistant vanished like the little sprite she was. He stood pressed against the wall, savoring the cinnamon-gum taste of her kiss and a lingering feeling of warmth in his body.

Saturday, 31

The first person to be concerned by Indiana's absence was Amanda. Knowing her mother's habits better than anyone, she found it odd that Indiana had not come back for Friday-night dinner—a ritual that had been observed, with few exceptions, since Amanda first went to boarding school four years earlier. Mother and daughter looked forward all week to seeing each other on Friday—especially if Amanda was spending the weekend with her father. Without Alan Keller—who had rarely staked a claim on Indiana's Friday nights, except during their trip to Turkey, or when he wanted to go to some special concert—Indiana had no reason not to be home for dinner. She would finish with her last patient, hop on her bike, and cycle up Broadway past the bars and the strip clubs, along Columbus Avenue, past the famous City Lights bookstore, home to the local beatniks, past the striking burnished copper facade of Francis Ford Coppola's Sentinel Building, and down toward Portsmouth Square, on the edge of Chinatown, where the old men of the Chinese community gathered for tai chi or to bet on tabletop games, and from there over to the Transamerica Pyramid—an unmistakable feature of the San Francisco skyline. At this hour, the financial district was undergoing its evening transformation, as offices closed and bars began to open. Indiana would cycle under the Bay Bridge connecting San Francisco to Berkeley, then past the new baseball stadium, by which time she was ten minutes from home. Sometimes she would stop off to buy something for dessert, but quickly got home and was ready to sit down and eat. Since Indiana was often late, and neither Amanda nor her grandfather could cook, Friday-night dinner relied either on pizza delivery or the kindness of Elsa Domínguez, who would often leave them something in the fridge. That Friday, Blake and Amanda waited until nine o'clock before they gave up and reheated a pizza, which by then was tough as cardboard.

"You think something's happened to Mom?" murmured Amanda.

"She'll be here. Your mother's over thirty—it's only normal that once in a while she should go out for a drink with her friends after a hard week's work."

"But she could have called! One of her so-called friends could have lent her a cell phone."

Saturday dawned under an ocher sky, and spring setting out its stall in budding magnolia blossoms, with hummingbirds hovering like tiny helicopters between the fuchsias in the garden. Amanda woke with a jolt, feeling a foretaste of some disaster, and sat up in bed, shaking off the memory of a nightmare in which Alan Keller was trying to rip the arrow from his chest. A thin, golden ray slipped between the curtains to illuminate the room, and Save-the-Tuna was purring contentedly, curled into a ball on the pillow. The girl picked the cat up and buried her face in her warm belly, muttering an incantation to dispel the lingering images of her nightmare.

Barefoot and wearing one of her grandfather's T-shirts for pajamas, she followed the smell of coffee and fresh toast through the house and padded into the kitchen to give the cat some milk and make a cup of hot chocolate. Blake was already there, watching the news in slippers and an old flannel robe, the same one he had worn seventeen years earlier, when his wife was still alive. Amanda deposited the cat in his lap and went up to the witch's cave via the spiral staircase. A moment later she was back in the kitchen, loudly announcing that there was nobody in her mother's bedroom, and the bed had not been slept in. It was the first time since Amanda and her grandfather could remember that Indiana had not come home without calling.

"Where could she have gone, Grandpa?"

"Don't worry, Amanda. You get dressed, and I'll drop you at your dad's and then go to the clinic. I'm sure there's a simple explanation."

But Blake could find no explanation. At noon, having checked all her usual haunts and called around to Indiana's friends—including Doña Encarnación, whom he did not want to worry any more than was necessary, and the formidable Celeste Roko, who answered the phone in the middle of a massage only because she saw that the call was from the man she planned to marry—with no results, Blake Jackson finally called his ex-son-in-law and asked if he thought it was appropriate to get the police involved. Bob Martín suggested he wait a while—the police were not likely to send out a search party for a grown woman who had spent one night away from home—but he promised to put out some feelers and call if he heard anything. Both men were afraid that Indiana was with Ryan Miller. Knowing her the way they did, they could list a number of reasons why that fear was justified—from the unbridled compassion that might move her to shelter a fugitive from the law to her troubled heart, capable of making her pursue another love to replace the one she had just lost. The possibility that neither of them dared to consider yet was that she was with Miller against her will, a hostage. He guessed that if that was the case, they would find out soon—when the phone would ring and the kidnapper named his conditions. He realized that he was sweating.

Pedro's secret cell phone vibrated in the pocket of his tracksuit pants while he was halfway through his daily four-mile run in Presidio Park, training for the triathlon he would have competed in with Ryan had things with his friend not become so complicated. Only two people could be calling him on this number: his fugitive friend, and Amanda Martín. He saw that it was the girl, changed direction, and carried on running until he got to the nearest Starbucks, where he bought a frappuccino—no substitute for a good maté, but useful for throwing anybody who might be following him off the scent—asked to borrow a cell phone from another customer, and called Amanda, who put her grandfather on the line. The conversation with Blake Jackson was just four words: Dolphin Club, forty minutes. Pedro trotted back to his car and drove to the Aquatic Park, where he was lucky enough to find a parking space, then walked nonchalantly into the clubhouse, his bag over his shoulder, as he did every Saturday.

Jackson took a cab to Ghirardelli Square, then walked to the club, mingling with the tourists and families out enjoying one of those magnificent spring days when the light over San Francisco bay is positively Mediterranean. Pedro was waiting for him in the dim lobby of the club, apparently studying the table on which the members of the Polar Bear Club kept track of the distance they had swum over the winter. He signaled to Blake, who followed him up to the cramped locker rooms on the second floor.

"Where's my daughter?" Blake asked.

"Indiana? What makes you think I'd know?"

"She's with Miller, I'm sure of it. She hasn't come home since yesterday, and she hasn't called either. This has never happened before—the only explanation is that she's with him and hasn't called because she's trying to protect him. You know where Miller is hiding out—get a message to him from me."

"I'll give him a message if I can, but I could swear Indiana's not with him."

"Don't swear anything, just talk to your friend. You're aiding and abetting a fugitive—you're guilty of perverting the course of justice. Tell Miller that if Indiana doesn't call me by eight o'clock this evening, you'll be the one to pay."

"Don't threaten me, Blake, I'm on your side."

"Okay, all right," the old man stammered, trying to hide the panicked choke in his voice. "Sorry, Pedro, I'm a little tense."

"It'll be difficult to talk to Miller—he's constantly on the move—but I'll try. Wait for my call, Blake. I'll call you from a pay phone soon as I know something."

Pedro led Blake down the hallway that connected the Dolphin to its rival, the South End Rowing Club, so that he could go out by a different door from the one he had used himself, then went to the beach, where he would have some privacy. He called his friend and explained the situation. As he'd thought, Ryan had no idea where Indiana might be. The last time he had spoken with her, he said, had been from the loft apartment on Saturday, March 10, the day Alan Keller's body was found. While in hiding, he had thought about calling her a thousand times, had thought about risking everything and showing up at the Holistic Clinic. The strange silence that had come between them was getting more unbearable by the day. He needed to see her, to hold her, to tell her that he loved her more than anyone or anything in his life and would never leave her. But he could not make her an accessory. He had nothing to offer her until he could catch Alan Keller's murderer and clear his name. He told Pedro that after securely erasing the contents of his computers and leaving the loft, he had called Amanda, convinced either that Indiana had forgotten her cell phone or that the battery was dead.

"They were together, so I got a chance to speak to Indiana. I told her I didn't kill Keller—I admitted I punched him, and that I had to hide because of the evidence incriminating me."

"What did she say?"

"That I didn't owe her an explanation, because she had never doubted me, and she begged me to give myself up. Obviously, I said I couldn't, and I made her promise not to turn me in. It wasn't exactly the right time to talk about our relationship—Keller had only been dead a couple of hours—but I couldn't help it. I told her I loved her, and that when everything was cleared up I was going to stop at nothing to win her back. But none of that matters now, Pedro. The important thing is to rescue her."

"She's only been gone a couple hours—"

"She's in serious danger!"

"You think her disappearance is related to Keller's death?"

"I know it, Pedro. And from the details of Keller's murder, I'm pretty sure we're dealing with the killer responsible for the other murders."

"I don't see the connection between Indiana and that serial killer."

"Right now, Pedro, I don't see it either, but believe me, it's there. We have to find Indiana right away. Put me in touch with Amanda."

"Amanda? The girl's pretty shaken up with what's happened, I don't see how she can help you."

"You will."

April

*T*he deputy chief, dressed in his gym clothes and with his
daughter in tow—Amanda had refused to stay behind, and
had brought Save-the-Tuna along in her basket—set out for North
Beach. Though it was Sunday, and Bob knew his assistant had no
obligation to work, he called Petra from the car, explained what had
happened, and asked her to get the names and phone numbers of all
the therapists who worked at the Holistic Clinic, of Indiana's patients, and of Pedro Alarcón, all of which were on a list somewhere
in the homicide detail. Ten minutes later he was double-parked in
front of the Holistic Clinic with its green walls and murky yel-
lowing windows. He found the front door open, since some of the
therapists saw patients on weekends. Amanda had withdrawn into
a childlike state, walking around with her head down, the hood of
her parka pulled over her eyes, sucking her thumb, ready to cry at
any moment. She followed the deputy chief up the two flights of
stairs and scaled the ladder leading up to Matheus Pereira's attic, to
ask him for a master key to Indiana's treatment room.

Matheus, who looked for all the world as though he had just got out of bed, answered the door naked apart from a frayed towel slung loosely around his waist to hide his private parts. His dreadlocks were as tangled as the snakes of Medusa, and he wore the vague expression of someone who has smoked something more interesting than tobacco and can't quite recall what year it is. But his disheveled look did nothing to detract from his elegance. With his glinting eyes and full lips, he was all muscle and bone, as beautiful as a Cellini bronze.

The Brazilian's rooftop shack would not have looked out of place in a Calcutta slum. Pereira had built it out of bric-a-brac by the same process he used to make his artwork. Nestling between the water tank and the fire escape on the flat roof, a jumble of cardboard, plastic, zinc sheets, and chipboard panels, the lean-to looked like a living organism. Inside, the floor was mostly bare concrete, with a jumble of linoleum scraps here and there and a few threadbare rugs. A warren of twisted spaces that served various functions, the place could be transformed at the drop of a hat by taking down a piece of oilcloth or moving a folding screen, or by reorganizing the boxes and crates that comprised most of the furniture. Bob decided on first look that it was an airless, filthy, and doubtless illegal hippie den, but deep down he had to admit that it had its charm. The daylight filtering through the plastic sheets gave it the feel of an aquarium. The large canvases streaked with primary colors, which looked so aggressive in the building's foyer, took on a more childish aspect up in the attic; and the mess and grime that anywhere else would have been repellent could be accepted there as an artist's caprice.

"Pull up your towel, Pereira," Bob ordered. "You can see I'm here with my daughter."

"Hey, Amanda," the painter said, positioning himself to block his visitors' view of a marijuana plantation behind a partition made of shower curtains.

Bob had already seen it, just as he had smelled the unmistakable pungent tang that suffused the attic, but he turned a blind eye; he was there to talk about other matters. He explained the reasons for his precipitous visit.

Pereira had spoken to Indiana as she was leaving on Friday afternoon, he said. "She told me she was going to meet some friends at the Rossini, then head home when there was less traffic."

"She mention any of the friends' names?"

"I don't remember. Truth is, I wasn't paying much attention," Pereira replied vaguely. "She was the last one to leave the building. I locked the front door at eight. . . . Or it could have been nine." It didn't look like he was about to provide any useful information, perhaps suspecting that Indiana was involved in something and not wanting to make it easier for her ex-husband to find her.

But the deputy chief's tone suggested it would be better to cooperate, or at least appear to, and sure enough he pulled on his trusty jeans, grabbed a bunch of keys, and led them to Treatment Room 8. He opened the door and, at the request of Bob, who did not know what he might find inside, waited with Amanda in the hallway. Everything in Indiana's room was in perfect order: the towels in a pile, clean sheets on the massage table, the vials of essential oils, magnets, candles and incense, all ready to use on Monday, and the little plant the Brazilian had given her as a gift sitting on the windowsill, looking as if it had recently been watered. From out in the passageway Amanda, who could see the laptop on the reception table, asked her father if she could open it, as she knew the password. Explaining that she might smudge the fingerprints, Bob went down to his car to get a plastic bag and some gloves. Out in the street, he remembered Indiana's bicycle and went round to the side of the building, where she usually locked it to a metal railing. With a shiver, he saw that the bicycle was chained up there. He tasted bile in his throat.

Danny D'Angelo was not on duty at the Café Rossini that day. Bob Martín questioned a few of the waitstaff, who weren't sure whether they had seen Indiana; the place had been packed that Friday afternoon. He also passed around a photo of Indiana, which Amanda had on her cell phone, to the kitchen staff and the customers, who at that hour were enjoying their Italian coffee and the best pastries on North Beach. A few of the regulars recognized her, but they couldn't remember seeing her on the previous Friday. Father and daughter were on the point of leaving when a man with reddish hair and rumpled clothing who'd been sitting at one of the tables at the back, jotting on a yellow notepad, approached them.

"May I ask why you're looking for Indiana Jackson?" he asked.

"Do you know her?"

"You could say that, although we haven't been introduced."

"I'm Bob Martín, deputy chief, Personal Crimes Division, and this is my daughter Amanda." He showed the man his badge.

"Samuel Hamilton Jr., private detective."

"Samuel Hamilton?" asked the deputy chief. "As in the famous detective from the Gordon novels?"

"He was my father. He wasn't a detective, though, he was a reporter, and I fear the author rather exaggerated his skills. That was back in the 1960s. My old man passed away, but for many years he lived off the memory of his former glory—or his fictional glory, I should say."

"What do you know about Indiana Jackson?"

"Plenty, Deputy Chief, including that she was married to you, and that she's Amanda's mother. Allow me to explain. Four years ago Alan Keller employed me to follow her. For my sins, a large portion of my income is provided by jealous spouses and partners who get suspicious—it's the most tedious, distasteful aspect of my work. I couldn't give Mr. Keller any useful information, and he suspended the surveillance, but every couple of months he would call me up again with another attack of jealousy. He was never convinced that Ms. Jackson was faithful."

"Did you know that Alan Keller has been murdered?"

"Of course—it's been all over the media. I'm sorry for Ms. Jackson—she loved him very much."

"We're looking for her now, Mr. Hamilton. She's been missing since yesterday. It seems the last person to see her was a painter that lives at the Holistic Clinic."

"Matheus Pereira."

"That's the guy. He says he saw her in the afternoon, that she came here to meet some friends. D'you know anything?"

"I wasn't here yesterday, but I can give you a list of the friends that Ms. Jackson saw regularly in the last four years. I've got the information at my house—I live nearby."

Half an hour later Hamilton arrived at the police department, carrying a thick folder and his laptop, excited that for the first time in months he had something interesting to work on—something other than following people who had breached the terms of their bail, or spying on couples with a telescope, or threatening poor wretches who couldn't pay their rent or the interest on a loan. His work was tiresome, with none of the poetry or romance about it that it has in books.

Petra Horr had given up on her day off and was in the office trying to cheer up Amanda, who seemed to have shrunk to half her usual size and was silently crouched on the floor, hugging the basket in which she had stowed Save-the-Tuna. That morning, Petra had been in her bathroom, dying her hair three different colors, when she got the phone call from her boss, and had hardly had time to rinse and throw some clothes on before shooting off on her motorcycle. Wearing shorts, a faded T-shirt, and gym shoes, and without the gel she usually spiked her hair with, the deputy chief's assistant looked like a girl of fifteen.

Bob Martín had already arranged for the forensics team to take prints from Indiana's computer and then go to the Holistic Clinic to get samples. Amanda sank deeper and deeper into the hood of her coat as she listened to her father give out his instructions, even with Petra explaining that these were standard measures for gathering information and didn't mean that anything serious had happened to her mother. Amanda only responded with moaning sounds, frantically sucking her thumb. Seeing that the girl was regressing further as the hours passed, and fearing she would be back in diapers if it carried on, Petra picked up the phone on her own initiative and called Blake Jackson. "We still don't know anything, Mr. Jackson, but the deputy chief is dedicating all his energy to finding your daughter. Could you stop by the department? Your granddaughter would feel better if you were here. I'll send a patrol car to get you. It's the April Fool's Run today, and half the streets are closed off."

Meanwhile, Hamilton had laid out on Bob's desk the copious contents of his file, a complete history of Indiana's private life. There were notes on where she went and when, transcripts of tapped phone conversations, and dozens of photographs—most of them taken at a distance, but clear enough when they were enlarged on the screen. There were members of her family, patients from the clinic (including the poodle), and friends and acquaintances. Bob felt a mixture of disgust at the way this man had spied on Indiana, disdain for Alan Keller, who had contracted him, professional curiosity about this valuable material, and the inevitable pain of being confronted with the intimate secrets of the woman for whom he felt such a fiercely protective affection. He was deeply moved when he saw the photographs: here was Indiana on her bicycle, or crossing the street in her nurse's scrubs; there she was talking with someone, or on the phone, or shopping at the market. He saw her tired, he saw her happy, he saw her asleep on the balcony of her apartment above her father's garage. He saw her carrying a giant cake for Doña Encarnación, and arguing with Bob himself in the street, indignant, her hands on her hips. Indiana, with her vulnerable, innocent look, with the flushed cheeks of a young girl, looking as beautiful as she had at fifteen, when he had seduced her behind the bleachers of the school gymnasium with the same idleness with which he had done everything at that time. And he hated himself, as he looked at the photos, for not having loved and looked after her the way she deserved, for having blown his chance to make a loving home for her where Amanda would have flourished.

"What do you know about Ryan Miller?" he asked Hamilton.

"Apart from the fact that he's wanted for questioning about Keller's death, I know that he had a liaison with Ms. Jackson. As it was very short-lived and happened when she and Keller had split up, she wasn't being unfaithful, so I didn't mention it to Mr. Keller. I like Ms. Jackson—she's a good woman. And there aren't many of those in this world."

"What's your view on Miller?"

"Mr. Keller was jealous enough for half the city, but of Miller more than anybody. I wasted hundreds of hours watching him. I know a thing or two about his past, and I know his habits, but it's a mystery to me how he earns his money. I'm sure he lives on more than his wounded veteran's pension, that he's comfortably off and travels overseas. His apartment is protected with a high-tech security system, and he owns a number of firearms—all of them legal—and goes to a shooting range twice a week to practice his marksmanship. His dog never leaves his side. He has very few friends here, but he's in contact with the other guys from SEAL Team Six. He broke off with his lover a few months ago—Jennifer Yang, Chinese American, single, age thirty-six, bank executive, once appeared in Indiana Jackson's treatment room, threatening to throw acid in her face."

"What do you mean?" Bob interrupted. "She never told me about that."

"At that time Indiana and Miller were just friends. I suppose Miller had mentioned to Indiana that he had this girlfriend, just to put some kind of name on it, but he hadn't introduced them, so when Jennifer Yang arrived at her treatment room trying to scream the place down, Indiana thought the woman had got the wrong door. Matheus Pereira came down from the attic when he heard the noise and got Yang out of the building."

"This woman got a police file?"

"Nothing. If I were you, Deputy Chief, I wouldn't waste my time with Jennifer Yang. Let's get back to Ryan Miller—I'll make it as short as I can. His father reached a high rank in the marines, where he had a reputation for being strict, even cruel, with his men; his mother committed suicide with his father's service pistol, though in the family it was always said to have been an accident. Miller followed his father's footsteps into the navy, had an excellent service record and medals for bravery, and was given honorable discharge after losing a leg in Iraq in 2007. He was duly decorated, but quickly sank into drugs, alcohol—all the usual stuff for cases like his. He got back on his feet, and now he works for the government and the Pentagon, but I couldn't say in what, possibly espionage."

"Miller was arrested for violence in a club on the night of February eighteenth. He injured three people. Do you think he was capable of killing Keller?"

"He may have done it in a fit of rage, but not in that way. He's a Navy SEAL, Deputy Chief. He would have confronted his rival, given him the opportunity to defend himself—he would never have used poison."

"How d'you know about the poison? That was never made public."

"I know a lot of things: it's my job."

"So maybe you know where Miller is hiding."

"I haven't looked for him yet, Deputy Chief, but if I do, I'm sure I'll find him."

"Do it, Mr. Hamilton. We need all the help we can get."

Bob Martín closed his office door so Amanda wouldn't hear him, and let Samuel Hamilton in on his suspicion that Miller could have kidnapped Indiana.

"Listen, Deputy Chief," said Hamilton. "Since I found out that the police were looking for Miller, I've dedicated all my time to following Ms. Jackson, just in case the two of them met. I haven't got much work at the moment, so I've got time to spare. I've watched Ms. Jackson so many times that I would almost call her a friend. Miller's in love with her, and I thought he would try and get close to her, but as far as I know, there's been no communication between them."

"Why do you say that?"

"You know Ms. Jackson better than I do, Deputy Chief: you can see right through her. If she was helping Miller, she wouldn't be able to hide it. Besides, her habits haven't changed. I know what I'm talking about here: I can tell when a person is hiding something."

While Bob looked over the files the private detective had brought him, Blake Jackson arrived in Petra Horr's small office, harassed and out of breath. He saw his granddaughter in a ball on the floor, her head on her knees, so diminished she looked like a heap of rags. Without touching her—he knew how inaccessible the girl could be—he sat down beside her and waited in silence. After five minutes had passed, although to Petra it seemed like hours, Amanda pulled a hand out from the folds of her clothes and felt around for her grandfather's hand.

"Save-the-Tuna needs some fresh air, something to eat, and to do her business," he said to her, as though soothing a frightened animal. "Come on, sweetheart, we've got a lot to do."

"My mom . . ."

"That's what I mean, Amanda. We have to find her. I've told all the Ripper players to log on in two hours. They all agree that this has priority, and they're already working on it. Come on, girl, up you get, let's go."

He helped her get to her feet, straightened her clothes out a little, and picked up the basket with the cat in it. Just as he was walking out, Amanda's hand in his, Petra, who was talking on the phone, motioned to them to stop.

"They've got the prints off the computer, and they're bringing it up right now."

An officer brought the laptop to them in the same plastic bag Bob had taken it away in a few hours before. He handed them the lab report, which confirmed that only Indiana's fingerprints had been found. The deputy chief took the computer out of its bag, and they all gathered around his desk while Amanda, who was as familiar as its owner was with its contents, opened it up wearing latex gloves. She had started to thaw out a bit now that she felt useful, and pulled her hood back from her face, although her expression was still forlorn. Indiana, who couldn't tell one piece of software from another, used only a minimal portion of her computer's capacity—for e-mailing, tracking each patient's history and treatments, accounting, and little else. They read through all her e-mails from the twenty-three days that had passed since Keller's death, and found nothing but mundane correspondence with the usual people. Bob asked Petra to copy them, as they would have to scrutinize them for any revealing detail. Suddenly the screen went black. Amanda cursed under her breath; she had already come up against this problem.

"What's happening?" Bob asked.

"The Marquis de Sade, Mom's pet pervert. Watch out, you're about to see the gross stuff this freak sends her."

She was still speaking when the screen lit up again, but instead of the graphic sex and twisted acts of cruelty that Amanda was expecting, a video started, showing a winter landscape somewhere in the northern hemisphere, illuminated by the moon—an icy, snow-covered clearing in a pine forest, the wind whistling through it. A few seconds later a solitary figure emerged among the trees; at first it looked like a shadow, but as it approached across the snow, they could make out the silhouette of a large dog. The animal prowled in circles, sniffing the ground. Then it sat on its haunches, raised its head to the sky, and greeted the moon with a baleful howl.

The whole thing was over in less than two minutes, and everyone was perplexed except Amanda, who got up, shaking all over, her eyes wide and a strangled cry stuck in her throat. "The wolf, the sign of the killer!" she managed to stammer, before doubling over and vomiting on her father's ergonomic chair.

More than once, Indiana, you've told me that you trust to your good fortune, that you think your mother's spirit keeps watch over your family. That would explain why you don't make plans for the future or save a single cent—you live day-to-day, happy as a clam. You're even free of the worries that would affect any normal mother, because you assume that Amanda will succeed by her own merits, or with help from her father or grandfather; you're even irresponsible with that. I envy you, Indiana. Fate hasn't smiled on me, I've got no guardian angels. I'd like to think my mother's spirit looks after me, too, but that would be childish. I'm alone, and I look after myself. I'm careful, too: it's a hostile world, and I've been bitten by it.

You're very quiet, but I know you can hear me. Maybe you're plotting something? Well, you can forget it. When you first woke up on Saturday night, it was so dark, damp, and cold, and the silence was so pure, you thought you were dead and buried. You weren't ready for fear. But unlike you, I know very well what fear is. You'd slept for twenty-four hours, and you were confused, and you haven't had much clarity since then either. I let you scream and shout for a while, so you'd understand that nobody was going to come and rescue you; and when you heard your own voice resounding inside this giant fortress, panic silenced you. I have to gag you when I go out, although I'd prefer not to—the glue on the tape is going to sting your skin. It's possible that while I'm away you'll wake up and then pass out again—it's one of the effects of the drug I'm giving you so that you'll be comfortable. It's for your own good. It's just benzodiazepine, nothing harmful, although I do have to give you a high dose. Convulsions or a respiratory block are the only possible complications, but they're rare. You're strong, Indi, and I would know: I've been researching and experimenting for years. Do you remember how you got here? You probably don't remember a thing. That's normal: the ketamine I gave you on Friday causes amnesia. It's a very useful drug—the CIA has experimented with using it in interrogations, and they've found it less problematic than torture. Personally I abhor cruelty, and the sight of blood makes me dizzy. None of the delinquents I've killed suffered more than was strictly necessary. In your case, the sleeping pills are helpful, because they make the time pass, but tomorrow I'll have to bring the dosage down so there's no risk of harm, and so that we can talk. I can still hear you muttering something about a mausoleum—you think you've been buried—even though I've explained the situation to you. The pain in your belly will pass; I'm also giving you painkillers and antispasmodics. I'm concerned about your well-being. As I've told you, this is no bad dream, Indiana, and you're not going mad. It's normal at this stage for you not to remember what's happened in the last few days, but you'll remember who you are and start to miss your daughter, your father, and your former life. The feeling of weakness is normal, too, and it will pass. Have patience; but you won't get better until you eat. You need to eat at least something. Don't make me do anything unpleasant. Your life is no longer yours, it belongs to me—and I'm in charge of your health. I'll be the one who decides how, and how long, you live.

Tuesday, 3

T hanks to Ripper, which kept her busy, Amanda managed to recover from the terror that had gripped her when she first realized that the Wolf had taken her mother. None of her father's arguments could convince her that Indiana's absence was not related to the previous spate of crimes, and in fact he did not even believe his own reassurances. The symbol of the wolf was the only thing in common between Indiana's disappearance and the killer, but it was too clear to ignore. Why Indiana? And why Alan Keller? The deputy chief had a feeling that none of the experience and knowledge he had built up over his long career would be of use; he just asked that his sixth sense, which he had so often bragged about, didn't let him down now.

As Amanda was still having panic attacks, Blake Jackson called the school to explain the family drama to Sister Cecile and tell her that his granddaughter wasn't in a state to come back to class. The nun gave the girl permission to be out of school for however long she needed, said she would pray along with the other nuns, and asked to be kept up-to-date. Blake did not go to work either; all his time was taken up with looking after Amanda and playing Ripper, which was no longer a simple pastime but an appalling reality. The players were faced with the mother of all role-plays, as they called the desperate search for Indiana Jackson.

Bob could only conclude that the killer was a methodical and implacable psychopath of exceptional intelligence, one of the cruelest and most complex criminals he had heard of. He often said that his day-to-day work was simple, because he could rely on his network of informants—who kept him up-to-date on the criminal underworld—and because most petty criminals were already on file. They were reoffenders, drug addicts, and alcoholics locked in a cycle, or else just stupid, they left a string of clues behind them, tripped up on their own tails, betrayed and informed on each other, and eventually collapsed under their own weight. The real problem was with the top-flight criminals—the ones who could wreak havoc without even getting their hands dirty, who evaded justice and died of old age in their own beds. But in all his years of service, Bob had never been faced with a character like the Wolf; he didn't know what category to place him in, what motivated him, how he chose his victims and planned each crime. He felt a tight ball in his stomach, and sensed that the Wolf was nearby, that he was a personal enemy. Keller's death had been a warning, and Indiana's disappearance a direct attack. The horrifying idea that the killer might set his sights on Amanda put him in a cold sweat.

Since Indiana disappeared, the deputy chief hadn't returned to his apartment. He ate the cafeteria food, or whatever Petra brought him, slept in an armchair, and showered in the department gym. On Monday Petra had had to go and get him some clean clothes and take the dirty ones to the laundromat. She didn't take a break either; she'd never seen her boss so fixated that he even let his appearance go, and that worried her. Bob usually kept his football player's physique intact on the machines in the gym, smelled of a cologne that came at $200 a bottle, paid too much for his haircuts, and had his shirts tailored in Egyptian linen. His suits and shoes were impossibly expensive. If Bob felt like it, which he invariably did, he could seduce any woman—apart from Petra herself, of course.

Early on Tuesday morning, when Petra arrived at the office and saw her boss, she let out a yelp of surprise: his mustache, lovingly cultivated over the course of a decade, was gone.

"I haven't got time to worry about facial hair," he growled.

"I like it, boss. You look more . . . human. The mustache gave you a kind of Saddam Hussein look. I wonder what Ayani'll think."

"What the hell is she going to care!"

"I imagine it must kind of tickle with the mustache when . . . Well, you know what I'm saying."

"No, Petra, I have no idea what you're saying. My relationship with Mrs. Ashton is limited to her husband's murder investigation."

"Well, if that's true, I'm proud of you, boss. It wasn't a good idea for you to be involved with a suspect."

"You know very well she's no longer a suspect. Richard Ashton's death is linked to the other cases—the similarities with the other crimes are undeniable. Ayani is no serial killer."

"How do you know?"

"Jesus, Petra!"

"All right, all right, don't get annoyed. But can I ask why you broke up with her?"

"No, you can't, but I'm going to answer anyway. We were never together in the way you're suggesting. And that's the end of this absurd interrogation. You got it?"

"Sure, boss. Just one more question. Out of curiosity. How come it didn't work out with Ayani?"

"She's physically and emotionally traumatized, and she has issues when it comes to . . . to love. The day Elsa Domínguez came to tell you about the dogfights, and you called me, I was with Ayani. We'd eaten dinner at her place, but after the food, instead of having a romantic moment like I'd hoped, she put on a long documentary about genital mutilation and told me all the things she's had to suffer because of it, including two operations. She never had sexual relations with Richard Ashton—that was laid out in the marriage contract. Ayani married him for financial security, and he married her to make people envious, so he could wear her like a fancy watch."

"But I can't believe Ashton would have stuck to the terms of the contract when they lived together," said Petra. "And that'll be why they fought so much."

"That's what I think, although she didn't tell me that. I understand Galang's role now—he's the only man Ayani truly allowed to get close to her."

"Like I told you, boss. Hey, you want a coffee? I can tell you spent the night here again. You got raccoon eyes. Go home and get some rest, and if there's any news I'll tell you right away."

"I don't want any coffee, thanks. I'm starting to think whoever killed Keller in Napa isn't behind the five murders in San Francisco. It's just a hunch, but it could be that Ryan Miller killed Alan Keller out of jealousy and copied the Wolf's methods to throw us off the scent. Amanda could have told him any details that weren't in the press. My daughter's up to her eyes in this, and she's got a soft spot for Miller. God knows why, must be that dog of his."

"If Amanda had been speaking to Miller, we'd already know about it."

"You sure? That girl could make fools out of all of us."

"I doubt that Miller would have gotten rid of Keller in such an unmilitary way, or left a trail of evidence behind him. He's a smart man: trained to be stealthy and secretive, and to carry out the toughest missions with a cool head. I just don't think he'd incriminate himself in such a stupid way."

"That's what Amanda thinks," the deputy chief admitted.

"So if it wasn't the Wolf or Miller, who could have killed Keller?"

"I don't know, Petra. And I don't know who's responsible for Indiana's disappearance, either. Miller is still the logical suspect. I've put Samuel Hamilton on to checking an idea of Amanda's: Staton, the Constantes, Ashton, and Rosen all worked with children. It's a clue that could lead us to the Wolf."

"Why did you ask for Hamilton's help?"

"Because he can investigate without using the resources of the department, which are at capacity. And because he's experienced. I got a good feeling about the guy."

In their various cities around the globe, the Ripper players, including Jezebel, had dropped everything to devote all their energy to studying the cases at hand, each using his or her particular skills. They stayed in constant contact with their cell phones and got together on Skype whenever they came across some new clue, often in the middle of the night. As the job was so urgent, Abatha started to eat so that she would have enough energy, and Sir Edmond Paddington got up the courage to leave his room—which he had been closeted in for years on end—to go and talk in person with an old retired Irish policeman from New Jersey who was an expert in serial killers. Meanwhile Esmeralda and Sherlock Holmes, in Auckland, New Zealand, and Reno, Nevada, respectively, scoured all the available information again, from the bottom up. It was Abatha, in the end, who found the key that would open Pandora's box.

"As Sherlock Holmes explained to us in a previous game," said Jezebel, standing in for Ryan and Pedro, "all the bodies except for

Rachel Rosen's—which was found three days after her death—presented rigor mortis, allowing time of death to be calculated. We know for sure that five of the victims died around midnight, and we can assume the same is true of Rosen."

"What use is that to us?" asked Esmeralda.

"It means the killer only strikes at night."

"Perhaps he works by day," said Sherlock Holmes.

"It's because of the moon," Abatha cut in.

"How do you mean, because of the moon?" asked Esmeralda.

"The moon is mysterious; it signals the movement of the soul from one incarnation to the next," the psychic explained. "It represents femininity, fertility, imagination, and the murky waters of the unconscious. The moon affects the menses and the tides."

"Make it quick, Abatha—let's get to the point," Sir Edmond Paddington interrupted.

"The Wolf attacks under the full moon," she concluded.

"You're rambling, Abatha. Explain yourself."

"Permission to speak?" asked Kabel.

"Hench, I order that from now on you speak whenever you have something to say," said the games master impatiently. "Don't wait to ask permission."

"Thank you, mistress. Have you noticed there's only one murder each month? Maybe Abatha's right."

"All the crimes took place on the night of a full moon," said Abatha, more assertively than usual, as she'd had half a doughnut.

"You sure?" asked Esmeralda.

"Let's see," said Jezebel. "I've got almanacs from 2011 and 2012 here.

"The Wolf struck on October 11 and November 10 of last year, then January 9, February 7, and March 8 this year.

"Full moon!" Jezebel cheered. "There was a full moon on every one of those nights!"

"Do you think we could be dealing with some kind of creature that's half human, half beast, and metamorphoses when there's a full moon?" Esmeralda was excited at this new possibility.

"Me and Pops studied lycanthropy when we got bored of vampires," Amanda said. "D'you remember, Kabel?"

"The wolf-man is both more aggressive and more intelligent than any other lycanthrope," recited Kabel. "He has three forms he can inhabit: human, hybrid, and wolf. He's antisocial, lives alone, and prowls by night. In hybrid or wolf form he's carnivorous and wild; but in his human form he can't be told apart from other people."

"That's a fantasy," said Colonel Paddington. "We're not playing anymore: this is real."

"In the hospital I was admitted to last year there was a guy who used to turn into Spiderman," Abatha offered. "They had to keep him tied down so he wouldn't jump out the window. Our killer thinks he's a wolf-man."

"You mean he's crazy," said Amanda.

"Crazy?" said Abatha. "I don't know—they say I'm crazy too."

There was a long silence while the players digested that piece of information. It was interrupted by Esmeralda, asking one of her typical questions.

"What happened on the full moon in December?"

Bob Martín panicked for a moment when his daughter called him at five in the morning with a story about the wolf-man and full moons. The girl was even stranger than they thought; the moment had come to call a clinical psychiatrist. But a few moments later, when he compared the dates of the crimes with the phases of the moon, according to the explanation she reeled off at him, he said he would look through police files for December 10 of the year before—a full moon—and the rest of that week. The whole thing was starting to get so fantastical that he hardly dared delegate it to one of his detectives—besides, they were busy with the pending investigations and the couple of FBI agents, who had somewhat complicated the smooth running of the Personal Crimes Division. So he asked Petra Horr. Thirty-five minutes later, his assistant put what he had asked for on his desk.

On the night in question, there had been various deaths from unnatural causes in San Francisco: fights, accidents, suicide, an overdose. In other words, the usual tragedies. But one case caught the attention of the deputy chief and his assistant—an accident that had happened at the only campsite in the city, described in the typically curt language of a police report. On the morning of December 11, the few campers staying at the Rob Hill Campground complained to the attendant that there was a smell of gas around one of the trailers. As no one answered when they knocked on the door, the attendant broke in—and there he found the bodies of two tourists, Sharon and Joe Farkas from Santa Barbara, California, who had died of carbon monoxide poisoning. No autopsies were carried out, since cause of death seemed clear: an accident that happened because the couple was drunk and didn't notice a butane gas leak from the kitchenette. There was a half-emptied bottle of gin in the trailer. The police managed to track down a brother of Joe Farkas's, from Eureka, who arrived two days later to identify the bodies. The man wanted to take the trailer, but it was confiscated by police until the case file could be closed.

Bob charged one of his detectives with making a background check on the victims, finding Joe Farkas's brother and talking to the Santa Barbara police; then he ordered his team of forensic investigators to comb the trailer for anything that might help them. He immediately called his daughter to thank her for the lead about the couple who died under the December full moon.

"It's another execution, Dad, just like the others. The trailer was a gas chamber for the Farkases."

"Alan Keller was poisoned."

"That's a form of execution too. Socrates, for example."

"Who?"

"A Greek guy who died way back. They made him drink hemlock. And the Nazis used cyanide to kill a bunch of generals who fell out of favor. But none of that's going to help us find Mom."

"Kidnapping is a federal offense. There are police looking for her all over the country, Amanda. Turn on the TV, and you'll see her picture on all the channels."

"I've seen it already, Dad. Some people have already called to say they're thinking of us, and Elsa's come to stay with us until they find Mom. Did you question her patients?"

"Of course—that's all routine procedure—but nobody can tell us anything. None of them are suspect. Answer me honestly, sweetheart. Do you think Indiana's gone off with Ryan Miller? Both of them have disappeared."

"Why don't you get it, Dad! The Wolf's got her!"

"Right now that's just a theory—but I'm giving it due consideration."

"It's three days till the next full moon, Dad," said the girl. "The Wolf's going to strike again." A sob choked her as she spoke.

Bob promised to keep her up-to-date on every step of the investigation. When she answered that she would look for her mother by herself, he assumed she was referring to Ripper, and felt a vague sense of relief, as though the heavens had come to his aid. He was starting to take those kids seriously.

Wednesday, 4

The deputy chief kept his promise and called his daughter at 7:00 a.m. to let her in on the new details uncovered by Samuel Hamilton. Ed Staton, the security guard who'd had a number of accusations lodged against him for physical abuse of children under his charge at Boys' Camp, and who was fired in connection with a boy's death in 2010, had got work shortly after that in a school in San Francisco, thanks to a letter of recommendation from the judge Rachel Rosen.

The woman—known as the Butcher, for the draconian sentences she handed down to the minors who appeared in her court—was frequently invited to speak at reform schools, some of which had received hundreds of complaints about mistreatment of their pupils. California, straining under the weight of a burgeoning prison population, subcontracted its youth correctional services out to other states, and thanks to Rosen, Boys' Camp and other similar private facilities enjoyed a continuous influx of clients. She couldn't be accused of taking kickbacks or bribes; her remuneration appeared in the form of her public speaking fees or as gifts—theater tickets, cases of liquor, holidays in Hawaii, Mediterranean and Caribbean cruises.

"There's something else you'll be interested to know, Amanda," said the deputy chief. "Rachel Rosen and Richard Ashton knew each other professionally. The psychiatrist did psychological assessments on kids referred by the courts and Child Protective Services."

"And I suppose the Constantes took in kids that Rosen sent them."

"That wouldn't be the judge's responsibility," her father explained, "but you could say there's an indirect link between them. Get this, Amanda. In 1997 a complaint was made against Richard Ashton, and then quickly hushed up, for using electroshock therapy and experimental drugs when treating a minor. He had some dubious methods, to say the least."

"You need to investigate the Farkases, Dad."

"We're on it, sweetie."

/////////////////////

You should be more awake by now, Indi—you're obviously very sensitive to the medication. And you could show me a little more gratitude, you know: I try to make you as comfortable as possible in the circumstances. It's no Hotel Fairmont, I'll admit, but you've got a decent bed and fresh food. The bed was already here, it's the only one; the rest are stretchers for the wounded, just a piece of canvas between two poles. I brought you another box of pads and some antibiotics for that fever of yours. A fever that's starting to interfere with my plans, by the way: you're not really drugged out, and it's high time you woke up. I'm only giving you a cocktail of painkillers, sedatives, and sleeping pills to keep you calm. The dosages are perfectly normal, nothing that should lay you out like this.

Make a bit more effort to be present. How's your memory? Do you remember Amanda? She's a curious child. And curiosity is the root of all sin, but also of the sciences. I know a lot about your daughter, Indiana—for example, I know that right now she's dedicating herself to finding you. And if she's as clever as everybody thinks she is, she'll find the clues I've left for her, but she'll never find them in time. Poor little Amanda, I do feel sorry for her: she's going to blame herself for this for the rest of her life.

You should appreciate how clean you are, Indiana. I've taken the trouble to give you a sponge bath, and if you were a little more cooperative I could wash your hair too. My mother used to say that virtue begins with hygiene: clean body, clear mind. Even when we were living in cars or trucks, she always arranged things so we could take a shower every day: for her that was as important as having enough to eat. We've got a hundred barrels of water here that have been sealed since World War II. And you won't believe it, but there's also a large, beautifully carved wooden frame, with a beveled mirror, not a single scratch on it. And the blankets are from that period too. It's amazing that they're still clean and in a reasonable state—you can tell they're not moth-eaten. Trust me, I'm protecting you from insects too, and I'm not going to let you get lice or catch some infection. There must be all kinds of horrible insects around here, especially cockroaches, even though I fumigated the room properly before bringing you here. I couldn't fumigate the whole place, of course: the grounds are huge. There are no rats, because the owls and cats deal with them. There are hundreds of owls and cats that have lived here for generations. Did you know that outside, there are wild turkeys everywhere, too?

After bathing you, I put your beautiful nightgown on you, the one Keller gave you and that you were keeping for a special occasion. And what occasion more special than this one? I had to throw your pants away, though—they were all bloodied, and I can't spend my time washing clothes. Did you know I've got a key to

your apartment? I have the underwear that disappeared from your
closet—I wanted a memento of you, and took them, having no
idea they'd be so useful to us now. Life is a funny thing! I can get
into your apartment whenever I want—the alarm your ex-husband
installed is a joke. In fact, I was there on Sunday, and I went down
to your father's place and took a look at Amanda, who was curled
up asleep with her cat. I thought she looked pretty well, although
I know she's been worried and so she hasn't been to school—with
good reason, poor girl. I've got a key to your treatment room too,
as well as the password to your computer—Remember I asked you
for it to get movie tickets, and you gave it to me without batting an
eyelid. You're very careless, although I admit you didn't have any
reason to suspect me.

I'm going to have to gag you again. Try and get some rest. I'll
come back tonight, because I can't come and go at any old time. You
won't believe it, but it's morning outside. The walls of this room are
tarpaulins made from some strange material, rubber or black can-
vas or something. They're heavy but flexible, and airtight—that's
why you think it's aways night here. The roof is a little collapsed in
some parts of the fortress, and a little light gets through in the day,
although it doesn't get as far as here. You'll understand that I can't
give you a lamp—it would be dangerous. I know that the hours are
dragging, and you wait for me anxiously. You're probably afraid that
I'll forget you, or that something will happen to me and I won't come
back, and then you'd die of starvation, tied to your bed. But no, Indi,
nothing's going to happen to me. I'll be back, I promise. I'm going to
bring you some food, and I don't want to have to force it down you.
What would you like to eat? I'll get you whatever you want.

///////////////////////

The clock on the deputy chief's wall was a relic from the 1940s
that the homicide detail kept for historic reasons, and for its un-

swerving Swiss accuracy. Bob Martín, who had hung it opposite his desk alongside some photographs of Mexican singers—among them his father with his group of mariachis—could feel his blood pressure rising as the metal hands marked out the passing seconds. If Amanda was right, and she almost certainly was, he had until Friday night to find Indiana alive—just two days and a few hours. His daughter had persuaded him that finding her mother would also mean catching the vicious psychopath that was loose in their city, although he could not figure out the link between Indiana and that murderer.

At 9:00 a.m. he received a call from Samuel Hamilton, who the day before had gone about comparing the list of friends from Indiana's laptop with his own. At 9:05 the deputy chief put on his jacket, ordered Petra Horr to follow him, got in a patrol car, and headed for North Beach.

At the Holistic Clinic, everybody had already seen the photograph of Indiana Jackson on the television or in the papers. Some of her colleagues were discussing this in the hall on the second floor, by the door to Treatment Room 8, which was sealed off with yellow police tape. Petra Horr stayed with them, taking down their details, while the deputy chief sprinted up to the third floor and leaped nimbly up the ladder that led to the roof terrace. Instead of knocking on the dilapidated door, he kicked it open and went right up to Matheus Pereira's bed, snorting angrily. Pereira was lying in his clothes, with his boots on, sleeping the deep sleep of his peace pipe. The painter woke up in midair, with Bob Martín shaking him like a rag doll in his football player's hands.

"Tell me who Indiana left with on Friday!"

"I already told you everything I know . . . ," said Pereira, still half asleep.

"You want to spend the next ten years behind bars for selling narcotics?" the deputy chief hissed, inches from Pereira's face.

"She left with a woman—I don't know her name, but I've seen her around here a couple times."

"Give me a description."

"If you let me go, I can draw her."

He picked up a piece of charcoal, and a few minutes later handed the deputy chief a portrait of the Russian babushka.

"You jerking me around, you piece of shit?" Martín roared.

"That's her, I swear to you."

"She called Carol Underwater?" asked the deputy chief. That was the name Samuel Hamilton had given him—it didn't appear in Indiana's e-mails, which Petra had copied before the computer was stashed with the rest of the evidence.

"Yeah"—Pereira nodded—"I'm pretty sure she's called Carol. She's friends with Indiana. They left together—I was downstairs in the hallway, and I saw them go out."

"Did they say anything to you?"

"Carol told me they were headed to the movies."

Martín went down to the second floor and handed the drawing around to the tenants of the clinic. A few confirmed they had seen the woman with Indiana from time to time. Yumiko Sato added that Carol Underwater had cancer and had lost her hair during her chemotherapy, which explained the scarf over the Russian peasant's head.

When he got to his office, the deputy chief tacked Pereira's sketch to a bulletin board across from his desk, where he had laid out any other information that might help him in the search for the Wolf and Indiana. Keeping it in sight all the time like that, he was bound to think of something. He knew that in the past a surfeit of evidence and a tight deadline for solving a case had stopped him thinking clearly. And this time it made him sink even deeper into anxiety. He felt like a surgeon forced to perform a risky operation on a loved one: Indiana's life was hanging on his skill.

At the same time he trusted his hunter's instinct—the part of his brain that allowed him to detect invisible clues, guess where his prey had been and where it would go next, come to conclusions that had no strict logic but were almost always right. The display board helped him make connections between different aspects of the investigation, but more than anything it kindled in him that hunter's instinct.

Since Amanda first started talking about a serial killer, Bob Martín had met a number of times with forensic psychologists from his department to look over similar cases from the last twenty years, especially in California. This sort of systematic killing was not spontaneous behavior: it was a response to fantasies that been incubating for years until something triggered a decision to act. Some were out to punish gay people or prostitutes, others driven by racial hatred or some other fanaticism; but the Wolf's victims were so disparate that they seemed to have been chosen at random. He wondered what beliefs, what kind of image of himself, the Wolf had—whether he saw himself as victim or executioner. We are all heroes in our own stories. What was the Wolf's story? To catch him, the deputy chief would have to think like the Wolf. He would have to become him.

At midday Petra Horr came to tell him that she couldn't find a single piece of evidence that Carol Underwater had ever existed. There was no driver's license, vehicle, property, credit card, bank account, phone number, or employment history under that name, and she wasn't registered as a cancer patient in any hospital or clinic in the San Francisco Bay area or the counties around it. It could be that whoever had access to the laptop to upload the wolf video had deleted the relevant e-mails, or that the two had only ever communicated by phone. As they hadn't found Indiana's cell phone, Bob Martín applied for a warrant to force the phone company to trace calls from the number, something that would take a day to process. For now, Carol Underwater, who so many people had seen in recent months, was a ghost.

Nobody troubled to tell Celeste Roko that Indiana had disappeared. She only found out several days later, when she got a hysterical phone call from her friend Encarnación Martín, who had already been to pray to Saint Jude about finding her daughter-in-law. "Didn't you see Indiana on the television? My poor little Amanda! You've no idea how much it's affected her! The girl's a nervous wreck, she thinks her mom was kidnapped by some wolf-man."

Celeste, who a few weeks earlier had seen Ryan Miller's photograph on the television, showed up at the Personal Crimes Division determined to speak with the deputy chief. When Petra Horr tried to stop her, Celeste had her against the wall with a single shove. Petra had a lot of respect for astrology, so she stopped short of using her martial arts to hold her back. Celeste burst into Bob Martín's office, brandishing a folder that contained two star charts that she had just done and a comparative reading of the two. She explained to him that in all her years studying the stars, and human psychology through the works of Carl Gustav Jung, she had never seen two people so psychically compatible as Indiana Jackson and Ryan Miller. They had been together in previous lives, she said, had even been mother and son recently, and were destined to come together and split apart again and again until they could resolve their psychic and spiritual conflict. In this present incarnation, they had a precious opportunity to break that cycle.

"Well, whaddaya know!" snarled Bob, furious at the interruption.

"It's true. I'm telling you for your own good, Bob, because if Indiana and Ryan have escaped together, which must be what's happened, because it's written in the constellations, and you try and separate them, you'll mess up your karma big-time."

"Fuck my karma!" Bob yelled, beside himself. "I'm trying to do my job, and you come and disturb me with this bullshit. Indiana didn't run off with Miller—the Wolf kidnapped her!"

Celeste was stunned. For the first time in years, she didn't know what to say. When she had managed to rally herself a little, she put the star charts back in the folder, picked up her crocodile-skin handbag, and took a few shaky steps backward on her stiletto heels.

"I don't suppose you'd happen to know what this wolf-man's star sign is, would you?" she asked timidly from the doorway.

///////////////////

Open your eyes, Indi, and try and pay attention to what I'm telling you. Look, this driver's license from 1985 is the only existing photograph of my mother. If there were others, she destroyed them: she was very careful about her privacy. There are no photos of me before I was eleven, either. Everybody looks like a criminal on their driver's license, and this one's just as bad: my mom looks sloppy and fat, even though she wasn't. It's true she was carrying a couple extra pounds around that time, but she never had this lunatic's face, and she was always turned out impeccably, not a single hair out of place. She was obsessive about that, and her work demanded it anyway. The habits she drilled into me have been my guiding principles in life: cleanliness, exercise, healthy food, no smoking or drinking. When I was a little girl I couldn't go out and play sports like other children, I had to stay in the house; but she taught me the benefits of gymnastics, and that's still the first thing I do when I wake up. You'll need to do a bit of exercise soon yourself, Indiana, you ought to move around. But we're going to wait until your bleeding has stopped and you feel a little more yourself.

I had the best mother a person could ask for. She was utterly devoted to me: she adored me, looked after me, protected me. What would have become of me without that saint of a woman? She was both mother and father to me. At night, after we'd eaten and gone over my assignments, she'd read me a story and we'd pray. Then she would dress me for bed, kiss me on the forehead, and tell me I was her darling little girl. In the mornings, before she left for work, she would show me what I had to study, and give me a tight hug good-bye, as though she was afraid we'd never see each other again. If I didn't cry, she'd give me some candy. I'll come back soon, sweetie, be good. Don't open the door to anybody, pick up the phone, or make any noise, because the neighbors have already started to mutter about us—you know how mean people are. The security measures were for my own good, as there was so much danger out there, so much violence and crime, so many accidents I might have, so many germs to catch. Trust no one: that's what she taught me. And the days were long. I don't remember how I made the hours pass in my first few years—I think she would leave me in a playpen or tie me to the furniture with rope, like a dog on a leash, so that I wouldn't hurt myself. She always left toys and food within easy reach. Later, when I was older, she didn't need to. I learned to keep myself occupied. By the time I was six or seven, when she was out, I'd clean the apartment and do the laundry, but I never cooked; she was afraid I would cut or burn myself. I'd watch TV and play too, but first I would do my homework. My mom was a good teacher, and I learned fast; that's why, when I finally went to school, I was better prepared than the other kids. But that came later.

Do you want to know how long you've been here, Indi? Just five days and six nights, which in the span of a human life is nothing at all, especially if you've spent them asleep. I had to put diapers on you. It was better that you slept at first, because the alternative would have been to keep you in a hood and handcuffs like you were at Guantánamo Bay or Abu Ghraib. They know how to do things in the military. The hood is suffocating, people have gone mad wearing those—and the handcuffs are painful, they make your hands swell up and your fingers go purple. The metal gets embedded in the skin, and the wounds can get infected. In other words, it's a mess. You're in no state to put up with any of that, and I don't intend to make you suffer more than I have to; but you have to cooperate with me and behave yourself. It's for your own good.

So, I was telling you about Mama. People said she was paranoid, that she had a persecution complex, and that that was why she kept me locked in the house, why we were always on the run. But it's not true: Mama had good reasons to do what she did. I used to love those journeys: the gas stations, the diners we'd stop at, the never-ending highways, the changing landscape. Some nights we'd sleep in motels, other times we'd camp. We were free as birds! We'd set off without a plan, stopping in whatever town we liked. We'd stay there for a while, setting up as best we could with the money we had, in a room at first and then moving into something nicer if she found work. I didn't care where we ended up—all rooms looked the same. My mother always got work. She was well paid and well organized, didn't spend much, and saved it all up—so she'd always be prepared when we needed to head off somewhere else.

//////////////

At that moment, the *Ripper* players were opening new lines of investigation. The games master had updated them with every detail of the police operation, the latest mystery being Carol Underwater, to whom Amanda owed nothing less than her precious Save-the-Tuna.

"I thought it was interesting that a formal complaint was made against Richard Ashton for child abuse in 1997, and another against Ed Staton in 1998," said Amanda. "I sent my henchman to make some inquiries."

"The deputy chief's up to his neck in it, so I didn't want to bother him, but Jezebel's got access to all kinds of information, and she helped me. I don't know how you do it, Jezebel—you must be an expert hacker, a real digital pirate—"

"Does this have something to do with the present discussion, Hench?" asked Esmeralda.

"Apologies. The games master thought there was a link between the two complaints, and with Jezebel's help we were able to confirm that there is. And there's a connection with the judge, Rachel Rosen. Both complaints were brought to juvenile court by a social worker, and both were about the same kid, a Lee Galespi."

"What do we know about him?" Esmeralda asked.

"That he was an orphan," said Denise West in her role as Jezebel, reading from the piece of paper given to her by Ryan. "He went through a number of institutional settings, but he struggled in all of them. He was a difficult child—diagnosed with depression, paranoid fantasies, incapable of socializing. He was assigned to Richard Ashton's care, and Ashton treated him for a while, but the social worker made a complaint against Ashton for using electroshock therapy. Galespi was a shy kid—traumatized, and constantly bullied by the cruel kids in his school. There are always a few of those brutes around. At the age of fifteen he was accused of starting a fire in a school bathroom, while the kids bullying him were inside. Nobody was hurt, but Galespi was sent to a reform school."

"And I take it it was Rachel Rosen who sentenced him," said Sherlock, "and that the reform school was Boys' Camp in Arizona, where Ed Staton worked."

"You guessed it," replied Jezebel. "And the same social worker made a complaint against Ed Staton for sexually abusing Lee Galespi, but Rosen didn't take him out of Boys' Camp."

"Can we talk with the social worker?" asked Esmeralda.

"Her name is Angelique Larson," Jezebel told them. "Retired, lives in Alaska, where she got a job as a teacher."

"Well, there is such a thing as the telephone," the games master intoned. "Hench, get that woman's number."

"That won't be necessary," said Jezebel. "I've already got it."

"Excellent—why don't we call her?" Esmeralda asked.

"Because she's not going to answer questions from a bunch of kids like us," warned Colonel Paddington. "If the police called, that would be a different matter."

"It can't hurt to try," said Abatha. "Who's gonna step up?"

"I would, but I think Grandpa's voice—I mean, Kabel's voice—would be more convincing. Go ahead, Hench, call her and tell her you're the police. Try and sound like you got some authority."

Blake Jackson was reluctant to pose as a police officer, as he thought it might be illegal, so he introduced himself as a writer—which was only a half lie; he was starting to get serious about fulfilling his lifelong dream and becoming a novelist. Angelique Larson turned out to be such an openhearted, kind woman that Hench regretted deceiving her, but by then it was too late to turn back. She remembered Lee Galespi well; he'd been in her charge for a number of years, and his case was one of the most interesting of her career. She talked with Blake Jackson for a full thirty-five minutes, telling him everything she knew about Lee Galespi. She hadn't heard from him since 2006, but up to that time they had always been in touch around Christmas. Angelique and Blake were like good friends by the time they put the phone down; he could call her again whenever he wanted, she said, and wished him luck with his novel.

Angelique Larson remembered every detail of her first encounter with Lee Galespi, and often turned it over in her mind—that child had come to represent the sum of her work, with all of its frustrations, punctuated with rare moments of satisfaction. Hundreds of poor souls like Galespi would be rescued from some horrible situ-

ation by Child Protective Services, only to come back again in an
even worse state—more damaged, less hopeful, and more withdrawn every time—until they turned eighteen, lost what scant
protection they had received, and were thrown out on the street.
For Angelique, all those children merged with Galespi, and they
passed through the same stages: shyness, distress, grief, a terror
that slowly transformed into rage and rebellion, and then finally a
sort of coldness or cynicism. At that point there was nothing anybody could do—you had to say good-bye to them, but it felt like
you were throwing them to the lions.

Larson explained to Blake that in the summer of 1993, a woman
had a heart attack at a bus stop. During the commotion it caused
in the street, before the police and an ambulance could get there,
somebody stole her purse. She was admitted to San Francisco
General Hospital without any papers, unconscious, and in a criti-
cal state. The woman was in a coma for three weeks before dying
of a second major cardiac arrest. The police arrived shortly after
and identified her as Marion Galespi, sixty-one years old, a shift
nurse at the Laguna Honda Hospital and resident of Daly City, to
the south of San Francisco. Two officers presented themselves at
her address, a modest block of low-income housing. When nobody
answered the door, they brought in a locksmith, who couldn't
open it because it was bolted twice from the inside. Some of her
neighbors came out into the corridor to see what was going on, and
that's when they learned how their neighbor had died. They hadn't
missed her, they said; Marion Galespi had only been in the building a few months and wasn't the friendly type. In fact, she hardly
said hello when she shared the elevator with someone. One of the
bystanders asked where the girl was, explaining that a daughter
lived there too, but nobody had ever seen her because she never
went out. Her mother used to say that the girl was mentally handi-
capped and had a skin disorder that was aggravated by sunlight, so

she was homeschooled. She was shy and obedient, and sat quietly at home while her mother went to work.

An hour later the fire department set up a telescopic ladder in the street, broke a window, entered the apartment, and opened the door for the police. The austere home consisted of a living room, a minuscule bedroom, a kitchen built into one wall, and a bathroom. The furniture was minimal—although a number of suitcases and boxes were scattered around the place—and the only personal possessions were a color picture of the Sacred Heart of Jesus and a plaster statuette of the Virgin Mary. The place smelled stale and looked completely uninhabited, and yet the door was locked as though the owner had stepped out to buy some milk. In the kitchen they found cereal boxes, jam jars, milk bottles, and an orange juice carton, all of them empty. The only signs that the girl had ever existed were her clothes and some school notebooks; there was not a single toy. The police were ready to leave again when one of them thought to take a last look in the closet, pulling the clothes apart on their hangers. Crouched on the floor was the girl, huddled like an animal beneath a heap of rags. When she saw the man, the creature howled so frightfully that he didn't dare to prise her out of her hiding place by force, and had to ask for help. It took a woman police officer some time to persuade the girl to come out. Thin, filthy, and unkempt, she had a deranged look. Before she had taken three steps, she collapsed in the policewoman's arms.

Angelique Larson first saw Lee Galespi in the hospital, three hours after her dramatic rescue from the Daly City apartment. She was in an emergency ward, hooked up to a drip and half asleep, but attentive enough to anybody who came over to her. The resident physician who admitted her said that she seemed malnourished and dehydrated; though she devoured cookies, custard, Jell-O, and anything else they put in front of her, she vomited it all up immediately. Despite her weak state, she defended herself like a wildcat when they tried to take off her dress to examine her. The doctor decided it wasn't worth restraining her—it would be better to wait until the tranquilizers she had been given took effect. The girl shrieked whenever a man came near, the doctor told Larson. The social worker took Lee by the hand, explained who she was and why she was there, told her she had nothing to be afraid of and that she would stay with her however long it took for her family to arrive. "Mommy, I want my mommy," the girl repeated, and Angelique Larson didn't have the heart to tell her then and there that her mother had died. When Lee Galespi was in a deep sleep, they undressed her so the doctor could examine her. It was only then that they discovered she was a boy.

Galespi was transferred to the hospital's pediatric department while the police searched in vain for relatives. Marion Galespi and her son seemed to have appeared out of thin air—they had no family, no past, no roots. The boy suffered from allergic eczema and alopecia, and was in need of dental treatment, fresh air, sunshine, and exercise, but he showed no sign of physical or mental illness, contrary to what his neighbors in Daly City believed. His birth certificate, signed by a Dr. Jean-Claude Castel, which was dated July 23, 1981, recorded that the birth had taken place at home in Fresno, California, and that the baby was a Caucasian male weighing seven pounds and measuring twenty inches.

In January 1994 Dr. Richard Ashton filed his initial psychiatric assessment of Lee Galespi with the juvenile court. The boy had a normal level of physical development for a pubescent male and an above-average IQ, but he was held back by serious emotional and social problems and suffered from insomnia and an addiction to the tranquilizers his mother had used to keep him calm during his confinement. It had been a battle to get him to cut his hair and wear boys' clothing—Galespi insisted he was a girl and that "boys were bad." He missed his mother, wet the bed, cried frequently, and always seemed afraid—especially of men, which brought conflict into the therapist-patient relationship and meant that eventually hypnosis and drugs had to be used. His mother had kept him locked in the house and dressed him as a girl, teaching him that people were dangerous and that the end of the world was near. They were always moving: the boy couldn't remember or didn't know in what cities he had lived, and could only say that his mother worked in hospitals or geriatric care homes and would often change jobs "because they had to leave." The psychiatrist finished by saying that, in light of his symptoms, the patient Lee Galespi would need electroshock therapy.

The social worker explained that psychotherapy was proving counterproductive because the boy was terrified of Dr. Ashton, but Rachel Rosen did not seek a second opinion; she ordered that the treatment be continued, and that Galespi be settled in a home and attend school. In a report dated 1995, Angelique Larson noted that the boy was a good student but lacked friends; he was bullied for being effeminate, and his teachers found him uncooperative. When he was thirteen, he arrived at the home of Michael and Doris Constante.

///////////////////

I can tell you're thirsty, Indi. So as a reward for how good you've been, I'm going to give you some orange juice. Don't try and get up, just suck on the straw. That's it. What, more? No, one glass is enough for now, I'll give you a little more before I go as long as you eat the food I brought you. It's rice and beans—you'll need it to get your strength

back. You're shivering—you must be freezing cold. It's very damp down
here; there are even parts that are flooded where the groundwater has
seeped through. Goodness knows how long you've been frozen half to
death. I left you wrapped up good with a couple blankets—I even gave
you woolen socks—but you started wriggling and managed to get out
from under the covers. You need to stay still when I'm not here; struggling's not going to help you. The straps are tight, and however hard
you try, you won't be able to get free. I can't keep an eye on you all
the time—I've got a life out there, as I'm sure you can imagine. I've
explained the situation to you quite a few times, but either you ignore
me or you forget. So I'll say again that nobody's going to find us here:
we're in the middle of nowhere, in a building that's been abandoned for
years. The property is fenced off, and it's impossible to get in; even if you
weren't gagged, you could shout yourself hoarse and no one would hear
you. You're quiet as a mouse, so maybe you don't need the gag—but I
can't take any risks. What are you thinking? You might as well give up
any fantasies you have about escaping, because in the unlikely event
of you managing to stand up, you won't be able to get out. This little
nest I've created is screened off with black drapes, but it's in an enormous basement of reinforced concrete and iron pillars. The door's made
of iron, too, and I've got the key.

    You seem a little groggy. Maybe you're sicker than I thought—it
could be the blood loss. What's up, Indiana? Maybe you're not
afraid anymore? Have you given up? Your silence is frustrating,
because the whole purpose of your being here is that we can talk
and come to understand one another. You remind me of those Tibetan monks who escape from the world by meditating. They say
that some of them can control their pulse, their blood pressure,
heartbeat—even die at will. Is that true? This is your opportunity
to put into practice those techniques you're always recommending to
your patients: meditating, relaxing, and all the rest of your cherished New Age garbage. I can bring you magnets and essential

oils, if you like. While you're meditating, by the way, why don't you use the time to reflect on the reasons you're here, on how willful and evil you have been? I know you're sorry, but it's too late to go back now. You could promise me that you realize all your mistakes and that you're going to mend your ways—you could promise me anything you like, but I'd have to be a fool to believe you. And I assure you: I'm no fool.

Thursday, 5

After listening to the rest of the Lee Galespi story, the Ripper players decided unanimously to tell the deputy chief about him. Amanda dialed her father's cell number straight away. When there was no answer, she called Petra Horr, who told her that the FBI had called the whole homicide detail in for a meeting.

"They think we're sabotaging them with the Miller investigation," said Petra. "They've lost a lot of time, and they haven't found anything. I suggested they enjoy it while they're here and do a bit of sightseeing, and let's just say they didn't take it well. They aren't the laughing type."

"Maybe Miller went to Afghanistan," said Amanda, hoping to throw Petra off the trail. "He talked about some debt of honor he had over there."

"They want us to look for Miller as though we had nothing better to do. Why don't they find him themselves? That's why they got everybody under surveillance. Nothing's private any more in this fricking country, Amanda, you know that? Every time you buy something, use your cell phone or the internet or a credit card—hell, every time you blow your nose—you leave a trail, and the government knows about it."

"You sure?" asked Amanda, feeling alarmed. If the government and her father knew that she was playing Ripper with Ryan Miller, she could end up in jail.

"No doubt."

"Tell my dad to call me as soon as he gets out of his meeting—it's urgent."

Bob Martín was dialing her number twenty minutes later. In recent days he had grabbed what sleep he could on the sofa in his office, subsisted on coffee and sandwiches, and had no time to go to the gym. His body felt stiff, as though he was wearing a suit of armor, and he was so irritable that the meeting had ended with raised voices. He hated that bitter woman Lorraine Barcott, and that Napoleon guy drove him nuts with all his little tics. Amanda's voice, which could still touch him like it did when she was a little girl, soothed his nerves a little.

"You wanted to tell me something?" he asked her.

"You tell me your news first."

"We've had the Farkas trailer impounded since December, but nobody had checked it, because the department's had other priorities. We analyzed the bottle of gin that was inside, turns out it was spiked with Xanax. And you know what else we found, Amanda?"

"A stuffed toy wolf."

"An album of holiday photos of places the Farkases had been—they traveled through a number of states before settling in California. There was an interesting postcard signed by Joe's brother, dated November fourteenth last year, suggesting they meet up in San Francisco in December."

"What's interesting about it?"

"Two things. First, the picture on the postcard is of a wolf. Second, the brother swears he never sent it."

"So, the Wolf made a date to kill them."

"Absolutely. The only thing is, the postcard means nothing as evidence. It wouldn't stand up to the slightest examination."

"So throw in the Xanax and the full moon."

"Say the Wolf gets into the trailer on some kind of pretext—I bet he brought them the liquor as a gift, 'cause he knew they liked a drink. The gin is spiked with the drug. He waits for it to knock them out, maybe a half hour, then turns on the gas before walking out. He leaves the bottle so it looks like just the kind of accident a pair of old drunks would have, which is exactly what the police assumed it was."

"That doesn't get us any closer to the Wolf, Dad. We've got thirty-nine hours to save Mom."

"I know, sweetheart."

"Hey, I got news for you too," said Amanda, in that excited tone Martín had come to respect in the last few weeks.

His daughter's news did not disappoint. He immediately called the director of Child Protective Services, who couriered over the file on Lee Galespi that Angelique Larson had compiled over the seven years the boy was in her care.

On a separate sheet, written by hand, the social worker reflected that Lee Galespi had suffered much, and that the people at Child Protective Services, like everyone else who ought to have helped him, had failed him time and again. She felt she had done little for him herself. The only good thing that had come Lee Galespi's way in the whole of his wretched existence was the $250,000 of life insurance left to him by his mother. The juvenile court had set up a trust fund for him, which he would be able to access when he turned eighteen.

///////////////

I've brought you chocolates to cheer you up—they're the same ones Keller used to bring you. Weird combination, chocolate and chili.

Sugar is bad for you, it makes you fat. You've never worried about your weight—you think those few extra pounds make you look voluptuous, don't you? Well, take it from me, when you're forty they just make you look fat. Right now you think it's funny. You're very beautiful. I'm not surprised men lose their heads over you, Indiana, but beauty is not a gift, like they tell you in the fairy tales, it's a curse. Remember Helen of Troy, who set off a bloody war between the Greeks? Fate almost always turns against beauty. Then there's Marilyn Monroe, the quintessential sex symbol, a depressive and a drug addict who died alone. It's something I know a lot about. Femmes fatales captivate and repel me, they fascinate and scare me, like reptiles. You're so used to being the center of attention, to being worshipped and desired, that you don't even realize the suffering you cause. Wanton women like you strut around, arousing, seducing, and tormenting other people with no sense of honor or responsibility. Nothing in the world is worse than unrequited love: it is a cruel torture, a slow death. Just think about Gary Brunswick, a good man who selflessly offered you his love; or Ryan Miller, whom you tossed aside like garbage—not to mention Alan Keller, who died for you. It's not fair. You have to pay the consequences, Indiana. These last days, I've been studying you closely, from the scar on your buttocks to every fold of your vulva. I've even counted your beauty spots.

///////////////

Lee Galespi spent two years with the Constantes until a routine medical exam found cigarette burns on the boy. Although Galespi refused to say what had happened, Angelique Larson concluded that this had probably been the Constantes' way of teaching him not to wet the bed. She took the child away from them, but did not succeed in having their foster care license revoked. Not long afterward, Galespi was sent for a year to Boys' Camp in Arizona. Angelique Larson begged Rachel Rosen to reconsider her decision—a camp notorious for its brutality and its harsh military-style discipline was utterly unsuited to a vulnerable, traumatized child like Galespi—but Judge Rosen ignored her pleas.

Every one of the letters Larson received from the boy while he was in the camp was censored using a thick black marker, so in December 1998 the social worker decided to visit him in Arizona. Boys' Camp did not allow visitors, but Larson managed to get a court authorization. Lee was pale, thin, and withdrawn, and there were extensive cuts and bruises on his arms and legs. The counselor, an ex-soldier named Ed Staton, said that was normal, since the boys exercised outdoors; besides, Lee often fought with the other inmates, who hated him because he was a whiner, a crybaby, and a faggot. "But I'll make a man outta him, sure as my name's Ed Staton," the counselor had said.

Angelique insisted on talking to Lee alone, but she could get nothing out of him. To every question he robotically answered that he had nothing to complain about. She spoke to the nurse who worked at the camp, a fat, unsympathetic woman, who told her that Galespi had been on a hunger strike, that he wasn't the first to resort to such tricks, but he'd quickly given up when he discovered how unpleasant it was to be force-fed through a tube. In her report, Larson wrote that Lee was in a terrible state—"He looks like a zombie"—and recommended that he immediately be removed from Boys' Camp. Once again her pleas to Rachel Rosen fell on deaf ears, so she lodged a formal complaint against Ed Staton, which also came to nothing. Lee Galespi served out his sentence of one year in that hell.

When he came back to California, Larson had him fostered by Jane and Edgar Fernwood, an evangelical family who welcomed him with a kindness he had long since ceased to expect from anyone. Edgar Fernwood, who worked as a builder, took the boy on as an apprentice, and he began learning a trade; Lee Galespi finally seemed to have found a safe haven in the world. In the two years that followed, he got good grades in high school and worked part-time with Fernwood. Fresh-faced and with blond hair, he was short and skinny for his age, a shy, solitary boy who enjoyed comics, video games, and action movies. Once Angelique Larson asked whether he still believed that "boys were evil and girls were good," but Galespi didn't know what she was referring to; he had blocked from his memory that period when he had wanted to be a girl.

In the dossier there were photos of Lee Galespi, the last taken in 1999, when the boy turned eighteen and Child Protective Services ceased to have responsibility for him. Rachel Rosen decided that, given his behavioral problems, he should not receive the insurance money left to him by his mother until he was twenty-one. That was the year that Angelique Larson retired and moved to Alaska.

Deputy Chief Bob Martín set his team to tracking down Lee Galespi, Angelique Larson, and the Fernwoods.

//////////////////////

I've brought you some Coke. You need to drink lots of fluids, and a bit of caffeine might perk you up, don't you think? Come on, Indi, don't make this difficult. If you're refusing to eat and drink because you figure I'm trying to drug you, think about it—I could just inject you the way I did with the antibiotics. It was the right thing to do—it brought down your temperature, and you're not bleeding so much. Give it a little time, and you should be on your feet again.

Anyway, I'll carry on with my story, because it's important that you get to know me, get to understand my mission. This press clipping is from July 21, 1993. The headline reads: "Girl Chained Up by Mother Almost Starves to Death." The story that follows is a string of lies; it claims that an unidentified woman died in the hospital without revealing the existence of her daughter, and that a

*month later the police discovered an eleven-year-old girl who had
been kept locked up her whole life and . . . it says they discovered a
gruesome scene. Lies! I was there and I can tell you that the place
was neat and tidy, there was nothing gruesome about it. Besides it
wasn't a month later, it was only three weeks, and what happened
wasn't Mama's fault. She had a heart attack and never regained
consciousness—how could she let people know I was all on my
own? I remember exactly what happened. She went out first thing
like usual—she'd made breakfast for me, and she reminded me to
double-lock the door, and not to open it to anyone for any reason.
When she didn't come home at the usual time, I thought she'd been
held up at work, so I had a bowl of cereal and watched TV until I
fell asleep. I woke up really late, and when I saw she still wasn't
back, I started to get scared, because Mama had never left me alone
for this long before, and she'd never stayed out all night. I spent
all day watching the clock, waiting for her to come home. I prayed
and prayed, my heart cried out to her. She'd always told me never
to answer the phone, but I decided that if it rang again I'd answer,
because if something had happened to Mama, someone would probably call me. But no one called, and she didn't come back that night
or the following morning. The days went by—I counted them off
on the calendar taped to the fridge door. Eventually the food ran
out and I ended up eating the toothpaste, the soap, wet paper, anything I could put in my mouth. The last five or six days I survived
on nothing but water. I was desperate—I couldn't understand why
Mama had abandoned me. I dreamed up all sorts of explanations: I
thought maybe it was a trial to test my obedience and my strength;
maybe Mama had been attacked by criminals or arrested by the police; maybe this was punishment for some sin I'd committed without
realizing. How much longer could I last? I figured it wouldn't be
long before I died from starvation or from fear. I prayed and prayed
and I called out for Mama. I cried a lot and I offered up my tears to*

Jesus. Back then I believed, just like Mama; now I don't believe in any god—I've seen too much evil in this world for that. Later, when I was found, everyone asked me the same questions: Why didn't you leave the apartment? Why didn't you ask for help? The truth is, I didn't have anyone to turn to. We had no family, no friends, we didn't know the neighbors. I knew that in an emergency I should dial 911, but I'd never used the telephone, and the very thought of talking to a stranger was terrifying.

Twenty-two days later, help finally arrived. I heard the banging on the front door, men's voices shouting: "Open up, it's the police!" That just scared me even more, because Mama had drummed it into me that the scariest people of all were the police, that never, under any circumstances, should I go near anyone in uniform. I hid in a closet I'd converted into a little den, making a nest out of clothes. They came in through the window, they smashed the glass, they invaded the apartment. . . . Then they took me to the hospital, where they treated me like a laboratory animal, performing humiliating tests on me, forcing me to dress as a boy. Nobody took pity on me. The cruelest of them all was Richard Ashton: he did experiments on me, gave me drugs, hypnotized me. He screwed with my brain and then diagnosed me as crazy. You know what electroconvulsive therapy is, Indi? It's a terrifying thing, an unspeakable thing. It was only just that Ashton should suffer it in the flesh—that's why he had to be executed by electrocution.

I was sent to various children's homes, but I couldn't bear any of them because I was used to Mama's love, because she had raised me by herself; I couldn't stand to be with other children, they were dirty and messy, they stole my things. The home run by the Constantes was the worst. Back then, Michael Constante still drank, and when he was drunk, he was terrifying; there were six children in the foster home, all of them more fucked up than me, but it was me he really hated. He couldn't stand the sight of me. If you knew the things he did to punish me. . . . His wife was just as bad. They both deserved the death penalty for their crimes, that's what I told them. They were drugged up, but they were still conscious—they recognized me, they knew what was going to happen to them. Every one of the eight offenders had time to hear me out; I explained to every one why they had to die—except for Alan Keller, because the cyanide worked too quickly.

You know what date it is today, Indiana? Thursday, April 5. Tomorrow is Good Friday, when Christians commemorate the death of Jesus on the cross. Back in Roman times, crucifixion was a common method of execution.

///////////////////

Blake Jackson, who had not been to work for days, dropped by the drugstore to check that everything was all right. Although he trusted his employees, they still needed a boss's supervision. In a moment of inspiration he decided to phone Angelique Larson again. He'd felt a rare affinity with her. He was not a man of romantic leanings—in fact, he had a horror of emotional entanglements—but there was no danger of that with Angelique: they were separated by about three thousand miles of varied terrain. He imagined her swaddled in furs, teaching the alphabet to Inuit children with her dogsled parked outside her igloo. He went into his study and dialed the number. The woman did not seem surprised that this supposed writer had called her twice in a few short hours.

"I've been thinking about Lee Galespi . . . ," said Blake, furious with himself that he hadn't prepared an intelligent question.

"It's such a sad story. . . . I hope you can make use of it in your novel."

"It will be the backbone of my novel, Angelique, I can promise you that."

"I'm glad I could be of help."

"But I have to confess, I haven't written the novel yet, I'm still at the planning stage."

"Really? Have you got a title?"

"I'm thinking of calling it Ripper."

"Is it a crime novel?"

"In a way. Do you like the genre?"

"There are others I prefer, to be honest, but I'll read your book anyway."

"I'll send you a copy as soon as it comes out. Tell me, Angelique, is there anything else you remember about Galespi you think might help?"

"Hmm . . . There is one thing—it's a minor detail, and maybe it's not important, but I might as well mention it. Are you recording?"

"I'm taking notes, if that's okay with you. So, what's this detail?"

"I always had my doubts about whether Marion Galespi was Lee's mother. When she died, she was sixty-one, and the boy was only eleven, so that would have meant she had given birth at fifty—unless there was some mistake in the birth certificates."

"Well, anything's possible with fertility treatment. These days in California you'll sometimes see a fifty-year-old woman pushing triplets around in a stroller."

"Not up here in Alaska. Anyway, in Marion's case it doesn't seem likely she would have had fertility treatment—she was in poor health, and a single woman. Besides, the autopsy revealed she'd had a hysterectomy. No one bothered to check where and when she'd had the operation."

"Why didn't you raise your suspicions, Angelique? They could have performed a DNA test on the boy."

"I didn't say anything because of the life insurance. I thought if there was any doubt about his parentage, Lee might lose the money Marion left for him. The last time I spoke to Lee, Christmas 2006, I told him that Marion had been obese, that she suffered from diabetes, high blood pressure, and heart problems, and that sometimes such conditions can be hereditary. He assured me that he was in very good health. I casually mentioned that by the time he was born, most women Marion's age would have been through menopause, and I asked if he knew about her hysterectomy. He knew nothing about the operation, but said he'd also been surprised by his mother's age."

"Have you got a photo of the kid?"

"I've got lots, but the best one was sent to me by the Fernwoods in 2006, on the day Lee was finally allowed to cash the life insurance check. I can send it right now. What's your e-mail?"

"I can't tell you how much you've helped me, Angelique. Do you mind if I call again if I think of anything else?"

"Of course, Blake—it's been a pleasure talking to you."

Blake Jackson hung up and called his former son-in-law and his granddaughter. By this time, Bob Martín already had a preliminary report on his desk about the Farkases, and listening to Blake, he was able to cross-reference his story with the recent discoveries. Without setting the phone down, he scribbled "Marion Galespi, Tuscaloosa city," followed by a question mark, and passed the note to Petra Horr, who punched it into her database. Bob explained to Blake that the Farkases were also from Tuscaloosa, Alabama, had had minor run-ins with the law—possession, petty theft, DUI— and had drifted for a while, living in various states. In 1986, in Pensacola, Florida, their five-week-old daughter had died, smothered by a blanket while they were in a bar, having left her alone. They had spent a year in prison for child endangerment. They moved to Del Rio, Texas, where they lived for three years, then to Socorro, New Mexico, where they stayed until 1997. Joe managed to get occasional work as a laborer, and Sharon worked as a waitress. They kept moving west, with brief periods spent here and there, until they finally settled in Santa Barbara in 1999.

"And listen to this, Blake: in 1984, their two-year old son disappeared under suspicious circumstances," said the deputy chief. "The child had already been hospitalized three times—the first time at ten months, with bruises and a broken arm that the parents claimed were the result of a fall. Eight months later he was readmitted with pneumonia, having arrived at the emergency room severely malnourished and running a high fever. Police interviewed the parents, but no charges were brought against them. The third time, at two years old, the boy was admitted with a skull fracture, bruises, and broken ribs; according to the parents, he had been knocked down by a motorbike that had fled the scene. Three days after he was released from the hospital, the child vanished. The Farkases seemed devastated and swore that their son had been kidnapped. He was never found."

"What are you saying, Bob?" asked Blake. "Are you suggesting this kid could be Lee Galespi?"

"If Lee Galespi is the Wolf—and if, as we believe, the Farkases were victims of the same killer—then there has to be a connection between them. Hang on a minute—Petra's just brought me something she's found on Marion Galespi."

Bob skimmed through the two pages passed to him by his assistant, then read the relevant part aloud to Blake Jackson: in 1984 Marion Galespi worked as a nurse in the pediatric unit of Tuscaloosa General Hospital. That same year she suddenly quit her job and left the city. Nothing more was heard about her until her death in Daly City in 1993, when she was listed as the mother of Lee Galespi.

"There's no need to look any further," said Blake Jackson. "Marion snatched the child to save him from abusive parents. She was a single, middle-aged woman with no children, and I think that the boy became her reason for living. She moved away and brought the child up as a girl, keeping 'her' locked in the house so she would not be found, terrified that at any moment the authorities might take him away. I'm sure she truly loved the child."

"So the Wolf is the Farkases' missing son," said Bob.

In the hours that followed, the deputy chief discovered that it was as difficult to track down Lee Galespi as it had been Carol Underwater. The Fernwoods, like Angelique Larson, had heard nothing from him since 2007. He had invested half the insurance money in buying a derelict house on Castro Street, which he had renovated in the space of four months and sold to a gay couple, making a profit of more than $100,000. Over the next eighteen months, he repeated this operation twice. In the last message from him, at Christmas, he announced that he was planning to try his luck in Costa Rica for a while, though there is no record of a passport ever being issued in his name. Bob's team was able to track down a state license as contractor and surveyor dating from 2004, both still valid, but could find no work undertaken other than the house on Castro Street.

///////////////////

I'm sure you agree, Indiana, your real parents aren't the people who gave birth to you but the people who raise you. I was raised by Marion Galespi—she was my only mother. The others—Sharon and Joe Farkas—never behaved like parents to me: they were a couple of itinerant alcoholics, and it was their neglect that killed my little sister. They beat me so badly that if Marion Galespi hadn't saved me, they would have killed me, too. I searched and searched until I found them, and then I waited. I got in touch with them last year when I had everything prepared for my mission. Then I introduced myself to them. If you could have seen how emotional they were at having their son back! They had no idea of the surprise I had in store for them.

What sort of monster hits a baby? You're a mother, Indiana, you know the fiercely protective love children inspire. It's a biological impulse. Only unnatural creatures like the Farkases could mistreat their children. And speaking of children, I wanted to congratulate you on Amanda—she's a very bright girl, and I say that with respect and admiration. Like me, she has an analytical mind. She enjoys intellectual challenges; so do I. I'm not afraid of Bob Martín and his team—like all cops, they're incompetent. They close maybe one out of three murder cases, and even then they don't necessarily arrest and convict the real culprit. It's much easier to make the police look like fools than it is your daughter.

I should point out that I really don't fit the profile of the psychopath, as I've been labeled. I'm a rational, sophisticated, educated individual. I read, I study, I keep myself informed. I spent many years planning this mission, and when it's completed, I'll go back to living a normal life, far away from here. To tell the truth, the mission should have ended in February with the execution of Rachel Rosen, the last offender on my list, but you complicated my plans and forced me to eliminate Alan Keller. It was a last-minute decision; I wasn't able to prepare things with the same attention to detail as I did in the other cases. Ideally your lover would have died in San Francisco at precisely the appointed hour. If you want to know why he had to die, the answer is that you're to blame: he died because you took him back. For months I had to listen to you talking about Keller and then about Miller. Your confidences and stories of emotional entanglements turned my stomach, but I memorized them because I knew they would be useful. You're the sort of slut who can't live without a man: hardly had you dumped Keller than you rushed into the arms of Ryan Miller. You disappoint me, Indiana. You disgust me.

It was the soldier who was supposed to die so that you would be free, but he survived because you dumped him without so much as an explanation. You could have told him the truth. Why didn't you tell him you were pregnant by Keller? What was your plan? A termination? You knew Keller never wanted children. Or did you think you could convince Miller that the kid was his? I didn't think you'd have been able to tell him that—then I realized that it wouldn't have put him off; he would have happily taken responsibility for another man's child, it's part of his hero complex. I had a lot of fun reading Celeste Roko's astral chart for him.

Knowing you, Indiana, I think you'd decided to be a single mother, like your father advised. Only two people knew your secret, your father and me, and neither of us could have predicted Keller's reaction. When he asked you to marry him in the Café Rossini, he knew nothing about the pregnancy—you'd only just found out yourself. Two days later, when you told him, he started sobbing at the very thought of being a father, something he'd thought would never happen. It was like a miracle. He convinced you to accept his ring. What a truly grotesque scene that must have been!

I never intended to induce a miscarriage, Indiana—that was an accident. Just one little dose of ketamine to keep you calm, to get you to come here with me, it wouldn't have done any harm, but then I had to keep you drugged for days on end, and that's probably what triggered it. You gave me a terrible scare. On Monday when I came, I found you lying in a pool of blood and almost passed out—I never could stand the sight of blood. I feared the worst, that you'd somehow managed to kill yourself, but then I remembered you were pregnant. For a woman of your age, the chance of miscarrying is between 10 and 20 percent; it's a natural process that rarely requires medical intervention. I did worry about the fever—we managed to sort that out with antibiotics. I took good care of you,

Indi. You have to understand I couldn't let you bleed to death: I have other plans for you.

//////////////////////

Studying the photo of Lee Galespi that Angelique Larson had sent her grandfather, Amanda felt nauseous. There was a metallic taste in her mouth—the taste of blood. She was convinced she knew the face, but she couldn't quite place it. Having shuffled through various possibilities, she gave up and asked her grandfather, who said he thought it looked a bit like that woman with cancer who gave them Save-the-Tuna. On the spur of the moment they headed down to the Café Rossini, since they knew that Carol Underwater spent hours there reading, killing time between her hospital appointments or waiting for Indiana.

Danny D'Angelo, theatrical as ever, greeted them with an effusive display of affection; he had not forgotten that when he was ill it had been Blake Jackson who had taken him in and looked after him. He sobbed as they talked about the awful turn events had taken. He couldn't believe that Indiana had simply disappeared; she had to have been abducted by aliens, there was no other explanation. . . . Amanda interrupted, setting the photo down in front of him.

"Do you know who this is, Danny?"

"Looks to me like Miss Thing—that Carol woman, you know, Indiana's friend, when she was younger."

"But this is a man," said Blake.

"So's Carol. C'mon, anyone can see that."

"A man?" yelped Amanda. "Mom didn't realize, and neither did we."

"Really? I thought Indi knew. Your mom's away with the fairies half the time, honey, she never notices a thing. Hang on, I've got a photo of Carol that Lulu Gardner took. You know Lulu—I'm sure you've seen her around, a kooky old broad, goes round taking photos of people in North Beach."

Danny rushed off to the kitchen and reappeared a minute later with a color Polaroid of Indiana and Carol sitting at a table by the window, Danny himself crouching next to them.

"Transvestism is a subtle art," Danny explained. "Some men, when they cross-dress, can look hotter than a supermodel, but that's rare, and usually it's obvious. Carol isn't trying to look stunning; she just wants to feel feminine. She deliberately chooses frumpy, old-fashioned clothes because they hide her body better. Anyone can dress like a dog. Oops! Sorry, shouldn't be so bitchy about someone with cancer. Though strangely, that sort of helps, because you can forgive the fright wigs and the hideous scarves she wears. Or maybe she hasn't got cancer at all; maybe that's just part of her role as a woman, or maybe she does it for the sympathy. . . . There's a name for that, when people pretend to be ill. . . ."

"Münchausen syndrome," said Blake, who, being a pharmacist, had seen it all.

"That's it! The difficult thing when you're trans is changing your voice, because men have thicker vocal cords than women. That's why Carol always talked in a whisper."

"Mom thought it was something to do with the chemotherapy."

"Oh please! It's a trick of the trade—TVs all try to sound like Jackie Kennedy, God rest her."

"The guy in the photo has blue eyes, but Carol's eyes are brown," said Amanda.

"Right—I've no idea why she wears those mud-brown contacts, they look awful. They make her eyes bulge."

"Have you seen Carol lately?"

"Actually, now you ask, I haven't seen her for a couple days. But next time she's here, I'll tell her to call you."

"I don't think she'll be coming back, Danny."

///////////////////

I haven't dressed like a woman for a long time, Indiana, and I did it just for you, to gain your trust. I needed to get close to Martín—I needed details of the investigation, because what little they feed the media is usually inaccurate—and I knew you could help me with that. You and Bob make a strange pair of divorcees; very few couples who are still married get along as well as you two. But that wasn't the only reason; I was hoping you'd grow to love me, to depend on me. Have you never noticed that you don't have any female friends? Almost all your friends are men, like that cripple soldier; you needed a girlfriend. The cancer was an inspiration, you have to admit—you were so desperate to help me that you let your guard down. How could anyone be suspicious of some poor thing with terminal cancer? It was easy to pump you for information, but it never occurred to me that your daughter would prove useful too; if I believed in luck, I'd say she was a godsend, but I prefer to believe that my plan paid off. On the pretext of finding out how she was getting on with Save-the-Tuna—what a stupid name for a pet—I visited your daughter a couple of times, and sometimes we'd talk on the phone. I was always careful, so as not to alarm you, but I'd talk to her about Ripper, and she'd fill me in on everything she'd found out. She had no idea the favor she was doing me.

///////////////////

Grandfather and granddaughter rushed from the Café Rossini to the Personal Crimes Division with the photo of Carol Underwater Danny had given them. Amanda was so panicked at the thought of how much this person knew about her mother that she could barely speak, so it was left to Blake to explain to Bob Martín that Carol and Lee Galespi were the same person. The deputy chief urgently summoned his team and the two criminal psychologists in the department, and called Samuel Hamilton, who showed up fifteen minutes later. Everything pointed to Lee Galespi being guilty of the killings, as well as of kidnapping Indiana. They worked out that although Galespi had been brooding for years on getting revenge on the people who had abused and mistreated him, he had not decided to act until Angelique Larson sowed doubt in his mind that Marion Galespi—the only person who had ever truly loved him—was not his mother. He traced his biological parents, and when he finally found them, he realized that his misfortunes had begun the day he was born. It was at this point that he quit his job and cut himself off from his friends. Lee Galespi officially disappeared and spent several years preparing for what he believed was an act of justice: ridding the world of these depraved human beings so they could never vent their rage on another child. He lived frugally and had saved some money, so he was able to support himself until he had achieved his goal, spending his every waking hour planning the murders—from acquiring the drugs and the guns to learning how to kill and leave no forensic evidence.

"Galespi disappeared off the face of the earth and reappeared a year ago to kill Ed Staton," explain the deputy chief.

"By which time he was Carol Underwater," Blake chimed in.

"I don't think he committed the crimes using a female persona," suggested one of the psychologists. "As a child, Marion Galespi drummed into him the idea that 'girls are good and boys are evil.' It's likely he committed the crimes under his male identity."

"Then why did he pass himself off as a woman?"

"It's difficult to know. Perhaps he's a transvestite."

"Maybe he only did it so he could befriend Indiana," said Blake. "Carol Underwater—aka Lee Galespi—was obsessed with my daughter. I'm pretty sure that it was Lee, dressed as Carol, who sent her the magazine in which she saw Alan Keller with another woman and broke off their relationship."

"Revenge is the motive in all of the killings, except Keller's."

"It's the same killer, just a different motive," ventured the other psychologist. "He killed Keller because he was jealous."

Blake explained that Indiana trusted Carol and had told her all about her private life. How sometimes Carol/Lee would sit around in the waiting room while Indiana was with a patient. She would have had every opportunity to access her computer, read her e-mails, see her diary, and plant the S&M videos and the video of the wolf.

"I saw them together often at the Café Rossini," Samuel Hamilton interjected. "On Thursday, March eighth, Indiana must have told Carol that she was having dinner with Alan Keller in San Francisco—after all, she told her most things about her life. Carol/Lee had all afternoon to go to Napa, gain access to the house, lace the two glasses with cyanide, then hide somewhere, wait for him to get back, and, once he was dead, shoot the arrow into him."

"But she couldn't have known that Ryan Miller would show up to talk to Keller," said Amanda. "She probably saw him, or at least heard him from wherever she was hiding."

"How do you know when Miller went to the house?" asked her father, who for three weeks now had suspected that his daughter was hiding something from him; perhaps the time had come to tap her cell phone and her laptop.

"Simple logic," Blake cut in quickly. "When Miller got there, Keller was still alive; they argued, Miller punched him and then left, leaving his prints everywhere. Very convenient for the killer. Then Keller drank the poisoned water and died. But I don't understand why the killer shot an arrow into the corpse."

"For Lee Galespi, this was another execution," explained one of the psychologists. "Alan Keller had harmed him, had stolen Indiana from him and therefore had to pay. The arrow through the heart is an obvious message: Cupid as executioner. Just as sodomizing Ed Staton with the baseball bat was a reference to what the man had done to him at Boys' Camp, and burning the Constantes to the fact that they'd burned him with cigarettes when he wet the bed."

"Matheus Pereira was the last person to see Indiana and Carol together on Friday afternoon," said Hamilton. "I went to talk to Pereira because I've had something going round and round in my head."

"What's that?" asked the deputy chief.

"Carol told Matheus that they were going to the movies, but according to Mr. Jackson here, Indiana always ate dinner at home on Friday nights."

"So she could see Amanda when she got back from school," said Blake Jackson. "Hamilton's right—Indi would never have gone to the movies on a Friday night."

"Indiana is tall and heavily built," said the deputy chief. "Carol couldn't have taken her against her will."

"Unless she gave her something to make her compliant and sub-missive," said Hamilton. "I'm talking about a date-rape drug. It didn't strike Pereira as unusual seeing the two of them together, but when I mentioned the possibility that Indiana might have been drugged, he confirmed that she had seemed a bit out of it, that she didn't respond when he said hello, and that Carol was holding her by the arm and leading her."

By eleven fifteen everyone was tired and hungry, but no one thought of sleeping or eating. Amanda did not need to look at the clock on the wall of her father's office, having trained herself over two years to be able to tell the time: her mother had a little over twenty-four hours left to live.

Ryan did not get any sleep that night either: he was glued to his computer, looking for some thread he could pull to unravel the tangle of riddles he was faced with. The programs he used for work gave him access to any data in the world, from the most secret to the most trivial. In a matter of seconds he could find out what had been said at the latest meeting of the directors of Exxon-Mobil, PetroChina, and Saudi Aramco, or today's lunch menu for the members of the Bolshoi Ballet. The problem was not finding answers; it was knowing which questions to ask.

Denise West had sacrificed one of her chickens to make a delicious fricassee, which she had left in the kitchen with a loaf of whole-wheat bread to see him through the night. "Good luck, kid," she said as she kissed him on the forehead, and Ryan blushed—though he had been living here for two weeks, he was not used to these spontaneous displays of affection. The days were warm now as spring approached, but the nights were still cold, and the sudden shifts of temperature made all the boards in the house creak like the joints of an arthritic old woman. The only sources of heat were the living room fireplace and a gas heater Denise trailed with her from room to room. Accustomed to his freezing loft, Ryan did not need it. Denise went to bed, leaving him still staring at his computer screen, Attila at his feet. Since the dog could only be exercised on Denise's four acres lest he attract attention, he had gained some weight and, living with two house dogs and several cats for the first time in his harsh life, begun to smile and wag his tail like a common pet.

At two in the morning Ryan polished off the chicken stew, sharing it with the dog. He'd tried to do his Qigong exercises but couldn't focus. His mind was racing, and he couldn't think clearly; any attempt at reasoning things out was interrupted by images of Indiana. His skin was burning up, and he felt like screaming, like pounding on the walls. He had to do something—he needed instructions, orders, a tangible enemy. This silent, senseless waiting was worse than the thunderous roar of battle.

"I need to calm down, Attila. The state I'm in, I'm no use to anyone." Overwhelmed by the idea of failure, he slumped onto the sofa and forced himself to rest. He tried to breathe the way Indiana had taught him, focusing on every breath, using the techniques he had learned from his Qigong master. Twenty minutes passed, and still he could not sleep.

And then, in the reddish glow of the fire's dying embers, he saw two figures: a girl of about ten and a young boy she was holding by the hand. Ryan froze. He did not blink, did not dare to breathe, for fear of startling them. How long the vision lasted it was impossible to say, perhaps only a few seconds, but it was as real as if the children had traveled from Afghanistan to visit him. On previous occasions they had appeared to him as he had seen them in 2006, in the heat of battle, cowering in a trench, a little girl of four clutching a baby; but that night in Denise West's house he saw not ghosts from the past, but the children themselves—Sharbat and her brother, as they were now, six years later. When the figures withdrew with their usual discretion, the soldier felt as though his heart was finally free from the vise in which it had been trapped for the past six years, and he began sobbing with relief, with gratitude that Sharbat and her brother were still alive. They had survived the horrors of war and the pain of being orphaned, and they were waiting for him, calling to him. Silently, he promised them that he would come as soon as he had finished his last mission as a Navy SEAL: rescuing the only woman he would ever love.

Sleep caught up with Ryan a moment later, and he dozed off, his cheeks still wet with tears.

///////////////////

I hope you can forgive me for deceiving you in my role as Carol—as I said earlier, it was a whim, I meant no harm by it. All I wanted was to be closer to you. More than once I thought you'd realized that Carol was a man and simply accepted the situation, the way you accept most things, but the truth is that you were never interested in looking at me, in really getting to know me. To you it was a superficial friendship, but to me it was as important as my mission.

As I'm sure you understand, Indiana, disposing of Ed Staton, the Farkases, the Constantes, Richard Ashton, and Rachel Rosen could not go unnoticed: it was important that the public understand. I could have killed them and made their deaths look accidental—no one would have bothered to investigate, and I would have had no reason to worry—but from the very first, my intention was to send a message to perverted individuals like them who have no right to live in society. It had to be absolutely clear that my victims had been tried, sentenced to death, and executed. I succeeded—though there was a moment with the Farkases when it almost failed; the police didn't analyze the contents of the bottle of gin, even though I left it there deliberately. I only just found out that your ex-husband was the one who discovered that the liquor was drugged. Three months later! That should tell you how incompetent the police are.

It was a crucial part of my plan that the murders get maximum news coverage and terrify anyone with a guilty conscience, but journalists are lazy—and the public is indifferent. I needed to find a way of attracting media attention. Then, last September, a month before the first killing, the execution of Ed Staton, I saw Celeste Roko doing her daily horoscope on television. She's a great performer, you have to hand it to her. She managed to convince me, and I don't believe in astrology; her show really deserves its popularity. It occurred to me that I could use Celeste Roko to drum up the publicity my mission needed, so I sent her five short messages, announcing that there would be a bloodbath in San Francisco. I assume she discounted the first message as a joke, the second as the work of a madman, but when the messages kept coming, she would *have paid attention—if she's as professional as she claims—and studied the heavenly bodies.*

You have to understand, Indiana, that suggestion is a very powerful tool. Madame Roko gazed at the stars and saw what she expected to see: evidence of the bloodbath I had foretold in my letters. And so, of course, she found that evidence, the same way that when you read your horoscope, you always find something true. The predictions are so vague that people who believe, like you, can interpret them to mean anything they want. Perhaps Madame Roko had seen the prophecy scrawled in blood across the sky and decided to warn the public, just as I hoped. Okay, Indiana, for the sake of argument I'll admit it might not have happened that way. Which came first, the chicken or the egg? Perhaps my mission truly was decided by the position of the planets. In which case it was fated from the moment I was born. It was inevitable; I am only fulfilling my destiny. We'll never know, will we?

Friday, 6

*A*t four in the morning, when Amanda had finally dozed off on her grandfather's bed, covered with his jacket, and with Save-the-Tuna sleeping on the pillow, the cell phone Blake Jackson had prized from her hand and set down on the nightstand rang. Blake, who could not sleep and was sitting in the darkness watching the minutes pass on the luminous digital clock, gave a start, initially in the wild hope that it was Indiana, that his daughter was free, and a second later panicked that it would be bad news.

Sherlock Holmes had to repeat his name before Blake realized who it was. This was something that had never happened: one of the unspoken rules of Ripper was that there was no independent contact between the players.

"It's Sherlock Holmes," yelled the boy in Reno. "I need to talk to the games master."

"This is Kabel. What's up?"

Hearing her grandfather's voice, Amanda woke up and took the phone from him.

"Master, I've got a lead," said Sherlock.

"What is it?" Amanda was completely awake now.

"I found out something that might be important: *farkas* means 'wolf' in Hungarian."

"What did you say?"

"You heard. I was looking up the word for 'wolf' in various languages, and discovered that in Hungarian, it's *farkas*."

"That doesn't help us find out where my mom is."

"No, but it means that the killer adopted the wolf as a symbol because he's related to Sharon and Joe Farkas. He had to know them before he murdered Ed Staton, because he left the sign of the wolf—*farkas*—at every crime scene."

"Thanks, Sherlock. I hope it turns out to be useful."

"Good night, master."

"Good night? This is the worst night of my life!"

After she hung up, Amanda and her grandfather considered this new piece of information.

"What was the name of the little boy the Farkases lost?" asked Amanda, who was so scared now her teeth were chattering.

"Come on, sweetie, calm down and try to get some sleep. You've already done more than enough—we need to leave it to the police now."

"Do you remember his name or not?" Amanda shrieked.

"I think he was called Anton. That's what your dad told me."

"Anton Farkas, Anton Farkas . . ." Amanda muttered to herself pacing the room.

"That's the same name Joe Farkas's brother gave," said her grandfather, "the one who identified the bodies. You don't think—"

"The letters branded onto the buttocks of the Constantes!" Amanda interrupted. "They were his initials."

"*F* on Michael, *A* on Doris."

"That depends on how they were positioned on the bed. *A, F*: Anton Farkas."

"The card found in the trailer had the same name on it. It was an invitation to a party at the Rob Hill campground on December 10. But in his police statement, Joe Farkas's brother denied having sent it."

"He was telling the truth, Grandpa—he didn't send it. His nephew, Sharon and Joe's son, did. Don't you get it, Kabel? The Farkases didn't come to San Francisco to see Joe's brother. The person they met in that trailer was their long-lost son, also called Anton, like his uncle."

"You need to call your dad," said Blake.

"Hang on, give me a minute to think. . . . We also need to contact Ryan, and it would be better to do it by phone."

Blake Jackson dialed the cell phone number Pedro had given him. The phone only rang twice, as though the Uruguayan was expecting the call.

"Pedro? Sorry for calling so late." Blake handed the phone to his granddaughter.

"You have to get a message to Ryan right now. Tell him *farkas* means 'wolf' in Hungarian. The Farkases' son was called Anton. Lee Galespi knew his real name, and who his parents were, when he drew up the list of people he intended to kill. I suspect the reason there's no record of Lee Galespi or Carol Underwater is because he's using his real name. Tell Ryan that Anton Farkas is the Wolf. You need to track him down in the next twenty hours."

Then Amanda called her father, who had gone back to his apartment for the first time that week and dozed off on his bed, still wearing his clothes and his shoes.

"You need to arrest Anton Farkas, Dad. You have to get him to tell you where he's taken Mom. Rip out his fingernails if you have to, you hear me?"

"I hear you, kid. Let me talk to Blake."

"Hey, Bob," said Blake.

"This is in my hands now, Blake. I'll get the entire San Francisco force and every other force in the Bay Area out looking for every Anton Farkas they can find, and I'll put a call in to the FBI. I'm worried Amanda is about to have a breakdown. Could you give her something to calm her?"

"No, Bob—we need her to be clearheaded for the next twenty hours."

///////////////////////

At 10:00 a.m., having been careful to turn off video streaming, Ryan contacted the Ripper players on Skype. He could not ask Denise to play the part, since, it being market day, she had set off early with her crates of free-range eggs, chickens, and jars of jam, and would not be back until the afternoon.

"What happened to your webcam, Jezebel?" asked Amanda, who was sitting with her grandfather in the kitchen with a single laptop.

"I don't think there's time to fix it right now. Can you hear me okay?"

"Loud and clear," said Colonel Paddington, "but your voice sounds odd."

"I've got laryngitis."

"Let's get to the most recent updates, players," said the games master. "Kabel, you're up."

Blake summarized what had been discussed by the homicide detail. The players already knew that Carol Underwater was really Lee Galespi, and that the police had been unable to track him down. Blake also explained what Amanda had discovered about Anton Farkas.

"I called Jezebel last night and asked her to track down Anton Farkas," said Amanda, not mentioning that they had spoken again a couple of times this morning. "She's the best investigator we have."

"I thought we agreed that no player should be given an advantage," said Paddington grumpily.

"We've got no time for formalities, Colonel. The battle has already started. We've only got until midnight, and we don't know where my mom is." Amanda's voiced was choked with emotion.

"She's alive, but her aura is very weak," said Abatha in a sleepwalker's drone. "She is in a large building. It's cold and dark—I can hear screams. I can also sense the spirits protecting the master's mother."

"What have you managed to find out, Jezebel?" Sherlock Holmes interrupted.

"Well, what info I have, I owe to Sherlock and Amanda," said Jezebel. "Thanks to both of you, we're a lot closer to solving this thing."

Jezebel went on to explain that, fortunately, Anton Farkas was not a common name. There were only four people with that name in California: Joe Farkas's brother in Eureka; an old man in a retirement home in Los Angeles; a man living in Sacramento; and someone else in Richmond. He had called the first number and got a recorded message: "You've reached Anton Farkas, licensed builder and property surveyor. Leave a message, and I'll get back to you as soon as possible." When he called the second number, he got the same recording: they were the same person.

"This is the most important lead we've had," said Colonel Paddington.

"There is no street address listed for Anton Farkas in either city," said Jezebel. "Only post-office boxes."

Amanda and Blake already knew that, not only from Ryan but also because Bob Martín had phoned to tell them. The address of anyone renting a mailbox is confidential, he had explained, and he would need a warrant to get it. He then pointed out that he had no jurisdiction in those cities, but that when they had found out what was happening, the two FBI agents—who did not need a warrant— had immediately offered to help. Right now, Lorraine Barcott was in Richmond, and Napoleon Fournier III was in Sacramento.

What Blake and Amanda did not know was that Ryan Miller and Pedro Alarcón had found out something else.

"Did you say Anton Farkas was a property surveyor?" Esmeralda asked Jezebel.

"That's right, and that's why I decided to take a look at the list of recent surveys signed off by Anton Farkas in Sacramento and Richmond, where he had to be working. There is a state list of surveyed properties. One of them immediately corresponds to Abatha's description: Winehaven. It's a derelict property in Point Molate that was a famous winery until it closed in 1919. During World War II, it was used by the navy. These days it belongs to the Richmond city council."

"Very interesting," said Paddington.

"It's a vast abandoned building. The navy used to house officers in the old workers' cottages, and they converted the storage cellar into a military barracks and built an air-raid shelter,"

"You think it would be possible to hide a kidnap victim there?"

"It would be perfect. The navy hasn't used it since 1995, so Winehaven's been uninhabited since then. No one knows what to do with the place; there was some vague plan to turn it into a casino, but it never got off the ground. The workers' cottages are still there. The main building, which looks like a medieval fortress built of red brick, isn't open to the public, but you can see it from the Vallejo ferry, which passes close by, and from San Rafael Bridge. Last March, the San Rafael council hired Anton Farkas to survey the property."

"Anton Farkas, or Lee Galespi, or Carol Underwater—whatever you want to call the Wolf—could be holding my mother in any of the abandoned houses, or in the fortress itself," said Amanda. "How are we going to find her without a SWAT team?"

"If I were the Wolf and was looking for a lair, I'd choose the air-raid shelter," said Colonel Paddington. "It's basic strategy."

"The houses are boarded up, and they're all close to the road. They would be no use as a hideout. I agree with the colonel—the Wolf would choose the air-raid shelter. Since Anton Farkas was hired to survey the property, he would know how to get into it."

"What's the next step?" asked Esmeralda.

"We need to tell my dad!" shouted Amanda.

"No." Jezebel stopped her. "If Anton Farkas has got your mom in Winehaven, we can't alert the police. They'll storm the fortress like a herd of buffalo, and they'd never get to your mother in time."

"I agree with Jezebel," said Colonel Paddington. "We have to do something ourselves. We have to take him by surprise."

"No point counting on me," said Esmeralda. "I'm in a wheel-chair in New Zealand."

"I suggest we ask Ryan Miller to help," proposed Jezebel.

"Who?" said Esmeralda.

"The guy accused of killing Alan Keller."

"Why him?"

"Because he's a Navy SEAL."

"Miller is probably halfway across the world by now," said Sherlock Holmes. "He wouldn't have been stupid enough to stay so close to the scene of the crime with a police manhunt going on."

"He didn't commit any crime," Abatha interrupted. "We know that now."

"He might have stayed in the Bay Area to try to track down the Wolf," suggested Kabel, signaling to Amanda to be careful what she said. "I don't think he trusts the police."

"So, how do we find this Navy SEAL?" asked Esmeralda.

"I'll take care of that," Amanda reassured them. "I'm the games master."

"I know this man will help us—I can see it in my third eye," said Abatha.

"Assuming he's free," said Colonel Paddington, disappointed that he was in New Jersey, since the situation clearly required a military strategist of his caliber.

"Let's assume the master manages to track down Ryan Miller," said Esmeralda. "How is he going to get into Winehaven?"

"The Navy SEALs managed to get into Osama bin Laden's compound in Pakistan," muttered the colonel. "I don't think Miller will have much of a problem getting into a derelict warehouse in Richmond."

"The Bin Laden operation took months of planning, the assault was led by a group of Navy SEALs in helicopters with further air support, and they went in intending to kill," Sherlock Holmes said ominously. "This would be an unplanned operation by one man to rescue someone, not to kill. The most difficult thing to do is to recover a hostage alive: it's been proven."

"Have we got an alternative?" asked Esmeralda.

"No. But, for a Navy SEAL, this is child's play," said Jezebel, and immediately regretted the words because it was bad luck to boast about an operation in advance, as more than one soldier had learned.

"We'll meet up again at six p.m., California time," said Amanda. "In the meantime, I'll track down Miller."

///////////////

Four of the Ripper players signed out of Skype, while the games master and her henchman stayed online with Jezebel—or rather, Miller—listening to his plan of action. The SEAL explained to them that Winehaven was made up of a number of buildings and that the biggest, which housed the old wine cellars, was three storeys high, and had a cellar where the navy had built the air-raid shelter. The windows were covered with metal grilles, the door that led to the shelter from the bay side was blocked with a pair of crossed steel bars, and the whole property was fenced off for fear it would be used for a terrorist attack on the neighboring Chevron oil refinery. A security guard did a few circuits at night, but he never went into the buildings. There was no electricity, and according to the last inspection report, by Anton Farkas, the place was unsafe: it often flooded during storms or when the tide was high in the bay. The floorboards were loose, there was rubble where parts of the ceiling had fallen in, and large holes in the floors.

"Do you know what the shelter's like?" asked Blake.

"More or less, although the plans don't make it very clear. The cellar is huge. There used to be an elevator, but it's not there any more, so there must be a staircase. According to the plan drawn up by the navy, the shelter can accommodate a whole regiment of soldiers and officers, as well as a field hospital."

"How are you planning to get in?" asked Amanda.

"There's a door on the second floor that you can see from the path," Ryan replied. "Pedro's just called me, he's at Point Molate, says he photographed the door with a telescopic lens from the fence. It's made of iron and locked with industrial padlocks that he says are easy to break open. But then, any padlock is a piece of cake for him."

"I'm assuming Pedro'll go with you," said Amanda.

"No, he'd only get in the way. Pedro doesn't have my level of training. He should be careful, too, because your dad has a detective following him—I don't know how Pedro slipped away and got to Point Molate, or how he's going to get me what I need from where he is."

"Can he teach you to open the padlocks?"

"Yeah, but it's one of those sliding metal doors—if I try to open it or break a window, it'll make a lot of noise. I'll need to find another way in."

///////////////

I'm glad you're finally awake, Indi. How do you feel? You're weak, but at least you can walk—it's just there's no need to. There's a beautiful day dawning outside. It's mild, the water's clear, not a cloud in the sky, and a breeze is picking up—ideal for sports. There are hundreds of sailboats out in the bay, and there's always a few of those crazy people skimming over the water on their kitesurfs. There are a lot of gulls out, too—and man, what a racket! That means the fishing's good, so all the ancient Chinese guys will come out on to the shores to fish. We're near an old whaling station, the last one in the US, it's been disused for forty years. They used to bring in whales from the Pacific, and you could still find a few in the bay a century ago. The bottom of the bay's a carpet of bones. They say that back in the day, a team of forty men could reduce a humpback whale to oil and stewing meat in an hour, and that the smell reached all the way to the city.

Did you know we're just a few meters from the water? What am I saying—how would you know if you haven't been able to go outside? There's no beach here, and the property can't be reached from the bay. This was a navy fuel depot in World War II, and you can still find mildewed old instruction manuals lying around, and medical equipment, and the barrels of water I mentioned to you the other day.

Your daughter's good fun, a real sharp girl. Playing with her is keeping me on my toes: I've left clues for her, and she's found almost every one. I'm sure it's occurred to her that the Wolf is Anton Farkas, which will be why the police are going after him now.

They're going to find nothing but some mailboxes and phone numbers, though—an illusionist's trick. I've mastered the art. When I found out they were looking for Farkas, I knew that sooner or later Amanda would link the property surveyor with this fortress. She'll never do it in time, though—and anyway, I'm ready.

Good Friday has come at last, Indi, so your captivity ends today. Don't think I've dragged it out to punish you, though: you know that cruelty disgusts me, it only creates confusion, filth, and chaos. I would have preferred to spare you this trouble, but you didn't want to see reason, you refused to cooperate. I didn't just pick today at random, or because I felt like it—I chose it from the lunar calendar. Dates matter, and so do rituals: they give human actions meaning and beauty, and they help to fix them in our memories. I know I've got my rituals. I always carry out my executions at midnight, for instance—that mysterious moment when the veil separating life and death is lifted. It's a shame that there are so few secular rituals left in modern life—they're all religious now. Take Christians, who are celebrating Holy Week with solemn rites as I speak. They observe three days of mourning to commemorate Christ's crucifixion—we all know that—but not very many people know what crucifixion really is. It's a slow death: utter torture. The condemned man is tied or nailed to two planks of wood, one vertical, the other horizontal—at least that's the well-known version, but there are other sorts of cross too. It can take hours or even days for him to die, depending on the method used and the victim's state of health. The cause of death can be exhaustion, septicemia, cardiac arrest, dehydration, or a combination of any of those. It can be loss of blood, too, if the convict has wounds, or if his legs have been broken, which was sometimes done to speed up the process. There's a theory that the position of the outstretched arms, holding up the weight of the body, stifles the breath, and that death is caused by asphyxiation, but it's never been proven.

////////////////////

It was a sunny day, spring was in the air, with bursts of color on all the market stalls. Among those stalls strolled a crowd of shoppers in light clothes and high spirits, buying fruit, vegetables, meat, bread, and various delicacies. At the entrance to the market a blind girl wearing the distinctive cap of Mennonite women was singing in a heavenly voice and selling CDs of her songs; a hundred yards farther on a Bolivian band, with their indigenous clothes and Andean instruments, entertained the crowd.

At midday Pedro Alarcón, wearing shorts, sandals, and a straw hat, walked up to the white canopy under which Denise West sold products from her farm and her kitchen. The detective from the homicide detail who had been trailing Pedro for some days had taken off his jacket and was fanning himself with a pamphlet about ecological living that someone had put in his hand. Hidden in the crowd a few yards off, he watched the Uruguayan flirt with the stall owner—a mature, attractive woman dressed like a lumberjack, with a gray plait of hair hanging down her back—but didn't see him give her his car keys. The detective sweated as he followed Pedro, who strolled from stall to stall buying a carrot here, a spray of parsley there, with infuriating slowness. He had no idea that meanwhile, Denise was on her way to the parking lot to get a package out of Pedro's car and put it in her truck. The detective saw nothing strange in his subject stopping by the stall again to say good-bye to the woman he'd been making eyes at as he left, and he suspected nothing as Pedro got his keys back.

Denise closed her stall early, took her canopy down, loaded her gear into the truck, and headed for the location Pedro had given her, by the mouth of the Petaluma River, a huge expanse of rivulets and swamps. She had trouble finding the place. She had been expecting something more like a shop selling water sports equipment, but it turned out to be a house so dilapidated it looked abandoned. She brought her heavy vehicle to a halt in a mud puddle. Not daring to drive on for fear of getting stuck, she honked her horn a few times, and as if by magic a bearded man holding a rifle appeared less than a meter from her car window. Still pointing the gun at her, he shouted something incomprehensible, but Denise hadn't come that far to fall at the first hurdle. She opened the door, getting down with some difficulty because of the pain in her joints, and faced the man, hands on her hips.

"You put that rifle down, mister, 'less you want me to come take it off of you. Pedro Alarcón told you I'd be coming. I'm Denise West."

"Why didn't you tell me before?" he growled.

"I'm telling you now."

"You got what's mine?"

She passed him the envelope that Pedro had given her. The man counted the bills slowly, and when he was satisfied he put two fingers to his mouth and let out a loud whistle. A few moments later two well-built young men arrived, carrying a pair of big canvas sacks, which they dumped unceremoniously in the back of the vehicle. Just as Denise had feared, the truck had sunk into the mud; but the three men didn't dare refuse her when she told them to get behind it and push.

Denise got home at dusk, by which time Ryan had carefully packed his gear, just as he used to for his missions as a Navy SEAL. He felt as confident as he did in those days, too—even though he didn't have his brothers from SEAL Team Six with him, or a choice of forty different weapons. He had memorized the floor plans of Winehaven. The winery had been founded after the 1906 earthquake, when Point Molate was populated only by a handful of Chinese families who fished for shrimp and were quickly evicted. Grapes would arrive on great barges from the vineyards of California, to be processed by more than four hundred permanent workers. They had to produce half a million gallons of wine per month just to quench the immense thirst of the rest of the country. The business was promptly closed down in 1919 on the passage of Prohibition, which would last thirteen years. The fortress lay abandoned for more than twenty years, until the navy converted it into a military base, whose plans Ryan had obtained without difficulty.

Denise and Ryan hauled the sacks down from the truck and opened them on the terrace. The first contained the frame, the second the hull, of a Klepper kayak—a direct descendant of the canoes used by Inuits. Instead of wood and sealskin, though, its folding hull was made of plastic and aluminum, and covered with waterproof canvas. There was no boat more light, quiet, or practical than that Klepper, which was ideal for Ryan's purposes—he had often used it in his time in the navy, and in choppier waters than the San Francisco Bay.

"Pedro sent you this," Denise said, handing Ryan the packet she had taken from the Uruguayan's car.

Inside was a harness for Attila, and the beige cashmere sweater Alan Keller had given to Indiana a few years ago. Pedro had found it in Ryan's truck and decided to keep hold of it when he got rid of the vehicle, as Ryan had told him to. He had left the truck in a garage, hidden in the abandoned shipyards of Hunter's Point, where a gang of highly skilled criminals would give it a makeover before selling it in Mexico.

The time had come to put the sweater to use.

"You already know what I think of all this," said Denise.

"Don't worry, there's good visibility."

"And quite a wind."

"In my favor," parried Ryan, but he avoided mentioning the possible risks.

"This is some show you're putting on, Ryan. Why are you going alone into the Wolf's mouth? Quite literally, in fact—"

"Male arrogance, Denise."

"You mean you're a maniac," she murmured.

"You don't get it. The truth of it is, that heartless bastard has Indiana, and the only way of getting her out alive is to take him by surprise, without giving him time to react. There's no other way."

"What if you're wrong, and your friend isn't sitting hostage in the winery like you think? Or maybe the Wolf will kill her the moment you come close—if he hasn't done it already, that is."

"That's not going to happen, Denise. The Wolf is ritualistic: he's going to wait until midnight, like he did with all the other murders. This is going to be easy."

"Compared with what?"

"He's a paranoid psychopath working alone, armed with a Taser, some narcotics, poison, and a few arrows. I doubt he can use an air rifle. And come on: the guy dresses as a woman."

"Sure, honey, but he's committed eight murders."

At 6:00 p.m., the games master told the Ripper players that they had found the Navy SEAL, and outlined the plan, which was met with enthusiasm by Sir Edmond Paddington, and with doubt by Sherlock Holmes. Abatha was even more incoherent than usual, being psychically whacked out by the strenuous effort of reestablishing telepathic communication with Amanda's mother. There was some interference, she explained, and the messages she was getting were very vague. In the first few days she had visualized Indiana floating in the sidereal night, and they were able to talk, but Indiana's spirit was no longer moving freely through space. It was her own fault too, Abatha admitted, or at least the fault of the five hundred calories she had eaten the day before, which had bent her aura out of shape and set her stomach on fire.

"Your mom is still alive, but she's getting desperate. In those conditions, I can't enter her mind."

"Is she suffering?"

"Very much, Master," replied Abatha, while Amanda could only sob.

"Have you thought about what will happen if Miller fails?" Esmeralda interrupted.

For a long minute, nobody replied. Amanda could not consider the possibility of Ryan failing; there would be no second chance. As night closed in, her doubts grew, stoked by her grandfather, who was starting to seriously consider calling up Bob Martín and confessing everything.

"This is routine stuff for a Navy SEAL," said Denise West in her role of Jezebel, although her tone lacked conviction.

"The plan is a good one from a military point of view," said Paddington firmly. "But it's risky, and should be monitored from the ground."

"Miller's friend Pedro Alarcón will do that with his cell and a GPS," Kabel pointed out. "He'll just be a mile away, ready to intervene. The games master and I will stay in close contact with him."

"And how can we help?" asked Esmeralda.

"Well, you can pray," said Abatha, "or else send positive energy to Winehaven. I'm going to try again telepathically. I need to tell Amanda's mom to hang in there and be strong, that help is on the way."

The remaining hours of daylight passed at a torturously slow pace for everyone, but especially for Ryan. Through his telescope he watched the fleet of sailboats on the bay, counting the minutes until they would set course for their docks. At nine, when there was no traffic left on the water and the last ferry had left for Vallejo, Denise West dropped him, along with Attila and the kayak, at Sonoma Creek, a tributary of the Napa River. It was a starless night, but with a full moon—a brilliant disc of pure silver rising slowly over the hills in the east. She helped him get the kayak into the water and then said an unemotional farewell, wishing him luck. She had already told him what she thought about his plan. The Navy SEAL felt well prepared: he had a Glock .45 semiautomatic, the best possible handgun for this mission. He had more lethal weapons hanging on the wall of his loft, but he didn't miss them; none would have been as much use as the Glock for rescuing Indiana. He also had his KA-BAR service knife—the same model that had been used since World War II—and his standard-issue first-aid pouch, more out of superstition than anything else, since a tourniquet had stopped him bleeding to death in Iraq (Attila did the rest). He had asked Denise to buy the best night-vision goggles on the market, costing a mere thousand dollars—he would depend on them entirely once he was inside Winehaven. He'd dressed all in black—trousers, T-shirt, sweatshirt, and shoes—and smeared his face with black boot polish. In the darkness, he was all but invisible.

He had calculated that if he rowed at a speed of four to five knots, it would take him a few hours to cross to Point Molate. That left him a good margin before midnight. He trusted in the strength of his muscles, his experience as an oarsman, and his knowledge of the bay. Pedro had inspected the surroundings of Winehaven and warned him that there was no beach or pier, that he would have to climb a rock face to get to the property, but it wasn't too steep, and he thought Attila could do it too, even in the darkness. Once inside the old winery, he would have to move quickly and stealthily or he would lose his advantage.

He went through the plans of Winehaven again in his head as he paddled the calm waters of the strait. Sitting in the bow of the kayak, upright and attentive, Attila scanned the horizon like any good sailor would.

Fifteen minutes later, the kayak was entering the San Pablo Bay and heading south. Ryan needed no compass: he oriented himself by the faraway lights of the shores on both sides and the navigation buoys that marked the routes for ships and tankers. The kayak could move through shallow waters, which would allow him to carve out a direct route to Point Molate without fear of running aground, which is what would have happened with his motorboat. The day's pleasant breeze had become a north wind, and it was at his back, although that was of no help to Ryan; because the tide was coming up strong with the full moon, and the wind cut against the direction of the water, stirring it up into waves. As a result he had to paddle harder than that stretch of water would normally have required. The only other vessel he saw for the whole of the next hour was a cargo ship heading toward the Golden Gate and the Pacific Ocean.

Ryan was unable to see the pair of rocky outcrops peppered with gulls' nests that marked the point where the San Pablo Bay gave way to the San Francisco Bay, but he intuited where they were because the waters were even choppier. Continuing a little farther, he saw before him the lights of the Richmond–San Rafael Bridge, which seemed much closer than they in fact were and which he would use to orient himself, and the glow of the old lighthouse on one of the two Brothers islands, which had become a boutique hotel for adventurous tourists. Winehaven would lie to his left a little before he got to the bridge, and as there were no lights, he would have to stick close to the shore so as not to overshoot. He carried on paddling into the waves, indifferent to the strain on the muscles of his arms and back, the steady rhythm of his oar strokes never faltering. He only stopped once or twice to wipe off some of the sweat soaking his clothes and to drink a bottle of water. "We're doing good, boy," he assured Attila.

The SEAL felt the familiar heightened state that comes before a fight. When he said good-bye to Denise West, he had given up any illusion that he was in control of his circumstances or that he had foreseen all the possible risks. A battle-hardened soldier, he knew that escaping a combat situation unharmed was a matter of luck, and that the most highly trained fighter can be killed in an instant by a stray bullet. During all his years at war, he'd been aware that he could be injured or killed at any moment; he woke up grateful every morning, and at night he bedded down prepared for the worst. But this was not the high-tech, abstract, impersonal sort of war he was used to: this would be a brief skirmish, an idea that increased his excitement and anxiety. He wished for it now—he wanted to see the Wolf face-to-face. He was not afraid of him. In fact, there was no civilian he feared. He could not have been better prepared. He had kept in good shape, and that night he would be facing a man on his own—he was sure of that, because no serial killer ever uses accomplices. The Wolf was like something out of a storybook—he was absurd, deranged, and certainly no match for a Navy SEAL. "D'you think I'm underestimating the enemy, Attila? Sometimes I get too proud, too arrogant." The dog didn't hear him, but stayed rigidly in his position, his one eye fixed on their goal. "You're right, buddy, I'm getting distracted." He focused on the present—on the water, on the rhythm of his arms, on the plan of Winehaven, on the luminous dial of his watch. He did not think about the engagement, or run through the risks again, or recall his brothers from SEAL Team Six, or consider the possibility that Indiana was not in the air-raid shelter. He needed to get Indiana out of his head: distraction could be fatal.

The moon was already high when Ryan brought the kayak up in front of Winehaven—a hulking mass of brick with thick walls, turrets, and crenellated parapets. It looked like a castle transplanted from the fourteenth century into the placid San Francisco Bay, and in the soft white glow of the moon it had a gloomy, ominous look. It was built on the hillside, so from where Ryan stood, the facade looked twice its real height. The main entrance, on the side where the road was, went straight on to the second floor. There was one floor above that, another below, and the basement.

Ryan jumped into the water, which came up to his chest, and tied the fragile vessel to a rock before taking out his weapon, his ammunition, and the rest of his equipment. He put on his sneakers, which had been tied around his neck, signaled for Attila to follow him, and helped the dog up the slippery rocks. Once the two were on dry land, they ran the forty yards that separated the building from the water. It was 11:35 p.m. The crossing had taken longer than expected, but if the Wolf was faithful to his habits, time was on Ryan's side.

Pressing himself to the wall, he waited a few minutes to make sure everything was calm. The only sounds were the hooting of an owl and some wild turkeys moving in the grass—he wasn't surprised to hear them, as Pedro had warned him about the flocks of these big clumsy birds on the grounds of the estate. He crept forward in the shadow of the fortress, rounded the turret to the right, and came out in front of the southern wall, which he had chosen, looking at one of Pedro's photographs, because it could not be seen from the path the guard walked along. At its lowest point, the wall was between forty-five and fifty feet high, and an iron drainpipe channeled water down it from the roof. When Ryan strapped Attila into his service harness—an improvised jacket with holes for the dog's legs and a hook at the back—he felt the animal's nervous tension. Then he understood: the dog had a memory of wearing another harness just like it. "Easy boy, this is gonna be nothing compared to a parachute jump," he whispered, as though the dog could hear him, and stroked his head. "Wait for me here, and don't even think about going after the turkeys." He hooked the rope that hung from his waist to Attila's harness and signaled to the animal to wait.

Praying that the drainpipe would hold his weight, Ryan started to climb, propelling himself with the muscles in his torso and arms and balancing his body with his one leg, as he did when he swam. The prosthesis was no help at times like this. The pipe turned out to be firmly attached—it creaked but did not yield to Ryan's weight. He quickly got to the roof. From here he could take in the immense surface area of the building as well as a spectacular moonlit view of the bay, with the lights of the bridge off to his right and the distant glimmer of the city of San Rafael ahead. He gave a short tug on the rope to alert Attila, then started to raise him slowly, being careful not to knock him against the wall. As soon as he could reach the dog, he lifted him over the lip of the wall and unhooked the rope, though he left the harness on. In that brief climb, Attila regained the courageous spirit that had won him his medal. No longer nervous, he was ready for orders and bursting with energy, with a look of wild anticipation that Ryan had not seen in him for years.

On the surface of the flat roof, Ryan could see three glass domes, one for each part of the building. He would have to enter by the first one, slide down to the upper floor of Winehaven, and find the elevator shaft that ran through all the floors to end down in the air-raid shelter. He silently thanked Pedro for his attention to detail—his friend had sent him shots of the exterior, including the skylights. Removing a few thin metal slats from the ventilation grille at the bottom of the glass dome was easy, as they were rusted and loose. Sticking his head in so he could light up the opening with his flashlight, which he had decided to use as little as possible, he calculated a distance of about five meters. He dialed Pedro and spoke to him in a whisper.

"All good. I'm on the roof with Attila—we're about to go in."

"You've got about fifteen minutes."

"Twenty."

"Be careful. Good luck."

Ryan put Attila's night-vision goggles on him; he had kept them as a memento after the dog wore them in the war, never suspecting they would be put to use again. He could see Attila was uncomfortable, but as he'd worn them before, he suffered in silence. They would not make much difference—the animal had poor eyesight—but he was going to need them. Ryan hooked the rope to the harness, stroked the noble beast, gave him a signal, and proceeded to lower Attila into the dark space that opened up before them.

As soon as he could feel that Attila had touched the ground, Ryan tied the other end of the rope to the metal frame of the skylight and used it to go down himself. "Okay, buddy, we're inside," he murmured, pulling on his new goggles. It took his eyes a few seconds to get accustomed to the shifting, shadowy images he could see in red, yellow, and green. He turned on the infrared flashlight strapped to his forehead and was able to get more of a feel for the enormous room he now found himself in, which was something like an airplane hangar. He took the harness off the dog—it would be useless from now, as the rope was still hanging from the skylight. From here on in he would have to trust to the accuracy of the plans drawn up in 1995, to his experience, and to luck.

The goggles allowed him to move forward, but they provided no peripheral vision. The dog would use his instinct and sharp sense of smell to alert Ryan to any danger. He went deeper into the room, avoiding the debris scattered over the floor; about ten yards farther on, he could make out the large metal cage where before there would have been a service elevator like the one in his loft. Next to the elevator shaft was a small iron staircase, just as he had pictured. He assumed that the Wolf's hideout would not be on this floor, or on the one below it, as they both received some light during the day—from the skylights, the elevator shaft, and the gaps in the boarded-up windows. His cell had no coverage now; he'd lost contact with Pedro. They had foreseen that possibility, but he cursed under his breath all the same; the only support he had now was his dog.

Attila hesitated before the steep, narrow staircase, but he started to go down it carefully when he was given the signal. While preparing for the mission at Denise's house, Ryan had thought of bandaging Attila's paws to minimize the noise, but he decided it would make the animal hobble, and settled for clipping his claws. He didn't regret the decision; the dog needed good grip on these steps, or he'd slip.

The main level was vast, stretching across all three of the buildings that made up the fortress. Ryan resisted the idea of exploring it: there was no time for that. He had to stake everything he had on one bet: the shelter in the basement. He stopped, listening in the darkness, with Attila at his side. In the absolute silence that reigned there, he thought he heard the voice of Abatha, the anorexic girl who had described that bizarre place so accurately from a clinic in Montreal. Spirits of the past are protecting Indiana, she had said. "I hope you're right," murmured Ryan.

The next flight of stairs turned out to be a little wider and more solid than the first. Before they went down it, Ryan took the plastic bag he was carrying out from under his T-shirt, took out Indiana's beige sweater, and put it under Attila's nose. He smiled at the thought that even he would be able to follow the trail of that smell that was so characteristic of her, a mixture of essential oils that she called the "scent of magic." The dog sniffed the wool and lifted his head to look up at his master through his goggles, indicating he had understood. Ryan returned the sweater to the bag so as not to confuse the dog, and put the bag under his T-shirt again. Attila put his nose to the floor and went down the next flight of steps with the same caution as before. The Navy SEAL waited, and when he was sure the dog hadn't come across anything alarming, he followed.

He found himself in an area with a lower ceiling and a concrete floor—it had probably been used as a storehouse, first for barrels of wine and later military equipment and fuel. He felt cold for the first time, and remembered his clothes were wet. As far as he could see with the goggles, there was nothing but scattered debris—barrels and other old junk, huge sealed crates, wooden wheels for winding hoses or rope around, an old refrigerator, and some chairs and desks. Indiana could be held hostage in any corner of this floor, but Attila's behavior told him they need not waste time here: he was crouched down with his nose on the steps, awaiting orders.

The infrared image picked out an opening and the first steps of a twisted, dilapidated staircase, which according to the plans ought to lead to the shelter. The air stank of enclosed space and stagnant water. Ryan wondered if Attila would be able to follow Indiana's scent in such contaminated air, but he got an answer immediately: hackles raised, every muscle tensed, the dog was ready for action. There was no way of guessing what Ryan would find in the air-raid shelter. The plans showed only four thick walls, a hole where the elevator had been, and the positions of some iron pillars. One of the navy plans had provisional partitions for a hospital, some offices, and the officer's quarters drawn in. Those would complicate matters considerably: the last thing the SEAL wanted was to get lost in a maze of tarpaulins.

Ryan understood that he was finally, as Denise West had put it, in the Wolf's mouth. In the ominous silence of the fortress, he could hear the beating of his heart like the ticking of a clock.

The opening that led to the staircase was merely a hole, just a foot and a half wide. He would have to bend down to half his height to squeeze under a metal bar before he could get to the rusty iron steps. It was hardly going to be a graceful maneuver, he thought, given his size and the nuisance of his prosthetic leg. The infrared beam did not reach the bottom, and he didn't want to give himself away by turning on his flashlight. He hesitated, torn between creeping down, careful not to make any noise, and hurling himself down into the hole to save time. He inhaled deeply, filling his chest with air, and swept all thoughts from his mind. From that moment on he would act only on instinct, propelled by hatred for the man who had Indiana in his power, and guided by the knowledge and experience written into him in fire and blood during the war—the automatic response that his instructor from Hell Week had called muscle memory. He breathed out, took the safety off his pistol, and gave his companion a few pats on the back.

Attila started to go down.

If the Navy SEAL had hoped to make a surprise attack, the click of Attila's claws reverberating in the depths of the cellar put paid to that. He counted the dog's paces to get an idea of how far down the staircase went, and the moment he thought Attila had reached the bottom, he crouched low to get under the bar and hurtled down the stairwell, his pistol in his hand, with no regard for the noise it made. He made it down only three steps: the fourth gave way with a crash, and his prosthesis dug into the rusted metal. In a flash of clarity he realized that, if he'd still had his leg, the sharp edges would have ripped the skin right off. He tried to yank the prosthesis out, but the carbon-fiber foot was jammed between the pieces of the step, and he had to use his hand to loosen it. He couldn't leave his prosthesis behind: he would need it. He had lost precious seconds, and the advantage of surprise.

In four long leaps he was at the bottom, crouched down and whirling in a circle to scan as far as his goggles allowed him to see, his Glock gripped in both hands. At first glance it seemed he was in a smaller space than the other floors, but he soon realized that the walls were hung with dark tarpaulins: the partitions he had feared. He had no time to evaluate the obstacle, because at that moment he clearly saw the silhouette of Attila stretched out on the ground. He called out to him, his voice choked. He could only guess what had happened: the shot might have been muffled by the step breaking, or by a silencer. The animal lay on his side, motionless, his legs stiff and his head thrown back in a strange position. "No!" cried Ryan, "no!" Overcoming the impulse to run toward the dog, he crouched, scrutinizing the small area around him for his enemy, who was doubtless close by.

He was at the foot of the staircase, by the metal grille of the elevator cage. He was exposed on all sides; he could be attacked from any angle. It could hardly be a worse scenario: the center of the shelter was a vast empty space, but the rest was divided up, creating a labyrinth for Ryan and the perfect lair for the Wolf. At least he could be sure that Indiana was close, though: Attila had identified her scent. He had not been wrong to guess that Winehaven was the Wolf's hiding place, and where he was holding Indiana prisoner. As his infrared light, able to pick up human body heat, showed nothing, he worked out that the man must be hiding behind the canvas of one of the tents or partitioned rooms. Only the darkness and his black clothes protected him—as long as the Wolf didn't have night-vision goggles too. He was too easy a target: he had to leave Attila for now and find some kind of cover.

The soldier hunched low and ran to the right. The position Attila had fallen in meant he had probably been hit from the left, so his adversary ought to be there. He reached the first enclosure, and with one knee on the ground he surveyed the terrain, thinking of his next move. Checking the enclosures one by one was not possible. It would take time, and he could not move between them, ready to fire, because the Wolf might be waiting in any of them, ready to use Indiana as a shield.

Of all the risks that Ryan had envisioned when he planned the Winehaven mission, losing his faithful companion did not feature. For the first time he regretted his decision to go and face the killer alone. Pedro had warned him more than once that arrogance would be his downfall.

The minutes seemed endless as he waited, alert to the slightest sound, the slightest disturbance, in the shelter. He needed to know the time, to know how long there was until midnight, but he didn't dare take his watch out from under the sleeve of his sweatshirt; the dial would shine out in the darkness like a bright green searchlight. He decided to go as far as the wall to get some distance from the Wolf—who must be close to the staircase, where he had shot at Attila—and force him to show himself. He was sure of his aim: he could easily hit a moving target at twenty yards, even in limited visibility like this. He had always been a good marksman, with a sharp eye and a steady hand, and since he left the army he had trained rigorously at a shooting range, as though somewhere in himself he knew he would need the skill again.

He stole along next to the tents, aware that he could have guessed wrong—his enemy might be inside one of them, able to attack him from behind—but with no better ideas. As quickly and as stealthily as his prosthetic leg allowed, with all his senses heightened, he advanced, stopping every two or three paces to assess the danger. He resisted thinking about Indiana or Attila, concentrating instead on the situation, and on his body. The adrenaline was making him pour with sweat, the shoe polish stung his face, and the straps of his goggles and headlamp pinched his skin—but his hands were dry. He felt in full control of his weapon.

Ryan had gone nine yards when he saw, at the far end of the cellar, a bright, shimmering glow he could not identify. The night vision goggles were magnifying the light; he pushed them up onto his forehead and tried to adjust his eyesight. A second later he recognized what it was, and a strangled cry rose from his belly. In the far-off depths of that enormous black space was a circle of candles whose flickering flames cast their light on a crucified body. The figure hung at the intersection of a pillar and a crossbeam, its head slumped onto its chest. He recognized the golden hair: Indiana. Without a second thought, he ran toward her.

The Navy SEAL did not feel the impact of the first bullet in his chest, and he managed several more paces before he fell to his knees. The second shot struck him in the head.

///////////////////////////

Can you hear me, Indiana? It's Gary Brunswick, your Gary. You're still breathing. Look at me. Here I am, at your feet, where I've been since I first saw you last year. Even now, at the hour of your death, you're so beautiful. . . . That silk shirt, it flatters your figure—it's light, elegant, sensual. Keller gave it you for making love in, and I've put it on you so you could wear it while you atone for your sins.

Lift your head a little, and you'll see your soldier: he's that heap on the floor where I'm shining my flashlight. The dog fell farther off, at the foot of the stairs, but you won't be able to see it from here. The Taser finished off that awful creature—the electric shock is lethal in an animal that size. Your soldier's hardly visible, all in black. Or can you see him? It doesn't matter—he can't interfere with our love now. This has been a tragic love story, Indiana, but it could have been a beautiful one if only you had let it. In this week we've spent together, we've gotten to know each other as though we'd been married for years. I gave you the opportunity to listen to the whole of my story, so I know you understand me now. I had to avenge the baby that I was, Anton Farkas, and the child I was—Lee Galespi. It was my duty, my manifest moral duty.

Did you know I haven't had a migraine in three weeks now? We could conclude that your treatments have finally turned up some results, but there's another factor we can't ignore: I'm free of the burden of revenge. I've been bearing that responsibility for years—imagine the damage it's done to my nervous system. You know those migraines better than anybody. I've suffered from them ever since I started to plan my mission. The killings gave me this delightful feeling: I felt light and euphoric, as though I had wings; but within a few hours the headaches would start up again, and I thought I would die of pain. Now that everything's done, I think I'm finally cured.

I admit I wasn't expecting visitors so soon—Amanda's smarter than I thought. I'm not surprised the soldier came on his own, though: he thought he could easily beat me, and he wanted to make a show of rescuing his damsel in distress. When your ex-husband arrives with his bunch of halfwits in tow, I'll be far away. They're going to keep looking for Anton Farkas, but at some point Amanda will realize that the Wolf is Gary Brunswick. She's observant: she recognized Carol Underwater in a photograph of me from when I was Lee Galespi. My guess is she'll keep thinking about those photographs and eventually put two and two together, and understand that Carol Underwater is also Gary Brunswick, the man she played chess with.

I'll repeat what I told you yesterday, Indi: once I'd finished taking revenge, I was looking forward to telling you everything, explaining to you that your friend Carol and your most faithful client, Gary Brunswick, were the same person; that my birth name is Anton Farkas, and that under any identity, as a man or a woman, whether Underwater, Farkas, Galespi, or Brunswick, I would have loved you just the same, if only you had let me. I dreamed of us go-

*ing to Costa Rica. It's a welcoming place, peaceful and warm, and
we would have been happy there; we could have bought a little hotel
and lived off the tourists. I offered you more love than any man
you've had in all your thirty-three years. Hey—I've just realized
you're the same age as Jesus was when he died! I'd overlooked that
little coincidence. Why did you push me away, Indi? You humiliated me, made me suffer. I wanted to be the man of your life, and
instead I've had to settle for being the man of your death.*

*It's very nearly midnight, when your Calvary will end, Indi. Just
two minutes now. It ought to be a nice, slow death, but as we're in
a hurry and I can't hang around, I'm going to give you a little help
dying—although the sight of blood makes me queasy, as you know.
No one could accuse me of being bloodthirsty. I'd like to spare you
the pain of these last two minutes, but it's the moon that will dictate
the exact moment of your death. It'll be nice and quick, a shot to the
heart: none of that spear-in-the-side stuff that the Romans did to
their convicts on the cross, who always took so long to go. . . .*

//////////////////////

Attila brought Ryan back from the dead with two licks to his face.
The dog had taken the full force of the Taser charge as he reached
the last step of the staircase, where Brunswick lay in wait. He was
unconscious for a few minutes, utterly paralyzed for a few more,
and it took him a while longer still to struggle to his feet, shake
off the confusion the electric charge had triggered, and remember
where he was. Then he felt the call of his most powerful instinct:
loyalty. His goggles had ended up on the floor, but his sense of
smell led him to the spread-eagled body of his master. Ryan felt
Attila nudging him with his head, trying to bring him around,
and he was still disoriented when he opened his eyes. But the last
thing he had seen before he fell was fresh in his mind: Indiana on
the cross.

Not since he had come back from the war five years ago had Ryan so needed recourse to the extraordinary determination that had allowed him to become a Navy SEAL. The most powerful muscle is the heart: that much he had learned in Hell Week. It was not fear he felt then, but a great sense of clarity. The head wound must be superficial, he thought, or he would be dead—but the wound to the chest was clearly serious. No tourniquet in the world is going to save me this time, he thought. I'm fucked. He closed his mind to thoughts of the pain and all the blood he must be losing, shook off the immense feeling of weakness that kept telling him to rest, to abandon himself, as he had in Indiana's arms after they made love. "I'm not ready yet," he told death, pushing it to one side. With the dog's help he raised himself up on his elbows, looking for his weapon, but he couldn't lay hands on it; he assumed he must have dropped it as he fell, and there wasn't time to look for it now anyway. He wiped the blood from his eyes with his sleeve, and saw, some fifteen yards away, the Golgotha scene that was burned into his retina. Next to the cross stood a man he did not know.

For the first time, Ryan gave Attila the signal he had never given before in earnest; one that they had practiced when they were playing or training. A sharp clap on the back of the neck, as he pointed to the man in the middle distance. It was an order to kill. Attila hesitated for a moment, torn between the desire to protect his friend and the obligation to obey. Ryan gave the signal a second time. The dog leapt forward, swift and true as an arrow.

Gary Brunswick heard the sound of running and figured out what was happening. He turned and fired into the darkness, hoping to hit the beast that was already in the air, leaping right for him. The bullet was lost in the vastness of the cellar, and the dog's fangs closed around the arm holding the weapon. Brunswick screamed as the pistol fell from his hand, and desperately tried to free himself, but the weight of Attila knocked him to the ground. Releasing the man's arm, the dog sank its titanium fangs into Brunswick's throat, shaking its head savagely, tearing at the wound. Brunswick lay splayed on the floor, his throat ripped out, blood pulsing ever more weakly from his jugular.

Meanwhile, using his arms Ryan dragged himself along— approaching Indiana with excruciating slowness, calling to her and calling to her again, his voice growing fainter. He would lose consciousness for a few seconds, and as soon as he came to, he would drag himself a little farther. He knew that he was leaving a trail of blood on the cement floor. He made the last few feet thanks to Attila, who dragged him by his clothes. The Wolf had not nailed his victim to the cross, as the pillar and the beam were made of iron; instead he had lashed her wrists to them, suspending her a couple of feet from the floor with her arms outstretched. Ryan kept calling, Indiana, Indiana, but there was no reply. He did not try to ascertain whether she was still alive. With a superhuman effort, the Navy SEAL managed to get to his feet, leaning on the pillar and supporting himself with his carbon-fiber leg; the other was failing him now. He wiped his eyes with his sleeve again, but realized it was not just blood and sweat that were clouding his vision. He unsheathed his KA-BAR knife, and proceeded to cut one of the ties around Indiana's wrists. He kept the knife razor-sharp and knew how to use it, but it took him more than a minute to cut through the leather strap. Indiana's lifeless body fell on top of him, and he was able to support it only because her other wrist was still lashed to the beam. He held her up with an arm around her waist while he attacked the other strap. With the last of his strength, he finally cut through it.

The two of them were still standing. From a distance, it looked as if they were locked in a loving embrace, she yielding to him languorously, he pressing her to his chest in a gesture as possessive as it was tender; but the illusion would only have lasted a moment. Ryan slipped slowly to the floor, without letting go of Indiana; his last thought was to protect her from a fall.

*A*manda Martín convened the Ripper players one final time so that they could close the game and say good-bye. In two days she would be at MIT, dedicating herself fully to reconquering Bradley, and studying in any spare time she got, so there would be no room in her life for role-playing games.

"Yesterday Kabel and I went to drop my mom off at the airport," said the games master. "She's gone to Afghanistan to try and find two kids in a village."

"What for?" asked Esmeralda.

"To keep a promise she made to Ryan Miller. She doesn't know the names of the children or of the village, just that it's close to the border with Pakistan. But she's getting help from a group of Navy SEALS who were Ryan's buddies."

"Then she'll find them," said Colonel Paddington, for whom the Navy SEALs were demigods.

"Those kids have been waiting for Ryan Miller for six years," said Abatha.

"How d'you know?" asked Esmeralda. "Can you read their thoughts?"

"I haven't tried," replied the psychic. "I know because the games master told us his story. You guys have bad memories."

"Mom dreams about Ryan almost every night," Amanda said. "She's more in love with him now that he's dead than when he was alive—right, Kabel?"

"That's right. Indiana's a changed woman. I don't think she's ever going to get over Alan Keller and Ryan Miller's deaths and all that horror she suffered at Winehaven. And I'll never forgive myself for what happened to Miller—we could have prevented it."

"I'll never forgive myself either," Amanda agreed. "If I'd told my dad a little sooner, Ryan would be alive. The police arrived ten minutes too late. Ten minutes!" she exclaimed.

"The Navy SEAL saved your mother and died like a hero," said Sherlock Holmes. "He chose to run unnecessary risks, refused to accept help from anyone." He went on, musing, "Maybe he had a death wish. . . ."

"That's not true!" Amanda argued. "Ryan wanted to live, he wanted to marry my mom, and he wanted to go and see the kids in Afghanistan. He didn't want to die for a moment!"

"What's going to happen to the dog when you go to MIT?" asked Esmeralda.

"I'll keep him," Kabel said. "Attila puts up with me and with Save-the-Tuna, but he's got a lot to recover from too. He'll stand stock-still for hours at a time, staring at the wall. He looks like a mummy."

"He's mourning too," Abatha reassured him. "The spirit of the soldier can't get away because Indiana and Attila are keeping him here. They have to let him go."

"Maybe when Mom keeps his promise, Ryan can say good-bye to us and continue his journey," ventured Amanda.

"Are we going to play Ripper again some day?" asked Esmeralda.

"We could hook up in the winter vacation," suggested Sir Edmond Paddington.

"Unless there's something gruesome we need to investigate before then," added Sherlock Holmes.

"And meanwhile Ķabel is going to write our story," said the games master, by way of farewell. "A novel. It's called *Ripper*."

$\mathscr{A}$cknowledgments

$\mathcal{T}$*his book was born on* January 8, 2012, when my agent, Carmen Balcells, suggested to my husband, Willie Gordon, and me that we cowrite a crime novel. We tried, but within twenty-four hours it was clear the project would end in divorce. So he stuck to his own work—his sixth detective novel—while I shut myself away to write alone, as always. Still, this book would not exist without Willie: he helped me with the structure and the suspense, and he supported me when I wavered. Some others I would like to thank for their help:

Ana Cejas is the white witch who inspired the character of Indiana.

Robert Mitchell is the Navy SEAL of the book, although he has two legs and a clear conscience.

Sarah Kessler was my fabulous researcher.

My son, Nicolás Frías, revised the text to comb out the frequent consistency errors that my readers chalk up to magical realism.

My granddaughter, Andrea Frías, initiated me into the mysteries of the role-playing game of "Ripper."

The forensic expert Dr. D. P. Lyle answered my questions about homicide, weapons, drugs, and poisons, never bothering me with moral scruples.

The psychologist Lawrence Levy helped me develop the most important character of all: the villain.

Captain Sam Moore taught me about the waters around San Francisco.

My daughter-in-law Lori, and Juliette, my assistant, protected me from the world while I wrote.